Blue Knights in Black Armor

Lt. Dan Marcou

Holt, Michigan

S.W.A.T.
Blue Knights in Black Armor
by Lt. Dan Marcou

Published by
Thunder Bay Press
Holt, Michigan 48842

First Printing June 2008

15 14 13 12 11 10 09 08 10 9 8 7 6 5 4 3 2 1

ISBN: 978-1-933272-12-2

This is a work of fiction.

Printed in the United States of America
by McNaughton & Gunn, Inc.

This book is dedicated to the memory
of thousands of fallen officers.
They wore their uniforms with pride
and in that uniform they died.

Table of Contents

Acknowledgments

I would like to extend a special thanks to Chief Edward Kondracki, who allowed members of the La Crosse Police Department to pose for the cover and interior photographs. Officers who posed are Corrie Korn, Andrew Rosenow, Matt Malott, Jacob Jansky, Tony Leque, Gary Clements, and Todd Fischer.

Thanks also to Sheriff Randy Stammen for agreeing to be pictured in this book.

Photographs were taken by Dan Marcou, Joe Smith, and Vicki Marcou. Graphic design and editing by Julie Taylor.

I would also like to thank Christa Modderman and Nathan Marcou for their inspiration and feedback.

Prologue

Sir Humphrey lowered his head and removed his black helmet. The sweat stung his eyes as he whispered his prayer, "Dear Lord of Mercy, I fight for my king and my country. I hope I shall survive this battle on this muddy field of Agincourt, but the numbers do not favor us. I hope my actions on this day will tarnish neither my honor nor my soul. Lord, give me the strength to leave this battlefield to once again favor my family with my presence. If this not be your will, give my soul the grace and wings to find a home with you and the saints on this Holy St. Crispin's Day."

Humphrey was shaken from his most deep and fervent prayer by shouts, "The king! The king! Long live the king!" Sir Humphrey started to rise from his knee as he raised his head and then abruptly dropped down to his knee again and lowered his head, for his eyes had met King Henry's. The king sat astride his magnificent horse not five feet from where Sir Humphrey had knelt in prayer. His armor was not the armor of a king but the armor of a warrior leader, who shared the dangers of battle with his army. He shared the hardships of the march, and he had felt the sharpness of the sword and survived.

His armor was the armor of a brother warrior, and his words were the words of an honorable brother knight. His voice was loud and regal. The words stretched out across the battlefield and beyond. They filled each knight and every bowman's heart.

"My brave soldiers, some of us have seen our last sunrise, ate our last meal, and are about to say our last most sincere prayer, for we are marked to die. This time we all ask ourselves why we must fight and possibly die on this St. Crispin's Day. Is it for gold? Is it for fine garments or land? I say No! I do not covet any of these."

"I am covetous of something that can only be found on this battlefield this day. That is the honor of fighting beside each of you. I hope that each of you seek the same honor for when such honor is fought for and won, it overcomes death and outlives life.

This honor will be carried by those who survive this day in our hearts and in our minds, and it will be marked on our bodies in the wounds we receive and the scars they become."

The king's countenance suddenly changed, and there was a harshness and disgust in his face that showed the words he was about to speak did not come easily, "If there be any among you who wish to secure a long life more than honor and flee from this fight, do so now. I will bid you leave and give you enough crowns and a passport for passage home. Leave now, for we who have stomach for the fight do not wish to die among you." The king paused and no man moved from his spot.

The king's face changed once again, and he adjusted his seat in his saddle to stand in his stirrups. He was the embodiment of courage, and all of his soldiers leaned forward as one to hear his words, certain that they would bring courage to them. "Those of us who stay and fight on this day and outlive this day will pause on all future St. Crispin's Days by drinking ale in memory of those we will leave here on this field of battle. We will stand tall when others mention that we fought here together. All men in your presence will feel small knowing that they were not here and find themselves in the presence of one that was."

"And the amazing feats of bravery that shall be done on this day will be the grist of lore around campfire and hearth for as long as there is an England. They will speak of the bravery," the king then made eye contact with each knight as he named them slowly, "of Bedford… Exeter… Warwick… Talbot… Salisbury… and my dear brother Humphrey. What deeds, what great deeds, what great feats you will all perform today that will enable your countrymen that could not be here to say they too are Englishman like those who carried the shield, sword, and longbow at Agincourt."

As the king's eyes met Sir Humphrey's, the good knight knew that his prayers had been answered. He would leave this field in body or in spirit, but either way, he would leave with honor as the brother to a king. Humphrey had never heard such a loud silence. He was in the midst of ten thousand heavily armored men quiet, all straining to see and hear the king. Each man was trying to draw some of his strength to help them make it through this terrible day.

The king then paused to look at his men, his brave men. Those that survived the day would later say, "I was afraid as I have ever been, and then the king looked me straight in the eye. Me! And he told me they would speak of the brave deeds I would do on the battlefield forever, and the fear was washed away like creek scum over a waterfall." Each man would report the same feeling of courage breathed into them by their beloved king, their beloved brother.

The king continued, his voice booming and then riding on the breeze to every knight, page, archer, and camp follower.

"This story shall the good man teach his son;
And Crispin Crispian shall ne'er go by,
From this day to the ending of the world,
But we in it shall be remember'd;
We few, we happy few, we band of brothers;
For he to-day that sheds his blood with me
Shall be my brother; be he ne'er so vile,
This day shall gentle his condition:
And gentlemen in England now a-bed
Shall think themselves accursed they were not here,
And hold their manhoods cheap whiles any speaks
That fought with us upon Saint Crispin's day." [1]

The silence continued until all at one moment the meaning of every word filled the gentled beating heart of every man on that forever-to-be-remembered field of battle, and at one moment ten thousand men, as if scripted, roared a throaty response, "Brothers! Brothers! Brothers! Brothers!"

The king gently spurred his horse slowly along the line of soldiers, and the chant continued until throats were hoarse and the king had taken his position in the center of the line.

Sir Humphrey turned his face with new courage and determination toward the task at hand. Sir Humphrey was a knight sworn to give his life for his family, his neighbors, his country, and

---

1. William Shakespeare, Henry V, Act IV, scene iii.

his king. He gave this oath, but today he would fight as a brother beside his brothers.

On this day that would be remembered for all time, October 25, 1415, he was a honorable knight, the brother of a king. He wore his black armor with pride. As he readied to face the fight of his life, he picked up his helmet. Sir Humphrey of Gloucester would survive the day because of King Henry's words. King Henry would survive the day because of Sir Humphrey's deeds.

After the echoes of the shouts of these courageous men had faded, Sir Humphrey of Gloucester dropped to his knee one last time before he would stand and fight and whispered his battle prayer, "Thank you, God, for my wife, for my family, and for my life. May I do my best until I am laid to rest. Amen."

Humphrey set his helmet upon his head and gazed out the visor. He mounted his horse, which was black as Humphrey's armor. He followed his king on the advance. He marveled at the way Henry's armor appeared hot white in the morning sun, so sharp was the contrast to Humphrey's black armor. Both carried a shield with the lion crest. Humphrey's was black with a red lion, and the king's was white with a red lion. They rode toward an enemy that appeared to be struggling in the muddy plowed field it had ridden into. Henry shouted, "Forward, my brave men! Let us ride forward to victory!"

Henry hit the line of French knights hard, cutting a swath through them with his sword and courage. Henry and his horse fought as if they were one. Humphrey slashed and cut trying to stay close to his king, but no one could match Henry on this day, in courage and ferocity, fighting as if he were ten, no, twenty knights. Suddenly, Henry's horse reared backward and fell from a lance thrust deep into the noble steed's heart. The king stayed with the steed all the way to the ground and somehow dismounted standing, but standing in the midst of knights on horseback is merely a momentary station stop between life and death. The king parried one sharp blow with his sword and another with his shield as the enemy engulfed him, recognizing the opportunity to realize sweet victory with the death of this noble knight-king.

Humphrey slashed, cut, recovered, and slashed his way to his king. When Sir Humphrey reached King Henry, the warrior-monarch was on his back blocking blows with his battered, but intact, shield. The enemy, in their excitement to be the one who killed the king, had lost focus and could not finish the job. Their tunnel vision did not afford them the opportunity to see swift death arrive in the figure of Sir Humphrey, whose armor was as black as the night he was about to send them into.

Humphrey killed each knight close to King Henry with no need for a *coup de grâce*. Each died after receiving the first blow. Each fell to the ground as dead as Julius Caesar.

Henry made it to his feet after receiving the reprieve offered by Humphrey, and both knights stood back to back and fought all comers holding thusly the advanced ground they had gained until they were joined by the rest of the English army.

Both warriors fought until there was no one left to fight. All who dared challenge them for this piece of ground now lie dead upon it and would soon lie dead under it. The two knights then leaned one against the other, slowly lowered to the ground, and sat exhausted, breathing the air of sweet life in the presence of horrible death. The day was won by this outnumbered band of brothers who did not fight for a country but fought for each other.

The noble knight Exeter rode up to Henry and Humphrey and exalted, "Sire, the day is ours. Your courage gave us all heart, and we have defeated the French in total." Exeter dismounted, approached, and dropped to a knee stating, "Sire, may I speak?"

"Speak, Exeter," gasped the king, as he removed his helmet to reveal his hair matted with the sweat and blood earned in the battle.

"As I approached the fight that you were engaged in, it appeared as if you were in white armor and then black and then white and then black, and I was so transfixed by this vision I almost could not concentrate on the fight before me. I thought, how could the king's armor change in color so? What kind of magic was this? Then I saw the truth was there were two of you fighting as one like I have never seen before and feel I shall ne'er be granted the privilege to see again."

The king looked to Exeter and then looked about the harvest of this day's work. After a long while he quietly spoke, "Noble Exeter, you give me pause to think. I think you saw what has always been and shall always be. There will always be knights clothed in honor and virtue to protect those who could not breathe free if not for these knights. Some of these knights will have to always be in black armor to wage battle in dark places with dark enemies who do dark deeds to those lambs these knights have sworn to protect. I have seen it in a dream. There will always be a need for knights who will follow us throughout the ages, knights in black armor who fight as one."

Chapter One:
"My Friends Call Me Stumpy"

As always, when Sergeant David Compton entered the room, the kidding around and activity ended, and everyone sat up, took out a pen, and readied themselves for what "the man" had to say. Sergeant David Compton was a shift sergeant who made things happen. He did it by leading from the front, beside, and behind, and he would always be in the best place when and where he was needed. He was as reliable as a Swiss watch and twice as tough.

"Tonight, I want the SWAT team to get your reports done early. We will be serving a warrant toward the end of shift. I will fill you in later," began Compton.

Compton then paused for effect and said, "Listen up! The next item is for everyone. For the thirty-plus years I have been a cop, periodically someone gets the idea to work a car-deer accident and fill out a state accident report indicating that it is a fatality and one Jane Doe was the deceased victim. This has happened over and over again throughout my career. I am quite certain it has been happening for as long as there have been cars and deer running into them and, of course, accident reports and cops who like to get a laugh at the sergeant's expense. In each of these cases the investigating officer thought it was the funniest idea in the world until their sergeant did not laugh. In fact, the sergeant did not laugh with extreme prejudice. In our most recent case, the jolly jokester turned the report in. The report was signed by the sergeant and sent to records. It was logged in by records and sent to the state. It was logged in by the state, and La Claire was reported to have one more traffic fatality last year than they should have had. The State of Wisconsin had one more fatality than they should have had. The mistake has now been discovered, and who can tell me, this is for a free soda now, guys and ladies, who can tell me how many are laughing now?" asked Compton, looking around.

Stanley Brockman raised his hand and Compton called on him, "Go ahead, Stanley. How many people are laughing?"

"Well, Sergeant, I want the free soda, so I'm going to say none," said the incorrigible Stanley Brockman.

"You are correct, Stanley, but since you clearly have something else on your mind and I do not want you to feel compelled to interrupt in your effort to share, go ahead and say it," Compton said holding his hands up in the air and motioning as if he was conducting and orchestra.

"Well, Sergeant, I know the answer is none, and that is my final answer, but… I still think it is pretty fucking funny," said Brockman, and everyone in the room was laughing the painful restrained, compressed, and contained laugh.

"Stanley, you are correct again, but since everyone knows who did this and I cannot say," Compton directed the orchestra once again…

Nearly everyone in the room recited, "Jared Jackson."

"And everyone knows exactly how many days off the offending unnamed officer received without pay, which I am, once again, not inclined to say," Compton directed the orchestra once more.

Again, nearly everyone present recited, "Five days no pay."

Compton then completed his oratory, "Therefore, this is officially not funny. Remember, once a report gets turned in to records, signed, it is an official document. It can be supplemented but not tossed. Save humor for other venues. God knows there are enough opportunities to be funny in this life besides official police reports."

"Amen," said the union president, who had to fight to keep Jared Jackson from losing his job. "Heads almost rolled on this one guys."

"Unofficially, it always has been and continues to be fucking hilarious," said Brockman. "In case this is my last line-up, I do not want to go to meet St. Peter with a lie on my lips."

When Officer Dan McCarthy left line-up on this night, he had a trainee with him. McCarthy was a veteran of eight years on the La Claire Police Department and he was field training officer.

McCarthy watched as his young charge did the squad check. Officer William Shepherd walked around the squad talking to himself as he checked off the squad check list, "No damage... check, headlights working... check, taillights working... check. That's it. Everything is in order." Shepherd looked for approval toward his field training officer. "We're ready to hit the road." He proclaimed.

As Shepherd's field training officer, it was McCarthy's responsibility to keep this young rookie alive tonight and for the rest of his career. While they were together, Shepherd would constantly be training in the very real world of police work. It would be at times boring and at times dangerous and unforgiving. The trick was that you never knew what you were going to get. You never knew what was behind door number three. "We're good to go then?" asked McCarthy.

"Yes, sir. I think so, sir." responded Shepherd, less certain than he was just a moment ago.

McCarthy opened the front door of the squad and reached under the driver's seat and pulled out a magazine filled with live ammo and held it up for Shepherd to see. He slipped the magazine into his belt. Going to the backseat, McCarthy slid it forward, held up his search-and-rescue knife, and slid it into its pouch. Tilting his head and smiling he asked, "When do we check those seats?"

"Before we hit the road and after every transport and before ending our shift," answered Shepherd. "I'm sorry. Damn! There's not a box on the form for that," said Shepherd.

"This is how we learn, by making mistakes when it doesn't count so that we don't make them when it does. There's a box waiting for officers that make mistakes when it counts. The good thing about checking boxes is it's a routine. The bad thing about routines is nothing in the real world is routine. If we face our tasks like they are a routine, we will appear thorough, but we will become complacent. Bad guys are waiting for complacent cops. Pay your dues in training, pay attention on the street, and you will be a bad guy's worst nightmare… a prepared, professional cop."

"Sorry," lamented Shepherd one more time for effect.

"Did you learn something?" asked McCarthy.

"Yes, I did," answered Bill.

"Then there's nothing to be sorry for. Anytime you learn something and no one gets hurt that's a perfect start to a shift," said McCarthy, sliding in behind the wheel of the cruiser. "You can call me Dan. There's no need to call me 'sir;' I work for a living and there are no stripes on my sleeve. Call me Dan."

"Yes, sir, Dan. You can call me Shep. My friends call me Shep," said the young officer as he slipped on his seat belt while McCarthy adjusted the mirror and checked the spotlight one more time.

"OK, Shep. Does that mean we are friends?" asked McCarthy.

"Absolutely, if you say so," responded the rookie.

"Can't have too many of those, especially in this line of work. The general public will not be lining the streets to tell you how much they love you, you know." McCarthy looked behind him and backed out. "If you want that, become a fireman." He swung around and then pulled up to the driveway of the police ramp and slid seamlessly into traffic. "I will drive first tonight and do reports. You will drive the last half and do reports. Tomorrow night you will drive the first half and do reports, and I will drive the second half and do reports. When I decide, you will begin driving more and more and doing more and more of the reports until you get to the point where it will totally be your shift and I will be watching in awe. Remember, there is no rush. We will ease you into to it. If you have any questions, ask. There are no stupid questions. I am here to teach you, help you, and guide you into this very complex and dangerous profession that you have chosen, and I demand that you stay alert, stay awake, and stay positive! Why do I want you to stay positive?" asked McCarthy.

"Umm, because ahh it's more fun and I heard you think police work is fun," offered Shepherd.

"Who told you that?" asked McCarthy.

"Brockman. He said, 'You're riding with McCarthy tonight. He thinks police work is fun.'" answered Shepherd with a smile.

"No, he didn't." answered McCarthy.

"Yes, he did. That's exactly what he said," the young officer said defensively.

"What Stanley Brockman said to you was that you were working with McCarthy tonight and he is a fucking nutcase who thinks police work is fun. Is that a little more accurate?" McCarthy looked toward his partner to check for the reaction.

Shepherd fidgeted in his seat, looked at McCarthy, opened his mouth, and shut his mouth without saying a word. Shepherd then slowly turned away when his eyes met McCarthy's. Shepherd did not confirm, nor deny, the truth spoken by McCarthy with anything but his body language and silence.

"Staying positive is a discipline in this profession. You are going to arrest fathers who sexually assault their children. You are going to cut down teenagers who hang themselves because their parents made them do their homework instead of letting them go to the mall. You are going to have people call you pig, motherfucker, and Nazi because you issue them a parking ticket. Sometimes they will say these horrible things to you when the only thing you have done to them was save their life. You have to stay positive. Not only is it healthier, but when you get negative, you get lazy. When you get lazy, you don't pay attention. When you don't pay attention, you miss little things and big things, and you're not there when someone needs you. You make big mistakes when it counts. You stop being a bad guy's nightmare and you become a bad guy's dream cop." McCarthy paused for effect. "Are you excited to be here?"

"Yeah! All I ever wanted to be is a cop," declared the rookie.

"Hold that thought for another thirty years. If you think about it, why shouldn't police work be fun? You're outside. You get to catch bad guys, real bad guys. You get to drive fast and rescue damsels in distress. The damsels don't live in castles; they live in low rents and trailer homes, but they are still damsels, and they are still in distress. Instead of being princesses, they are welfare moms with missing teeth and homemade tattoos, but they are still damsels in distress, and you get to rescue them. This job is easy to love, but the world and some of your fellow officers are going to try to convince you every day of your career that you hate it. Don't believe it and stay positive, and you will be halfway to your goal of being a great cop." McCarthy then shifted total attention to the sights and sounds on his beat.

After a long silence Shepherd asked, "When you are out on the street, what are you looking for, Dan?"

"I'm looking for everything. If you are looking for nothing you'll probably find nothing. If you are looking for some *thing* you'll probably find nothing. If you are looking for everything you'll find something." McCarthy turned down River Street and slowed his speed slightly below the speed limit letting his eyes scan up, down, left, and right as he drove. River Street was the heart of the bar district in Downtown La Claire.

La Claire was a picturesque city of fifty-five thousand people nestled between the Mississippi River and bluffs. The downtown area bustled during the day and hustled at night, but the population that did the hustling at night and the population that did the bustling during the day were as different as night and day. McCarthy loved the sights, the sounds, and the smells of the night shift. He even loved the people of the night shift. He called them his law enforcement family. He would say, "They are little bit dysfunctional, but they are my family. They might as well be family. I spend as much time with them as with my own family."

McCarthy loved training new recruits. He felt duty-bound to train them right as he was trained by his best friend Randy Stammos. McCarthy had rode his first night with Stanley Brockman and had decided that night to never buy into the cynicism that made Stanley miserable. The cynicism made Stanley angry, bitter, and less of a cop.

McCarthy knew that police work was an emotional drain, but he discovered riding with young recruits was like hooking a dying battery up to a charger. Their enthusiasm was unbridled and spilled over. You could not help become a little enthusiastic also sitting next to someone with a smile on their face. Dan was sure that on their first night out every last one of them would be bouncing on the seat if not for the seat belt.

"I cannot believe I am sitting here," said Shepherd.

"Excuse me?" said McCarthy.

"I cannot believe I am sitting here next to Dan McCarthy. I have wanted to be here for a long time and have read in the papers for years every article about police work. You can't help but notice, if you wanted to do police work in La Claire, you would want to do it with Dan McCarthy." Shepherd paused, bit his lip and took a breath. "Now I'm here with Dan McCarthy. Wow!"

McCarthy slowed the squad. "Look there."

"Where?" the newest member of the La Claire Police Department asked. "I don't see anything," he answered snapping his head about trying to figure out what McCarthy was pointing out. He didn't have cop eyes yet. He would see some day, but not this day.

"On Diamond Street, there was a guy slumped over the wheel." McCarthy slowed and pulled into the Subway lot, but because River Street was one-way, he could not turn around. Before deciding on how best to get back to Diamond Street in the traffic, the blue Chevrolet pulled off Diamond and turned onto River Street causing the cars on River to screech to a halt to avoid striking the Chevy.

As the car passed McCarthy and his young charge, the driver had a glazed look on his face and was slumped over the wheel. McCarthy pulled to the driveway exit of the Subway lot, and all other traffic stopped to let in the marked squad. It was one of the moments that all drivers say, "Where's a fucking cop when you need one?" In this case, where was the cop? Right there! These drivers were only too anxious to have the marked patrol car take up pursuit of the driver who had made them all say at least two of George Carlin's "seven words you can't say on the radio."

"Generally speaking, we do not make traffic stops in this area around bar time because of the potential for a crowd gathering, but we are going to hit the lights on this guy before he kills somebody!" exclaimed McCarthy, hitting the lights. "255 10-38 (traffic stop) on River just south of Diamond."

"10-4, 255," came the immediate response from Lydia, the 911 center dispatcher working tonight.

The driver of the Chevy either ignored the squad's lights or just did not see them because he continued on his way drifting between the two lanes without really occupying either. The driver seemed content using the whole road since his hard-earned tax dollars helped pay for it. After two blocks, McCarthy hit the siren and the driver stopped in his tracks. McCarthy had been anticipating such a possibility; it is likely, however, that someone else might have hit the rear end of the Chevy. The driver then slowly pulled to the curb and bounced up over it, stopping partially on the sidewalk. The driver's head slammed sharply forward and backward repeatedly as if it was mounted on a spring and finally came to a rest slumped against the seat.

As McCarthy cautiously approached and made contact with the driver, he attempted to account for both hands of the driver because every trainer told him, "Watch the hands. The hands kill." McCarthy could not see the hands, and he was shocked to discover that the driver had no hands and no arms. The driver, a skinny, long-haired gentleman, swung his head toward McCarthy and smiled big, then proclaimed in one booze-filled breath, "You got me. I'm drunk and I don't have a license. I fucked up and I'm all fucked up!"

McCarthy could see why the man was slumped over the wheel. He had been steering the car with two short stumps that extended out from the shoulder stopping short of where the elbows would have been. "Sir, I'm Officer Dan McCarthy of the La Claire Police Department; the reason I stopped you was because your driving was erratic."

"Erotic. Just because I'm truly fucked doesn't make my driving erotic. Ha ha ha ha ha! Snort!" laughed the driver at his own joke. The laugh was similar to the concept of a no-armed man driving, in that McCarthy had never experienced either before and was not quite ready for it.

"You say you do not have a license; what is your name, sir?" asked McCarthy.

"My name is Thomas Kraft, but no one calls me by my given name. Everyone calls me Stumpy. You can call me Stumpy," answered the driver, somehow managing to get the door open.

"Step over to sidewalk um, ahh… Stumpy," said McCarthy as he assisted Stumpy out of and around the car. Stumpy reached the sidewalk and stood in place as best he could. He swayed back and forth as if there was a strong wind blowing in two separate directions at one time. McCarthy was somewhat hesitant because nothing had prepared him for a traffic stop of a man with no arms. He looked at his young trainee and noticed Shep was willing to watch on this one. His eyes and mouth hung open in disbelief.

"Say, Stumpy, how much have you had to drink tonight?"

"I don't drink," said Stumpy with a slur, "not since they invented the funnel! Ha ha ha ha ha! Snort!"

"There is that laugh again. It's going to take a real effort to get used to that laugh because obviously I am going to hear it again," thought McCarthy. The laugh was more than a sound or a noise. It was an experience. Stumpy's whole body took part in the laugh as if it was music and his body bounced, wiggled, and contorted to dance to the tune.

McCarthy could see that this stop was being noticed and a crowd was gathering. Crowds on River Street at bar time were never good for police officers. They always consisted of two types of people. The first type was stupid people acting drunk, and the second type was drunken people acting stupid. Very few people in either category ever chose to be pro-police. McCarthy decided it was best to arrest Stumpy and continue the investigation in a place and time different than here and now. There was no issue about probable cause. Stumpy was absolutely driving dangerously, and the cause was, indeed, probably alcohol poured copiously into the body of a man with no arms and then placing that man behind the wheel of a motor vehicle. Probable cause was not the issue.

"Say, Stumpy, I'm going to place you under arrest for operating a motor vehicle while intoxicated, could you spread your feet for me, please." Stumpy complied with a smile and McCarthy found nothing of consequence on his search. He instinctively reached for his handcuffs and paused, almost embarrassed.

"Go ahead, Officer, put those cuffs on. You'll have to do it yourself because I can't give you a hand. Ha ha ha ha ha! Snort!" Stumpy laughed so hard at that one that he nearly fell over. McCarthy even had to laugh, and he looked at the crowd gathering and noticed they were also enjoying the show.

Entertained as the crowd was, McCarthy knew that he needed to move this arrest elsewhere, quickly. He motioned Stumpy toward the backseat of the squad car and eased him ever-so-carefully into the car. Shepherd parked and secured Stumpy's car for him and then ran back to the squad, joining Dan and Stumpy for the ride to the station.

As he drove through the heavy traffic, McCarthy recited to Stumpy, "You have a right to remain silent, anything you say can and will be used against you. You have a right to an attorney. If you can't afford an attorney one will be appointed for you at La Claire County's expense if the court decides you are entitled to one without charge. If you decide to answer questions now without an attorney present, you can stop any time during the questioning. Do you understand your rights?"

"Not much chance of that happening." chimed in Stumpy.

"Do you mean answering questions?" queried McCarthy.

"No. Remaining silent. I can't keep a word my brain thinks of unsaid anymore than I can keep a fart unfarted. Ha ha ha ha ha! Snort!" Stumpy was clearly going to be more fun than trouble tonight unless there was some drastic change in his temperament, which can happen to people under the influence. McCarthy thought that unlikely in this particular case. Stumpy was unadulterated fun wrapped up in a very unique package.

"This is cool. I ain't never been in a police car before," said Stumpy excitedly. "I never been arrested. Never even got so much as a parking ticket before."

"Have you driven before?" asked Shepherd in disbelief.

"I have been driving for seventeen years, and I have never been stopped once by the police," bragged the no-armed Jeff Gordon.

"I suppose you had bad luck tonight because you have been drinking," reasoned Shepherd, who seemed amazed by the Stumpster.

"No. You'd have a harder time catching me driving sober than driving drunk." Stumpy said with great sincerity. "I am always drunk. I even wake up mostly drunk and have drink right away to seal the deal."

"Have you ever had a license?" asked McCarthy.

"No. Would you give me a license? In case you haven't noticed, I don't have any fucking arms! Ha ha ha ha ha! Snort!" Stumpy laughed at that line but with much less body English. "Hurry this up. I was on my way to my violin lessons. Ha ha ha ha ha! Snort!" The body English indicated that Stumpy really liked that one.

McCarthy found Stumpy to be a happy-go-lucky drunk, who was a gentleman throughout the night — a drunken gentleman to be certain, but a gentleman nonetheless. He let Shepherd practice his field tests. Stumpy blew hard into the Intoxilyzer puffing out his cheeks, crossing his eyes, and turning his face red. He hit the DWI lottery testing out at .30 which was so high it showed he was a seasoned drinker to be still on his feet. It was over three times the legal limit of .08 in Wisconsin.

McCarthy at one point asked if he could sign a rights form. Stumpy said, "Sure." He then picked up the pen and held it expertly between his stumps. His chest muscles were amazingly flexible, and he had obviously learned long ago to overcome this personal challenge.

"Necessity is the mother of invention," thought McCarthy. McCarthy closely scrutinized the signature and marveled, "Your handwriting is better than mine!"

"Handwriting? It's not handwriting. It's stump writing! Ha ha ha ha ha! Snort!" quipped Stumpy, "Stump writing. I kill myself. Ha! Snort, snort!" Stumpy was truly his own best audience. "No shit. I kill myself. One of these days I am going to laugh so hard that I'll piss my pants and drop over dead. Speaking of pissing my pants, can I take a piss?" asked Stumpy. "I have to piss like a racehorse." Stumpy proclaimed as he squirmed in his seat.

"Sure. Follow me," said McCarthy. McCarthy motioned for Stumpy to get up and directed him to the bathroom. When they reached the bathroom, Stumpy managed to do his thing without any help, and what McCarthy saw could not be described. Words fall short. It would be like describing how man got to the moon, landed on the moon, walked on the moon, and got back to earth. It was a series of complicated maneuvers that were difficult to explain but led to success. When he finished, Stumpy did everything he did to accomplish the task in reverse order to put it back. "I didn't fucking spill a drop," he bragged.

As he tucked it away he joked, "I hate to let that monster out. It has such an appetite I am afraid I might not get it back in unless I feed it. My friends call me Stumpy, but my intimate lady friends call me…" He looked around as if someone else might discover his secret and he whispered, "Stretch. Ha ha ha ha ha! Snort!"

After Stumpy was released to a friend who agreed to take him home and see to it that he did not drive, McCarthy was approached by Sergeant Dave Compton. He was the most experienced wise old man on the shift. Compton stayed on nights because he liked the action. He liked the young people, and he felt he could make a difference. Compton was "my favorite sergeant" to every officer who ever worked for him and always would be. He was the best.

"Hey, McCarthy." said Compton.

"Yes, Sergeant Compton," said McCarthy with respect. This show of respect was not demanded by Compton. He deserved it, earned it!

"Finish your reports and then suit up. Like I said at line-up, we have a no-knock warrant to serve toward the end of shift. I'll give everyone the details at the briefing in the line-up room. We want to get this guy in handcuffs while he's still wearing his early morning piss hard on." Compton then headed toward the command room. "Shep. You can come along to drive the van and watch our wheels."

"Yes, sir!" said Shepherd with a huge smile, like a kid who was just told by his dad that he could steer the boat for the first time. He turned to McCarthy and exclaimed, "I'm driving the SWAT van!"

"Yes, you are. See, I said you'd be driving the second half of the shift. We'll get our reports written, and then I will fill you in on what is expected of you." McCarthy said quickly as if there was now a sense of urgency about getting these reports finished.

As they walked back to the report rooms, they met Stanley Brockman. Brockman was one of McCarthy's least favorite training officers. When Dan thought back on his shifts working with Brockman, he would have to admit that he learned a great deal, for Stanley Brockman did manage to serve as a bad example. Brockman was a man fighting cynicism one day and giving into it on most others. Stanley looked like the cat that ate the canary; McCarthy could see that Stanley had something clever to say — at least Stanley thought it was clever.

"OK, Brockman, say it," said Dan McCarthy motioning with both hands as if to say, "Bring it on. Get it over with."

"I just thought I better tell you since you are training this rookie, you better train him right." Brockman said making Shepherd cringe at the suggestion that he was a rookie, even though he knew he was.

"Say it, Brockman. Get it over with and say it." said McCarthy with impatience in his voice.

Brockman was undeterred."Well, any trainer would tell you that it is not a good habit to get into. I noticed that your last prisoner you brought in was, ahem, not properly handcuffed." Brockman stood up a little bit and hitched up his duty belt with both hands, proud that he could entertain himself and take a shot at McCarthy at the same time.

Unexpectedly, and without missing a beat, Shepherd stepped up to play this ball, "I wouldn't worry much about that sir. I was with Officer McCarthy when he arrested that man. He searched him extremely well and discovered he was," Shepherd paused, looked back and forth between McCarthy and Brockman, and then with the timing of Chris Rock served his backhand smash, "he was unarmed. Ha ha ha ha ha! Snort."

Dan McCarthy split a gut and high-fived Shepherd. "Well played William Shepherd. Well played."

Even the incorrigible Stanley Brockman had to concede, "Well played, kid."

Chapter Two: No Prisoners

McCarthy buttoned his black tactical uniform shirt over his level two second-chance vest. The bullet resistant body armor was one of the most expensive pieces of equipment that the SWAT tactical operator wears, but all cops know it is "cheaper than a funeral." McCarthy tied in his bloused bottoms of his black tactical pants at the bottom and strapped on his belt. He adjusted each set of handcuffs and replaced each back into its case. He checked his TASER, did a spark test, and replaced it in its holster, cross draw, opposite his firearm. Dan shook his pepper spray and placed it back in the holder. McCarthy tied his tactical shoes and strapped his gas mask holder securely to his left leg. McCarthy made sure all of his magazines were fully loaded with duty rounds and turned them properly in each magazine pouch to allow for quick access under stress. He checked his baton and secured the flap over it to keep it in place.

McCarthy had a routine that was anything but routine. He went through it when time permitted. Dan snapped his helmet and double checked all of his equipment. He checked to make sure his police markings and badge patch were clearly visible on his uniform. Tonight the black would be coming in handy because they would be hitting the target house just before dawn.

La Claire Police Department had a very well trained and well equipped SWAT team. Like most agencies, its members held jobs all over the department. Even some larger agencies discovered that officers who did nothing but SWAT became stale waiting for the "Big Call." Smaller agencies could not afford having a large contingent of officers doing nothing but SWAT, so as a practical matter SWAT team members came from the patrol division, the detective division, administration, community services, and even school liaison officers.

McCarthy dropped to a knee and closed his eyes, quietly alone in the locker room and said his prayer, "Thank you, God, for my life, for my family, and for my wife. May I do my best until I'm laid to rest. Amen." McCarthy rarely asked for anything in his prayers. He figured the big guy upstairs had already done so much for him. He had a beautiful wife, his son Nate, who was his buddy, and his darling little dawdler Christa. His daughter Christa took her time with everything and always had a smile on her face. He called her his darling dawdler because she was always the first one in with a smile and the last one out, still smiling. McCarthy already felt blessed with all that he had. People had tried to kill him on more than one occasion, and he had survived. If that happens to anyone and they really give it some thought, it gives one perspective.

McCarthy then rose from his silent prayer and he reached for his cell phone. He called his wife, Victoria. "Hello, Hon."

"Hi, Sweetheart. Is everything OK?" asked Victoria in a sleepy voice just wrested from a dream. McCarthy pictured her eyes half filled with sleep, her tousled blonde hair and her warmth and softness. You could not separate the two. She was always so warm, so soft, so… "Honey, are you still there?"

"Sorry, Vic, I am going to be late today. I won't be able to take the kids to school." McCarthy said.

"What's up? Late arrest? Reports? SWAT?" queried Victoria.

"SWAT. We have a warrant. Love you, Honey. I will be home as soon as I can." McCarthy loved what he was doing, but he was wishing he was home in bed after hearing Victoria's voice. He loved her phone voice. It was friendly, loving, and sensual. Her phone voice always made him want to be with her when he heard it. Then she said it. She did not know she was part of his mental survival readiness. "I love you. Be careful, Sweetheart."

McCarthy then answered mentally, "Bad guys better be careful." It was McCarthy's ritual to get his mind prepared for where his body was about to take him. She would say, "I love you. Be careful," before every shift no matter how she felt. She would not let him go out of the house without telling him to be careful.

McCarthy had learned this preparedness ritual from Sergeant

Dave Compton, who had practiced it with his wife. Sergeant Compton had recently lost his wife of thirty years to cancer. McCarthy recognized Compton to be the strongest man he knew because Sergeant Dave Compton loved his wife more than life itself, and when he returned to work after his funeral leave, there was absolutely no change in his demeanor. It was unusual. It was uncanny. It was almost unsettling. That was Dave Compton though. The strongest man McCarthy ever had met. Except for the dusting of gray in his dark hair, Compton looked just like superman, without a cape.

Dan McCarthy closed his eyes and hung up the phone. He took a breath in through his nose and held it a moment. He then breathed out through his mouth pushing the breath out with the muscles of his abdomen. He placed his black Kevlar helmet on his head and adjusted the strap.

McCarthy then started his stretching routine. Calls on the street did not allow time for officers to stretch before things got physical. Cops get into foot chases in full gear. They get involved in full contact combat, even sometimes make flying tackles, and never get a chance to stretch first.

Everyone knows bullets sometimes kill cops, but very few know how many die from heart attacks during very physical activities. Many more cops are put out of business by back injuries doing things that pro football players, wrestlers, and boxers do, except with no protective equipment and no time to warm up. McCarthy liked to stretch before SWAT calls when time permitted. He ended his stretching with some controlled front and side kicks into mid air. He was mentally kicking an imaginary person his own size in front of him. He would start his kicks with a slow smooth precision and build power, with each practice kick.

The door to the locker room swung open just as McCarthy had finished his last front kick and set it down "McCarthy! Did you take your battle piss?" inquired Sergeant Compton as he entered in full gear. Compton was the officer in charge of the SWAT team. When the team was formed, the mayor said he did not want the SWAT team called SWAT because it was "too harsh sounding." In a world where freedom of speech has been quashed by the term politically correct, the people in that world have become obsessed with inventing new terms that sound nicer than old terms. Governments and businesses pay individuals and committees fortunes to think of new words to call old items, ideas, concepts.

In fact, a "new idea" with the mayor was, as the mayor would call it, "a synergistic thing and thinking out of the box." Thinking out of the box was the practice of the brilliant in the eyes of the mayor.

The mayor asked the officers present for alternative names for the team other than SWAT. He invited them to, "Think out of the box. Do not have your minds chained by convention. Think out of the box," the mayor repeated.

Compton immediately responded, "Your honor, while thinking out of the box, I have thought up a new name for the SWAT team. Your honor, how about we call it the Fast Action Response Team."

The mayor smiled at such a quick and sincere response, which obviously showed at least one person present was a true modern professional capable of thinking out of the box. At least one person present agreed with him on this issue that called for a certain amount of political correctness. "Good idea. The Fast Action Response Team that would be..."

"The FART team, your honor," said Captain Hale, who was head of community services and a master of politically correct speech with everyone except officers, those below him in rank. Hale cast a truly disdainful look in the direction of Sergeant Compton. "This was an apparent attempt at humor by Sergeant Compton. Sergeant Compton, a good joke requires proper timing and this is poor timing for humor such as this," lectured Hale in his most condescending tone he could muster.

"Respectfully, sir," followed up Compton, "You can call a fart perfume, and it is still a fart. You can call a SWAT team a boy choir, but it will always be a SWAT team and everyone will know it. Why not just call it that? There is a time for politically correct semantics, and I do not feel that the naming of a SWAT team is the time to be politically correct."

Eventually Compton's point was made and the team was called The La Claire Police Special Weapons and Tactics Team. It was an example of why Compton would always be a sergeant. He was honest, and most politicians cannot handle the truth. There are politicians in politics. There are politicians in police departments. Compton was too honest for the politicians inside and outside the department.

Sergeant David Compton would remain a sergeant, and the officers would be the benefactors of Compton's career "stagnancy" as some would put it. Compton did not call it that. He would always say, "Find a job you love and you never have to work another day in your life." Compton loved police work, and his affliction was contagious. He knew that in McCarthy he had found another carrier of that enthusiasm.

"Battle piss? No, Sergeant, I did not." answered McCarthy, already heading down the hall. When time permitted, Compton always recommended taking a "battle piss." Once the entry was successfully made, it would be a long time before anyone would have a chance to use the bathroom if things went well. If things did not go well, no one wanted to get shot with a full bladder. It increased the possibility of a life-threatening infection. Compton was a Marine who had been to war in Vietnam. He was a warrior who had lost friends who had survived the battle wounded but had died later from infection. It was all a part of his "prepare for the worst and hope for the best" philosophy, which he practiced on a daily basis. This philosophy was always demonstrated by Compton but especially showed prior to the SWAT team rolling.

When McCarthy returned to the briefing room, Compton began speaking. He was obviously waiting for McCarthy's return, but he made no mention of it. Compton was always careful not to get a laugh at someone else's expense. He then began as McCarthy seated himself. "We are looking for this man," Compton had put together a PowerPoint presentation on the pre-dawn raid, and a picture of a ruddy-faced felon flashed on the screen, "Harley David Slade. He hates the government, he hates the courts, and he hates us. He will have a weapon within reach wherever he is in his house." Compton advanced the PowerPoint to a screen showing a run-down, white two-story home that was poorly maintained. "It's early. We want to hit the door at 5:58 AM so we catch him the way I like to catch them." He turned to Stammos as if the briefing was rehearsed.

"Still takin' his mornin' nap and before he has taken his mornin' crap," answered Stammos. McCarthy looked at Stammos and Stammos acknowledged the glance with a wink.

Stammos was one of the SWAT team's team leaders. On this call out, he made the plan and now would give the plan to the team. He stepped forward and continued.

"We will take two marked units for possible pursuit and later for transport. The SWAT unmarked van will contain the entry team. Officer Shepherd will be driving. Stand up, will you, Shep. Officer Shepherd is the newest member of our department. He is in field training."

Shepherd hesitated, stood up, and proudly smiled.

"At least this one is old enough to shave," commented Officer Gary Carpenter, who was sitting here on this day thanks to the new technology of Kevlar in his Second Chance Vest and the age-old warrior spirit. He had been shot through the arm and into his chest by a 20-gauge slug several years earlier. Although he was knocked down, he stood himself up again. Carpenter was referring to the heavy "five o'clock shadow" on Shepherd's face. His beard grew fast, thick, and black. It gave the rookie the grizzled look of a veteran "You got it!" We will stop the transport on 1200 Oak. There is a stone wall and bushes, and we will be able to approach unseen. There are no lookouts and no visible cameras. You guys on the perimeter will stack first and separate here, cutting through the yard at 1215 Oak. The entry team will hit the door here. Dooley will breach after what, Dooley?"

"After I check the door first," responded Officer Dooley. "Opening an unlocked door is faster and quieter than any breaching device yet invented."

Stammos continued, smiling at Dooley's answer, "Dooley will breach, and then we announce. This is a no-knock warrant because

Slade is known to be armed. After Dooley, it will be Brockman with the shield, Carpenter with the Benelli, Stammos, that's me," said Stammos looking at the name patch on his tactical uniform, "with the MP5, and, McCarthy, you will be with your hand gun and will handle anything physical that does not rise to deadly force. You will be the hands-free guy taking all comers."

McCarthy listened to Stammos' briefing as he subconsciously checked his equipment again. He checked his radio and made sure it was on the SWAT channel. 911 Dispatch had designated a dispatcher assigned to this operation.

"The SWAT van will park, and the entry team will stage here and get into the stack, while the marked units will park here and here," Stammos used the laser pointer on a schematic of Slade's house and neighborhood. You will arrive precisely at the moment that the team calls out moving. One officer from each marked unit will approach here to cover the perimeter, and one will stay with the marked unit in the event that we have a pursuit. I want Hartley and Lusk behind the wheel. You two will handle negotiations if it turns into a breach and hold stand-off. Did you load your gear?" asked Stammos.

"I have enough equipment to get us started quickly if we need," answered Hartley.

"Questions?" asked Stammos. He was met with the tense silence of a pride of lions who were about to pounce on their unsuspecting prey.

"Ok, let's mount up and get ready to roll. You know what day it is today, guys?" asked Compton. There was no answer. "It's St. Crispin's day. October 25," said Compton to a room full of blank stares.

"What the fuck… St. Ritz Cracker Day. Who the fuck… what is that?" asked Brockman, who sounded genuinely puzzled. McCarthy could hardly recognize Brockman's voice devoid of sarcasm.

"On October 25 in 1415, a badly outnumbered group of English knights defeated a much larger French army on the fields of Agincourt. The battle was immortalized in a speech from a

Shakespeare play, *Henry the Fifth.* You read Shakespeare, don't you, Brockman?" asked Compton.

"I once had a pork sandwich made from a pig named Hammmmlet!" answered Brockman, his voice once again recognizable, generously laced with sarcasm.

"Anyway," continued Compton, "King Henry V gave a speech before the battle. Many of his knights wore black armor just like you guys. He said to them,

We few, we happy few, we band of brothers;
For he to-day that sheds his blood with me
Shall be my brother; be he ne'er so vile,
This day shall gentle his condition:
And gentlemen in England now a-bed
Shall think themselves accursed they were not here,
And hold their manhoods cheap whiles any speaks
That fought with us upon Saint Crispin's day." [2]

"I think of that speech often. It says because we risk what is near and dear to us and count on each other, it makes our bond special. We do not have to bleed today to be brothers. Let's stay safe together. Let's say our SWAT prayer." Everyone bowed their heads. "Whether we are five or ten, good women and men, and we can count on each other to come back again, and one more thing, good God," Compton paused and as one they all ended the prayer with the volume and intensity of any SWAT team at prayer, "Amen."

"Let's roll!" shouted everyone. They moved deliberately and expertly exactly to where they needed to be. A well-oiled SWAT team is like a macho ballet in motion. It is a highly trained, highly motivated group of modern knights. Make no mistake about it. The knights of old were the policeman of their time. The policemen and policewomen of modern day are the knights of today. The tactical operators are in top physical condition and the most highly trained of all police officers. Their movements are practiced

2. William Shakespeare, *Henry V*, Act IV, scene iii.

so often together as a team they appear choreographed.

The vehicles pulled out of the police ramp, and Compton radioed dispatch, "Dispatch we are 10-76 (en route)." Dispatch was already aware of the location the team was headed. An ambulance was standing by at a location close to the scene to allow for a quick response if needed. All other units on the street could not help but listen to the SWAT channel. They knew the team was going out. You could not miss the activity at the station. There was a tension that could be felt, but not explained, by every officer listening to the radio, whether they were in the SWAT van approaching the target or in a squad working a beat.

Shepherd pulled silently up to the spot where he had been directed to stop. He hit his mark perfectly. The team exited at the staging area silently and stacked in a column perfectly as directed by Compton with a thumb up. The last man in the stack tapped up the line, and when Dooley received the tap, he adjusted the "Thunder-shock 2000" in his two hands and tightened the grip. The Thunder-shock 2000 was his battering ram of choice. It was his ram. It was his favorite ram. Dooley moved and the rest of the stack followed, quickly, quietly, smoothly, as if they were attached by some unseen cord.

The approach to the house was like a ride at Seven Flags. It started slowly and sped up click———click——click——click—click—click–click-click.

As they reached the sidewalk leading to the door, every member of the entry team could smell the marijuana. It was as plain to them as smelling the onions on the roadway beside a large onion field just before harvest. "Wow, the mother-lode," thought McCarthy. "*The mother-lode!*" Click—click–click-clickclick!

Harley David Slade was awake. He did not sleep much. Morning was the time he watered his plants. The house was not just Harley David Slade's home. It was his greenhouse. It was his place of business. He did not make sales from his house. In this house he grew the plants, dried the plants, separated the seeds, and weighed and bagged the plants. Each of these functions was done as a separate operation in a separate room.

Harley David Slade was a successful businessman, in his point of view. He had been the child of a vagabond biker, whose only legacy was to name his son after his favorite and only possession. Harley David Slade was named after his father's Harley Davidson motorcycle. Slade did not know his father and had never met him. The name was unique just like Harley David Slade. Harley liked his name. It was one of the few things in life he liked.

Slade's mother was a seventies' flower child, who also passed on a legacy to Harley. She passed on her love of "the plant," as she called it. She never liked to refer to it as weed because she felt marijuana was not a weed. She would say, "A weed is an unwanted plant that is ugly and serves no purpose." She would say, "Marijuana was a plant, which was a gift from God with powerful healing qualities. We have a God-given right to smoke the plant." Slade's mother felt the government illegally kept marijuana from the masses because it was afraid that the people would live up to their potential and realize there would be a perfect world if there were no governments. Her legacy to her son was a love of "the plant" and a hate for the government.

Nearly the entire house was used for the manufacture of "the plant." Harley ate in the kitchen and slept in the a corner of the living room in the midst of his product. He was not sleeping now though. The voice had awakened him again.

Slade was a deep thinker and a dark dreamer. He was the proverbial "loner." Harley had smoked marijuana all his life. His mother smoked it while she was nursing him, and he had no memory of a life without marijuana in it. It entertained him as a youth, and now it soothed him as a mentally tortured adult. Harley was certain without it, his dark dreams would turn into a horrific reality, which both scared him and intrigued him. He wore his paranoia on his sleeve. A simple, "Good morning," from a passing stranger on the street would go unanswered and be met with a stare of puzzlement. Slade would spend the rest of the day pondering the innocent stranger's meaning, motive, and next move.

Harley David Slade was a dangerous man. He knew it. The La Claire police knew it, but for some reason very few others could see it. He quietly maneuvered about the world barely noticed. If anyone would ask, "What's the deal with Slade?" The answer would be, "He's quiet. He's a loner. He doesn't say much. You hardly notice he's around. He's the perfect neighbor." To some, the perfect neighbor is someone they rarely see and never hear. If that was true, then Slade was, indeed, the perfect neighbor.

If not for his marijuana, he would have no world. He grew it to smoke it. He sold it to grow it. He cleaned up a strip joint after hours and hung at its bar nearly every evening. The joint's name was RUMPlestiltzkin's on the south end of River Street. It was affectionately called "The Rump" for short. At a glance, Slade did not fit in, but then again, he never fit in anywhere. He had no desire to fit in anywhere. He was there nearly every day from about 6:00 PM to close. He would help the bartender close up, and then he would clean up.

Slade was paid to clean up, but that is not how he paid for his weapons, house, car, and van. The Rump was where he quietly sold his product. No one gave Harley a second thought. He was good for the Rump's business because he had a high quality product. He became a fixture at the bar. At six feet three inches, 215 pounds, he was a rather imposing fixture. He wore cowboy boots, blue jeans, and an army jacket whether he was inside or out, winter or summer. His dope was beyond good. It was beyond real good. It had a great, fast, and pleasantly long-lasting high.

When the drug investigator Detective Sergeant Brickson tested the marijuana that his informant bought from Harley David Slade, he popped the second ampoule in the field test packet and yelled, "Bam! This is some quality shit!" The clear liquid in the plastic packet exploded into a bright violet instantly. The THC, which is the magic potion inside marijuana, heavily occupied Slade's product. "That's what I'm talking about," shouted Brickson to his partner Jefferson. "This warrants a warrant!" exclaimed Brickson.

On this morning, Harley had just gotten home after cleaning

the bar, and he was tending his hybrid cannabis plants. Slade's plants were the most important living things he cared for in his dreary life. He nurtured them, talked with them, and shared his home with them. He was closer to them than any human.

There was one human that was worthy of his attention. In the world inside his mind, he did have a girlfriend of sorts. Darla Darling was the moniker she worked under. It most probably was not her given name. Darla was one of the strippers at the Rump. This was the perfect relationship for both Harley and Darla. Harley worshipped Darla from the seat next to the stage as she danced, kicked, twirled, and disrobed at the Rump. Darla did not know she was Harley's girl any more than Harley knew that he had just sold a quantity of his product to a police informant. Harley similarly did not know his simple life was about to be drastically altered.

Click—click–click-clickclickclick… Smash! Dooley hit the sweet spot on the front door with his Thunder-shock 2000. He had wielded the ram so efficiently that it had "key to the city" painted across its length. "Police! Search warrant! Down! Down! Down!" Every member of the team shouted in unison as it filed through the door and poured into the house. It was all you could hear up and down the entire street. It jarred every neighbor awake for one square block.

Slade froze for one interminably long second as the team members thought, "What next?"

"Police! Get down now!" ordered Stammos with the menacing MP5 submachine gun pointed at Slade. The LASER sight was in the dead center of Slade's forehead. In a blink, Slade spun and ran down a hallway. He disappeared as he pivoted into a bathroom, and when he was safely inside the bathroom, he slammed and locked the door. Stammos and McCarthy followed but backed off when they heard a shotgun round being cycled by a pump action into the chamber of a 12-gauge shotgun. Stammos positioned himself at the corner by the entrance of the hallway. He covered the door, motioned a hold for the rest of the team, and shouted loudly, "Gun!" Stammos thought, "Who the fuck keeps a shotgun in their bathroom?"

Randy signaled silently for the shield man to bring the shield forward. Brockman came forward and positioned himself at the corner of the hallway, and Stammos nestled himself behind and beside Brockman. Stammos radioed through his head mic while still covering the door, "Suspect Harley David Slade has barricaded himself in the first floor bathroom. He appears to be armed with a pump-action shotgun. All units hold your positions. I want Jim Hartley at my position. Have him come through the entry point. Send in another shield with him." Stammos then called to Slade, "Harley David Slade. This is Officer Randy Stammos of the La Claire Police Department. Put down your weapon and come out slowly with you hands up. Do it now!"

"You put down your guns and leave my house. Do it now!" shouted Slade in response.

Officer James Hartley came in with Jefferson holding the second shield. Stammos motioned them to the opposite side of the hallway entrance, and they quickly crossed and fell into a mirrored position across from Stammos. Hartley had his weapon out, but even though they all came prepared for a gun fight, everyone was hoping he could work his magic.

Everyone liked Jim Hartley. If he could look a suspect in the eye and get one complete sentence out, there probably was not going to be a fight. Every member of the La Claire Police Department SWAT team was cross-trained as a tactical member and also were trained negotiators. Hartley was a communications master. Compton always said, "If you are talking, you are probably not shooting. If we can all keep them talking, a police shooting might be avoided. Regardless, we are going to prepare you on the team for all eventualities."

Most of the team members were on the team for their tactical skills primarily and their negotiator skills secondarily. Compton did not want one dimensional personalities on his SWAT team. Hartley was one of the four team members whose primary job was a negotiator. He brought a bullhorn with him. The bullhorn was annoyingly loud and distorted the voice badly. It was not the best way to conduct a conversation which might result in a deadly encounter. Hartley would rather not use the bullhorn, but he preferred the bullhorn to yelling. If a suspect had to resort to yelling to communicate, it usually had a tendency to wind them up tighter than a Swiss watch.

"Harley David Slade, this is Jim Hartley of the La Claire Police Department. I'm here to help see that this situation does not get any worse than it is. Mr. Slade… Harley. Can I call you Harley?" asked Jim.

"Sure. That's my name," came Harley's response.

"Great!" Jim thought. "The walls are thin enough so that we can talk and hear each other, but that means they are thin enough to shoot through." That concerned Hartley deeply and inspired him to snuggle a little closer behind his shield man. "Harley. How about you just come out of there, and we can end this right now?"

Jim would say later at the debrief that he should have taken more time to establish a rapport. He thought by the sound of Slade's voice, when asked about his name, that he was already second guessing his actions and was ready to come out. Jim said at the debrief later, "Hindsight being 20-20, I would say now that my judgment was wrong. I should have spent more time on the rapport building."

"Yeah. I'll come out now. I'm counting down from ten, and if you guys are not out of my house, I am coming out shooting," growled Slade in a voice that was sinister as death itself.

"10 – 9 – 8,"

"Stop and think about this Slade," called Hartley, now shouting.

Stammos made his athletic frame smaller, like a clenched fist tightening just before a punch.

"7 – 6 – 5,"

"Shit!" whispered Brockman to nobody… to everybody. He brought the shield up and re-gripped it as he peered through its window while he attempted to pick up the front sights on his

Glock through the window on the shield.

There was a pause in the counting, and the door opened. The muzzle of a shotgun extended out of the doorway, pointed at a ninety degree angle to the officers at the end of the hallway. The longest ten count anyone on that team had ever heard continued.

"4 – 3 – 2 – 1," then… nothing. The number one seemed to hang in the air floating above the muzzle of the shotgun.

Stammos focused on the spot where Slade would have to appear if he did exit. He could easily figure it by the position of the barrel and the size of Slade. He waited. He breathed. He shouted one last time, "Police. Drop the gun. Do it now!"

"Blast off!" shouted Slade.

With a frantic thrust, the shotgun barrel came around the corner and then Stammos saw it. He was so focused that all he could see was the shotgun and the green of Slade's shirt.

It was all so surreal. Ten seconds that felt like ten minutes. The movements seemed so slow and deliberate and so unlike the high speed desperate movements that they would have looked like if played back by a replay camera.

"Brrrap," spit Stammos' MP5. He did one controlled trigger squeeze on auto, and they later found that all three rounds he fired hit their intended target. The green fatigue shirt was floating down the hallway away from the team. Then, like a prom dress in May, it dropped to the floor. The shotgun disappeared back into the bathroom from whence it came.

"Shots fired," called Jim Hartley.

"Hold your positions," barked Stammos.

"What happened?" asked Brockman.

"I just shot the guy's shirt. He tied it to the gun and shoved the gun out the door way.

"I just shot the guy's shirt," repeated Stammos keying the mic for the benefit of the remainder of the team holding the perimeter. "The suspect is barricaded again. He is still armed."

"Don't shoot. I'm coming out," shouted Slade.

"I want to see your hands first. I want to see your empty hands first, and step out slowly turning away from my voice," ordered

McCarthy, leaning out high over Stammos, who quickly opened the action on his MP5, switched to a full magazine, and then slammed the bolt home. The practiced movement was over in a second at the most.

Slade stepped out slowly with his hands in the air. "Don't shoot. I put the gun down," Slade reported.

Slade then did everything McCarthy asked him to, and he did it immediately and quickly. He had found out what he wanted to know about these SWAT guys. He was prepared, now, to be arrested. He had wrapped his mind around it when he saw his shirt ripped from the barrel of the shotgun. McCarthy ordered, "Walk backward slowly… hands higher. Higher! Now drop to your knees. Put your hands flat on the floor in front of you. Walk backward on your knees until you're flat on your stomach. Place your hands in the small of your back. Point your fingers to the sky. Lay your left ankle inside the back of your right knee. Point your left toes to the sky. Turn your head to the left. Now, do not move!"

McCarthy slid into a leg lock and applied the handcuffs as quickly and as smoothly as Stammos had reloaded his MP5. To anyone watching, they looked like SWAT, and to Slade it felt like SWAT, even though this was his first arrest at the hands of a SWAT team.

Slade had tied his shirt to the shotgun to see what would happen if he went charging out of the door. He wondered if he would be able to get a shot off and take one or two with him. He wondered how fast these guys would react. Slade was like a swimmer who was just trying the water by dipping his toe in. He got his answer in less than one second, with three well-placed shots. Slade looked at his shirt lying dead at the end of the hallway. "That could be me right now. What a waste. I'm not leaving this world for no reason like the Beetles' song," he promised himself, "A Nowhere Man."

Slade did not want to die on this morning. He did not even want to kill. He did not want to go to jail either, but this morning, he would. He would get out. He would have a chance for revenge. "Next time, I will be the one dressed in black. I will be the one with the gun. If they want war, they shall have war!" Then Slade warned in a muffled voice as he talked into the carpeting, "War on drugs? I'll give you a fucking war on drugs!"

The words were muffled and unintelligible but were foreboding in their tone. After McCarthy handcuffed and then searched Slade while he was covered by Stammos and Hartley, Slade turned his head and looked at McCarthy. "He's smiling," thought McCarthy. "This man is smiling. This man is a very dangerous man."

Slade looked at the name patch on McCarthy's uniform and said in an inquisitive tone. "McCarthy?"

"Sir, you are under arrest for manufacturing marijuana and reckless use of a weapon. You, sir, have a right to remain silent...." McCarthy could recite it by heart. He had done it a thousand times before. He now had a tone that made it less of a memorization and more of a conversation, like a friend giving another friend some advice on a used car he was about to buy.

The courtesy was lost on Slade. His home was invaded. His business was destroyed. He had read extensively on the "War on Drugs." Richard Nixon had declared the war on drugs. Slade had learned from his mother that war had been illegally declared. She would rail on constantly about it as they smoked the magic plant together. Slade was now on the floor. He had been taken prisoner in that unconstitutionally declared war. "I am now a POW. That means I must be a combatant. If I am a combatant, then I can inflict casualties," reasoned Slade as he lay there looking at McCarthy, "the enemy." Then he smiled bigger and said, "Good morning, McCarthy."

The rest of the team moved through the house clearing it. The place was a greenhouse for the largest in-door marijuana grow operation in the history of La Claire. Slade had made hundreds of thousands of dollars selling the best weed manufactured north of the Rio Grande. It was homegrown and American made. Harley David Slade was living the American dream. He had a small business, and he produced and sold his product. He even was the quality control officer, for he did not pass a day or night without sampling his wares. He would not think of selling foreign imports or outsourcing any of the labor. He would not have some

Punjab in New Delhi taking orders for him over the phone. He reconciled everything he did and had yet to be targeted in this war on drugs. Now that he was targeted, it was his turn to fight back. As McCarthy helped Slade to his feet, Slade looked at him and smiled again as he thought. "The difference between you and me, McCarthy, is when I launch my counter-attack I will take no prisoners."

MP-5

Chapter Three: "Do You Do Shirts?"

McCarthy and Shepherd grabbed one of the squad cars at the scene and transported Slade to the County Jail. Slade was quiet. After Randy had shot his shirt, Slade physically complied with every request, but McCarthy was especially uneasy about this prisoner. Harley did not say another word after wishing McCarthy a "Good morning." He smiled in the squad when he was transported to jail. He smiled as he walked into the jail from the car port. He smiled all the way to the booking counter. McCarthy found that preferable to a prisoner kicking and screaming all the way, but he knew that this was a very unnatural quiet. The look on Slade's face was called by police and military the "1000 yard stare." The body was present, but the mind was occupying another plane, dimension, galaxy, or possibly an alternate level of consciousness. Take your pick. He was not in the here and now.

The jailer tried to book him, but Slade would say nothing. The jailer sent him to a temporary holding cell since it was breakfast for the inmates, and the jailers were all busy. After McCarthy was gone and breakfast was finished, Slade allowed the jailer to book him. It seems like a cliché, but Slade would be out before reports were completed on his arrest. The truth in any cliché is what makes it a cliché.

Judge Alice was handling initial appearances today. It was Judge Alice's duty, in her eyes, to honor the framers of the constitution by letting out every criminal as quickly as absolutely possible, no matter what the crime. She was any criminal's dream judge. Dream judges heavily populate the criminal justice system and are the impetus pushing the criminals out the revolving door as fast as the cops of the world are pushing them in.

McCarthy took time to cover booking procedure and the jail procedure for Officer Shepherd since this was his first opportunity to take someone to jail on his first night as a police officer. Stumpy had been released without being booked earlier.

While Shepherd drove back to the police station from the La Claire County Jail, he said, "That Slade was quiet, but I sensed something very dangerous about him. I mean, beyond the fact that he had a shotgun. I felt he was an extremely dangerous man."

"That's great, Shep. Pay attention to those senses. I'm convinced that there is a portion of our brain sending us messages based on information processed in our subconscious. Some people call it a sixth sense. All I know is that it's beyond the hair on the back of your neck and so much more useful than goose bumps. There is a mental communication when something is not right, and your brain senses that your physical well being is endangered. Most people ignore it and it goes away when unused. Great cops develop it, and it gets them arrests. It keeps them alive. It also helps them remember anniversaries. Are you married?" asked McCarthy.

"Nah. I haven't found the right girl yet. Are you?" asked Shepherd.

"Yeah. I have two kids," answered McCarthy.

"Kids! Great! I want kids some day. I hope I am off nights before all that happens."

"Actually, nights are great for kids normally. They go to school and I sleep. They come home and I am up. They go to sleep and I go to work. SWAT call outs and court kind of mess things up, but my wife put her career on hold to raise the kids, and it really works out well." explained McCarthy.

"What now?" asked Shepherd when he pulled into the ramp of the police department.

"Just one more question. If I could grant your request right now and you could pick one of the four options, how would you answer? You could pick being a lousy cop, an average cop, a good cop, or a great cop. Which would you choose?"

Shepherd liked this. This was an easy answer. He answered without hesitation. "A great cop!" The smile on his face resembled the dog in the Garfield strip, Odie. McCarthy could see all of Shep's teeth, and his tongue was hanging out, and his eyes were bright even though he had been awake all night. The rookie got to drive a SWAT truck tonight. The SWAT team arrested a real bad guy, and he got to take him to jail. A shirt got shot, and, oh yeah, he arrested an intoxicated driver with no arms. He would not be able to sleep for three days. "I want to be a *Great Cop!*" Shep repeated since McCarthy failed to answer. Dan was savoring the look on the rookie's face.

"Abracadabra, you're going to be a great cop." McCarthy said waving his hand magically over the rookie.

"That's it?" puzzled Shepherd.

"It's almost that simple. I can wave my hand. I can train you. Your college professors taught you how to think about being a great cop. Your academy instructors and I have and will continue to teach you how to be a great cop. Now, all you have to do is decide to be one and work hard, and you will get there. There is one antidote to the magic I have just laid on you." McCarthy stopped talking and remained as quiet as Slade.

"What's the antidote? What will keep me from being a great cop?" asked Shepherd.

"Cynicism! Cynicism and negativity! Cops are immersed in violence, victimization, death, and hypocrisy. They have to work in the best criminal justice system in the world, but it is flawed because some of the people in it are flawed." McCarthy exited the squad and loaded up his gear.

The rookie followed his lead. He marked down the mileage on the squad in his notes and tripped after his field training officer. Shep looked at the SWAT uniform and thought, "Some day, I am going to be in one of those. Hold it rookie! You better make probation first. I have to learn how to walk before I learn to run." he mentally cautioned himself.

McCarthy continued, "Here's the deal. Nothing good comes from buying into cynicism. It negatively impacts on your job, your family, and even your physical and emotional well being. Staying positive in this career is a discipline. To stay positive you will have to discipline yourself. Slade will be out of jail before the reports are written, and some of the cops will complain and talk for a week about it. It is a fact. Live with it. Our job was to put him there. He's there. It is the system's job to keep them there. Start today realizing that the system is truly the best in the world, but it is flawed. We did our job well and no one got hurt." McCarthy stopped in stride, almost causing the rookie to run into him, "Got it!"

"Got it!" echoed Shep.

"Now, do you like your profession?" asked Dan.

"Yes, sir!" He answered enthusiastically, as if it was his first night on the job, which it was.

"Is it just about the most important job in the free world? Quite possibly even a sacred calling?"

"Yes sir!"

"Are you going to be a great cop?"

"Yes, sir!"

"Hold that thought for about another thirty years and you will be." answered McCarthy.

Stanley Brockman was standing just inside the entrance, and he had been listening to McCarthy with absolute disgust. He took a sip on his ever-present Styrofoam cup of coffee, and he just had to comment, "Hey, rookie. Keeping your sanity in this profession comes down to remembering TJIF. When that doesn't work remember IAB. Got it?" asked Brockman.

"What does that mean?" asked Shep, setting his gear down inside the hallway on the wall near the command room.

"This job is fucked!" Brockman said with feeling. "IAB means it's all bullshit!" Brockman took another sip of his coffee.

McCarthy then finished the lesson, "I started the shift with this message, and now I have ended it to make this point. You have to survive this job physically, legally, and emotionally. Skills, tactics, and attitude are three important keys to survival. By the way, Officer Brockman chose to help me make my point on his own. I did not ask him to back me up." McCarthy showed Shepherd where to hang up the keys, sign in, and place his radio in the charger.

Shepherd for some time wondered if Brockman and McCarthy had their shtick down. He thought it too coincidental that Brockman would serve as a bad example before the shift and after the shift to prove McCarthy's point so well. He would think that for some time, until he got to know Stanley Brockman.

McCarthy sat down and wrote his portion of the report on the Slade arrest. The arrest belonged to the drug investigators. They made the case and filed the paperwork and packaged the pounds and pounds of marijuana that was recovered. They also found $2000 in cash and eight firearms, besides the one that was used to threaten the entry team.

Sergeant Compton immediately started writing the over-all report on the SWAT team's action, and Stammos was writing his report explaining the reason he fired his weapon. Compton had already told Stammos, "Totally justified. Obviously, someone else will look at it and make a determination, but it was totally justified. Good job! Write it up." directed Compton with a friendly and sincere pat on the shoulder.

Every few minutes, officers entered the report room. Each one had something to say to the man who had just shot a shirt.

"Randy. Nice shooting! Thanks for covering us," said McCarthy.

"Thanks, buddy," replied Randy as he kept tapping away on the computer.

"Hey, Randy, that was cool, real cool. I haven't seen anything that cool since the hogs ate my little brother." said Dooley.

"Yeah, thanks. That reminds me, I've been meaning to ask you. Did your parents have any children that lived?" questioned Stammos.

"You be the judge." Dooley laughed and sat down at an unoccupied computer.

"Hey, Randy, next time hopefully Slade will be in the shirt." said Captain Jackson, who was in charge of the patrol division. He had heard the details of the shooting and thought he would stop in and reassure Stammos. He patted him on the back as he stepped in to reassure Stammos.

Then a dark cloud blocked the sun. Captain Hale of Community Services entered the room. Quiet engulfed the room and its occupants. "I think you will be all right on this one, but I certainly would have made sure of my target before I pulled the trigger," said Captain Hale.

"Target. Right, sir. I will keep that in mind when I am target shooting," said Stammos. Randy had slammed one by Hale without Hale even noticing that he had been put down. Captain Hale was the only cop in the room that missed the meaning of what Stammos had just said to him.

McCarthy looked up from his work station with disgust. "Hale must always think very hard before he speaks so doesn't accidentally say the right thing," thought McCarthy.

After Hale left the room, Carpenter yelled over to Randy, "Hey, Randy! I see you alter shirts. Do you alter pants too?"

Brockman then chimed in, "Randy could have altered the pants too, but Slade couldn't send them out. He was too busy shitting them." Everyone laughed. Everyone noticed Stanley Brockman was always a different person when he was with SWAT and talking SWAT. No one but Brockman knew how much he loved being on the SWAT team. He had ostracized so many people he worked with. He was a classic case of an officer that the experts would call over invested. He had no life and no identity but his identity as a cop.

His career was all he had, but it had been a disappointment. He had tried for an investigator's position but was turned down because he was not "self motivated."

He had written and tried repeatedly for a sergeant's position but could not write a good test. Then he tried out for and was appointed to the SWAT team. He had skills. Compton had known Brockman before the light flickered out. Compton thought Brockman's skills would benefit the team and the team would benefit Brockman.

As usual, Compton was right. The team was a life jacket for Brockman. He felt like he used to feel when he loved the job when he was with the team. Brockman was always good when he wanted to be, and he wanted to be good when he was with the team.

Stanley Brockman looked around the report room at all the cops in their black tactical uniforms. He looked down at his. He looked at the name tag. It said, "Brockman." He was a somebody in this uniform. He belonged to something important that had not lost meaning to him. He looked at each one of the black uniformed coppers. Some of them were still wearing their armor. Carpenter still had his helmet on.

"Why do you still have your helmet on, Gary?" asked Brockman.

"I got to look my best. I took it off, and I got helmet hair." answered Carpenter while he mockingly combed his helmet with an imaginary comb as if he was Fonzy from *Happy Days*.

Brockman laughed. He loved this part of the job. He loved being a part of the team. Brockman thought, "I might not like them, and they might not like me, but I don't have to like them because they are my family. Compton said it himself in his Saint Ritz Cracker Day Speech, 'We're a band of brothers.'" He smiled and took a sip of his coffee and said quietly but out loud, "Slade couldn't send them out. He was too busy shitting them," Brockman chuckled as he walked out of the report room sipping endlessly from his seemingly bottomless cup. "I kill myself."

But Stanley Brockman would never do that… as long as he had family. The SWAT team was the closest thing to family he had. Stanley was having a good night. He went out with his beloved SWAT team, one of two things in his world he had not soured on. He also managed to avoid writing a single report, even though there was a massive seizure of marijuana and there had been shots fired during the arrest. Now he was just killing time and getting paid on the "big clock."

Getting paid on the "big clock" was overtime in cop speak. They always felt like they were getting paid more closely to what they were earning when they got paid on the "big clock." For Brockman, anyway, it beat the hell out of going home to his empty home and staring at the ceiling for two hours before he could sleep.

Brockman started heading toward the front desk to see what the second thing in his life that he was not soured on was doing. That was the good looking and amiable secretary, Sandy. She was a gorgeous blonde who looked like a super model but acted like the girl next door. She seemed unaware of her beauty. Stanley was secretly in love with the woman, but the only person on the department that did not know this fact was Sandy. He was deathly afraid to ask her out. To be more correct, he was not afraid to ask her out; Stanley was afraid that if he did she would turn him down like all the others and that would end their relationship, such as it was. The relationship consisted of Stanley bringing her coffee, and a sweet roll occasionally, and standing around her desk awkwardly exchanging small talk for a few minutes. That wasn't much, but it was good enough for Stanley Brockman.

Just before Stanley's arrival, a strange man wearing a hooded sweatshirt came to the front desk of the La Claire Police Department. Sandy was working at the front desk and saw the man come in. His head was down, and she could not see his eyes because the hood was pulled forward and hid them. He startled her to her core when he suddenly appeared looking like none other than the grim reaper without the sickle.

The troubled man was Tyrone Baxter. Tyrone was a person with severe emotional problems. "Can I help you, sir?" said Sandy, who was always instinctively nice. She could not help it. It was in her nature to be nice. Even the "grim reaper" would have to prove himself grim to Sandy before he would be treated in kind and maybe not even then.

Tyrone did not hear her. Tyrone just maintained his stare. He appeared to be looking somewhere beyond the twilight zone. It would be difficult to know if being on some psychotropic drug would have helped Tyrone be more lucid, but being on nothing left him in the darkness of mental health oblivion.

Baxter stood next to a trash receptacle and unzipped his pants. He pulled out his penis and emptied his bladder with neither a word nor a whinny.

"Sir! Oh my God, this is the police department, sir! What are you doing?" She, of course, knew exactly what Tyrone was doing, but lacking something else to say in a situation such as this she felt something needed to be said. Sandy asked a second time, "Sir! What are you doing?" still knowing the answer to her question, but lacking the availability of another conversational option.

Just then Stanley Brockman arrived at the front desk. He had acquired a second cup of coffee for his beloved Sandy when he came upon a sight he did not expect and was not quite ready for. When he saw the urinating disturbed person, he thought. "Shit! The fucking grim reaper is taking a piss in front of Sandy. That can't be good." He radioed for assistance, "Could someone in the report room back me up. I will be making an arrest at the front desk of the police department."

Instantly, he could hear footsteps running down the hall toward him. He recognized the enthusiastic patter of McCarthy's sprinting feet. Brockman felt he needed to clarify to McCarthy how things were going to be handled. He wanted this arrest. He did not want to pass it off on someone else like so many others. This man had exposed himself in front of his beloved Sandy. This might be an opportunity to show Sandy he was a man of substance, a man of action. "McCarthy. I'll take this guy. He is going for lewd and lascivious and disorderly conduct and mopery with intent to fucking gawk. I know Tyrone. I have dealt with him before. He's a total wack job." Stanley informed McCarthy.

"Yeah, I've dealt with him before on a mental hold. It's all yours. I am just here to help," acquiesced McCarthy. He did not need another report to write.

After finishing urinating, Tyrone just let go of his rather large flaccid member and turned toward Sandy with a blank look on his face.

Brockman took Tyrone in an escort hold and said, "Hey, Tyrone. Just put your hands behind your back. That's the way to do it. You're a good man. Thanks," said Brockman as he brought Tyrone's arm back. McCarthy was on the opposite arm, and he brought Tyrone's other arm back. There was surprisingly no resistance. There was not even a flinch. Brockman fumbled nervously a bit with the handcuffs, being under the watchful eye of Sandy, but was able to apply them, check them for tightness, and double lock them without Tyrone making a peep. He just continued to stare toward that place that lies directly across the street from Never-Never Land.

"Tyrone, what's going on here tonight?" asked Stanley. Tyrone said nothing. He just stared blankly ahead.

Brockman stood for as moment with his prisoner in tow, allowing Sandy to gaze upon his manliness and his proficiency. Instead, it allowed Sandy extra time to gaze upon Tyrone's stately exposed member.

"Stanley," Sandy whispered as she pointed toward Tyrone's love lizard hanging out of his pants portal.

A stunned Stanley Brockman spun Tyrone into a half circle to turn away from Sandy. Tyrone did not react and was non responsive. McCarthy and Brockman walked him to the back and searched him after Brockman put some gloves on. When Stanley reached Tyrone's exposed pocket rocket, Stanley carefully maneuvered Tyrone's pants zipper opening down around and over Baxter's one-eyed snake and carefully zipped up the enclosure. Stanley did this without even brushing up against Tyrone's water horse even once. When it was away, Brockman sighed a sigh of relief as if he was a bomb tech who cut the blue wire and did not hear an explosion.

Tyrone Baxter was acting even stranger than usual. Strange did not get someone to a psyche ward. The courts had decided in the seventies that it would be much better for the mentally ill if it was more difficult for police to place protective holds on them. Stanley Brockman said once, "The way hospitals and the courts handle mentally ill people kills more people than shark bites, but you never see anyone complaining about it."

Tonight, Tyrone was headed for jail until he looked at Brockman and said, "Let me go. I need to kill someone." That was all he said, but it was more than enough. Stanley did a charges pending report on Tyrone and gave him a ride to La Claire General Hospital.

Within seventy-two hours, Tyrone was released from the hospital as a patient "not suitable for treatment." He would not talk to the doctors. He was not violent, and he was totally cooperative. He was then transported to La Claire County Circuit Court and was released from custody on the charges of disorderly conduct. The District Attorney did not charge the lewd and lascivious. "He took it out to urinate, and therefore, the exposure was not sexual in nature," he would explain to the media at a later date.

When Stanley returned to Central Station, he bought another cup of coffee for Sandy and set it on the desk in front of her.

"I should be buying you a cup of coffee. Your timing was perfect. Thanks for being there, Stanley." She said smiling and laying her hand on his arm.

"I uh, well, you know, um, I guess that's, ah, what I get paid the big bucks for," said Stanley, overwhelmed by the touch of Sandy's hand. "Ask her out for breakfast," said his little voice. "Sandy, do you ever eat breakfast after work?"

Sandy, by now, was looking at her computer screen. "No. I can't sleep if I have anything to eat after coming home from working nights." Her eyes never left the screen.

"Me neither. I guess I'll see you," said Stanley as he turned to walk away, hoping that she would call for him to come back.

"Bye, Stanley. Thanks again," said Sandy with a smile.

"You call me anytime," said Stanley. "Anytime for anything!" Stanley walked away.

Anytime was surely going to be some other time than now. Stanley didn't mind though. She smiled and touched his arm. That was enough for Stanley Brockman.

Chapter Four: "We Did It!"

Harley David Slade stood before Judge Alice six months to the day after his business was shut down. The investigators were unable to make the total impact on Slade that they would have liked to. Slade did not keep much of his money in the bank. His cash flow was still very much intact thanks to the fact that Slade did not trust the banks. Harley David did not trust the government, his neighbors, or even God. Slade trusted himself and the voice he heard consistently echoing inside his head.

Slade stood before Judge Alice, who was a judge and, therefore, a lawyer. Of all the people in the world, he trusted lawyers the least. He had begrudging respect for the police because he felt he must. They were the "grunts" that he faced across the line in this war he was in. He was a grunt also in this "War on Drugs" he was engaged in. He had studied the tactics he would need to employ. He learned to apply them well. He learned subterfuge and spent the last six months doing everything he needed to do to survive this moment. He needed to stay out of prison at all costs. He went to work every day and did not sell any marijuana. He did not need any more money because he had more than enough to survive one more year, and that was all he needed. The war would be over for him and many more in one year or two at the most.

Slade and the voice had fantasized about his plan to wage war for some time, but now he had put the plan down on paper and began preparing for the moment the tide of battle would shift in his favor. Up to this point, Harley David Slade had kept his fantasies, his thoughts, his plans, and his preparations from all but his trusted voice.

"Mr. Harley David Slade, before I pass sentence in this matter do you have anything to say?" asked Judge Alice, who hoped every person before her would say the magic words to allow her to show unreasonable and dangerous leniency that was the trademark of "Wonderland." The police called her, "Alice in Wonderland," because visiting Judge Alice's court was like stepping through the looking glass where anything, but reality, could happen. The criminals usually faced sweet, compassionate, and forgiving Alice. The police and prosecutors usually met either the Queen of Hearts or the Mad Hatter. The story was she was a product of Berkley. When she was at the Lawyer's Bar parties, she would boast of having had Angela Davis as a professor. Davis was a seventies' radical who was strongly tied to a group accused of killings of cops and judges. Alice felt a kinship toward these "down with the man" types and wished she could have been young enough to have carried a banner with the anti-everything movement of the '60s and '70s.

Alice discovered a better way to lift up the downtrodden and stick it to "the man." She had become "the man." She was a circuit court judge, and she was about to lift up one more downtrodden soul to a better life after he had been knocked down and felt the sting of this jack-booted bunch of thugs. Even Judge Alice had standards. Harley David Slade would have to do the dance. He would have to jump through her hoop. He would have to grovel and say the magic words.

Now Harley David Slade stood before Judge Alice. He had asked for a substitution of judges until he received Judge Alice. Criminals clambered to go before Judge Alice for sentencing. It was an absolute "no brainer." Jack Sloan, Harley's attorney, arranged for nearly all of his clients to appear before this benevolent judge.

"Your honor, I respectfully stand before you a *changed man.* I have *learned the hard way. I have learned from my mistakes.* I have not committed a crime since the incident, and *I have successfully completed treatment.* I feel that I have been rehabilitated by taking a long, hard look at myself. I finally and forever have *given my soul up to the Lord and he has rehabilitated me.* If you can see fit to give me '*one more chance,' I will not let you down.* If sent to prison, I believe I will only come back a worse man *because prison does not rehabilitate.*"

Judge Alice felt flushed. She could not speak initially because she could not remember how long it had been since she had heard all seven. She felt as if she could do Meg Ryan's scene in the deli in the movie *Harry Met Sally* without even acting. "My God," she said to herself after checking her list, "he even has them in order. Let's see," she slid her personal sentencing guidelines sheet out from under the clutter.

Mercy is called for when the person facing me shows:

1. (S)He is a changed man/woman.
2. (S)He has learned from his/her mistakes.
3. (S)He has successfully completed treatment.
4. (S)He has given his/her soul up to the Lord (optional).
5. The Lord (optional) has rehabilitated.
6. If (s)he is given one more chance, (s)he will not let me down.
7. (S)He knows that prison does not rehabilitate.

Her honor then covertly slid the sheet back into hiding and began to pontificate for what seemed to Harley to be an eternity. The voice cut in, drowning out the droning voice of Judge Alice, "Look how she is talking down to you. She is a part of this war also. Look at her go on and on and on, immersed in her self importance. At the first opportunity, you must add her to the list along with the rest. In fact, put her up to number two on the list of all military and strategic targets. Add her barracks and her man if she has one. He will be acceptable collateral damage. Anyone living in a military barracks in time of war is an acceptable target."

Slade agreed with the voice but resisted the urge to acknowledge it here in court.

Judge Alice came to an exciting conclusion. "Therefore, I am giving you one more chance. I better not see you in front of my bench again. I am sentencing you to five hundred hours of community service and five year probation. You will be given jail time of… time served."

"Thank you, your honor," said Slade, turning away quickly. The smile left his face. He immediately discarded it since he no longer needed it. It had served its purpose.

"You did it!" said the voice, who was his mentor, his confessor, and his constant companion.

"We did it!" answered Harley David Slade.

"We did it!" exclaimed Jack Sloan, Slade's pony-tailed, fake-tanned, fancy-suited, court-appointed attorney.

Slade was startled to see Sloan next to him. He had forgotten about him. Slade looked at him and then looked beyond him.

The voice then snapped Slade back into his alternate reality. "Never mind him. He's a lawyer. He feeds at the same trough as the rest of your enemies. If they hadn't targeted you, he would be out of work. Get the hell out of here now! We have to talk." Slade obeyed and scurried quickly through the crowded courthouse looking beyond everyone he met.

Sloan shook his head and turned to his intern, "You want to be an attorney? This is the most thankless job in the world. I just saved that man from a certain prison term, and he doesn't have a simple thank you for me."

After surveying the sudden change of Slade's demeanor, Sloan's intern was moved to editorialize, "He kind of looked a little crazy."

"Shh, keep that under your hat. You play the mentally incompetent card as a last resort," said Sloan in a hushed voice. "We didn't need it today. We had Judge Alice and her seven steps to better living out of prison. That's always the better option." Sloan slipped his file into his briefcase and tried to follow his client out of the courtroom, but when Sloan and his hapless intern reached the hallway, Slade was nowhere to be found.

"How in… What the fu…?" Unable to find Slade, the pony-tailed attorney turned his attention to his intern. "Kid, do you want to be a defense attorney someday?"

"Yes?" responded the acne-scarred protégé.

"Then you have to learn that this is an adversarial system. Since guilt was not the issue, it was the prosecutor's job to see to it that Harley David Slade was sent to prison. It was our job to see to it that he did not received such harsh treatment, even if it was well deserved. Harley, who had a marijuana manufacturing plant in a residential area less than one thousand feet from a middle school and who taunted police with a shotgun, has now walked out of court with time served." Sloan pondered the enormity of the task that had been given to him this case. "I worked my ass off to get him before Judge Alice. Initially, I did not want the loon to say a word, but he insisted and, quite frankly, he scared me a little so I said go ahead. First, I coached him for no less than an hour on his little speech. Most people would have thought Harley David Slade would be on his way to prison for five years for what he did. Not this time. It was our job, no, our duty to see to it that he did not. Son," and Sloan put his hand up for a high five that the intern reluctantly delivered, "we did it!"

Chapter Five:
Madison Brown

At the same moment Slade was scurrying from the courtroom, Officer Dan McCarthy stepped into lane three of the indoor firing range located in the basement of the La Claire Police Department. He breathed slowly in through his nose and pushed the air out with the muscles in his abdomen. He looked at the target and always found it difficult to stand and look at the image of a man who was pointing a shotgun at him and have to wait to have someone else tell him when it was OK to shoot.

Officer Madison Brown stepped into lane number four and breathed in through her nose and pushed the breath out with the muscles in her abdomen. Madison Brown was the daughter of a Los Angeles cop. She was the granddaughter of a Los Angeles cop. She was a three-year veteran of the La Claire Police Department. When someone would inevitably ask, "Why would you leave LA to come live in Wisconsin and freeze your ass off for four months a year?"

Madison would simply answer, "I love five things about Wisconsin: winter, spring, summer, fall, and last but not least, the Green Bay Packers."

This was not a total lie, but it most certainly was not the whole truth. She did like the four seasons. She also loved the Green Bay Packers, but she had grown up the daughter of a police officer. Her father was an honorable man who was highly principled and dedicated to his profession, as most police officers are. She grew up watching a rabid media, which was notoriously biased against the police, discredit the entire Los Angeles Police Department over a few bad officers in the ranks. The media there swooned over cop killers, and the now-and-forever-famous "motorist" Rodney King. Four cops were tried twice for "the Rodney King beating," and the city burned while the Los Angeles Police were being crucified for being first too aggressive and then not aggressive enough. It cut deep into her father's pure and blameless heart. Her father aged twenty years his last five years on the department.

It pained her to watch the slanderous portrayals of Los Angeles Police in movies like *Training Day*. If that was what Hollywood thought of their police, she wanted nothing to do with them. She knew better. The cops she knew were her heroes. She had been at picnics with them. She had gone to the beach with them. She had attended funerals for them, and she had helped nurse her father back to health each time he was injured in the line of duty protecting the same people that so maligned him. Her father was her hero. He had taken a bullet in a gun fight with a notorious gang banger. Her father had put the gangster down and covered him until back-up arrived. The shooter later received an early parole for writing a children's book behind bars and was interviewed on "Prime Time Special" by a gushing anchor woman Diane Lambheart [3] just a few years later.

Maddy looked on as her father watched the interview and subconsciously rubbed his old wound while a tear welled up in his eye. No one clamored to interview him when he took the bullet for his city. Now, the man who shot her father was making a female news anchor all wet on national television. The news anchor, Diane Lambheart, wounded her father more deeply and more permanently with her "Prime Time Special" than the punk ever could have with his "Saturday Night Special."

Maddy always wondered why everyone in the world knew who Rodney King was, but no one had ever heard of her father. She would emulate her father and grandfather but not in Los Angeles. Madison decided Los Angeles did not deserve her best effort.

All Maddy wanted was to be a cop. She wanted to be a great

---

3. In SWAT terms "lamb heart" has a significant meaning. Someone with a lamb's heart can never tell the difference between the honorable sheep dog and the wolf. Police are the honorable sheep dogs that would never harm the sheep. The sheep do not like the sheep dog, because they are always barking at them and keeping them safely together with the flock. Sheep cannot tell the difference between the honorable sheep dog and the wolf, yet they are drawn to the wolf.

cop, not just a good cop. She had ridden with McCarthy when she was new, and she had told him that all she wanted to be was a "great cop," and after three years she still wanted that. She wanted her father to be proud of her. She wanted to follow in his footsteps, but not in the city that disrespected the many police officers that lived and died to protect and serve the "City of Angels." The people, the media, and the city did not deserve their police department she thought. On her last visit home to see her father, she arranged a ride along with the Los Angeles Police Department. When she came home at the end of the ride along, she had found her father awake and she asked him, "Dad, how did you take it for twenty-five years in this city?"

"You do what you love to do because you love to do it, not because it is easy. Sweetheart, being a cop is more than a job. It's more than a profession. It's a calling. I think the priests and the police are the only ones keeping Los Angeles from becoming Los Diablos. I knew that, and that is how I made it twenty-five years." He looked at his little girl, all grown up, and brushed the back of his hand across her cheek. "Sweetheart, I raised you to be tough because I didn't want my daughter to be a victim. I want you to know that because sometimes people think fathers do that when they want a boy and were disappointed. I always prayed for a little girl, and my prayers were answered. I also sensed you were going to answer the call and put that badge on." He leaned forward and gave her a butterfly kiss with his eyelash and then took off his St. Michael the Archangel's medallion he wore every night on duty and put it carefully around her neck. "St. Michael, watch over my little girl." Then he kissed her cheek lightly. "Be careful out there."

"I will be, Dad," she said. Then she thought of what McCarthy had taught her, and she said quietly to herself as she walked away, "Bad guys better be careful."

Maddy was now a three-year veteran of the La Claire Police Department and was eligible to try out for the La Claire Police Department SWAT Team. She stood in the booth next to her former Field Training Officer Dan McCarthy. He wasn't much older than she, but there was something very fatherly about him.

Maybe it was the way he always treated her like a cop and never like a woman. He treated her like a back-up and not like someone he needed to protect.

McCarthy was in lane three and Brown was in lane four in the basement shooting range at the La Claire Police Department. McCarthy was shooting the SWAT team's entry level course with Madison, who was a SWAT team applicant. If she made the team, she would be the first woman placed on the team as a tactical operator.

McCarthy was already on the team, but Compton always had a team member go through the entry test to get the applicants used to the idea that this was a team effort.

"All right, shooters on the line, ready, ready on the left, ready on the right, ready on the firing line… *Gun!*" shouted Compton.

Compton had not had McCarthy and Brown charge the weapons. There was no round in the chamber. Under the stress, many applicants would become flustered when they would draw and fire their weapon and hear nothing. McCarthy and Brown fired as one, "click." Then, without thought, they slammed the palm of their hands to the bottom of their magazine, rolled their weapons to the side, and racked the action back, feeding a round into the chamber. Then they fired ten rounds to the body and two to the head, well within the required time limit. Both breathed slowly, looked left, and looked all the way around to the right as they dropped the magazine in the weapon and slammed another one home. "Clear!" they shouted as one.

"Return to ready," ordered Compton. "Recover to the holster." Both shooters scanned the area again to the left, to the right, above and behind. When all was clear, they returned their weapons to their holsters.

"Well done. All we need to do is drop you two into a pool put the funny rubber hats on you, and you could win a synchronized swim competition. That was not only deadly but also beautiful!"

After the full course was completed, Compton scored the targets. "Brown, you shot a 298 out of 300 possible. Brown, you were good enough. That was plenty good enough."

"McCarthy, you shot a 300 out of 300. What does Victoria say about you sleeping with that weapon every night?"

"I bet she says, is that a Glock in your hand, or are you just excited to see me?" quipped Maddy.

"Yeah, ahh, something like that," said McCarthy, turning red and laughing.

"McCarthy, I do not know if I can have you on my beloved SWAT team if Maddy can make you blush that easily," said Compton shaking his head. "Get your sweats on we are going to do the physical now."

The physical test for the SWAT team consisted of a series of events. McCarthy watched in awe as Madison Brown surpassed all his expectations. McCarthy scored 100% on nearly every event, which was something members of the SWAT team shot for every time they took the test, but to see a female score so highly amazed McCarthy.

McCarthy performed each event faster than usual, not because he wanted to beat her, but he was anxious to see what she would do.

She rapped off fifty sit-ups in a minute for 100%. She pumped out fifty push-ups in a minute for another 100%. McCarthy pushed up 295 at the bench, which was well over the 100%, but then he dropped his jaw as Maddy pushed up 215. He had never seen a woman do 215 before. Then came the pull-ups. Women rarely could do them. They would leap up and then hang from the bar, drop, and say "I can't do pull-ups. I have never been able to do pull-ups." Then they would run off and complain that pull-ups were an invention by men to keep women out of "the club."

Madison stopped at the bar and turned to Compton and asked, "How many is 100%?"

"Fourteen, Maddy," answered Compton looking at the sheet on his clipboard.

"Remind me to stop at fourteen," said Madison.

Compton counted out loud each pull-up, and McCarthy found himself counting out loud, also, in awe. "One, two, three, four, five, six, seven, eight, nine, ten, eleven, twelve, thirteen, fourteen, fifteen," and both of them realized she was not kidding. "Stop!" called out Compton.

Brown stopped and dropped to the floor landing like a female panther, coming down from a tree ready to strike its hapless prey.

"So many… women say they can't do those. That was amazing," said Compton marking the score 100% on the sheet.

"My father used to tell me, 'When anyone says… women can't do something, you remember can't is a four letter word. We don't tolerate its use in our family.'"

"You obviously are your father's daughter. Let's head out to the track for the Cooper Run," said Compton. "Let us see if you can impress me one more time."

Brown was a natural blonde with a natural wave to her hair. She wore it over the shoulder off duty, but on duty she wore it tightly braided. She was five feet eight inches and weighed 145 pounds, and she was built like an athlete. She carried her strength well and, in spite of possessing it, still maintained her strikingly feminine beauty.

Brockman had once said, "Maddy looks like that early morning television exercise guru Denise Austin, except with an attitude." Brockman had to elaborate, "I can see her on TV in black leotards telling her audience, 'I'm going to work out now, and if you want to eat potato chips and sit on the couch on your fat ass and watch, you just go ahead.'" Rarely did people agree with Brockman, but this time he was right. She did look like Denise Austin with an attitude.

On the run, Brown kept a nice pace but was unable to do the two miles in twelve minutes. She finished one-and-three-quarter miles in the twelve minutes, which still allowed her to be on the SWAT team. One thing Compton noticed was something he had never seen before. The run was a twelve-minute run. When twelve minutes were up, she was clearly one quarter mile away from the two miles required for the 100% score. She would finish receiving a 90% on this event, which would allow her to be on the SWAT team. What Brown did was to keep running. She wanted to know how much time she had to cut off to make the two miles in twelve minutes the next time.

McCarthy was cooling down from his run. He had stopped running after the twelve minutes were up and had finished ahead of Maddy. He then was surprised to see her run past him and continue to run after the time was up. Compton walked up to McCarthy, who was stretching his hamstrings in his cool down, and said, "I've never had anyone keep running before."

As Maddy crossed the finish line, Compton shouted, "thirteen minutes and twenty-nine seconds on two mile. Way to gut it out, Brown! Your dad would be proud of you."

"Looks like our tactical unit will be adding on a member. I was hoping a female would try out. It will help us greatly on the entries where we have females that need to be searched. She'll be good," said Compton.

"She'll be great!" agreed McCarthy.

Compton turned toward Maddy and asked, "Well, Maddy,… do you still want a pager strapped to your side 24/7 and to catch bad guys with one of the best SWAT teams in the country?"

"Yes, sir, Sergeant Compton!" replied Maddy, her face lighting up as if she were Cinderella and Prince Charming had just asked her to dance at the ball.

"Well," he held up his fist and said, "Congratulations! You are SWAT."

She bumped fists with Compton, jumped, and let out a whoop, "Thank you! Thank you! Thank you! Thank you!" Some girls dream of being rescued by a white knight in shining armor or dancing with Prince Charming. This proud daughter and third generation cop was not raised to be a damsel in distress. She did not want to dance with Prince Charming. Maddy Brown had her own dream… to be a great cop and become a modern knight in black armor. Her wildest dreams had just come true.

Chapter Six: "I'll Be OK, But I'm Shot"

"One last item," said Compton, just before ending line-up the night after the SWAT physical test of Maddy Brown. "You noticed I have put individual packets of Kleenex on each table in the line-up room. Feel free to take one. I have received a complaint from day shift that someone on night shift is using the side of the driver's seat as a depository for… their nasal discharge, aka: boogers, snot, dried post nasal drip. Whoever is doing this, cease and desist and use the aforementioned Kleenex." Then Compton warned ominously, "Do not make me resort to DNA testing to determine the perpetrator."

Stanley Brockman picked up the Kleenex and tossed it in his duty bag and looked self consciously around the room.

"Be careful out there!" said Compton after closing the line-up book.

"Bad guys better be careful," thought McCarthy.

"Bad guys better be careful," thought Madison Brown.

Then the shuffle started immediately after as the night shift officers packed up to hit the streets of La Claire. "Stay Safe, Stay Strong, and Stay Positive!" added Compton. "Hold it!"

Everyone stopped. Compton had something important to say by the tone of his voice, and when Compton spoke, everyone listened. "Speaking of strong, one of your own showed one of the strongest SWAT team entry level performances I have ever seen. Let's hear it for our newest member of the La Claire Police Department SWAT Team, Maddy Brown!"

Every member of the shift set down their gear and clapped for Maddy. Stanley Brockman continued drinking his coffee with one hand and clapped with his other hand. Stanley was able to flap his fingers down against his palm with one hand and make a loud clapping sound one-handed. It was an awe-inspiring feat to behold in itself.

Maddy suddenly looked like a shy school girl. She acknowledged the attention with a smile and a curtsey, which was executed with the grace of a prima-ballerina. It amazed every cop in the room. It was the first time anyone had ever acknowledged acceptance onto the SWAT team with a curtsey.

"Fuckin' A!" proclaimed Carpenter.

"How profound," commented Compton. "Did you say that when your wife gave birth to the twins?"

"Fuckin' A!" answered Carpenter sounding shocked.

"When you locked the squad keys in the car last week?" asked Dooley.

"Fuckin' A!" again replied Carpenter sounding disgusted..

"How bout when you got shot?" asked Brockman.

"Fuckin' A!" said Carpenter this time holding his chest and grimacing.

"How about when you caught Baby Jane in an alley last week going down on that seventy-five-year-old man for $25?" asked McCarthy.

"Fuckin' A!" said Carpenter, cocking his head and sounding puzzled motioning with his fingers indicating the length was about two inches.

"Carpenter, once again, you have proved to be the master of 'Fuckin'-A-Manship.' I believe you now own the word. No one has accomplished more with one word and a letter since Chef Boyardee cooked up his first pot of Spaghetti O's," said Compton.

"Fuckin' A, sir!" responded Carpenter in his most humbled and thankful tone. Gary Carpenter had truly mastered the language of "Fuckin' A" like few before him and quite probably no one after.

"How about you all hit the street and start earning your exorbitant wages protecting your adoring public?" offered Compton.

Maddy had shot out ahead, appreciative, but also embarrassed by the attention. With her squad check completed, she called in, "259."

"259 go ahead," answered the dispatcher.

"259, I'm 10-41 (beginning tour of duty) in car thirty-three on beat two," Maddy said, and then she hung up the mic and expertly steered off the ramp into medium traffic. She pulled up to a red light just one block from the police department and saw a large male shuffling across the street. She could not see his eyes because he was wearing a hooded sweatshirt and the hood was pulled up. He had an old-style boom box on his shoulder with the speaker up against his ear. The music was loud for the late hour.

"Looks like the grim reaper likes rap music," thought Maddy.

Maddy rolled her window down as the man crossed the street in the cross walk. She could see both of his hands as he slowly made his way across the street, but she could not see his eyes. If only she could see his eyes. They say, "The eyes are the window to the soul." If Maddy could have seen his eyes, she would have known she was in danger. She would have seen the eyes of a mentally ill man who had been repeatedly placed on mental holds by the police and repeatedly released. Tyrone Baxter was, according to the other residents at the Salvation Army Shelter, "one crazy motherfucker."

To the officers that dealt with him and put psychiatric holds on him for being dangerous, he was an "EDP" (Emotionally Disturbed Person), or a 10-96 (emotionally disturbed person), or to Stanley Brockman, "one crazy motherfucker."

Stanley Brockman was the officer who had put the last mental hold on Tyrone Baxter because he came into the La Claire Police Department and emptied his bladder into a garbage receptacle in front of Stanley's beloved Sandy. Then Baxter said nothing but, "I need to kill someone." Brockman gave Tyrone a ride to the La Claire General Hospital Psyche Ward. A mental health professional released him within seventy-two hours because he was, "not a proper subject for treatment." Baxter still faced charges for urinating at the front desk of the police department, so he was taken to court, where he stood mute with his eyes cast downward in apparent submission. The judge released him on a signature bond on a charge of disorderly conduct. The judge could not see Tyrone's eyes or he might have reacted differently.

The answer to the question, "Is Tyrone a dangerous man?" could be found in Tyrone's eyes. In many cases, cops did not have to ask one hundred questions to determine if a man was a "subject for treatment;" they only had to see the eyes. If only Maddy could see his eyes. Maddy canted her head to get a look at the face of the strange man with the boom box. When he reached the midway point of the cross walk, Tyrone suddenly veered right at Maddy and ran to the driver's side window, which had just opened. He brought the boom box down off his shoulder and slammed it into Maddy's face repeatedly until she leaned to her right side to avoid the blows.

Tyrone then smashed the broken and bloodied boom box to the pavement and pulled a Smith and Wesson .357 magnum. He fired six rounds at the officer, striking her four times, and swung open the door of the squad. Two startled college students, who witnessed the sudden unprovoked assault, later said Baxter's eyes were wide and they could see the whites all the way around. One of the students shuddered as he related, "The man growled like," then he swallowed hard and continued, "an animal was caged inside of him."

Tyrone pushed Maddy's body over in the seat and jumped behind the wheel of the car. He slammed the squad car door and accelerated away from the intersection loudly squealing the tires.

"God it hurts," thought Maddy. Then she remembered her instructor in a survival class she had recently taken, "If you feel pain, you are alive. If you are shot, you will survive. Most people shot do survive. If you believe you will survive, your odds of survival are much better. Believe it! You will finish the fight, and you will survive." The instructor made her repeat the words while she punched a bag and while she ran with the class. She said it over and over again. Her instructor's voice called to her as she bled onto her clipboard holding her notebook on which she had moments before written the words, "Be careful out there, you are going home after this shift." She looked at the clipboard, and lying on top of her notes was her medal. The medal her father had given her. She whispered, "Saint Michael, patron saint of police officers, give me strength."

She had been mentally and physically prepared for this moment by the example of her father. She had been mentally and physically prepared for this moment by the words of her trainer. They called to her as she bled onto the seat of the car. She moved a little at first and discovered she could move. "If you are shot, finish the fight. You will survive!" shouted her instructor. "Get-up-and-finish-the-fight," he ordered emphatically.

Tyrone was literally, "going nowhere fast." The squad was heading nowhere at a speed of 80-85-90 mph and climbing. Tyrone had intended to go to the La Claire Police Department and empty his weapon instead of his bladder tonight, but he came across a target of opportunity and just reacted. Now he would drive. There was no purpose to his sudden road trip. There, certainly, was no reason for the impromptu late night drive by this man who was "not a proper subject for treatment."

Officer Madison Brown managed to maneuver her Glock out of her holster. She saw Tyrone was not paying any attention to her. She now could see his eyes, and she knew, in fact, that he was not paying attention to anything at all. Maddy could see the blur of lights in the window and knew they were traveling very fast. There would be a terrible crash one way or the other, and she decided the car would crash now rather than later. She aimed as best as she could, considering the fact that she was lying crumpled on a car seat with multiple gunshot wounds in her vest and in her body. The crazy man was tearing through the city. He had to be stopped. "Bam! Bam!"

She thought, later, she fired once, but she had fired twice. Officers at the scene would later say there was one bullet wound, so she must have missed once, since two empty cartridges from her weapon were found on the floor of the crumpled squad. How could anyone blame her for missing once, considering the circumstances? The autopsy would later reveal that Tyrone Baxter died instantly from two bullets fired into his right temple.

They both entered Tyrone's troubled brain through the same hole.

Tyrone immediately slumped forward and then to the left, falling against the driver's door.

Maddy said to God and herself loudly, "God, dead man driving!" She braced herself for the crash and recited quickly, "Hail Mary full of grace the lord is with you. Blessed art thou amongst women and blessed is the fruit of the womb," the car hit a curb and went air born. "Jesus!" Crash!

The car stopped as suddenly as it started, and Maddy could not tell which pain she felt was from the smashing of the car, the gunshot wounds, or the beating with the radio. She could hear her instructor again wake her out of her stupor, "If you are shot, you will survive. Return fire, reload if needed, radio your condition and location."

She covered Baxter while grabbing the mic, and she breathed slowly in through her nose and out through her mouth, "God it hurts!" she cried out loud just before she keyed the mic. She felt where it hurt, and one of the bullets had struck and fractured her left clavicle. She put pressure on the wound with the side of the hand that was holding the mic. She consciously regained her composure, and all who heard the transmission would never forget it.

McCarthy would tell his wife later, "She was so calm. You would have thought she was calling in a parking complaint."

The report was simple, but revealing. "259."

"259 go ahead," answered dispatch.

"259. I'll be OK, but I've been shot," said Maddy in a voice as smooth as hot chocolate in Wisconsin in January. Maddy had just called in "10-41," four minutes earlier. This had been a short shift for Officer Madison Brown.

Four days later, two bullets were removed from Maddy in two separate surgeries. Two had been stopped by her vest. Maddy was lying comfortably sedated but awake and alert and surrounded by every member of the La Claire Police Department SWAT Team. They had all come up in uniform. All eyes were on Maddy.

Compton spoke, "We brought you this." He set a box wrapped in pink gift paper and a dark pink bow with a ballerina figurine on it, doing a curtsey.

"Can you please open it for me?" she asked as she pointed at her left arm and shoulder, heavily casted, tightly wrapped, and awkwardly slung.

Compton opened the package and inside was her black tactical uniform and helmet. On the left breast was the La Claire patch badge, and on the right above the pocket was the name, "Brown."

Compton said, "Get better quickly. We are saving a spot for you on the team. You can start as a negotiator until you are at full speed, and then we will get you back on the tactical team… that is, if you want."

"I'm coming back," she said with the same determination that got her weapon out of her holster four days earlier.

"These are for you from all of us," said McCarthy, setting a plant on the desk next to the window of her private hospital room.

Young Officer Shep came along and brought his camera. The entire team huddled around, behind, and in front of Maddy's bed for a La Claire Police Department SWAT Team picture. Maddy wore her helmet and her tactical blouse was laid over her badly bruised and abused chest.

"Say Cheese Heads!" said Shep when the camera was focused.

"Cheese Heads!" said the whole team, including its newest member Tactical Officer Maddy Brown.

"Thank you so much. I am coming back," repeated Maddy. Then something caught her attention on the television, as the team members shuffled out of the pose. "Can someone turn that up, please?"

Carpenter found the controls and was able to bring the volume up.

The familiar face on the television reported, "Good evening, America. I am Diane Lambheart of Prime Time Special. Tonight we are going to have a panel of experts discuss the recent rash of police shootings involving white police and African American men. In just the last four days, four African American males were shot *and killed* in American cities by American police. The shootings took place in Dallas, Texas; New York, New York; Los Angeles, California; and La Claire, Wisconsin. Our panel of experts will be discussing whether racism played a role in these police shootings.

The first panelist is the honorable Reverend..."

Carpenter turned off the television.

Maddy had gotten quiet. She still stared at the set as if Diane Lambheart was still bleating on, or possibly listening to the honorable Reverend Who-Gives-a-Shit explaining to America that race somehow had something to do with her shooting a man who had "not been a proper subject for treatment."

It was quiet for a long time in the room. Maddy lay there rubbing the bruised area right above her heart, where one of the rounds had been stopped by her vest. A tear welled up in her eye as she stared at the blank television screen.

Compton said quietly, "Madison Brown, you are a great cop. You have the heart of a lion. You are our hero."

What else could she be. She was her father's daughter.

Chapter Seven: Dark Dreams

The morning after his court appearance in front of Judge Alice, Harley woke up and sat bolt upright in his bed. The Dark Lord had paid him a visit. Harley could sense his presence.

He then heard the words resonate more clearly then ever before. "From now on you will speak when you are spoken to by your Dark Lord!" his voice booming like a kettle drum. "Never again will you conceal my presence. I will from this day forward be your strength instead of your weakness," proclaimed Harley David Slade's companion, mentor, and even master.

"If I let others know about you they will put me away, and we will have accomplished nothing. I can't tell others," whined Slade.

"I did not tell you to tell others. I said you shall not conceal my presence," answered Harley David Slade's own personal demon. "If I command you to speak, you will speak. If I ask you a question, you will answer. If I tell you to kill…" there was a long pause and then nothing.

Slade then finished the sentence, "I will kill." Then all was quiet. Slade got out of bed satisfied that he was on the right path. He knew what he had to do. This was no longer a dream. This was no longer a fantasy. The plan was taking shape. La Claire would know his name. All of Wisconsin would know his name. The entire country would know his name. The world would know his name. He was at war. They all had brought this war to his door step, and he would bring it to theirs. He would become more famous than Eric Harris and Dylan Klebold. More would die in La Claire than in Columbine.

Slade turned on the television, and the local news woman, Rachel Klein was standing with a badly smashed squad car impaled in the wall of a Dairy Queen. Klein was tense and excited. This was, indeed, real news, exciting news, possibly even hot enough for national news. Slade listened intently as he made himself a cup of coffee and rolled himself a joint.

"Behind me you see what is left of a La Claire police car that has obviously been totaled. Tyrone Baxter was driving the squad after he suddenly attacked Officer Madison Brown of the La Claire Police Department, while she sat at a stop light. Baxter pummeled Officer Brown with a boom box radio in an unprovoked attack and then shot her, hitting her several times. Baxter then climbed into the squad, thinking he had killed the officer and accelerated the vehicle, reaching speeds of between 95 and 100 mph. Officer Brown came to her own rescue and was able to draw her weapon and shoot Baxter, who was reportedly dead on the scene. The squad car careened out of control after Baxter was shot and crashed into the downtown Dairy Queen. No one else was injured, and miraculously, Officer Brown survived the beating, the shooting, and the car crash. She is listed in serious condition at La Claire General Hospital and is undergoing surgery as I speak. Back to you, Mark," reported Rachel Klein.

"Rachel, does the La Claire Police Department have any idea what Baxter's motive was?" asked Mark Schaefer of the La Claire Action News Team.

"No, Mark, they do not. Baxter has been hospitalized in the past for what is called Chapter 51 Holds, which mean the police have thought he was either a danger to himself or someone else, but in each case he was released."

"Clearly, looking at the wreckage, I would have to come to the conclusion that the police were dead right on Mr. Baxter. I am sure that Officer Brown would agree with me," said Schaefer, whose smirk showed he was proud of himself, owning the perfect 20-20 hindsight that is possessed by all newsmen. "Thanks for an excellent report. Now after this message, we will return to Bob Kaminsky and the weather."

Slade turned the news off. He would now have to wait for his main assault. He did not want to compete for the local news. He wanted to accomplish his mission in a slow news period. It would be during a time that people would least expect it. After an attack like this, cops are wary. It would be harder to pull one over on them.

"I'll put my supplies into hiding. I will reconnoiter my targets. When I hit, I will hit hard and come out of nowhere," Slade said out loud.

The Dark Lord did not respond. He was silent. Slade always took silence as affirmation.

Slade took one last slow drag off the doobie he was smoking, and he carefully put the blunt into the garbage disposal and ground it up. Since his arrest, Slade now only kept small amounts in his house, and that he kept near the disposal so that he could get rid of it quickly if he had to.

Slade spent the day on his computer doing research on the "War on Drugs." He confirmed that it was declared by President Richard Nixon. Slade took notes, "Nixon declares illegal war on drugs."

Slade read pertinent parts of the United States Constitution and confirmed once again that the war was declared illegally. He found words of Thomas Jefferson declaring that an oppressed people have a God-given right to revolt. He read St. Thomas Aquinas who said, "War must be a last resort to correct a grave injustice."

"A grave injustice my ass," Slade said out loud, "is smoking marijuana a grave injustice? Against whom have I committed this grave injustice?"

He was certain in what was right. If war was declared on him, he would fight back.

He shut down his computer and wrote a list:

1. Judge Alice.
2. All Circuit Court Justices.
3. Lawyers… scum of the earth.
4. Probation Agents.
5. Any cops who get in my way, especially that fucking McCarthy.

At the bottom of the page, he wrote, "Initiate hostilities by taking Judge Alice from her barracks to the set place of execution.

The place of execution will be the place of incursion."

Slade then laid down in his corner of the living room. The place looked so barren now, without his garden. The marijuana plants were beautiful to him. They were a source of income. The plants gave him meaning. Selling the dope was the only socialization he allowed himself. The marijuana calmed him. It calmed the Dark Lord. Slade could reason with him. Now his plants were gone.

Slade would not go to doctors. He did not trust them any more than lawyers. How could a truly paranoid person possibly trust someone who handed out pills, performed surgeries, and gave him one more voice he had to listen to? Slade would never see a doctor. He would never take their pills or pay their exorbitant prices while he had his life, his solitude, and his home-grown medication, marijuana. He looked around the empty room and said between his gnashing teeth, "The bastards took everything. I'll kill them."

"Sleep now. Your time will come," said the Dark Lord.

"My time will come," agreed Slade. He closed his eyes, slept, and dreamed *dark dreams.*

Chapter Eight: "Hey, You People, Get Back Over There!"

Ray Draper brought his gun up, and McCarthy saw the flash. He had not even realized he had drawn his weapon, but he realized he was looking down his sights. He squeezed the trigger, but it would not move. It was frozen. Draper was shooting and laughing, and McCarthy's weapon would not fire. "10-78 (officer needs assistance) 10-78! Shots fired." Beep! Beep! Beep! Beep! Beep! McCarthy jerked himself into an upright position, causing Victoria to roll suddenly off his shoulder. She never would get used to these wake-ups.

"Your beeper's going off," said Victoria, rolling over to the opposite side of the bed. She pounded her pillow and laid her head back down out of either disgust or exhaustion. McCarthy could not tell and would not have time to delve into it.

He looked at the code. "1025." 1025 was the page out code, which meant gear up and head to the station. McCarthy had an office in the house and a half bathroom adjacent to it in the finished basement of the house. He had his tactical uniform hung and ready to go. He was ready in less than ten minutes. Dan took a dry shower, which consisted of a good solid layer of Speed Stick deodorant under his arm and a splash of Old Spice. He brushed his teeth and slapped on his duty belt.

Victoria was up and kissed him by the door before he got out. She always did, no matter what time it was. "I love you," she said, and then she kissed him one more time, longer, and said, "Be careful."

McCarthy was glad she said it. It would be bad luck to break the string. "Bad guys better be careful," he thought to himself. "I love you too, Honey. I'll be home as soon as I can."

"Let someone else go through the door today, can't you?" pleaded Vicki as he ran down the sidewalk to his car.

"I don't know if there will even be a door," said McCarthy, which he realized wasn't helping Victoria at all.

As McCarthy rolled out of his driveway and headed toward the station, he looked at the time on his dashboard. The time was 4:30 AM. It was his night off, and he was enjoying the rare privilege of being able to sleep with his wife. "Well, I wouldn't have slept much longer anyway," thought McCarthy. The Ray Draper dream always woke him up, and it always kept him up. Ray Draper was a man who had shot his partner and been caught by McCarthy and Compton after going through one of those "doors" Victoria was talking about. While Draper was waiting for his sentencing, he escaped from jail. After a man hunt was unsuccessful, Compton had sent McCarthy out to find him. McCarthy found Draper, and there was a brief, but life changing and life ending, exchange of gun fire. McCarthy killed Draper.

"About six months since the last Ray Draper dream," thought McCarthy as he headed toward the station at sub warp speed. McCarthy did not want to be stopped for speeding on one of these call-outs. It would not only put another cop in a bad position but would also slow him down. He tried to drive as fast as he could without inspiring a traffic stop. If Stanley Brockman was beat cop, he could fire the retro rockets because Stanley Brockman was above traffic enforcement. If young Officer Shepherd was on the beat, McCarthy would have to stay within the range of general tolerance. Tonight, McCarthy did not know so he just made it quick and safe.

Upon arriving at the station, Compton and Stammos were already suited up and were ready to go. Carpenter and Dooley were arriving just after McCarthy. Gloria Dooley, Dooley's wife, was a police officer too. She was a negotiator on the SWAT team. They had met on the department and had been happily married for two years. She had moved almost immediately into Community Services, and she liked being a part of the team. She would say, "Being part of the team makes me feel like I am still doing real police work."

McCarthy could never figure out why people worked so hard to get into police work, and then when they got to it, worked so hard to be promoted to positions where they would then complain about missing "real police work."

"Hop in the SWAT truck. I'll brief you en route," said Compton.

They all loaded up into the back of the SWAT truck, which was an old army ambulance. It was in excellent condition and only had 10,000 miles. It belonged to a reserve unit and was made available when all units went to the Humvee-type vehicles. The military give-back program allowed local police agencies to get outdated military equipment that was still usable, and this truck was not even broken in. It was a great program. McCarthy had no sooner slammed the door, and Compton was out of the garage.

"It's Rick Cantwell. Do you know him?" asked Compton.

"I thought he was in prison," said McCarthy. "I put him in about four or five years ago," he added.

"I know him," said Dooley and Stammos.

"Might know him, but I can't say that I remember him," replied Carpenter, while Gloria shrugged her shoulders.

"He was involved in a domestic tonight. Life sucks in prison, and now life sucks outside. He smacked his wife around when he realized, even with his limited education, Ricky Cantwell Junior should be older than two years, seeing Ricky has been away for four years. Ricky would not need a DNA test to prove that. He smacked his wife. He smacked Ricky Junior. He smashed the TV and broke some plates. When officers arrived, he grabbed a couple impressive pieces of their Chicago Cutlery set and ran out the door. He now is in the middle of the parking lot of La Claire Central High School with two large butcher knives deciding if he is going to do himself or let us do him."

Compton paused in his briefing to hit the reds and maneuver through a red light. He did not use the siren. An approaching siren never helps in a tense situation. "Shift has the area cordoned off," Compton continued after clearing the intersection. "I am going to stay with the truck and assign team members as they arrive. Gloria, this will be close this morning, but I do not want you closer than forty feet, you got it?"

"Yes, sir," answered Gloria.

"Take what you need, bullhorn or whatever."

"Yes, sir. I probably will not need it at that distance."

"Gloria, get a squad between you and Cantwell. Stammos, I want you with the Model 870, loaded with super socks, OK?" talking to Randy.

"Less lethal," answered Stammos as he pulled the weapon and the special munitions down from the rack.

"Carpenter, I want you to be covering Cantwell with the Benelli, so we have a deadly force option in the worse case scenario."

"McCarthy. You are going to be the arrest team's team leader."

"Yes, sir," said McCarthy, the lightly fluttering butterfly wings in his stomach grew into bat wings.

"Make a plan. You may have to go suddenly. You may see an opening to move. Make sure when you do everyone knows what you are doing," said Compton.

As Compton pulled into the parking lot, he parked just inside the entry driveway. Ricky had taken a stand in the middle of the parking lot. It was still dark, but the parking lot was well lighted.

There were five officers in a line talking to Cantwell. Cantwell was standing with two very large butcher knives, one in each hand, at the ready. The officers confronting Cantwell were in a straight line and were about forty to fifty feet from Cantwell. McCarthy scanned the area and could see there was a healthy contingent of La Claire city officers and county officers keeping the inner perimeter containing Cantwell. They had isolated the problem and hopefully, now with the arrival of SWAT, the solution.

McCarthy told Dooley as they got out of the van, "Dooley, you take the shield."

McCarthy then saw Brockman jumping out of a squad car with another team member, Perry Gates. Perry was a tall likeable guy, who was quiet, but quick to laugh.

"Here is the plan, guys. Gloria, Stammos, and Carpenter are going to join the existing line as quickly as possible. Replace some of the officers in that line and send them to Compton for re-assignment. I want Gloria establishing a rapport immediately, if possible, unless you think someone there has the rapport. That's your call. Stammos and Carpenter join that existing line for the less lethal and deadly force option."

"Brockman, Gates," and just then Jim Hartley jumped out of his personal vehicle and exited fully geared up. "Hartley, glad you're here. See what we got?"

"Yeah, dispatch filled me in," said Hartley slightly breathless.

"Gloria, if you see something indicating that we better move fast, just say 'I think you should put the knife down because kids will be coming here soon.' Got it?" asked McCarthy.

"Got it!" said Gloria.

"Stammos and Carpenter, you need any further rules of engagement?" asked McCarthy.

"No," said both as one.

"If you see the arrest team and myself sliding closer then you should know I am going to move. If you hear me yell, 'Hey, you people, get back over there,' that will be the diversion and the signal that we are about to move on Cantwell. If he takes the bait, I will move. If I need you to shoot, Stammos, as a part of the move, I will call for 'Less lethal! Less lethal!' Otherwise, use those weapons as called for by the situation that develops."

"Questions?" There was silence. McCarthy took the silence as an affirmation. "OK, negotiation and cover team move!"

The three were in line in a flash. Gloria immediately noted that negotiations by the team on site had reached the point of every officer on scene taking their turn saying,

"Drop the knives!"

"Ricky, drop the knives!"

"Drop the knives, Ricky!"

"The knives, Ricky, drop them!"

As Stammos and Carpenter stepped into line, Cantwell sensed now was the time. He immediately moved on Stammos with both knives clutched menacingly in either hand.

"Drop them, now!" called Stammos.

"Less lethal, less lethal," shouted Stammos and the "Boom! Chick-chick. Boom! Chick-chick." Stammos fired the Model 870 sending two super sock rounds into the abdomen of Ricky Cantwell. The rounds were like the punch of a heavyweight fighter. They may kill but most probably will not, and that is why they are called "Less Lethal Rounds."

Stammos saw that the rounds had stopped Cantwell in his tracks, and he quickly slipped two more rounds from the sleeve in the butt stock and tactically loaded them into the magazine of the 12-gauge 870 shotgun. He did this without taking his eyes off Cantwell.

"Ooof!" exclaimed Cantwell, doubling, but he stood up, still holding both knives. Cantwell staggered back several steps. "What the fuck was that?"

"Those were bean bag rounds, Ricky. If you expect us to make your dreams come true and kill you tonight, I'm afraid you would be sorely mistaken. 'Sorely' is the operative word. We do not want to hurt you, but we can't let you hurt us either."

Gloria subtlety signaled to others in the line that she would be doing the communicating now. "I'm sorry, Ricky. Is it all right if I call you Ricky?" asked Gloria.

"Who gives a shit, go ahead," said Ricky, maintaining his grip on both knives while he rubbed the impact area of his stomach and glared at Stammos. He listened to Gloria intently.

"Good morning, Ricky. I'm Officer Dooley of the La Claire Police Department. You can call me Gloria. I can see that you are very upset this morning. I am here to help. What has got you so upset?" asked Gloria in a tone that could have been used to read children a bedtime story and sooth them to sleep.

"I am a convicted felon, just out of prison, and I can't get a job. My life sucks, and my wife is a whore. Other than that everything is fucking peaches and cream," said Cantwell sarcastically.

The other officers knew what to do. The negotiator was here. They breathed a sigh of relief, but no one relaxed.

McCarthy gave the rest their marching orders. He pulled a pen and small notebook from his pocket and drew the location of Cantwell and the line of officers. "Dooley, you have the shield. Hartley, you are hands free, and I am hands free. TASERS are out. The knives are too big and his coat is too heavy. I do not trust that the probes will do their damage with a layer of clothes like he has on. We have them just in case. Dooley, Hartley, Brockman, you and I will form a right angle extension from the left flank of the line, forward of the line, like this." He drew it onto the small diagram on his notebook pad. "If I see an opening coming, I will step forward gradually. The twenty-one-foot rule works for us. If he is not in a position to arm himself for any reason we can move faster in twenty-one feet than he can arm himself. If I yell, 'Hey, you people, get back over there!' you will know I might be moving. The command to move will actually be my movement, nothing else. If he gets the knives back into a position to use them, Dooley, stun the hell out of him with that shield. I will step aside for you. If I decentralize him then you, Hartley, should take the opposite side of Cantwell, and we will tighten him up. Brockman, you are the deadly force option in close if it goes bad. Questions?" asked McCarthy.

"So when are you going to make the move?" asked Hartley.

"Hopefully, he will lay down his knives and we will then go through the surrender ritual if he is compliant. I will only make the move if I see an opening and I am sure we will be successful. Sound good, Sergeant Compton?" asked McCarthy.

"Sounds good. Do it. Where do you want them?"

"The sniper there when one arrives," said McCarthy pointing to a porch across the street.

"Soon as one arrives, I will post him there," answered Compton.

McCarthy, Dooley, Brockman, and Hartley moved into position.

Cantwell noticed the approach. "Hey, McCarthy, how'bout you do me a favor and do me like you did Draper," shouted Cantwell.

"Talk to Gloria, Ricky," said McCarthy. McCarthy and Cantwell had history. McCarthy always treated Cantwell with respect. Cantwell hated the cop of McCarthy but respected him.

"Over here, Ricky. We can work this out. Now, if I'm not mistaken you are trying…" Gloria kept him focused on her. After time, she got him relaxed enough to speak.

The minutes in an open air stand off seem like hours. There is no yawning, stretching, putting your feet up, or just taking five for a "cup of Joe."

After an hour, Gloria got Ricky to put one knife down. When he did, the situation almost ended… badly. Cantwell dropped to his knees and turned the knife and pressed it against his stomach in a *Hara-Kari* manner as if he was a Samurai who had lost his honor in the eyes of the Shogun. There was nothing to do except hope the cut did not kill him and the team could get him to the hospital fast enough to save him.

"What about Ricky Junior?" shouted Gloria.

"He's not my fucking son!" shouted back Ricky, but he stopped. It was a risky move, but she stopped him in his tracks. Only Ricky knew for sure that at that moment he was going to spill his intestines all over the parking lot except for Gloria's intervention.

There was no good option. The super sock round had barely fazed Cantwell. They were too far away for pepper spray, and the wind was not favorable. It is not very defensible to shoot a suicidal person to save them.

"He doesn't know that. He will never know that. He has your name. I was adopted and never knew who my biological parents were, but I knew who my real parents were. They were the people that raised me," said Gloria. "To Ricky you will always be his dad."

This revelation brought Cantwell away from the ledge again. He still had the one knife in his hands, and the other lay on the ground beside him.

"Yeah, but your adopted parents weren't asshole loser fucking jail birds like I am," argued Cantwell.

"Good fucking point," thought Stanley Brockman.

"I'd like to sit down and talk to you somewhere else. You know kids will be coming here soon. This is a school parking lot," Gloria said glancing toward McCarthy. McCarthy got the signal, but an opportunity was still not available.

"No. I'm going to die right here, but I will talk to you a while. I wish one of you fuckers would just shoot me. Which one has the real ammo?" he then looked at McCarthy again, "McCarthy, you'll shoot me won't you?"

"No one wants to shoot anyone. Just talk to Gloria, Ricky. She really can help you," McCarthy said. He needed to have Cantwell focused heavily on Gloria.

Then Cantwell did the strangest thing. McCarthy could have kissed him for it. He set one knife on the ground and tipped the other upside down and placed the handle on the ground. Cantwell then entertained himself by spinning the knife by its tip like it was a little toy. Cantwell was tired. He was sore. He truly wanted to die, and these cops were not helping him a bit. He did not want to be shot again by the bean bags. They hurt too much. He did not want more pain. He wanted to die and end his pain. Cantwell was visualizing his funeral. The sun was coming up, and it was getting light. It would be his last sunrise. "I wonder how long it will hurt and how fast it will take before it will be over," he thought as he felt the tip of the knife.

McCarthy started his move. He stepped with his lead foot, and his back foot slid up slightly. The rest of his team did the same thing and fell in line beside him, giving the appearance that they had never even moved. Then again, he stepped forward slowly and slid his back foot along landing in stance, and the team followed his lead. Then he repeated this movement ever so slowly, again and again and again.

McCarthy and the arrest team had gotten to within fifteen feet of Cantwell, and Cantwell had not even noticed the move. McCarthy yelled like he had never yelled before, looking beyond Cantwell to an area far behind him, "Hey, you people, get back over there!"

Cantwell looked at McCarthy and without giving another thought looked in the direction that McCarthy was looking, wondering, "Who the fuck is he yelling at?"

It was all McCarthy needed. He was on the move and his team was moving with him.

Cantwell realized what was happening and got up, tried to pick up a knife, but he just couldn't find the handle. The knife just twirled off into another direction landing harmlessly a safe distance away. Cantwell bolted, but it was a very lopsided attempt to escape. He looked like a wounded gazelle with four black leopards on its heels. This was a brief and shining moment for the team. The end was no longer in question as it had been just moments before. In spite of himself, Cantwell would live.

Cantwell was able to get about twenty-five feet before he was hit by McCarthy. The two skidded into the pavement, and McCarthy immediately swept Cantwell's right arm into a painful rear compliance hold. Most people are right handed, and he knew Cantwell was like most people. If he had another weapon it would probably be hidden on his right side.

Then Hartley hit, but in the skidding spinning mass, he landed on McCarthy. If someone would have snapped a photo at that moment, Hartley and McCarthy would have looked like they were a couple on a honeymoon after a gay marriage in Massachusetts. "Jim get the… Get off me, left arm, left arm!" said McCarthy in a voice loud enough for only Jim to hear.

Hartley regained his focus and balance, and the misstep was only momentary. He moved to the left arm, and Cantwell was handcuffed. The incident was over. McCarthy found a buck knife in Cantwell's right pocket, but there were no other weapons on him.

"SWAT is 10-95 (subject in custody)," McCarthy reported to dispatch.

"10-4," answered the dispatcher.

"Ricky, are you hurt?" asked McCarthy.

"No. Well just where that fucking Stammos shot me with those God damn bean bags. That hurt like a motherfucker. Why didn't he just kill me? McCarthy, just shoot me. Can't you just shoot me?" pleaded Cantwell.

"Not going to do it, Ricky. We're going to get you some help. You will be going to La Claire General. They'll check you out and get you through this thing. OK?"

"OK, McCarthy. Hey, nice move. I totally fell for it, man. That will never work again," assured Cantwell.

"Hopefully, Ricky, we won't have to keep meeting like this, and I won't have to use all my best moves on you any more. I hope you get it together. Try hard. If you don't want to try for yourself, do it for Ricky Junior. He's got your name, man. That's your boy."

"I hit the little guy, man. I hit my little boy. I'm fucking scum. I don't deserve to live. Why don't you guys just shoot me?" Then Ricky began sobbing. He couldn't stop. "Just shoot me. I don't deserve to live."

Ricky was turned over to the original investigating officers by the arrest team. He was transported to the hospital in handcuffs by ambulance. After his two super sock related abrasions were treated, he was put on an emergency Chapter 51 Hold. The hospital was told that there were charges pending against Cantwell. After the hospital and the psyche ward did the best they could for Ricky, the system would then take over and do the best thing they could for Ricky Junior. Ricky Cantwell Senior would be going back to prison.

At Central Station, Compton told everyone, "We have scheduled SWAT training tomorrow afternoon at Angelo. We'll debrief this call-out there before we get started. I will get everyone there at that time, including shift, and we will talk about how we did. For now, tag your evidence, write your reports, get back to your beats, go home and sleep, or take a dump, whatever is next on your dance card. Pick whichever one applies to your needs and responsibilities and do it. See you at training."

McCarthy headed back home after he finished his report. He was very satisfied with the outcome. To him, this call was clearly about to end with either a suicide or a suicide by cop. This is the phenomenon whereby people without the courage to kill themselves put the burden on the police. They carefully orchestrate a situation where some poor police officer gets put in a situation where they have to shoot the coward or die themselves. Today, because of a perfectly executed plan, that did not happen. He was very satisfied with his team's performance.

When he got home, Victoria was busy making beds. She had taken the kids to school, and she had missed the early local news. Cameras had footage of the stand off and the arrest. The angle of the camera did not make the initial contact between Hartley and McCarthy look as it felt. In fact, the minor faux pas was imperceptible on camera. The arrest team appeared to move smooth, fast, and clean.

At any rate, Victoria had missed it. McCarthy snuck up behind her and stopped and just said, "Hi, Honey."

She jumped and gasped and spun and then slapped his chest, "Daniel McCarthy, don't do that. You scare me half to death when you do that." She slapped his chest again lovingly and then brushed it off and laid her head down on it. "Did you go through the door this morning?" She queried.

"Nope, just because you asked, I did not go through the door." He answered truthfully as he put his arms around her.

"Are you telling me the truth, Daniel McCarthy, because you know I can handle the truth, but I cannot bear to live another day with a man that lies to me," she said, squeezing her softness into McCarthy's hardness.

"I swear. I did not even go through the door today, cross my heart and hope to be partnered the rest of my career with Stanley Brockman," pledged McCarthy, crossing his heart and ending with the boy scout salute.

"With Stanley Brockman!? Oh my. Well, I guess I can believe you then." Then she leaned back into him and wrapped her leg around him, rubbing her calf against his calf. "I'm still tired. That pager woke me up so early, and I could not get back to sleep. I got the kids to school on time. They don't move as fast as when you are here," whined Victoria.

"You poor thing. You mean you had trouble getting my darling dawdler to school on time?" asked McCarthy rubbing her back.

"You know how she is. She sings when she should be brushing her teeth, she dances when she should be putting on her shoes, and when you get serious, she just smiles at you, and she is so cute when she's making herself late, I can't stay mad," said Victoria.

"What are we to do now?" asked Dan.

"I'd like to go back to bed," said Victoria. We have four hours before we have to pick up the kids from school. I would like to get three hours of sleep." She then sat slowly on the bed and leaned back, pulling him down to her.

"Whatever shall we do with the extra hour?" asked Dan McCarthy in a mock quandary.

"Well, I can tell you one thing for sure. We are done talking." She said kissing her husband long and softly.

"You, sir, are under arrest."

Chapter Nine:
Debrief. Hindsight Is 20-20

Classroom 103 was packed at the Angelo Training Facility. The entire SWAT team, the officers who were on the call, and Captain Hale were present for the debrief. Hale had been involved in the most critical part of the call-out in his mind, which was to prepare the press release. Hale disregarded the fact that the room was crowded and packed with a SWAT team that was about to have a very physical work out, and he lit up a Marlboro and took a long satisfying drag and blew it out the corner of his large overused mouth.

Compton stepped up to the podium. "I'd like to thank you all for coming to this debrief. This is a scheduled SWAT team training. The team will begin training after it is over. I will give you a synopsis on what happened. At 4:17 AM, third shift officers arrived at the home of Ricky Cantwell. He had beaten his significant other for having a baby with another man while Ricky was in prison. She attempted to keep this fact from him by naming the child Ricky Junior, but Ricky, apparently, was familiar with the nine-month gestation period in the species homo sapiens."

"Ricky was doing some homo sapiens himself while he was in Waupun, I am sure," said Brockman to a sprinkling of laughter.

"Thank you, once again, Stanley, for adding color to the black and white world of SWAT. To continue, Ricky armed himself with two large Chicago Cutlery knives and ran out the door as the initial officers arrived. They engaged him in a foot pursuit and were able to contain him in a parking lot for the duration of the incident. Good job, guys! A general 1025 page was made of the SWAT team, ordered by myself. I called in another sergeant to take over command of the shift while I took over command of the incident." Compton then referred to a PowerPoint of the intersection, and he showed the positioning of each unit and Cantwell. He clicked forward on the PowerPoint indicating times units arrived and the locations they were positioned at.

"The initial team response consisted of me setting up a command post here and the arrest team setting up at a ninety degree angle to the line of officers, who were negotiating. McCarthy was the team leader, and Gloria Dooley was the negotiator. McCarthy's plan was initiated, and Cantwell was successfully taken into custody."

"Plan? What kind of plan was that? Jump him!" retorted Hale with his usual obnoxiousness. He then blew a smoke ring, demonstrating to all he had mastered the ultimate in the arena of tobacco product showmanship.

"This guy represents us to the public?" commented Stammos to himself as if he did not realize he said the thought out loud.

"Since when do we jump guys with a knife? Wait! Let me correct myself. Since when do we jump someone with two fucking knives?" asked Hale with his hands in the air as if he was questioning the heavens.

"McCarthy?" asked Compton.

"Thanks for asking, Captain. Sergeant Compton made me the team leader, and we had limited personnel at the scene upon arrival. We had the deadly force option available along with less lethal. At one point Cantwell advanced on the line and was shot twice with super sock rounds. It hit Cantwell twice in the abdomen and was partially successful. It stopped the advance, but he tightened his grip on the knives. McCarthy stood up and moved to the front of the room and Compton stepped aside to allow McCarthy to occupy front and center.

"Why didn't you just TASE him?" asked Hale, taking a drink from his coffee and leaning back in his chair and nodding his head as if he was agreeing with himself.

"Cantwell had a long thick coat on. I was quite certain that the TASER arch would not have been effective, and we might move on him thinking the TASER had worked and found that it did not," said McCarthy.

"He had two fucking butcher knives. You should not have moved in on a guy with two fucking butcher knives. That's insanity.

I told someone that we should be doing the Chapter 51 Hold on you." Hale said in an angry tone of voice. "I would never have done anything as crazy as that."

"Respectfully, Captain, I would not have asked you to because you could not have done it, sir," interrupted Compton. "That is why I gave the job to McCarthy."

"You are talking to a captain, Sergeant," said Captain Hale with a tone indicating his disdain for the person and the rank.

"Sir, I am the officer in charge of the SWAT team which, by policy, makes me ranking member present in this debrief since this is a SWAT team matter. If that is not the case and I am mistaken, I would like to know now because if that is not the reality and I am not in charge of a simple debrief of a SWAT call-out, then I would be kidding myself in believing that I would actually have some control of an actual call-out as the policy states." Compton waited and then, "Captain?"

"Yeah, I suppose. I was just sayin' I wouldn't have done that. Continue, Sergeant," said Hale as he put his cigarette out in his Styrofoam coffee cup, once again the master of cigarette showmanship.

"McCarthy told me what he intended on possibly doing, and I approved, so I am ultimately responsible for what went right or what went wrong. This is a discussion to determine those issues." Compton then stepped to the side and sat down in a chair and finished, "Continue, McCarthy."

McCarthy then stepped toward the front and center again and said, "I discussed before approaching that Gloria should let us know with a signal whether she thought we should move or not. I wanted to know whether she thought she was getting anywhere. Gloria did an excellent job of keeping him from using the knife at one point. Although he did have two knives at the time we moved, he had set one down. The other he was twirling by the point with the handle on the ground. He was holding it loosely and spinning it like it was a toy top."

"We moved, without his knowledge, to within fifteen feet of him when I yelled, 'Hey, you people, get back over there!' That was the signal that we, as a team, would be moving if he bit at the bait and turned to look where the people I was yelling at were. He turned almost totally around, and then when he saw us coming, he lost his already tenuous grip on the knife totally. He tried to run, and we were able decentralize him and take him into custody. That was our plan. That was how we executed it, and the plan worked," finished McCarthy.

"Why did you have a female negotiating? Cantwell was pissed at a female. Maybe the negotiations wouldn't have failed if you would have had a man negotiating," said Hale lighting up another cigarette, leaning back in his chair and blowing the smoke out the corner of his mouth, obviously satisfied with his second counter.

Gloria sat straight up in her chair, looking as if she was about to put on the gloves. Compton merely had to step up to the center of the room and make eye contact with Gloria, and she sat back in her chair and crossed her arms. Dooley looked at his wife and chuckled at her. "Captain, Gloria Dooley is an experienced and well trained negotiator. Those negotiations were not a failure. She allowed us the time and opportunity to stage enough people and formulate a plan. She distracted him enough to allow our arrest team to move in close. She stopped him at one point from driving a knife into his gut by sharing personal information. By the way, Gloria, I did not know you were adopted?"

"I'm not," said Gloria.

"I thought you were not supposed to lie to people in negotiations?" carped Hale.

"We can, but only as a last resort. When a guy is about to drive a butcher knife into his heart, I consider it a last resort. I told him I was adopted, and it just came out, and it had an effect. We stopped that attempt," said Gloria.

"You stopped that attempt, Gloria. Nice job," said Compton.

"Continuing," said Compton, "the super socks fired by Stammos allowed us the time and opportunity to do something. I played the tape, and Cantwell was asked to put the knives down seventy-two times. He never complied. Negotiators buy us time. The SWAT team is called out for extraordinary situations. They are asked to bring them somehow to a successful conclusion. Gloria gave us the time. Stammos and his bean bags prevented one shoot situation. McCarthy recognized an opportunity and made a decision. He and the arrest team moved," said Compton. "They put their plan into action and it worked. Cantwell is in custody instead of in the morgue, and no one else was injured."

"I know I am Monday-morning quarterbacking," said Hale in a somewhat conciliatory manner, "but with 20-20 hindsight, I would have to say that move could have failed and someone could have been hurt. It may have made us have to shoot Cantwell. I'm the one that has to face the media and explain when something gets all fucked up. Me and nobody else but me," said the captain, uncrossing his arms, addressing the heavens, and then crossing them again.

"Respectfully, Captain, I saw an opening. I knew we could do it. The plan was discussed and implemented, and it worked. That is what SWAT is supposed to do. I considered everything you said and understand from your perspective you would have handled it differently. From my perspective, I would have to say I would do the same thing tomorrow given the same opportunity except under one circumstance," said McCarthy holding up his index finger and pausing.

"What would that be?" asked Compton.

"I wouldn't try it again with Cantwell. It won't work on him again," answered McCarthy sincerely.

"You're right. It won't work again. Next time we'll have to shoot him," agreed Hale looking around the room shaking his head as if he had been totally vindicated.

"Negotiations. Gloria, anything you would like to comment on?" asked Compton.

"Well, I did give McCarthy the signal, which was kids and school in the same sentence. I did that because I really thought it was going to end badly. I did something I do not do normally in negotiations. I only use it as a last resort. As I said earlier, I lied," said Gloria. "I told him I was adopted. I wanted him to project beyond his death to a child bearing his name being raised by strangers. I did it because I was certain it he was about to split open his stomach and spill his intestines all over that parking lot. I will not make it a habit, but it worked. He stopped what he was about to do." Gloria then looked about the room and then her eyes caught her husband Dooley's and they smiled.

"What do you all think?" asked Compton.

"I think it worked. We didn't bury anyone. The plan was made and the plan worked. I might not have done the same thing if I was planning it, but what was done worked," said Carpenter.

"If I would have been armed with a Benelli shotgun with a tactical load, I still would have shot him twice," said Stammos. "That's how close he was."

"Say, Stammos. Have you shot anyone today yet?" asked Dooley.

Stammos looked longingly at Captain Hale, who was oblivious and looking at his watch. "No, not yet, but it's still early."

Everyone in the room laughed except Compton and Hale. Hale looked up wondering what he had missed, and Compton smiled and contained a laugh because he knew it was the right thing to do. He had to look away when he saw how Stammos had worked his magic right in front of Hale and Hale was clueless. Compton had to turn away and suppress the laugh a second time. "This can't be healthy," he thought to himself, having difficulty holding the laughter in.

"Is there anything else?" Compton asked.

"I think you could have waited longer before moving. There was no rush. Maybe the negotiations would have worked," said Hale acting as if he had somewhere more important to be, but annoyed that someone was still talking making this meeting last longer.

"Gentlemen and ladies, I would like to thank Captain Hale for being here and making such an excellent point. What are the two things that can be argued in 100% of SWAT call-outs by anyone who was not there? Number one?" asked Compton throwing it out to the group.

"Why didn't you move sooner?" answered Dooley.

"Number two?" asked Compton.

"Why didn't you wait longer?" answered Brockman.

"We can always improve, ladies and gentleman, and that's why we debrief. Now, let's train."

As the group was gathering their gear and Hale hustled out of the room, McCarthy asked Compton, "What do you think, Sarge? Should I not have included that plan in our options?"

"McCarthy. Do not argue with success. I picked you that morning as a team leader because if anyone could get that guy into cuffs without shooting him, I knew it would be you. I never doubted you a minute. When he started twirling that knife, I actually started the McCarthy count down. I knew you were going. It's exactly like Hale said, 'Hindsight is 20-20' so use it. No one was hurt. The bad guy is in jail. It was a win. A big win." Compton held up his fist and McCarthy bumped it knuckle to knuckle. "Using 20-20 hindsight, I declare it was a job well done!"

The Stack

Chapter Ten: Perspective

It was a terrible turnout on a SWAT call-out. La Claire had a SWAT team that was part time, and that meant all members had another full time function on the department. There was never any guarantee how many would answer a page. Tonight was a Friday night at 6:30 PM. Try to find a friend to give away free basketball tickets to a game that starts at 7:00 PM and call them on Friday at 6:30 PM. You will not find too many takers because they will say, "It's Friday night. I have plans."

Compton would say on a call-out, "I'll be thrilled with twelve; I'll be happy with ten; I will get by with eight, and settle for six." This night fit that mold. Compton paged and called, and then called again. Many were working. Some had just sat down in front of the television and had started sipping a beer. One team member had a pretty rock-solid alibi. He was at his brother's wedding rehearsal dinner.

Compton was looking at six team members suited up in the classroom at the police department. He read off their names as if that would magically produce more, "Dooley."

"Here."

"McCarthy."

"Here."

"Carpenter."

"Here."

"Stammos."

"Here."

"Hartley."

"Here."

"Brockman… Brockman?… BROCKMAN!"

"Here."

"Why didn't you answer?" asked Compton.

"I was thinking that if you had to do a roll call with only six of us, maybe you didn't notice me sitting here, and if I stayed real quiet I could get out while the gettin' was good, 'cause I know what we are supposed to do tonight, and we sure as hell can't do it with six," said Brockman.

"Can't is a four letter word. We used to do this without a SWAT team. We sure as hell didn't form a team so that we could all come in after a page and tell people we can't do what they called us in for."

"What was I thinking? I just said 'can't' to a marine. Sorry, Sergeant," said Brockman.

"Tonight, I'll forgive Stanley Brockman for one reason. You answered the page, Stanley." Compton made a note on his sheet attached to his clipboard and then looked up, "Before we fill everyone in, is there any possibility we can get someone else?" asked Compton.

"Yes, sir," answered McCarthy, "but he's not SWAT."

"Who?" asked Compton.

"Shepherd. I was in the weight room and saw him there. I explained we were short, and he got his uniform on and is standing by in the event that he could be used for something," explained Dan.

"Tell him he will be rewarded for that enthusiasm with some overtime. Go get him."

"Right away!" said McCarthy. He then stood up and hustled out the door of the class room and nearly knocked Shepherd over, as he was standing around the corner just outside the door.

"Now that you have Shepherd, I can go then," said Brockman getting up and slowly heading toward the door in a mock tip toe motion.

"Sit your ass down, Brockman! I know your date tonight will still be waiting for you when you get home," said Compton.

"Yeah, he's got a date with the *Sports Illustrated Swimsuit Edition*," quipped Stammos.

"No, I saw him slipping out the back door of the Splendidly Sinful Sensations book store with the latest issue of *Junk in the Trunk*," laughed Carpenter.

"Aw, fuck you guys," whined Brockman.

The laughter was loud and made it sound as if there were more people in the room than there were. Brockman's whine was the frosting on the cake. It made him sound like a fifth grader responding to ribbing by his buddies on the playground.

Dooley, noticing the whine, knew they had hit a chink in Stanley Brockman's nearly impenetrable armor. Stanley had broken his own rule and let other cops know he was bothered. Dooley then chided, "I think we are on to something here. We struck a nerve." Dooley started singing, "Brockman and *Junk in the Trunk* sitting in the tree... K-I-S-S-I-N-G,..." and then everyone laughed as Brockman put his head down and covered it with both arms.

After listening to the laughing, he fired a return volley, "I know you are, but what am I?" It did nothing to help his cause. Everyone was now laughing, including Brockman.

McCarthy brought Shepherd into the room, and they both sat down watching the laughter. McCarthy said, "Damn! What did we miss?"

Carpenter said wiping his eyes, "It wasn't that funny, but it was. You had to be here."

"Damn. I wished I would have been here." McCarthy said to Shepherd.

"All right, you guys. Here's what we have," said Compton clicking the PowerPoint showing a U-shaped apartment complex that everyone recognized.

"1016 Henry Street," said most of the team upon seeing the photo.

"The targets are 1016 Henry Street, Apartment 204, 206, and 208. We have to hit all three apartments at one time," said Compton without emotion. He then paused and looked up as if he expected some type of reaction from the words he had just spoken.

"Yes, Stanley," said Compton. He knew the hand would belong to Stanley Brockman.

"How can we hit three apartments at one time with six people?" asked Stanley.

"Tonight, I will be the officer in charge and the team leader. I do not want to dump this responsibility on anyone else. Considering the unique layout and the unique problem we have been given, I think it can be done with what we have," said Compton, advancing the slide on the PowerPoint. It showed 1016 Henry from an aerial view, and he had three X's marked, and two Y's.

"The X's are the apartments. They fronted on the second story landing. Here is the back side of the apartments. The complex is built on a hill, meaning the drop from the windows in the apartment is not conducive for escaping. If the occupants jump, they break their legs at the very least. Therefore, we can get by with using two on the perimeter. I have arranged for Detectives Brickson and Jefferson to handle the perimeter. When we advise we are 10-23 (on scene) and moving, Brickson and Jefferson will secure the perimeter.

Compton then shifted the slide and showed a spot a block away and looked out into the small crowd, "Shep! Do you know this spot?"

"Yes, sir."

"Can you drive us to this spot and stop without making the tires squeal and the brakes squeak and avoid farting unless it's a real squeaker?"

"Yes, sir."

"Catch." Sergeant Compton tossed the SWAT van keys across the room and Shepherd, a former All State Receiver for La Claire High, caught the keys one handed.

"We are looking for this man." A stocky, angry looking black man in a Jamaican braid stared out at the small contingent of the La Claire Police Department SWAT Team. "He has only been in town for two weeks. His name is Jorge Castro. He goes by the street name 'Fidel.' He is from Chicago and is a member of the Latin Kings. He feels he is untouchable because he is the big fish in a little pond. He immediately moved his business into one apartment. He has his mother in another apartment and his girlfriend and their baby in another. He is renting 204, 206, and 208. You know the building layout. These three places are adjacent to each other and the landing over looks the lot. This is the bottom of the U and they are on the second floor."

"I have three keys for three teams. Team one: McCarthy, Stammos, you are hitting 204. You are on the bottom of the stack, Stammos!" Compton tossed Stammos the key and he caught it one handed. "McCarthy! You have to breach with the key and then enter first with the MP5. I will stand by outside with Thunder-shock 2000 and use it if any of the keys do not work on any of the doors. I cannot use the breaching shotgun because there is a small child in one of the apartments and we do not know which one. I will back up any one of the entries that need my help. Carpenter!" He tossed the key to Carpenter.

Carpenter stood up and caught the key in two hands behind his back. "Show off," said Brockman in a dead pan voice.

"Carpenter and Dooley, you will hit 206, and you will be in the middle of the stack. I will handle the breach if the key does not work. Brockman!"

"Catch those for me will you, Jim," Brockman said looking at Jim, who stood up and caught the keys which were about to hit Brockman in the face. "Nice catch, kid. There will be a little something extra in your paycheck next month," said Brockman, still dead pan.

"You two will hit 208, and you will be first in the stack," said Compton, giving Brockman a noticeable glare.

"Sergeant, should we be hitting three apartments with seven guys?" asked Brockman.

"Should we have handled a riot with nine a few years back, Stanley, or should we have run?" asked Compton.

"We didn't have enough sense to run," answered Stanley.

Compton reached into his pocket and pulled out a penny. I'll be damned. I had a penny in my pocket the night of the riot, and I have a penny in my pocket tonight. I was just shy of no cents then, and I barely have any cents tonight, so I say let's do it!" said Compton with enthusiasm. No one knew that the penny was an Indian Head penny that Compton carried to war and every night of his shift for luck. He would not carry more change than that for he would have been concerned about noise on the move, but he never went to work without it.

Compton gave one more directive. "Choose your own weapons on the entry. Remember earlier when you were all laughing about Brockman and his girlfriend, *Junk in the Trunk*. McCarthy, what did that sound like outside?"

"It sounded like there was about twenty guys in here whooping it up," said McCarthy, with Shepherd nodding his head in agreement.

"That's what I want when the doors go open. Yell as loud as you can 'Police! Search Warrant! Get down,' over and over again. To anyone in any other apartments it will sound like an army. You got it? We can do this thing. We are the La Claire Police Department SWAT Team. We don't know the meaning of 'can't.' When cops dial 911, we respond! We make the impossible possible. Can we do this thing?" asked Compton, building a crescendo of enthusiasm with each statement.

The entire team got pumped and responded, "Yeah, let's do it!" Compton rubbed the penny as he put it back into the pocket. They came together and said their prayer, maybe even more fervently than ever.

Compton put his hand on the others' and prayed, "Whether we are five or ten, we are all good men, and we can count on each other to come back again, and one more thing, good God," Compton paused. Then, as one, they all ended the prayer and quietly said, "Amen." Compton stood up and looked each one of them in the eye and then proclaimed, "Let's roll!"

The team stood by at a pre-arranged location waiting for word on the location of the target. Brickson and Jefferson had arranged a buy, hoping to target which apartment Fidel was in. Fidel did not want the buyer to come to his apartment. He arranged to make the sale in the Kmart parking lot and then apparently became wary about the sale.

"The informant says he's spooked. Fidel called the informant and said forget about it. The informant said Fidel is heading back to the apartment. He should be there in three minutes at the most. We are going to break off and set up for the entry if you can hit the target in three minutes?" Brickson said ending with a question.

"10-4. The team is 10-76 (en route) and should be moving in two and one half minutes if that is what you want," said Compton, motioning for Shepherd to drive.

"That's what we want. We will head to our positions and be there by the time you are. We are dressed in raid jackets. 10-4?"

"10-4," said Compton. "Do you know Brickson and Jefferson?" Compton asked the newest officer.

"White cop and black cop," said Shep.

"You got it. Brickson and Jefferson will be at their perimeter positions and wearing their raid jackets. Should not miss them unless there are shots fired and then miss them! OK?" suggested Sergeant Compton.

As the van rolled to a stop, everyone silently exited the van. "SWAT is 10-23 (on scene)," said Compton quietly on the radio.

"10-4, SWAT," responded dispatch also quietly.

Shepherd watched the team fall into their stack as previously ordered by Compton, and each man put a thumbs up as they lined up. When all were in line, Compton tapped Stammos, who tapped McCarthy, who tapped Dooley, who tapped Carpenter, who tapped Hartley, who tapped Brockman, and Brockman took a breath in through his nose and let it out through his mouth and then moved. They all moved as one. They rolled toward the three apartment doors as usual, into the unknown.

All three teams reached the doors without detection. The keys were quietly inserted simultaneously and worked on all three doors. There were no dead bolts and the doors swung open silently, and then the silence was broken by what sounded like the shouts of one hundred SWAT officers, *"Police! Search Warrant! Get Down, Down, Down, Down!"*

When McCarthy blew through the door he could see Fidel across the room on a couch. He was on the phone working a deal, and he dropped the phone. His eyes grew big and McCarthy shouted, "Get down on the floor! Do it now!"

Fidel started to the floor and then clearly had second thoughts. Fidel then put up his hands with his palms open and facing McCarthy.

"Police! Get Down! Do it now!" shouted McCarthy, but he had seen this before. His partner had been shot by a man that had performed this very act. McCarthy was ready for it this time. He stood his ground. He scanned for weapons and there were none.

Fidel moved closer and closer and closer, "Be careful, man. Don't shoot," pleaded Fidel in phony caution as he stepped within reach of his goal, which was the MP5.

"Bad guys better be careful," McCarthy thought out loud, and as Fidel started to close his palms around the MP5. McCarthy's thumb slipped to the safety and engaged the safety. He then slung his weapon tight to his body, brought his knee of his right leg up and thrust his right foot full power into the lower abdomen of Fidel, who walked right into the kick. "Down!" shouted McCarthy has he kicked Fidel hard in the guts, trying to shove Fidel's intestines out through his spinal column.

"Ooooffff" was the noise the air spit out along with a little bit of lunch that vomited out of Fidel's lungs and guts.

Fidel did not go down though. He spun off the kick like McCarthy had hit the sweet spot on a cue ball. Fidel bounced off the far wall and then spun instinctively to the bathroom, but he was caught around the waist by McCarthy, who kept the momentum of the spin going until Fidel was spun right into the carpet. "Down! Stay down. Stop resisting. You are under arrest!" ordered McCarthy and Stammos, who by this time had cleared the bathroom and two bedrooms and now had joined McCarthy. Both slung their weapons and handcuffed the two wrists of the dealer. "Clear 204!" said McCarthy, a little breathless.

"Clear 206!" said Carpenter.

"Clear 208," said Brockman after a pause. His dead pan voice had returned. There had been no one in 208. His dreams had come true. It went well and there was no problem. Now Stanley found himself terribly disappointed.

"Where's Fidel?" asked Brickson.

"He's 10-95 (in custody) in 204," responded McCarthy through the head mic.

"10-4," answered Brickson as he walked through the door.

"Fidel. Que pasa, mi amigo," said Brickson.

"Fuck you," answered Fidel.

"We'll see in a little bit here who's fucked," snorted Brickson with a laugh as he winked at McCarthy. "Are there any additional charges, McCarthy?"

"I will have a charge of resisting arrest, Brick. He fought pretty hard to get away, and then when that didn't work, he gave it the college try, attempting to get into the bathroom. I'd check the bathroom first," answered McCarthy. "There was a little drama when we met, but Fidel and I are getting along just fine right now," said McCarthy, slipping a pillow under Fidel's head after searching it.

Fidel looked puzzled by the act of kindness. Then he laid his head down on the pillow but kept an eye on McCarthy.

"Fidel are you hurt?" asked McCarthy.

"You kicked me pretty hard, but I can take it. No fucking cop going to hurt me. I'm only here, 'cause I lost my balance. Otherwise, I'd be kickin' yo mofuckin' ass right now," carped Fidel.

"Well, it was your job to get away and my job to arrest you. I don't think it was personal for you, and I can tell you it was not personal for me. The name is Dan or McCarthy, whatever you prefer. Can I call you Fidel?" asked McCarthy.

"Yeah… I s'pose," said Fidel.

"McCarthy!" said Brickson. "Bingo!"

McCarthy looked up. Brickson was holding a freshly cooked ball of crack cocaine rock the size of a sixteen inch kitten-ball. "With intent to deliver I guess," said McCarthy.

"I guess?" Then Brickson went to the doorway of the apartment and called to Jefferson, "Jefferson." He paused and then apparently when Jefferson was looking, he held up the huge ball of freshly cooked crack cocaine, "Check it out!"

"Whoa baby, Brick!" said Jefferson as he met Brickson in the doorway of the apartment. Jefferson was a muscular African American detective who was also on the SWAT team. This was his investigation, so he was in plain clothes. They both wore their brightly lettered POLICE raid jackets. "Do you want to talk to him?"

"Yeah. We don't need him to talk, but we'll see if he wants to help himself out of this big hole he dug himself into," said Jefferson half talking to Brickson and half talking to Fidel. McCarthy had searched Fidel and helped him to his feet.

Jefferson took Fidel out of the apartment and down to the station. Brickson stayed to complete the search of the apartment.

"McCarthy. See me in 206," requested Compton over the radio

McCarthy left Dooley with Brickson in 204 and entered 206. Two females were handcuffed on opposite sides of the room. Each was seated in kitchen straight-back chairs while Carpenter was searching the couch. There was a small boy with big brown eyes and curly black hair in a black sweat suit with the Batman emblem on his chest. His black sweat pants had two stripes on each leg. The boy looked frightened.

"McCarthy. Take care of the boy. He's little afraid," said Compton.

"What's his name, ma'am." McCarthy asked the young lady, who was the mother of Fidel's child. She was a beautiful young Hispanic lady with no bra. Her brown nipples protruded through her pink tank top with a fear induced rigidity. She had a very short blue jean skirt and spiked heels. She was dressed like a working girl.

Fidel pimped her out to his best customers. His best customers were anyone who could afford the $2000 for the "best experience in fucking ever. It will give meaning to your life," he would say. He would never bring it up unless someone showed interest and potentially had the cash to afford her. He made more money pimping her then all the robberies and burglaries he ever committed. It was easier. He used to have to pound on a safe all night to get it to give it up the $2000 it contained. He would only have to threaten to slap Louisa, and she opened up immediately giving up her treasures to all takers.

"Monty… his name is Monty," answered Louisa tentatively.

"Monty. Do you like Batman?" asked McCarthy pointing at the bat symbol.

Monty drew his head down and both his hands up to his mouth. He still looked at McCarthy cautiously.

McCarthy pulled out his pen and notebook. He always carried a pen and notebook even on SWAT calls. He began to quickly scribble something as he talked. "You know, Batman is a police man. He works in Gotham City, and he wears a black uniform just like SWAT. He carries all kinds of special equipment just like SWAT. Instead of a badge, he wears this symbol." McCarthy paused to tap the symbol on Monty's sweat shirt. McCarthy ripped out the page from his notebook. It was Batman. Not a cheesy reproduction, but Batman!

"Mommy, Mommy, Batman!" Monty erupted and ran over to Louisa and showed her the drawing. Louisa was squirming, twisting her $2000-a-tap money maker in the upright chair. McCarthy walked over to Compton and whispered to Compton as Louisa's attention was drawn to the Batman picture. "She's got it crotched."

"I'll call over a female officer to conduct the search. Are you sure?" asked Compton.

"Absolutely, she's squirming like a worm in a driveway after a spring rain. I saw it," said McCarthy.

McCarthy then did a few more drawings for Monty. After growing bored with the his new friend, Monty turned to his mother and whimpered, "Mommy, I'm hungry."

"You're hungry?" asked McCarthy.

"Yeah, my tummy says," answered Monty.

"When did he last eat?" asked McCarthy.

"We were just going to order a pizza when you guys decided to drop in. You should have called first. We could have ordered a couple more for you and had a party," Louisa worked another wiggle into a feigned sexually suggestive movement of her hips. McCarthy knew. Louisa did not know he knew she had "crotched" her "stash."

McCarthy checked and could find little in the house to eat. He did find some bite sized Oreo's in a bag. "Is this OK for now?" he asked Louisa.

"That's what he was eating when you guys… stopped by," said Grandma.

Monty then climbed up on McCarthy's lap while he drew. Every few minutes he tossed in a bite-sized Oreo, and he would use that opportunity to look McCarthy in the eyes and smile, showing he was very happy once again with his new friend.

Then Monty took hold of the television controls. He could not have been older than four, but he maneuvered the controls like a jet fighter pilot putting an F-16 through its paces. In no time he found the channel he wanted. It was the Kidz Music Channel. It was rock music for kids. Then it happened. *Perspective!* Every once in a while, a cop can obtain clear perspective and see the future. He can see that a guy dressed in dark clothes ducking into an alley is about to commit a burglary. He can see a look on a man's face and see he is about to smack his wife. Clear unobstructed perspective looking straight into the future. He can see some perp looking left and then looking right while he's digging for his wallet, and as the suspect goes into a lean, the cop knows he is going to make a run for it.

The Kidz Music Channel DJ announced, "Listeners, here is a classic little ditty by CCR called *Down on the Corner*. Let's see you kids dance." Monty did not have to be asked twice.

Monty dropped the controls and tucked his bag of bite-sized Oreos under his arm. He jumped off McCarthy's lap and dance he did. John Fogerty sang his heart out for Monty, "Out on the corner… Out in the street… Willy and the poke boys are playing… Seeing the nickels at their feet..."

Monty danced and twirled like a pro. He did not dance like a four year old. He danced like a young Michael Jackson, before he got all weird. Then Monty did a step that he must have invented because McCarthy had never seen it before. He planted one foot and the other lifted and shot back down as he spun round and round and round with the planted foot planted and pivoting while the other shot up and down and up and down, and Monty just kept smiling and spinning, smiling and spinning.

Pretty soon McCarthy and Compton could not help but clap

to the music and the Monty Show. Grandma and Louisa were now rocking back and forth and forward and back chanting rhythmically, "Go, Monty. It's your birthday. Go, Monty. It's your birthday. Go, Monty. It's your birthday," and then it struck McCarthy like a linebacker playing in his first Super Bowl.

Perspective! "My God!" thought McCarthy as he stopped clapping and watched the little Michael Jackson spin and kick and eat Oreos without missing a beat. "Grandma's handcuffed in the chair; she knows her daughter is a crack whore and her son-in-law is a major drug dealer. Momma is handcuffed in the chair rocking back and forth while she tries to camouflage a wiggle in now and then to force the crack rocks back up into her vagina, because that's where she keeps her own personal stash. Dad is down at the station rolling over on the people he bought his dope from. Monty? He's dancing and eating Oreos while his daddy is undoubtedly on his way to prison. A SWAT team is searching his home finding crack cocaine, weapons, and sex toys for his mother's lucrative business as a prostitute. Yes sir, Monty is dancing like nothing unusual is taking place in front of his young eyes. This is a regular Friday night in the life of Monty.

There it is, perfect *perspective* so unflinchingly clear that Dan McCarthy could see into the future. Fourteen years from now a SWAT team will be breaking down a door to arrest a criminal. Monty will be that criminal. McCarthy sadly saw Monty's future. He thought, "In about fourteen or maybe fifteen years, Monty will be the criminal lying handcuffed on the floor," after achieving a moment of perfect *perspective.*

Chapter Eleven: Gun!

Shepherd steered the squad off the ramp. This was a great night for Shepherd since McCarthy was no longer his field training officer but his partner. Shepherd still looked up to McCarthy and considered him to be his mentor. They were working central in what was called the "heavy car." Most cars were one-person units, but La Claire put out two-person squads to handle the "heavy calls," which were calls that needed two officers, at least. During the first shift that would be a warrant car. On second shift they would also work warrants. On third, they would look for trouble until trouble called, then toward the end of the shift they would work warrants, which meant they would actively seek out wanted people.

"What is the best way to find trouble? Do you remember?" quizzed McCarthy.

"Make lots of contacts. I remember. We're not looking for something…" Shepherd paused to make sure the words came out correctly. When Shepherd continued, McCarthy recited the verse along with Shep, "We're looking for everything. If we are looking for something we will find nothing. If we are looking for everything we will find something." McCarthy flashed a big grin at his protégé. "I'm impressed. You remembered."

"The saying and the doing are two different things," said Shepherd in a hopeless tone of voice.

McCarthy licked his finger and reached over and touched the steering wheel. "Sssssssssss!" exclaimed McCarthy as if the wheel was a hot griddle. "I'm telling you, Shep, you got the hot hand tonight. There's one now." McCarthy said pointing at a large beige Thunderbird with the red taillight lens showing white.

"Stop a cracked taillight lens? We're the heavy car," said Shepherd.

"Triage," said McCarthy.

"Tree what?" asked Shepherd.

"Triage. If all this turns out to be is a cracked taillight lens and the big call comes, then we can use triage and drop what we are doing and go to the heavy call. Right now, we are doing nothing and a cracked taillight lens is the heaviest thing going. Triage. That's how you take it from the saying and turn it into the doing. I am telling you. Make as many contacts as you can and then keep an open mind on each contact," McCarthy said as he motioned toward the vehicle, which was now noticeably drifting across the center line.

Shepherd hit the lights, and the driver stopped suddenly, jerking the T-bird into the curb. The chubby fifty-ish driver bounced quickly out of the vehicle for an extremely drunk man. His clothes were disheveled like he had dressed quickly and then gotten into a full contact cage fight. As the driver exited the Ford, he staggered toward Shepherd leaving the car door standing wide open.

Shepherd, seeing the hazard shouted to the driver, "Driver, shut your door!"

The driver stopped in his tracks and paused to compute what had just been said to him, and then he turned slowly and looked surprised at the door standing ajar. He returned to the door and slammed it shut, hard. He then met Shepherd between the cars. Shepherd began his questioning of the driver, who was clearly too intoxicated to be piloting this star ship.

McCarthy became curious. It was a common practice for drivers who were trying to hide something to exit the car they were in. This is often done to get away from something that was in the vehicle. It often was a good indication that the driver had something to hide.

McCarthy slowly made his way toward the vehicle, watching the developments of the Shepherd-driver conversation. All seemed to be progressing swimmingly there. The driver was piling up indicators of intoxication, giving McCarthy's young partner plenty to put into his report later. "Something is happening here. What is it?" thought McCarthy.

McCarthy reached the broken right taillight and could see by rubbings on the back of the car that the damage had been done by a violent fight that had taken place at the right rear corner of the vehicle. There was blood and red hair smeared about the trunk of the vehicle. The quarter panel had blood on it and was dented.

McCarthy then flashed his light through the passenger's side rear window of the Thunderbird and saw them. You couldn't miss any of them. They were neatly piled there on the backseat. There was the black coat. On top of the coat was a woman's red wig, the prescription glasses, the black high-heeled shoes, and the shovel. "Oh my God, a shovel!" thought McCarthy. McCarthy then shined his light on the driver's side of the backseat and was shocked, but not surprised, to see the butt end of an uncased rifle.

Just as McCarthy spotted the firearm, he noticed Shepherd was trying to convince the driver to stand in one place. He would not have it. He said, "I can straighten this out. I will show you." The driver turned and walked back toward the Thunderbird.

"Wait. Stay here, sir. Stop!" shouted Shepherd.

"Just a second, I'll show you," slurred the driver as he started to open the back driver's side door.

"GUN!" shouted McCarthy, drawing his weapon in a blur of a second and training it on the intoxicated driver, who would have some explaining to do if he survived the next few seconds.

Shepherd paused for a moment, placing his hand on his weapon. He then tugged urgently three times before working the weapon out. Even then he was not quite sure what was happening.

"Police! Do Not Move!" ordered McCarthy. "If you reach into that car I will shoot you," promised Dan McCarthy.

McCarthy then ordered the driver, "Get down on your knees!" The driver did this, almost crumpling instantaneously at the order. "Now put your hands on the ground." Once again, the driver fell forward, his hands slapping on the pavement. "That was very good. Now walk backward on your knees until you are flat on the ground." The driver just flopped on his stomach to this command. "Put your hands in the small of your back, with your fingers to the sky." The driver did this perfectly. "Now, don't move!"

"Cuff him." McCarthy said to Shepherd.

Shepherd moved in and quickly handcuffed the driver. During the search, he found that the driver had a small Derringer in his right front pants pocket. "Shit! Gun!" shouted Shep, recapturing his command voice.

After McCarthy read Miranda to the hapless looking driver, he did not beat around the bush. "I see the blood, the purse, the wig, and the gun, and I am wondering, where's your wife, sir?" asked McCarthy.

"She's at Gibbons Park," said the man looking at his feet with his head bobbing. A line of drool was dripping out of the right corner of his mouth.

"Is she alive?" asked McCarthy.

"I don't know. I hurt her. She pished me off, and I hit her hard. She fell. She didn't want me to drive, so she pished me off and I hit her. I pulled her into a bush and I went home, and I was going back to get her and, and, and… help her," said the drunk with his head bobbing like he was a doll on a dash board.

McCarthy leaned over to Shepherd, "Radio this in. Get a car over to Gibbons Park and have them beat the bushes for," he looked at the ID from the purse, "Rebecca Jones."

"My Becky. My bootiful, bootiful Becky," said the drunk as he began to sob and wail.

After ten minutes, Brockman called for an ambulance. "I've located the female. She is alive, but she is unconscious."

It was 4:00 AM before McCarthy and Shepherd had finished their reports.

"Do you think he would have killed her if we wouldn't have stopped him?" asked Shepherd.

"What do you think, Shep?" asked McCarthy.

"I think we saved a life tonight," said the young cop.

"I think we saved two lives tonight," said McCarthy. "I'll drive last half," said McCarthy. "Want to stop at Perkins or grab a sandwich at the Kwik Trip and check our businesses?"

"I would like to stay out. A sandwich is OK with me," said Shepherd.

McCarthy drove the squad out of the police ramp and headed toward the nearest Kwik Trip. As McCarthy piloted his "mop," his mobile observation platform, toward the Kwik Trip, he was keenly aware, as always, that his night was not yet over. He was keenly aware that he had no idea what the next moment would bring. That was the nature of police work.

Chapter Twelve: "They're Cute When They're Little"

At the same moment McCarthy was shouting for the chubby man to get down on the ground, the patrons at the RUMPilstilskins were all sporting a chubby as they watched Darla Darling on center stage. She was down to her G-string, and she was flinging her hips about like an experienced belly dancer to a Shakira song while a circle of men of all ages sat around the circular stage mesmerized by the dark-haired beauty.

Darla had started dancing to pay for her college. She had been a student at the University of Minnesota in Minneapolis, and she had worked all the clubs in that city. It was such a good living that each semester she carried a lighter and lighter load until one semester her degree and her dreams were put on hold. She would say, "I better make it while I can shake it."

Darla had worked the Minneapolis Clubs for a while and then the national circuit. She did a "Girls of the Big Ten" for Playboy and even a few "girl on girl" scenes in obscure porn movies. Now she had landed in La Claire. She was the popular featured dancer at the club. She liked the thought that she had a home after the years of travel.

Tonight she could see she owned the crowd. Every eye was on her. She could see the whites of the eyes… every eye. Their mouths were open, and they were unconsciously licking their lips as she shook her hips. The brown G-string matched her tan skin perfectly. She had natural breasts. They were a D cup, and they were her draw as well as the fact that she could actually dance. She would have mesmerized this group with her dancing even if she had her clothes on, but this group would not have gathered around a stage where a clothed woman was dancing.

Billy Mitchell was front and center. He was flush again after he had scored on a safe job out of town. He did most of his work out of town since he got back from prison. He was paranoid. He would say, "Fuckin' McCarthy's got my number. As long as he's in this town I'm takin' my business elsewhere."

Billy held up a $100 bill, and Darla danced her way over to Billy. She slid down near him on her left side folding up her left leg underneath her as she stretched her right leg straight up at a ninety degree angle to the left. She caressed her inner thigh slowly and all the men's heads shifted up and then down, following the entertainer's silk-gloved-covered hands. She then pulled out the G string, exposing the well trimmed natural bush, which held her obviously moistened womanhood. It was the object of his affection. Billy slipped the $100 between the G-string and the moistness, brushing her vulva lightly with the back of his hand on the way in and again on the way out.

Darla turned over and was on her knees in a snap doing a simulated act of love in front of Mitchell. She reached between her legs and rubbed herself and then removed the bill, exposing her vulva one last time to Mitchell while she blew him a kiss.

As Darla left the stage, Mitchell glanced about the room and his eyes met the angry glare of Harley David Slade. "Shit, he knows," thought Mitchell turning back to the stage as a slightly pudgy amateurish looking girl climbed onto the stage following Darla.

"He can't know," thought Mitchell, who was trying to look everywhere but at Slade. Mitchell was certain that his eyes would tell Slade the truth.

The truth was Mitchell got into trouble almost immediately after being paroled from Waupun State Penitentiary. Brickson and Jefferson had nailed him on a control buy. Mitchell was a nightmare on the loose for patrol officers because he was a burglar extraordinaire. As far as the drug guys cared, he was small potatoes because they were always looking for "Mr. Big," the "Mother-lode," and/or "The French Connection." Billy was a relative newbie to the drug world, but he knew he could make some fast cash. He made a sale, and "Bam!" — busted.

Brickson and Jefferson did a buy bust and flipped him for a

bigger fish. "Give us a name, Billy. It better be substantial, or you are on a fast wagon to Waupun." Brickson could see Billy was going to flip. His hands were wringing, sweat was dripping off his forehead, and he was as white as a Wisconsin prairie in January. "You know where they stick the ones in Waupun that come back so fast as you will be? They send them to the lower level, and I hear they have to actually pump them sunshine."

It was an easy decision for Mitchell. He would get anonymity, and he would be giving up someone he did not care for. Harley David Slade. Mitchell gave Brickson and Jefferson Slade. Slade lost his marijuana business and his shirt — literally — when Stammos blasted it. Mitchell thought it was great because he bought his freedom. Brickson and Jefferson were happy because they busted the biggest grow operation in the history of the city of La Claire. The women Mitchell was screwing were happy because he stayed out of prison. Mitchell reasoned Slade was happy because he was always pissed off anyway for no reason and now he had a reason.

Slade now was staring at Mitchell. "Fuckin' crazy bastard must know," thought Mitchell.

Slade did not know. If he knew, Mitchell would already be dead. All Harley David Slade knew was Mitchell was moving in on his girlfriend, Darla. Darla did not know she could not see other men. She rarely dated men from her gigs anyway. She was a dancer not a whore. She knew that she kept more of the money earned from dancing than she would get if she became a prostitute. Besides, in her mind, she was still just on a hiatus from college.

Mitchell bought a lap dance from her for $100 in the VIP room of the Rump. As she slowly grinded her naked sweet smelling flesh into the rock hard lump under his jeans he said, "Do strippers need boyfriends?" He could hardly keep his hands down at his side. He had to slide them under his legs to keep them off the exotic beauty.

"All women need boyfriends except for the ones that need girlfriends," whispered Darla as her hips moved as if she was on rocking horse. She was enjoying this ride. She'd gone longer than usual, and she had shut off the meter. Her breaths were coming now in short gasps. The pressure was building, and suddenly her mouth opened wide and she made not a sound. She did not want to give away what had just happened to her. She did not know if having an orgasm was a violation of professional lap dance etiquette. Her silence gave her secret away as she shuddered quietly.

Mitchell's excitement built right along with Darla's. Then he exploded. The pressure of the denim holding the in eruption added to the pleasure. It was the most pleasurable sexual experience in his life, and he had not even taken his clothes off.

Darla fell forward, dropping her head on his shoulder, and released a long breath that caused her body to shake and shudder as it poured out of her. Then she sat up and kissed him long… hard… and deep. She looked him straight in the eye and said, "This stripper needs a boyfriend. If it is you, we can never do this here again. I do not screw customers." She set her forehead against his and waited for his response.

"It's a deal! What do we do now… shake on it?" asked Mitchell with a wry, knowing smile.

"No. Tonight I am coming over to your place, and we're going to fuck until we fall asleep, and if you are my boyfriend we are going to wake up in each other's arms at about noon tomorrow and fuck some more," she said in a breathy phone sex kind of voice.

Billy wrote down his address and slipped it into Darla's hand and kissed her again. "I got to get out of here. I have to get some dry clothes on." He said as he pulled the crotch of his jeans away from his body. "I will be waiting for you at my apartment," said Mitchell, kissing her one more time.

"I'll see you there," said Darla lying down now, still naked and still on the couch.

Slade watched Mitchell from his perch at the bar. He watched him through the eyes of a predator.

At 4:00 AM as Mitchell looked down at the beautiful naked Darla, he wasn't sure what love was but thought if he could feel it

this must be what it felt like. He slid carefully out, unwrapping their bodies just so as to not wake up his very own Sleeping Beauty. He walked over to the window and opened the curtains so that there would be enough light for him to watch her sleep. He watched her breasts rise and fall with each breath. He even watched the beads of sweat he helped make as they evaporated off her skin in the night air.

Mitchell was a night person. He could not sleep. If it was not for Darla, he would be removing a window air conditioner from a business right now. He could take a night off. "Fuck it. I got no boss. I'm my own boss, and I'm takin' the night off," he whispered to himself as he gazed at the perfection that was Darla Darling's body. He picked up his cigarettes, tapped one out of the tight pack, and pulled it out with his lips. He picked up a lighter and brought it up to his cigarette behind his cupped hand. Just before he lit the lighter he caught a red glare. There was a familiar looking figure standing under the street light below, smoking. "Fuck! It's Slade!" said Mitchell as the fear coiled like an electric shock down his spine.

Slade had followed Darla to this spot. He knew when she did not go home that she would be seeing another man. Slade hated any of her dalliances, but after he stood outside and fumed, he would always forgive her. Even if they never spoke, she knew he loved her and she knew he had been hurt, but because he could forgive her, she loved him more. Slade did not want sex with women. There was something missing. He did not want sex with men either. He did not understand what was missing. He just knew something was missing.

The love affair with Darla was in Slade's mind. Slade's whole world was taking place before his eyes in his mind. Slade watched the house Darla had gone into and enjoyed his second love in life. He had lit up a marijuana cigarette.

"One day you will kill her," said the Dark Lord. "Not tonight, though. Not tonight."

"Never! I won't do it! Not Darla. Never Darla!" answered Slade as he took another toke on the doobie.

At 4:07 AM, 911 dispatch received a non emergency call. "La Claire Police Department. Can I help you?"

"Yeah. There is a guy, Harley David Slade, who has a hand gun, and he is in the 900 block of Lafollette Avenue. He's stalking someone. I think he wants to kill them," said Mitchell using a stolen cell phone with a handkerchief over the speaker.

"May I have your name please, sir, and who does he want to kill?" asked the dispatcher.

"Just send a cop over and stop him. Now!" Mitchell hung up. Billy crept up to the window and peered over the sill and watched. "Saying Slade had a handgun was a nice touch. That will get those fuckers out of the doughnut shops faster," thought Mitchell.

"255," said the dispatcher over the quiet radio channel.

"255 go ahead," answered McCarthy.

"There is a report that a Harley David Slade is armed with a hand gun in the 900 block of Lafollette. He is reportedly stalking someone there, but it is unknown who. Check it out and use caution," said the dispatcher.

"10-4," answered McCarthy shutting down the headlights. "We were real close, and we are 10-23 (arriving) and going in on foot."

McCarthy had parked around the corner from Lafollette, and he and Shep slowly unlatched the door and approached in the shadows. From behind a bush they could see Slade just standing and smoking. He dropped the marijuana cigarette to the ground and crushed it out with his foot. McCarthy and Shep were upwind of Slade and could not detect what it was Slade was smoking.

He slowly turned and walked toward the two hidden officers. He walked across the corner lot and looked as if he would nearly stumble into them. McCarthy reached to pull Shep back, but the kid drew his weapon and yelled, "Police! Don't move."

Slade stopped in his tracks, eyes wide.

"Get down on the ground. Do it now!" shouted Shep.

McCarthy thought, "Little too soon, but what's done is done."

Slade dropped quickly, and Shepherd holstered his weapon and patted down Slade. As he reached the waist band area he shouted, "Gun!" Shepherd pulled a small 25 caliber semi-automatic Raven

Arms handgun out of a holster that was on Slade's belt. In the right front pants pocket, Shepherd found a baggie with three marijuana cigarettes.

Shepherd handcuffed Slade. Slade said nothing. Slade said nothing all the way to the jail. Slade said nothing through the booking except to answer the questions of the jailer.

Mitchell watched the whole arrest from the window. He saw a familiar face, "Fuckin' McCarthy, you fuck. You are always at the right place at the right time. Don't you ever take a fuckin' break?" said Mitchell to himself out loud.

"What, Honey?" asked Darla.

Mitchell looked at Darla and stepped away from the window, allowing the light to wash across her smooth uncovered body. The excitement had aroused Mitchell's loins once again. "Nothin'," answered Mitchell.

"Come back to bed, tweetie," said Darla in the voice of a little girl that somehow made her even more sensual to Mitchell, "I'm so cold, brrrrrrr," she said wrapping her arms around herself causing her breasts to squeeze together and rise up like two mounds of ice cream with a chocolate kiss on top of each mound.

Mitchell shut the phone off and crawled in tight against her. "Cold my ass," Mitchell said. He slid his hands down between her thighs and felt her exotic orchid wet with the dew and in full blossom. "Thanks, McCarthy," he thought as slid his member deep into her. She arched and gasped sweetly as he entered her.

When they cleared the jail, McCarthy had a worried look on his face, but he was quiet.

Shepherd was pumped and then noted the concern on the face of his partner. "Something wrong, Dyno?" asked Shepherd.

"I hope not. I hope we have a named complainant," answered McCarthy.

"Why? Dispatch said…"

"I know what dispatch said, but they did not say they had a named complainant, and we did not ask. I hope they have one," McCarthy said as he tapped dispatch's number on the phone. "Hello, this is McCarthy. Do you have a complainant on that call?"

"Negative. The caller was anonymous. We redialed the number, and it is a cell phone and it's turned off."

McCarthy then called Compton and explained the situation.

"It could go either way," said Compton. "You have plenty of corroboration. It depends on the judge. It certainly is worth taking to court. The corroboration is there. Alice will dump it, but it should fly in every other court," said Compton. "He sits. It's too close for us to call now. He sits!" That was that. Compton could make a decision.

After McCarthy got off the phone, Shepherd asked, "What?

"The complainant was anonymous. We need corroborating observations and evidence to make an unknown complainant believable to the court. Otherwise, they'll toss the stop, and then because of 'fruit of the poisonous tree,' we lose the concealed weapon charge, and Slade walks with nothing."

"Do you think that will happen?" asked Shepherd.

"I don't know. It is a close call. The complainant said Slade was there with a gun, and Slade was there with a gun. I don't know what a judge will say. The judge that gets the case might not agree. Write it up good, partner. It's your arrest. Good pinch! Close call, but still a good pinch."

"We found three guns in one shift. Is that a record, Dyno?" asked Shep.

"It's your record. What counts is you took three guns off the street before they could be used in a criminal act rather than after the act because you were on the job, Shepherd," said McCarthy.

"Fuckin' A," said Shepherd.

"Fuckin' A," said McCarthy.

McCarthy looked at his partner smiling ear to ear. He still thought the ultimate fun in life was a man with a gun call. McCarthy looked again at his grinning young partner and thought, "I remember when staying positive was not such a discipline and I did not have to convince myself I was having fun." Shepherd looked at McCarthy and when he saw McCarthy looking at him his smile suddenly got bigger. McCarthy laughed to himself and thought, "God, cops are so cute when they're little."

Chapter Thirteen:
Man's Gift to Himself: Honor.

"Bob Waters, this is Officer William Shepherd. Friends call him Shep." Bob Waters had an easy smile and stepped around his desk to meet the young officer.

"Shep, this is Bob Waters. This man is your friend. If you are going into court, this is the man you want." Shepherd offered his hand and they shook hands warmly.

"It is nice to meet you, Shep. We will get to know each other well if you stay in La Claire," said Waters.

"I plan on staying a long time," answered Shepherd.

"From the reports, it sounded like you made the arrest. Is that right?" asked Waters getting quickly to business as always.

"Yes, sir," answered Shepherd, sitting in a chair after Waters moved a large pile of files precariously to another large pile of files sitting on the floor. He carefully turned them at a ninety degree angle with the files already on the floor, either to prevent a legal avalanche, or as some elaborate "Type A Personality" filing technique.

"How did you manage to latch onto a suspect before McCarthy?" asked Waters.

"Slade just kind of walked right into us, and I reacted," answered Shepherd.

"Well the issue today is the stop. This is a suppression hearing to throw out the stop. If the stop is tossed, the arrest is tossed and Slade walks. Jack Sloan is Slade's attorney, and he maneuvered the case into Judge Alice's court. You know Judge Alice, McCarthy. She sincerely believes that inside every criminal there is a brain surgeon, supreme court justice, or a fucking kindergarten teacher trying to get out, and the only ones stopping them is the oppressive jack-booted police. Today, that's you, Shepherd. If she has a hint of justifiable cause, she will toss the stop and suppress the evidence. This is a stop made on an anonymous complaint. You know that is a judgment call when it gets to this point, and the key syllable is *judge!* Shepherd, it will be your job to explain each point you observed that corroborated the anonymous complainant's information. I will ask you the questions, and you give the answers. Time, location, dress, suspect's name, gun found. Do you have any questions?" Shepherd was breathless. He had never heard such a staccato flow of words flow from another human being in his life. "Shepherd?" fired Waters one more time, impatient for an answer.

"Yes, sir. I will do my best," answered Shep.

"Dyno?"

"Yes Bob."

"The report says that Slade was smoking prior to the stop, and that he stomped it out. You later determined it was marijuana he was smoking. Are you sure you didn't get a whiff of the marijuana he was smoking before you made contact with him?" asked Assistant District Attorney Bob Waters. "If either of you detected the odor, then this anonymous complainant is not even an issue," probed Waters.

"I didn't," said McCarthy.

"I didn't either," answered Shepherd, following suit with a truthful answer.

"Dyno, are you sure you didn't but now as you think about it and play it back, you now remember that you did?" pressed Waters.

"I did not smell it before the contact," said Dan.

"Think about it again, because if you did, Bam! You have reasonable suspicion for the stop, and Slade is fucked. Truly, beautifully and literally fucked! He goes to prison on the previous marijuana manufacturing charges." Waters then smiled, "How about it, Dyno? Remember now?"

"No."

"Think. Are you sure?" said Waters with a smile getting bigger.

"I said no." said Dyno.

"Little eensy teensy whiff?" said Waters with a squeaky voice while pinching his thumb and index finger of the hand without the cigarette indicating just a pinch.

"Why do you do this all the time, Bob?" asked Dyno.

"It's cheap entertainment. It's the only time I get the opportunity to see you squirm. You don't do it on the stand. I am the only attorney that holds the secret on how to make Dan McCarthy squirm. Just suggest to him that he should lie. I love it. It makes me feel powerful." Waters was the only one in the room entertained, but that was OK with him.

"You know, Alan Dershowitz says that cops are taught to testi-lie all over the country," said Waters. "If he is telling the truth, then saying you smelled the marijuana when you didn't would be the easiest and smallest of lies."

"Alan Dershowitz is a liar. I wasn't taught that," said Shepherd indignantly, "and I just got out of the academy."

"Alan Dershowitz is a defense attorney. He was trying to prejudice every jury member he could when he said that on national TV. He might even believe his own bullshit," said McCarthy. "The cops I know do not lie on the stand. Not even Brockman. If you asked Brockman on the stand if he thought having children was constitutional right, he would tell you the truth. He would say 'I think only certain people should be allowed to reproduce, your honor. It should require a permit co-signed by the chief of police.' Brockman would tell you that even if it hurt his case because Stanley Brockman believes it." McCarthy shifted in his chair. He was becoming animated.

McCarthy then turned in his chair and spoke directly to the younger officer, "Shep, never compromise your honor or your integrity for the likes of Slade. If he walks today, big deal! You still have your integrity and honor. They are a cop's currency. You can sell them for a penny and you can't buy them back for a million bucks. Besides, if Slade walks, God made the world round so bad guys will come back. We'll meet him again and get another opportunity. We don't catch them all the time; we just catch them all," said McCarthy to Shepherd.

"Let's go see if Judge Alice appreciates all of this integrity when she sees it," said Waters scooping up a pile of files on the desk in front of him. "Over worked and under paid," said Waters, "is the lot of a career prosecutor."

"Just like cops," said Shepherd.

"Not hardly," quipped Waters, "I have nights, weekends, and holidays off. Do you?"

Shepherd laughed, "I like this guy. I'm glad he's on our side."

"Trust me," said McCarthy, "you don't ever want this guy on the other side."

"Never happen," said Waters. "I suffer from a debilitating condition. I like cops, and I hate criminals. I think they belong in prison."

"Which belong in prison, the cops or the criminals?" asked McCarthy.

"The criminals, however, I did try to entrap you into perjury earlier, McCarthy, but once again you didn't fall for it. So, I will just have to be satisfied with putting away criminals. Today I got a bad feeling about Slade. I think he'll walk," said Waters.

"I hope not, but I think you are right," said McCarthy as he stepped up his pace trying to keep up with Waters, who clicked down the hallway walking as fast as some people run.

"Judge Alice," said Waters.

"Judge Alice," said McCarthy.

Just two hours later after all the testimony was in, Slade sat devoid of emotion in front of Judge Alice as she made her decision. "Mr. Slade is a night worker. On his walk home, he stops under a street light to smoke. He testified that he did this so that he would not be thought to be lurking in the shadows. He has testified he has been stopped walking home many times for no apparent reason by the La Claire Police Department. An anonymous caller reports Slade is stalking someone but gives no name of the person being stalked or even their own name. How can the court find this caller credible when they do not even leave their name. I shall not chastise these officers for doing what they thought to be their jobs, but for all I know, they could have made the call themselves. I am not saying they did, but that is a real possibility. If the court allowed anonymous complainants to have total credibility, over zealous police could manufacture their own calls. Over zealous police pose more of a threat than over zealous criminals. Therefore, it is my ruling that the stop was without reasonable suspicion, and therefore, all evidence obtained from this stop are fruits of the poisonous tree and shall be suppressed. Mr. Slade, this was a close call, and if it was not for technical errors made by these officers, you would be facing prison with your record. I do not want to see you in front of me again, or you will be going to prison." Judge Alice struck her gavel as if that would work magic on Harley David Slade.

Slade's attorney Jack Sloan's artificially tanned face lit up. He looked to the heavens and mouthed, "Thank you, Lord." He then turned to Slade to receive his congratulatory handshake, and Slade stared straight ahead. He did not even look at Sloan. He glared at Judge Alice.

Harley David Slade was observing the world through his own prism. In his world, he was at war. He barely escaped being sent to the prisoner of war camp. Judge Alice was the contemptible keeper of the keys. She kept dangling them in front of him and smugly kept reminding him that she had the power over him to put him in prison at any time. He hated her. He hated her worse than McCarthy. The Dark Lord spoke, "When the counter-offensive begins, she dies first."

"Yes!" answered Slade.

"Yes!" mimicked Sloan, pulling back his handshake and turning it into a double fist shake of joy, as if Sloan was Brett Farve and he had just thrown a touchdown pass to one of his favorite receivers.

Judge Alice called for the next case, satisfied that she had just protected the public from one of the most over zealous policeman she knew, Dan McCarthy. "He is obviously teaching this new rookie, and I must show him there are boundaries they must operate within in my jurisdiction," she reasoned. Then she looked at Slade. He was still seated at the counsel's bench. He was glaring at her, and he had shown no reaction. Suddenly, she pictured him standing outside her house smoking at 4:00 AM, watching, watching, watching, watching.... It gave her a chill, and she shuddered and shook off the thought as preposterous. "Next case!" she shouted to the bailiff, shaking off the premonition.

Sloan shook Slade's arm and brought him temporarily into the real world. Slade stood up and realized that he was staring into the eyes of Judge Alice. He smiled.

Judge Alice then smiled back. She thought, "That smile is scaring the shit out of me, and I do not know why. It is just a smile." She shuddered again. Judge Alice was a sheep. The sheep can never tell the difference between the wolves and the sheep dogs. Slade was a wolf. Alice had not freed the children's book writer in him. She had freed the killer to do what killers do — kill.

Outside the court room, McCarthy spoke, "You know that Bob Waters knew I was going to tell the truth, don't you?"

"Yeah. That was pretty obvious. You two must have a history," said Shepherd.

"Absolutely. He's the man!" said McCarthy. "He's the man I want in there when things are tough. He knew I was not going to tell even a small lie under oath. He was using the experience as a learning moment for you. None of the dirt bags in this world are worth selling out for. I saw a movie once, *Rob Roy*." McCarthy stopped and turned toward Shepherd. "Have you ever seen it?" asked McCarthy.

"I don't think so."

"He was a Scottish hero. In the movie there is a scene where one of Rob Roy's sons asks him, 'Father what is honor?' Rob Roy answers, 'Honor is a man's gift to himself. All men that have honor are kings, but not all kings have honor.' Shep, this is an honorable profession if you do it with honor. It's the coolest thing in the world being one of the good guys, but it isn't easy. I am going to tell you something."

"Yeah?" said Shepherd.

"I knew on the night you stopped Slade that it was going to be a close call. I knew that all I had to do was say that I smelled the marijuana and the stop would be justified."

"Yeah?" said Shep.

"I was tempted. I thought, come on, McCarthy, who would know?"

"You were tempted?"

"Yes, I was, police work gives you plenty of opportunities to be a sinner or a saint. The temptation to take the easy path is always there. The best kept secret in the world is most cops take the difficult path. Most cops I know are saints, not sinners. You want to hear an old joke?"

"Yeah," said Shep.

"A lawyer dies and goes to Heaven. St. Peter meets him at the gates and says, 'Welcome to Heaven, I'm Saint Peter. God asked me to take you personally to your residence.'

'Great!' says the attorney. Then a golf cart appears, and Saint Peter buzzes through the gates and then takes a right up a hill following a beautiful country lane. Along the lane there are quaint little cottages. They are beautiful, and there are countless cottages as far as the eye could see.

'Who lives in all of these cottages?' asked the attorney.

'These are occupied by police officers and their families,' said Saint Peter.

'Wow. They are beautiful… kind of like an English country garden,' said the attorney.

Then when Saint Peter reached the top of the hill, there was a beautiful country estate, a mansion really. 'Here we are. This is your place,' said St. Peter, and then out of no where angels sounded a flourish of horns announcing the attorney's arrival.

The attorney was astounded. He had done well as an attorney, but never could he have imagined himself living in such a fine mansion as this, even in heaven. 'Saint Peter, why do I warrant such fine lodgings when all of the policeman were given nice but small little cottages?' asked the attorney in a truly puzzled tone.

'We get thousands of cops in heaven,' said Saint Peter, 'but you are our first attorney.'"

Shepherd laughed, "I get it… I get it."

"Did you learn something today?" asked McCarthy.

"Yes, sir. I learned the world is round," answered Shep.

"Really?" said McCarthy.

"I learned most cops are saints, and then I thought about

Captain Hale."

"Most, not all," piped in McCarthy, trying to maintain his credibility.

"I learned that you can sell your integrity for a penny and you can't buy it back for a million bucks," said Shepherd.

"Now your talking kid," said McCarthy.

"I learned that we catch all the bad guys, but not all the time."

"You're speaking the truth, Shep. Tell me more."

"I learned today that honor talked and Slade walked," then Shepherd stopped and looked at McCarthy and said, "and I feel like I'm one of the good guys. We just lost this case, but I feel great. Why?"

"Perspective. You have to keep perspective. You didn't lose a case today. You gave yourself a gift. Man's gift to himself: Honor."

Honorable modern knight Gary Clements
of the La Crosse Police Department
Second Chance Save Number 479

Chapter Fourteen: "Cease Fire!"

As McCarthy laid down to sleep, it was 1:30 in the afternoon. He was feeling pretty miserable about Slade walking out of court a free man. He knew that Judge Alice had the ability to rule in their favor with the case presented, but the police called her "Alice in Wonderland" because she lived in a fairy tale world when she looked at criminals. She was Alice to the criminals, but the cops always faced the Queen of Hearts screaming, "Off with their heads."

Victoria sat on the bed next to him. "What's wrong, Honey? You look a little out of sorts. Was it a bad day in court?"

"Yeah. Judge Alice let one go today that I think is going to kill someone some day. She could have put him in prison, and instead she cut him loose." Victoria brushed his hair lightly with her fingers. "It wasn't even that she let him go that bothered me. She made a comment about over zealous cops calling in false calls to give themselves reasons to stop innocent people for no reason."

"I've been shot at and missed and shit at and hit, and still all I am when I put on that uniform is a public pissing post." He then raised his voice, "Come one, come all. Bad guys, media, tax payers, step up and piss on Dan McCarthy's leg and tell him it's raining. He's got to take it because he is a PPP, which stands for Paid Police Person, which translates to Public Pissing Post. Step up, one and all."

"My, aren't we cynical today? You have told me that I am supposed to let you know when you are sounding like Stanley Brockman. Well, Stanley, where is my obnoxiously positive husband Dan McCarthy? We need him here," asked Victoria moving her gentle touch to his forehead. He yawned. She was working her magic.

"You are right. I have heard Stanley give that speech a hundred times. I am obnoxiously positive? You think?" asked McCarthy.

"I am sure that it is to some, but I love it most of the time. Sometimes I find it a little annoying, but not obnoxious. I sure prefer it to Stanley Brockman Junior, though." Dan's eyes were now starting to flutter. She leaned forward and kissed his forehead.

"Stanley Brockman Junior? Thanks for the heads up. I'll feel better in the morning." He then closed his eyes, and he was out in less than a minute.

As Victoria quietly slipped out the door and closed it noiselessly, she whispered to herself, "I wonder what that is like, to wake up in the morning with your husband next to you. That would be nice. Maybe that will happen some day." She had been the wife of a cop for eight of their nine married years, and he had been on the night shift for all of that time. There was no sense in complaining because there was no end in sight.

Beep! Beep! Beep! Beep! Beep! McCarthy woke up already on his feet. He looked at the clock and it was 3:30 PM. He snatched his pager from the table and saw the numbers 1025 calling for a general response to the station.

He dressed fast and grabbed his gear. Victoria was gone, picking up the kids from school. As he passed the refrigerator, he took the marker hanging from the eraser board and wrote SWAT and then a heart and a "U" and signed it Dan.

When Dan got into his car, he turned on the radio and knew immediately what was up. There had been an armed robbery at the Farmer's Co-op Bank in a community close to La Claire. A citizen followed the bank robber, without the robber noticing, and watched where he went. He was in room eight at the Settle Inn, a little old-style mom and pop motel on highway 41 in La Claire. It was one story and a line of doors, where the customers park in front of their door.

When McCarthy arrived at the station, there was a flurry of activity. The shift commander was briefing Dooley and Carpenter. McCarthy stepped into the briefing. "First Shift has been held over to handle day to day calls. Second Shift was sent straight out to the scene and perimeter. They have the suspect contained in room number eight. Compton set up a command post at the Kwik Trip just north of the hotel. The hotel has been evacuated. The only ones there were Mom and Pop Evans and the bad guy. Highway 41 has been shut down north and south. The state patrol is handling that."

"You guys take one of your own cars and come in from the north and see Compton at the Kwik Trip. He will assign you. There is an FBI Special Agent on the scene also."

"There is one snag. A national news chopper had been in the area doing a story on power lines that were affecting cows' milk production. They got wind of this, and now they are hovering over the scene. The problem is they are sending live shots of the scene to people all over the country and, oh yeah, *the bank robber!* Captain Hale said he will attempt to contact the news people and have them either stand down or stop using live footage.

"Is all the SWAT gear out there?" asked McCarthy.

Dooley answered, "The SWAT tactical gear is on scene. Compton took it out. Gloria already headed out with the negotiator's equipment also."

McCarthy and Carpenter rode in Dooley's Explorer. When they arrived, they discovered they were in the midst of organized chaos. Compton was always calmly at the eye of the storm. He never appeared shaken. He handled everything as if he had done it a thousand times before because most things he had done a thousand times before.

The chopper hovered overhead. "God that has to be an FAA violation," said Dooley.

"There's never an FAA cop around when you need one," said Carpenter.

"Dooley, Carpenter, McCarthy, get together with Stammos. He is putting together a team to deliver a throw phone. The suspect initially destroyed the phone. Initial responding officers were yelling back and forth to him. He says if we throw in a phone he will talk. See Stammos. He will assign you." Compton then was back on the phone talking to the chief.

Stammos was on the back side of the Kwik Trip. "McCarthy,

you are carrying the shield. We do not know what he might have. We know he has what has been described as a 1911 Colt 45, but he may have something bigger. We are using the big shield. You know it's heavy, so you will be hands free shield only. Got it?"

"You bet, Randy," answered McCarthy.

"Dooley, MP5. Carpenter, you're throwing the phone. Brockman, hands free in the event he surrenders, take him through the ritual; I will be carrying another MP5. Questions so far?"

"Stack?" said Dooley.

"McCarthy, shield; Stammos, MP5 right; Dooley, MP5 left; Brockman, hands free; Carpenter, throw phone. The sniper team is set up covering the move. After we deliver the phone, we will set up along the north wall in the event that an entry or the surrender ritual has to be facilitated," said Stammos.

"What about a breacher?" asked McCarthy.

"Thanks. I almost forgot. There will be no breacher. The bad guy is going to prop the door open for the phone. If it's not open, we will not deliver the phone.

"Propping the door open?" asked Dooley.

"Yeah it's either a real good sign or a real bad sign. We are going to go up there and find out which one it is. Be careful and stay behind the shield. Questions?" asked Stammos.

"Can I shoot that fucking chopper down?" asked Brockman.

"I wish. Everything we do is going out live and real time. If the bad guy has his TV on, he will be able to watch our approach and there is nothing we can do about it," said Stammos. "God bless freedom of the press. Let's do this," said Stammos.

Michael Mattix was a three-time loser. He was looking at life in prison. He was even looking at the possibility of death if they were able to connect him to the Farmer's Mutual Robbery in Liberty, Missouri, where he shot a bank president in the forehead when the man looked like he was reaching for an alarm.

Mattix had been out of prison for two years even though he

had eight years left to serve of a twenty-five year sentence for bank robbery. He skipped out on parole, and he had been on the run for most of that time. He could not tell anyone how many bank robberies he had done, but it was at least fifteen, maybe twenty. He liked to hit banks with the name Farmer in them, and he would hit them on Friday afternoons near closing. Hitting Farmer's banks was a big city prejudice. He thought very little of rural communities and felt he would less likely to be caught by "hicks."

Mattix did not know that La Claire was less than one hundred miles from Northfield, Minnesota. That was the town that Jesse James' gang rode straight into and was shot straight out of by that small farming community. Members of the James' gang were left littered across the state of Minnesota after that miscalculation. It was a farmer that managed to follow Mattix. This farmer did not need to belong to a neighborhood watch to know that he was responsible for the quality of life in his community. The farmer would later be called a hero, and he would say what all heroes always say, "I didn't do anything that anyone else wouldn't have done," even though he did what few ever do.

Mattix was caught off guard but not yet caught when he was called to surrender. He realized then that the news alert with aerial shots of a standoff with a bank robbery suspect was him. "Fuck!" he said. "Fuck! Fuck! FUCK!" was the response the officers received.

"Well, at least he's talking," said Compton.

Mattix could see from the live bird's-eye view that there was no escaping this little predicament alive. "I'm not going to fucking prison," he said to himself. Then he saw an out. He saw the SWAT tactical van show up. "I'll draw those fuckers in and take some with me," Mattix said to himself.

Then the phone rang. "This is Gloria Dooley of the La Claire Police Department, sir. I'd like to see if I can help you out of this situation without anyone getting hurt," Gloria said in her best, most empathetic negotiator's voice.

"Suck my big hairy dick, lady!" was his response, and then he ripped the phone out of the wall and threw it through the window of his room.

Mattix then readied himself for his final battle. He took some duct tape out of his bag. He checked the magazine in his Colt 45 and slammed it home. He checked his chamber and closed it on a shiny new round. He did a lot of shooting, and so his ammunition was always fresh, "I like my ammo fresh and hot." He once told a cellmate in prison, "Just like my mamma's home-baked bread if'n I was ever to have had a mamma that baked homemade bread." He didn't.

Mattix taped the pistol to his right hand and wrist so that he could not be disarmed. "Just like that bumper sticker. They'll have to pry this from my cold dead fingers," he said with a smile. "No way am I fucking going back to prison."

Mattix then poured himself a tall glass of Jack Daniels and drank it down. He poured another and sipped and enjoyed. Then he shouted, "Cops. Can you hear me?"

"Yes," called Gloria with her bullhorn.

"I'm sorry. I was pissed before. I want to talk. I don't want to shout, but now I don't have a phone," shouted Mattix through the broken window, baiting the hook.

"We can send in a phone," echoed Gloria.

"You got a sexy voice. I'd like to talk to you," shouted Mattix.

"I'll talk to you, but how are we going to deliver the phone?" asked Gloria.

"If you promise you won't rush in here and shoot my ass, I will prop the door open and you can throw it in. Then we will talk and work something out. I just don't want anyone to get hurt, especially me." That was the truth. Mattix didn't want to hurt anybody. He wanted to kill them all and leave them piled at the door. He did not want to be hurt either. He wanted to be dead.

Mattix didn't care if they rushed in or tried to deliver the phone. He was taking some cops with him. A SWAT team might be tough, but if they were expecting just to deliver a phone with no trouble, they might just give him an opening to kill a couple and wound a couple. Even if he did somehow survive, he would go back to prison with status. "Cop Killers" are the top of the food chain in prison. He sipped his Jack Daniels, "This is most likely my last drink," Mattix said out loud somberly and then finished the glass.

After finishing his drink, Mattix went back to work. He ripped down the curtain rod in the bathroom and used it to cautiously prop open the door to number eight. He kept the 45 hidden behind his leg in the event that he exposed himself momentarily. He did not want to die meaninglessly by justifying a sniper shot.

After propping the door, he turned the television so he could watch the SWAT team approach on TV. Then he slid under the bed. He duct taped his shooting hand to the bed, allowing for some movement but also insuring that his weapon would be aimed at the doorway even after he was wounded. "I will be able to kill as long as I have bullets and can squeeze the mother-fucking trigger," thought Mattix. Now he would watch the news and wait. He looked at the words on the top of the screen. "Live coverage, ain't that nice." He had a perfect field of fire at anyone coming into the fatal funnel of the doorway. The camera in the helicopter was keeping him informed of every movement of the police. He breathed in through his nose and out through his mouth and belched. "Yeah, Jack Daniels. I hope there is Jack Daniels in Hell."

McCarthy picked up the shield. It required both hands to carry, but it would stop everything this side of a 50 caliber. He looked through the window in the shield, which made the world look like it was under water. It didn't seem like it should be, but the window was also bullet resistant. His helmet protected the portion of his head which was above the shield. He felt everyone fall in behind him and then came the tap.

McCarthy took off at a quick walk. SWAT guys called it the "Groucho" because it looked like the way that the young Groucho Marx used to walk. It allowed a team to move quickly and smoothly and shoot on the move accurately.

"We've got movement," reported the announcer as the helicopter-cam followed every step of the team. "It looks like they are carrying some sort of explosive device in a black case," said the news man watching and reporting from a studio in New York City. He was referring to the throw phone, which was contained in a padded black case.

McCarthy's SWAT instructor, Logan Tyree used to say, "Smooth is Fast." It was true. SWAT teams moved as one and fought as one. Bad guys usually gave up when they came up against a SWAT team. The options were always there. They could fight, flee, posture, or submit, and when the SWAT team showed up they would usually submit. Mattix was a stone cold killer. He had submitted for the last time.

McCarthy followed the wall toward door number eight. It was propped wide open. Even though they were expecting exactly what they found, McCarthy got a feeling. It was overwhelming. He had learned never to ignore it. "Guys, something doesn't feel right," whispered McCarthy into his mic. "Let me clear this."

Mattix saw the arrival at the door on television and then he turned and focused on the bright opening from his dark lair. "Come on in, boys. I got it just the way you like it. Hot and fresh," whispered Mattix, grinning ear to ear.

McCarthy stayed tight behind the shield and leaned cautiously into the fatal funnel of the doorway peering through the shield's window.

Mattix was peering at the doorway waiting to see black, anything black. When Mattix saw the shield appear in the doorway, his heart leapt. "Fuck you and die!" he shouted. "Pop! Pop! Pop! Pop! Pop!" As the 45 spit out potential death from under the bed, to McCarthy, it sounded slow and distant. He saw the first round hit the window of the shield. He would wonder no more about the reliability of the shield's window.

McCarthy could sense members huddling around him at the doorway. He was their best cover. He could see wood chipping and splintering from the doorway being shot away by the rounds of the suspect. Then it came, "Brrrap. Brrrap. Brrrap," the sad song of the MP5. McCarthy could feel and hear the brass casings clinking off his shield and helmet but did not sense the gun fire. The clinking of the brass off his helmet seemed to last forever.

Through the damaged window, he could see the hand of the suspect holding the semi-automatic handgun, firing and firing. Then he could see his Glock appear in front of the shield, and it was firing. He was surprised that it was in his own hand. He could see the muzzle flash but could hear no noise from his weapon. He had passed again into the surreal world between life and death. He wondered which side he would exit on this time.

Dooley was firing from the left side of the shield. All he could see was the hand and the gun. "Brrrap, Brrrap. Drop the gun!" he shouted. "Brrrap. Reloading!" Dooley racked the action, removed the magazine, replaced the magazine and slapped the action shut.

Stanley Brockman dropped to prone. He didn't think about staying mobile. It never crossed his mind that his supine body would cause the rest of the team to fall and sprawl if any of them tried to retreat. It did not matter today though. Today there would be no retreat. Mattix had not left the door open for a retreat. In this gun fight, there would be no podium for second place. Brockman was the only one who could see Mattix clearly. He fired his Glock. Brockman could see all the rounds hitting. It was not like a Hollywood movie. It was real. Mattix was being chopped to pieces, but the gun was still there. He was somehow still holding the gun high. *"Drop the Gun! For God's sake, please Drop the Gun!"* screamed Brockman, in a high-pitched scream of horror. The muzzle was pointed right between Brockman's eyes. He could see it. It was a nightmare, but he was too busy to pinch himself. He was too busy shooting and did not think of retreating from the muzzle. He was frozen in that spot. Frozen on the trigger, Brockman was doing the only thing he could pull from his bag of tricks at that moment without a conscious thought. He was shooting and shooting and shooting.

Stammos fired from the right of the shield, "Brrrap. Brrrap. Drop the gun!" he shouted. Mattix would not drop the gun. Mattix was occupied at that moment, heading away from the light toward the shadow. He had exited the surreal world between life and death. Mattix was on his way to do time for his crimes. Mattix was dead. The duct tape held his arm in place. Duct tape was truly a miracle product. It held fast. It allowed a lifeless man to remain in a gun fight that he had lost a lifetime ago. It held Mattix's lifeless hand in place. The muzzle looked like a cannon to everyone in the doorway. The hand was still holding the gun, holding the gun, holding the gun. "Brrrap. Shit, still there. Reloading!" Stammos racked the action of the MP5 open and switched to the second magazine and slapped the action shut.

Then McCarthy thought, "Something strange is happening here, something very strange." He then shouted, "Cease Fire! Cease Fire!" The shooting stopped. It was quiet, but the hand and the gun were still there. The gun was suspended and twisted grotesquely from an unidentifiable bloody appendage. It was over.

"*Gun!*" screamed Brockman.

"No, Cease Fire!" shouted McCarthy.

"What do you see, McCarthy?" shouted Stammos.

"I can see the gun. It's still in his hand, but there is no movement. I am going to check it out." McCarthy then moved farther into the doorway and hit the lights on the shield. It was something he could never forget. The suspect was under the bed, and the rounds had not only killed him, but they had turned Mattix into a bloody, meaty, unidentifiable mass. McCarthy could see the gray identifiable duct tape holding the gun in place, still looking menacing and seeming to clash with the gray brain matter mixed with the bloody chunks of meat. McCarthy did not need a medical opinion on this. This man had robbed his last bank. "It's over. Has anybody been hit?" asked McCarthy.

There was a pause while everyone checked themselves, realizing sometimes you can be shot and not know it.

"Everyone's OK," said Carpenter, who was last in line. He had brought a throw phone to a gun fight. His Glock was at low ready, but he was out of position to do anything but watch. He saw the shooting but, like everyone else, could not understand what could possibly make four officers fire so many times. They did not see the muzzle. They did not see the hand. They did not have every cop's nightmare come to life in front of them, so they could not understand. There was a long silence.

The cameraman in the helicopter could not contain himself, "Holy shit, I got it all. Motherfucker, I got it all. This beat the hell out of cows standing next to power lines. I shit you not!" he screamed to the pilot.

McCarthy got on the radio, "Shot's fired. Suspect down."

"No shit," said Brockman to no one in particular, panting like he had run a marathon.

"Let's clear this place," said Stammos. "Move... Now."

The room was a small place to have your last drink in. The smell of fresh blood was heavy in the air and created a sickening mix with the Jack Daniels, which was a prominent smell since one of the rounds shattered the bottle. In less than ten seconds, the call came out, "Room is clear. Suspect is down. EMS is not needed. This is a crime scene. Lock it down," said Stammos.

"Now, all you guys. We are going to ease out of this place. Try not to move anything. Step over the brass. Leave the suspect DRT (Dead Right There)," said Stammos. "We won't be hearing a peep from him anymore today."

The television was still on. They stopped and gazed fixated on the screen like four-year-olds watching SpongeBob Square Pants. "He saw us coming. They shot footage of a SWAT team making an entry, and they put it live on TV, and this guy was watching us and waiting for us. They could have gotten us all killed," Brockman was absolutely right.

"All of us," said Carpenter.

"Killed," said Stammos.

"The weapon?" asked Brockman, looking at the weapon still sticking ominously out from under the bed.

"Leave it," said Stammos. "Leave the scene as it is. Guns don't shoot people. Live people shoot people. This one ain't going to be shooting anyone else," said Stammos.

The entire entry team stepped out, and for the first time heard the helicopter. They had never heard it, until now, and it head been hovering over them throughout the entire gunfight. The cameraman was still running live feed to the world. "Look at that guy," said Stammos quietly to McCarthy. "He's grinning. The horse's ass is actually grinning," Stammos said incredulously.

"Yeah and I bet he's got a hard on too," growled Brockman. Then Brockman did what everyone wanted to do, but no one but Brockman would do. He lifted his right hand slowly, ceremoniously up to the chopper and as he mouthed the words, "Fuck you," he flipped them "the bird" live on national TV.

"Ooooh, that's going to leave a mark, Stanley," said Stammos. Then he looked into Stanley's eyes. He slowly reached up to Stanley's out stretched arm and gently folded up Stanley's finger and put his arm around Stanley and gently patted his shoulder like a brother, for if they weren't before, they now were truly a band of brothers.

Then Stanley did one more thing that everyone saw nationwide live on national news. It was a real scoop. No one had ever seen Stanley Brockman do it before. The incorrigible Stanley Brockman… cried.

A Diamond in the Rough

Chapter Fifteen: Rush To Judgment

It was a media circus. The tape received as much air time as the North Hollywood Bank of America shooting, and some media pundits called it, "The Rodney King beating with machine guns." Chief Ray Johnson of the La Claire Police Department issued an initial statement to a swarm of reporters stating, "Initial indications reveal that this was a justifiable police shooting. We are going to be thorough with this, so please be patient. There is a great deal of evidence to process. We have not yet identified the suspect. He is a white male. He robbed the Farmers Co-op Bank. A witness followed him to the Settle Inn Motel on Highway 41 in La Claire. Police were called to the scene and contained him in room number eight. He initially threw the phone through the window and then asked to speak with our negotiator. He agreed to allow a phone to be delivered by members of our SWAT team. The suspect propped the door open to receive the phone, and members of the La Claire SWAT team attempted to deliver the phone. Instead of taking the phone, the suspect opened fire on the officers in what appeared to be a deliberate ambush. Four members of the team returned fire simultaneously. The suspect did not survive the gun fight. No officers were injured. That will be all for now, ladies and gentleman," said Chief Ray Johnson.

The reporters in the room that had converged on La Claire swirled around Johnson like piranhas in a feeding frenzy.

"How many rounds were fired, Chief?" asked the reporter from National Public Radio.

"How come such overkill, Chief?" called a voice from the rear.

"Why so many shooting at once, Chief?" yelled another.

"Why did they go up in the first place? Didn't they suspect that this desperate man might react badly to such an aggressive display of force by the police?" The Chief turned and thought, "I wish I would have brought Stanley Brockman to field that last question." Instead of answering, he tightened his lips and his hands crumpled the briefing sheet, all in an effort to hold in what he wanted to say so badly. What needed to be said, so badly, but could not be said by any chief or sheriff at any news conference even though every chief and sheriff has wanted to say it to reporters at least once in their career.

As Chief Johnson left the podium, he left the piranhas shouting. "Chief! One question!"

Then there was one glimmer of hope for the humanity of the media. Rachel Klein of the local news station called out, "Chief! Tell the officers that our hopes and prayers are with them, and thank them for their brave service."

The chief paused, looking initially shocked and then moved. His eyes found Rachel in the crowd, and he thought, "A dolphin swimming with the sharks." He put up his hand indicating halt to everyone still shouting, and with his other hand he pointed at Rachel as if he was directing cars in a massive traffic jam and said, "Thank you, Rachel. I will tell them."

McCarthy and the others had completed their statements and turned over their weapons because they had to be taken as evidence. Each one of the officers were read their Miranda Rights and told they could remain silent. They were interviewed by Detective Sergeant Brickson. They were then read their administrative rights and interviewed again by Detective Sergeant Joe Darnell. They were told they could not remain silent during this interview, which was internal.

When the investigators asked McCarthy at what point he decided to fire, he told the truth. He said, "I never really consciously made that decision. I just all of a sudden noticed a hand holding a weapon in the window of the shield, and I realized that it was my weapon, in my hand, and I was shooting."

"How many times did you fire at the suspect?" asked Detective Sergeant Darnell, an excellent investigator who showed little fondness in patrol officers. He acted as if they were a sub-species on most days.

McCarthy answered, "I would have to guess, and I won't. I have no idea how many times I shot."

"Did you hit him?" asked Darnell.

"I believe I did, just because I do not usually miss at that distance," answered McCarthy.

"Could you not tell the others were shooting?" asked Darnell.

"It is strange. It was like yes and no. I could hear the clinking of brass off my helmet, but not the shots. If I did hear them, I do not remember hearing them. It was all so bizarre," answered McCarthy. "I'm still sorting this out in my mind because I just now remembered the clinking of the brass off my helmet. I do not think I told anyone else about that," said McCarthy.

"I do not want to hear about anything you told anyone else. As I explained to you once already, there are two separate investigations, and they have to be conducted separately. There is one criminal investigation, and one in-house administrative investigation. One investigation is to see if someone should be criminally charged, and the other to see if someone should be fired or suspended." Darnell had started the interview in a very pleasant and even friendly tone, which McCarthy found unusual for Joe Darnell. This last statement was delivered in his usual "Do I have to explain everything to you over and over again, sub species person?" tone of voice.

"OK," said McCarthy. "Who's doing the investigation to determine if someone shot at us first, tried to kill us, and if we might be justified in returning fire to save our lives? Who's doing that investigation, because I would like to talk to them when you're done, Sergeant Darnell," said McCarthy with anger building up in him.

"Hey, McCarthy. It doesn't help your case at all to get defensive," said Darnell.

"Here is something for the record. I got defensive earlier when a bank robber that I was trying to deliver a throw phone to shot at my partners and me. My partners got defensive at the same time, and we returned fire. We continued to stay on the defensive, because the hand with the gun never dropped. We shot him a lot, because the hand did not drop, and the gun continued to be pointed at us. If we did not get defensive when we did, all five of us on that phone delivery team would be toe tagged right now and you would be talking to the bank robber. Respectfully, Sergeant, am I about done here?"

"McCarthy! Don't get smart with me. This is serious. I will tell you when you are done," snarled Darnell. "We've got a stiff with about fifty bullet holes in his body, and I'm going to find out why."

"One? Fifty? Under the circumstances, what really is the difference? He tried to kill us, and we defended ourselves, and he is dead and we are not," said McCarthy. "Frankly, Sergeant, you sound to me as if you wish it would have gone the other way. Sorry I couldn't have obliged you."

"Officer McCarthy, you will answer my questions when I ask and not before," ordered Darnell. "I don't need any bullshit from a patrolman who just took part in firing about seventy-plus rounds into one man."

McCarthy sat fuming and thinking, "Don't say it. Don't say it.... Fuck, you're going to say it."

"There might have been more, but the MP5 has only a thirty-round magazine." Then McCarthy thought, "Shit. Can't take that one back." Then McCarthy said seriously, "The guy shot at us. One flattened out in the shield right in front of my face. The gun was taped in his hand, and his hand was taped to the underside of the bed so that, to us, he never stopped being a threat. I called cease fire when something finally registered that he was dead. I don't know how it registered, but it did. The rest, I think, would have kept shooting and would have been justified to do so, but they stopped shooting because they trusted my judgment."

"Have you ever shot anyone before, McCarthy?" asked Darnell.

"Yes, I have, Sergeant," answered McCarthy. "You know I have. I shot Ray Draper, who shot at me several years ago," answered McCarthy.

"Did you like it?" asked Darnell.

"Did I like it? Have you ever shot anyone?" asked McCarthy.

"I'm asking the questions," barked Darnell.

"'Did I like it?' you ask. I liked it in the manner of I liked that

I walked away when someone was trying to kill me. I like being a cop. I like being a husband, a father, and a contributing member of my community. I didn't particularly enjoy shooting this man, nor did I particularly like shooting Ray Draper, but I do like raising my children. I want to see my son grow to be a strong man, and I want to dance with my daughter some day at her wedding. To make it to that part of my life, I had to shoot two men. My job description required it. Necessity required it. If all I had to look forward to in life is conversations with you, Sergeant Darnell, I most likely would have let them shoot me," said McCarthy as he crossed his arms across his chest and crossed his legs as he sat hard back in his chair and gritted his teeth.

After Joe Darnell made every one of the officers feel like criminals, instead of the heroes they were, they were sent home. They were placed on administrative suspension with pay. Even though it was standard procedure, it was never easy to give up your firearm and go on suspension. It sent all the wrong messages to someone who had just done as much for an employer as you can ask of anyone. They risked their lives and took a life. Then, without so much as a thank you, they were told, "Give me your guns, and you're on suspension."

McCarthy went home, and for two days he did exactly what he should not have done. He watched television. He sat on his couch with his feet up and went from channel to channel, mesmerized by the twenty seconds of horror. It did not look like horror from the vantage point of the smiling camera man.

McCarthy sat and jotted down some of the national media commentators remarks. One called it, "The Rodney King beating with machine guns." Another called it, "The Gunfight at the Nothing's OK Corral." McCarthy's least favorite was, "The Ready. Aim. Fire Fight."

"Should you be watching that over and over?" asked Victoria, breaking him out of his daze.

"Probably not," said McCarthy flipping to another channel showing Stanley Brockman flipping the bird to the helicopter.

"How are you feeling about all this?" asked Victoria, snuggling in next to him and laying her head against his shoulder.

"Truth? I'm pissed. I am so pissed. I feel like taking my badge into the station and shoving up Joe Darnell's ass."

"That would not be such a good career move," said Victoria brushing his temple.

"I know exactly what happened. I know we did nothing wrong, but Darnell acts like he wants to put us in prison." He threw a throw pillow hard into the wall across the room.

Victoria looked startled, "Dan!"

"What? It's a throw pillow, isn't it? I thought that was what they were for," explained Dan, putting his arm around his wife, realizing he had scared her. "Between Darnell and the media, I feel like I'm am this sane guy who is being judged by the residents of the secure wing at the psych ward."

The phone rang and Dan started to get up.

"I'll get it," said Victoria. "Like I said before, I'll screen your calls."

"Hello," said Victoria. "Just a minute, Chief, he's right here." Victoria handed the phone to Dan and said, "It's the chief. He would like to talk to you."

"Hello," said Dan.

"Hello, Dan. How are you doing?" asked Chief Johnson in a concerned voice.

"I've been better. I am worrying about Randy, Stanley, and Dooley. I am really concerned about Stanley, especially," said Dan.

"Stanley is going fishing. We arranged to get him out with Stammos. Stammos has a cottage on Lake Nelson in Hayward, and they are going to float around on the lake and catch walleyes until we finish this investigation," said the Chief.

"How is it going, Chief?" asked McCarthy.

"Preliminaries indicate that you guys have not a thing to worry about. For Christ's sakes it must have been a nightmare," answered the Chief.

McCarthy was shocked. Darnell had not given that impression to him at all.

The chief continued, "That muzzle sticking out from under the bed was still creeping out the investigators after you guys cleared the scene. Every time one of the investigators entered the room and saw that bloody hand holding the gun pointed toward the door, that son of a bitch almost got shot all over again. I am not going to cater to people who are so satisfied reporting bullshit. We are going to get it exactly right and then have a press conference to lay it out. The Wisconsin State Patrol Reconstruction Experts are on the scene and they are doing a computer crime scene mapping of the incident. It will be pretty dynamic. We will show it at the press conference and save the team a copy. You can play it at the SWAT Christmas party next year," Chief Johnson paused, waiting for a laugh, which never came.

"Thanks, Chief." said McCarthy, missing the attempt at humor.

"You guys really walked into it. You should have used the bomb, though," said Chief Johnson.

"We should have used the bomb? What bomb?" asked McCarthy.

"One commentator said it appeared as if the SWAT team was about to deliver an explosive device when they decided to open fire instead," said the chief.

"Explosive device?"

"The dumb bastard thought the throw phone was an explosive device," said the chief. "The local media has been great. They have not bought into the hype. This flood will recede just like everything the Mississippi has thrown at us, and when it does, we'll clean up the mud and the shit, and everything will be just like new," said the chief.

"Thanks again, Boss," said McCarthy.

"Wait. There was another reason I called. I think you should get out of town," continued Chief Johnson.

"Maybe," said McCarthy. "I don't know where to go though."

"How would you like a paid vacation? It wouldn't be a vacation for most, but for you, maybe. I took the liberty of signing you up in a Defense and Arrest Tactics Instructor's Course that starts Monday. How about it?" asked the chief. "It's at the Western

Technical College campus in Angelo, Wisconsin. I got you staying at the Radisson on the Mississippi in La Crosse. How does that sound?" said the chief. "Three presidents have slept there," the chief added for effect, "both Bushes and Clinton."

"That's where I went to college… the academy," said McCarthy in a matter-of-fact manner.

"I'll take that as a yes," said the chief.

McCarthy was silent. He wondered why he was not excited. He still felt like a pit bull chasing a rendering truck as it was pulling away. He had loved this job. He had wanted to be a DAAT (Defense and Arrest Tactics Instructor), but right now he felt like telling his chief, "Who gives a rat's ass!" Instead, he sighed and answered, "Yes, sir."

The chief recognized the melancholy in McCarthy's voice. He had heard it before in many officers at different times in their career. With some it came and went. With others it came and they went. Still others it came, it stayed, and they stayed. They became the ROD's. They would forever remain retired on duty. The walking emotionally wounded. He had never heard it in McCarthy's voice before. It did not surprise Chief Johnson. He had seen the news coverage. He had seen the grotesque, but deadly, looking hand dangling from the bottom of the bed. He had seen the menacing muzzle of the 45 staring, never blinking, at the fatal funnel that the officers had been sent to with that throw phone. He had seen the tape of the Darnell interview.

After Chief Johnson watched the tape of Darnell interviewing McCarthy, he called Darnell into his office. The conversation was a monologue, not a dialog. The chief had ended the proverbial ass chewing with Darnell by ordering him to, "Get the hell out of my office now. I wish you were in uniform so I could rip the God damn stripes from your God damn sleeves!"

The chief wanted to say more to McCarthy, but all he could say was, "Enjoy the class, Dan. Keep the TV off until you get back, OK? It's going to be all right." The chief's words were like a salve on a bad burn. The pain was still there, but the healing had begun.

Chapter Sixteen: La Crosse. God's Country

On Monday morning at 7:30, McCarthy was seated in a state-of-the-art classroom in Angelo, Wisconsin, just east of La Crosse. The room was inside a neat little brown brick building in the middle of what used to be an airfield. He felt at home. He had spent a great deal of time here as a criminal justice student, and then he completed the police academy here.

The place was like a Disneyland for cops and firemen. It had indoor and outdoor shooting ranges. It had an obstacle course, a driving track, a mat room, and a weight room.

It had the perfect bad guys to spar with. They were muscular men made of rubber with no arms and no legs. They couldn't out run you and they couldn't out fight you. It would be the last time recruits would see a perfect bad guy.

The best thing about the place, though, were the trainers. They were some of the best in the world, and most people could not find the place on the map. If you Googled the address, the computer could not find it either. The peaceful setting was filled with good memories for McCarthy.

He entered the room, and one of his old instructors, Logan Tyree, crossed the room immediately and extended his hand. "Hey, Dan, how are you doing?" said Tyree.

"Better now. It's great to be back," said McCarthy. Tyree had been McCarthy's Defense and Arrest Tactics Instructor. He had taught him Basic SWAT and Crowd Control. During the academy, Tyree had always run during lunch breaks and invited the students to join him. McCarthy was the only taker in the class. They ran "The yellow brick road." It was a trail that circumnavigated the property. They would run by a corn field, and then the trail would weave through genuine Wisconsin woods. It was not unusual to see a coyote tearing apart a rabbit or kick up a deer or wild turkeys.

It was called the yellow brick road because there were three large rocks painted yellow located on the trail. The first said, "Pride," the second said, "Integrity," and the last said, "Guts."

The three words' acronym spelled "PIG." Police officers in the seventies took to wearing little pigs, because they were called pig all the time. It took the sting away.

Tyree said on one of their runs, "In the seventies, we were called pig every night. Many of the people that called us pigs then are college professors, mayors, and congressmen. They are some of the same people that burned the flag and spit on the troops when they came home from war. It became so acceptable that even nice people called us pigs." Tyree kept running and then added, "I wish I was making that up."

Logan Tyree had also taught an early morning class for police officers and criminal justice students called *kei satsu jitsu*. Literally translated, it meant the police way of combat. McCarthy had never missed a class while he was in school. He became beyond proficient in take downs, throws, arm locks, and compliance holds. Tyree knew hundreds of them and was willing to share, and McCarthy was willing to learn. Tyree even let McCarthy teach the class a few times. Tyree and the other Defense and Arrest Tactics Instructor, Brian Noble, had become more than teachers to McCarthy and the other students, they were trusted friends and mentors. After a hearty handshake, McCarthy found his seat and sat down. "Damn! This is a dream come true, and I still feel like shit."

He thought, "I can remember sitting in here as a student hoping to be a DAAT Instructor some day. I wish I still felt like that. I feel like…"

"OhYahDA, my good friend!" said a familiar voice. McCarthy turned to see his old friend and Tae Kwon Do instructor Larry Kane waltz in the door. Kane was a part-time sheriff's deputy for the La Claire County Sheriff's Department and full time martial arts instructor.

"What are you doing here?" asked McCarthy.

"The sheriff thinks I might be able to teach self defense to his deputies." Then in a mock Korean accent he added, "Where he get such idea I not know."

"Maybe it's because you live in the basement of a martial arts studio and you hunt deer with a samurai sword," said McCarthy.

"I never actually hunted with the sword. I just asked the Department of Natural Resource Wardens if it was legal, and they said there was no law against it. I never actually killed a deer with it," explained Kane.

"Why didn't you tell me you were coming to this?" asked Dan

"I did not want to break your heart. I knew you wanted to come, and I knew you did not get the school when you asked for it," said Kane sincerely.

"After the shooting, the chief signed me up. I think he thought it might help… uh… take my mind off everything," said McCarthy.

"You did what you had to do, my friend. The bad guy just picked a fight with the wrong SWAT team, not suggesting that there is a right SWAT team to pick a fight with," said Kane.

"Tell World News Tonight that," said McCarthy.

"I think Brockman already issued a press release to them in sign language," said Kane squinting one eye and taking a thoughtful pose with his hand on his chin. Suddenly the middle finger popped up.

McCarthy laughed. They both laughed hard. It was the first time since the incident that McCarthy was able to laugh at "Brockman's first press release." He would never be able to think about it again without laughter.

Tyree then began to speak. It was 8:00 AM straight up. He always started on time and rarely let anyone out early. He said training was too scarce and too valuable to not take advantage of every minute offered. "This is the perfect size class. Twelve. It is divisible by two, three, four, and six. You will be learning working, and then you will be teaching. Everything you learn you will teach. DAAT is a system of verbalization skills coupled with physical alternatives. You will be teaching cops how to keep their names off criminal complaints, law suits, and most importantly, walls of honor. They must learn how to survive physically, legally, and emotionally and look like the good guys doing it. We will teach our trainees to show everyone respect and no one trust. They do not pay us to trust people. What does it say on the dollar bill?" asked Tyree.

"In God We Trust," answered Kane.

"Right and there the list ends. You will teach your recruits and veteran officers to show courtesy up to *Impact!* and beyond. We want them to know DAAT like they have black belts in DAAT. It is just as important for officers to have a black belt in dialog. Sun Tzu said the ultimate victory is to win the battle without fighting. Even so, there will always be those who must be taken physically. That's why DAAT is a system of verbalization skills coupled with absolutely necessary physical alternatives. Does anyone wish to report injuries they have now?"

"No, sir," they answered.

"Good let's keep it like that. DAAT Instructors are not here to cause injuries, we are here to prevent them. Let's get started," and Tyree led them to the mat room.

The days went fast: front compliance, rear compliance, angle kicks, front kicks, forearm strikes, punches, decentralization, falling, baton strikes, TASERs, pepper sprays, interview stance, defensive stance. They learned, they studied, they taught, they fought.

They all were pepper sprayed, and they laughed and pounded on the blue kick bags while blinded by the pepper spray. They were all hit with the TASER, and strangely, they laughed about that also, but no one could explain why later.

At times they all would lie on the mats soaking in their own sweat trying to catch their breath. They told politically incorrect jokes and war stories, and sometimes someone would "step on a duck," and they would all laugh. Little boys of all ages always find a loud fart hilarious when done in the company of a group. It was a timeless phenomenon. It was just as unexplainable as why they laughed at their own pain and misery during the pepper spraying and TASER.

Best of all, McCarthy did not have time to watch TV. He had no time to think about anything except learning how to be a Defense and Arrest Tactics Instructor. It was great. It was like hitting your head against the wall. When you stop, it feels great.

That was what this post shooting experience was like.

The night before the last day of class, Logan Tyree invited anyone who wanted to stay after for an experience in *Kei Satsu Jitsu*.

"What exactly is *Kei Satsu Jitsu*?" asked one of the student-instructors.

"It literally means 'The Police Way of Combat.' I am so arrogant I invented a martial art. It is not like any other martial art. It is a system that contains no techniques. In the martial arts there are no bad systems. In law enforcement there are no bad defensive tactics systems. I hear other instructors in both the martial arts and law enforcement saying the system they sell is the best and everything else doesn't work. *Kei Satsu Jitsu* is a philosophy of training. If you practice it, you agree that law enforcement is dangerous. You agree that you will be putting yourself in harm's way, and your life and safety depend on your ability to defend yourself. Other people's lives also depend on your ability to defend them. *Kei Satsu Jitsu* is a system that is no system. It is a system that is every system. You decide that as long as you wear the badge you will practice and train and expand your skills and ability to honorably protect yourself and others."

"It is crucial that you win and win honorably. You must maintain the status as a good guy. When you win with technique, you look like a good guy. The bad guy knows he lost to someone more skilled than him and might not try it again. You gain respect and even fear. There is a fine line between respect and fear, and I have always preferred one and settled for either but demanded compliance where compliance was required."

"The class tonight is voluntary. I offer it free to you and will not think badly if you choose to not attend. That will not reflect on your certification. I feel strongly that instructors should know more than their students and strive to learn more about their disciplines. Do you have any questions?"

It was 4:00 PM, which was quitting time. There has never, in the history of police training, been a question asked at quitting time. There was silence.

"We're done," said Tyree. The room cleared except for two. McCarthy and Kane were still sitting before Logan Tyree. "I am not shocked that you stayed. I am not shocked that the others left, but I am pleased." Tyree pulled out a boom box and an old, used cassette tape. "You know what this means?"

"Conan?" asked Kane and McCarthy.

"Conan," said Tyree.

The mat room was large. When you talked, there was a slight echo, which was a little annoying, but when a fall was crisply executed, the slam of the body hitting the mat was sweet music.

The three put on the RedMan chest protectors. They slipped on their sparring gear, including shin protectors, headgear, and slipped in the mouth pieces.

"OK. You remember how this is done?" asked Logan.

"Remind us," said McCarthy.

"This is tiring but extremely beneficial. It is good training, and it clears the mind and cleanses the soul," said Tyree. "We will turn the music on. This is the entire soundtrack to the movie *Conan the Barbarian*. Once it starts, two of us will spar. When one starts getting tired, they will tap out and another will begin. When someone else gets tired, they will tap out and the other will step in. We will spar until the entire soundtrack is played. We will contact spar, but all contact will be light everywhere except the torso. We are padded there, so we can pop each other pretty good. Are we good to go?" asked Tyree.

McCarthy stepped up to Logan Tyree and said, "Let's go."

Kane started the music. Tyree tapped his groin area, "Cup check."

McCarthy tapped his, "Check."

Tyree slipped his mouth guard into his mouth and put two gloves in the air, and McCarthy slipped his mouth guard in and tapped gloves. They both keuped, a barking sound designed to let the air out of the lungs. This began the long match.

All three had anticipated they were not going to be joined by other class members on this evening. They wore their *Dobaks* (martial arts uniforms). All three were affiliated with the American

Kyuki-Do Federation. All three had earned black belts, but Kane was a master and a sixth degree. Sparring was his specialty. Tyree and McCarthy had been veterans of many street confrontations. This had given them a very straightforward approach to fighting.

Their punches were straight, fast, and furious. Their kicks were delivered to the torso and primarily were the front kick and the side kick. Whenever they tied up, there would be a flurry of knees. When one would put too much weight in a certain direction, the master combatants would react in the blink of an eye. The throws were crisp, and the body hitting the mat could be heard in the parking lot by criminal justice students coming out of the shooting range.

"What's going on up there?" one asked Brian Noble, the student's instructor.

"That's what happens to our students that give me lip," said Noble.

"What's wrong, you can't handle us yourself?" pimped the student.

"Yes, but I like to watch," said Noble grinning. "In your case, if you keep it up, smart guy, I'm going to make an exception and beat you like a red headed stepchild." The student laughed as he entered the building, keeping a constant curious eye in the direction of the echoes of slamming bodies and keups upstairs in the mat room.

When Kane tapped in, the style was different. He was the veteran of many tournaments and point fighting. His technique was crisp, yet graceful, like a ballet dancer on steroids. He could spar longer because he was efficient. He could see openings and capitalize like a cobra striking. It didn't help to take him down because he could fight on the ground as well as he fought on his feet. He bore no observable weakness. These were three worthy opponents.

When it was all over, the three sat on the mats, leaning back on their elbows. Their black uniforms had somehow become even blacker for they were soaked in sweat.

Finally, the topic came up. "You don't seem yourself, McCarthy," observed Logan Tyree. "Would you like to talk about it?"

"I don't feel myself," answered McCarthy.

"Give it time," said Kane. "It's only been two weeks."

"I feel like I want to quit. Like all those years, the Stanley Brockmans of the world were right. TJIF, the job is fucked. The world is fucked up. It's all bullshit and I feel like a fool running around loving the job and trying to help people and telling people and recruits to stay positive because it's a lie. Police work dumps you in this big pile of shit, and eventually if you wallow in it long enough, you will smell like shit, and your world will be shit. That's how I feel, and I don't know how to stop feeling this way. I…" McCarthy stopped. He felt a wave of emotion, and he could not speak and control it at the same time. He just rode the wave and became silent.

"Do you still like the martial arts, Dan?" asked Logan.

McCarthy had regained his composure and was happy for the change of topic. He hoped no one had notice the wave. "Absolutely, it's a part of my life. It's a way of life," answered McCarthy.

"Do you like sparring?" asked Tyree.

"Yeah, tonight was the most fun I've had with my clothes on in years," answered McCarthy, with a modicum of excitement back in his voice.

"If you love sparring so much why did you tap out? You tapped out several times tonight and one of us took your place. Why did you stop?" asked Tyree.

"I had to. We all had to. We were exhausted. My arms got tired. My legs got tired. I had to rest and recover," explained McCarthy. "You tapped out too. So did Master Kane," said McCarthy showing Kane the respect warranted by the number of stripes on his black belt.

"But you still love the martial arts?" asked Tyree.

"Yeah. I think I even love it more than when I came in here. This was a blast," answered McCarthy sounding more like himself.

"A police career can be like this sparring session. It can be too long for most. Even though you love it, it kicks your ass sometimes. When you get knocked down, you get backup. When you can't handle it yourself, you call for backup and it will be there. Cops love to backup cops. They love it when you tap them in to help. There isn't another call they answer faster than an officer needs assistance call. Just like this sparring session, it kicks your ass sometimes, but if it doesn't kill you, it makes you stronger. It sometimes takes time to get perspective when the call is a tough call. When you survive and get perspective, if you were meant to be a cop, a blue knight, an honorable sheep dog, you know you will love the job again. Do you remember in the academy what I said about staying positive?"

"It's a discipline," answered McCarthy.

"It's a discipline. Just like the martial arts. Keeping a positive attitude is crucial to enjoying the job, life, and staying the great cop that you are. But, hey… it's a discipline!" said Tyree, putting his fist against the palm of his open hand and bowing slightly. "You made it even more difficult on yourself. You joined SWAT. You were a blue knight, but then you chose to wear the black armor. Sometimes cops have to dial 911 and call SWAT, because the shit is really about to hit the fan. You, Dooley, Stammos, and Brockman handled a tough call. You handled it well. It was so unique and so tough that the world is having trouble dealing with it and digesting what happened. They are treating you like you did something wrong, and that is wrong, but they are sheep. They do not understand the sheep dog and cannot recognize the wolves as being dangerous. You know that. Take some time to think, recover, and remember. You were born to be a cop… a sheep dog… and a blue knight. You have exceptional skills and deserve to wear the black armor. If you feel like this, can you imagine how Stammos, Brockman, Dooley, and even Carpenter feel. Carpenter, who had to stand and could not do anything but watch. I am thinking they would like a little backup from a cop that went through the same thing that they did…. Let's get a pizza." The three quietly pushed themselves off the mat and gave each other the martial artist handshake.

The next day was a short day. The written test seemed easy, but that was because the material was learned well. They not only had to learn it, but they had to teach back what they had learned.

McCarthy reached his hotel room at the Radisson in La Crosse. He was on the third floor on the river side of the hotel.

He watched the La Crosse Queen paddle down the Mississippi and gazed at the bronzed lifelike statute of the children standing waving at the riverboat. Real children were feeding ducks near the statue, and a small toddler just learning to walk waddled after a duck, who tried to run and then flapped its wings to propel itself forward, away from near death as the toddler fell flat on his face. The father picked him up and tried to comfort the crying child as the amused father attempted to suppress a laugh. McCarthy did not need to suppress the laugh from his third-floor window. He just laughed out loud.

He then dressed to run. He put on his running shoes and dressed in the jersey of the best quarterback in the history of pro football, number four Brett Favre. He put his Packers baseball cap on backwards, and he began to run.

McCarthy ran lazily along the Mississippi until he reached the large statue of Hiawatha. The statue had clothing and hairstyle from all the Native American tribes that lived and traded with the white man on the very spot that the statue stood. The city received its name because the tribes played a fast moving physical game that the French traders called La Crosse.

McCarthy followed the path and turned away from the Mississippi and followed the La Crosse River. He ran through the large wetland preserve in the middle of the city. Developers repeatedly argued to fill it in and slap parking lots on top of this land because it was "just a swamp." As McCarthy enjoyed the peaceful warbles, tweets, and chirps of the birds, he was glad that they had not turned this beautiful wetland into a sprawling complex of buildings and parking lots.

McCarthy ran a large sweeping circle that took him through the marsh and to the base of the large precipice that guarded La Crosse for a millennium. The white settlers had called it Grand Dad's Bluff. He turned and headed back toward his hotel on Main Street.

He could have made it to the hotel, but as he approached Saint Joseph's Cathedral he thought, "I think I'll tap out and ask for backup."

The cathedral was a special spot. He and his wife Victoria had been married there. His son and daughter had both been baptized there. It was a huge white-gray gothic style church, except much more ornate than the traditional gothic.

McCarthy entered the church, which was open and empty. It was dark, but natural lighting peeked through the colorful stained glass windows. McCarthy took off his hat and touched the sponge of the holy water fountain and crossed himself. As he looked up, he saw in a window a manger scene and under it the words, "He dwelt among us." McCarthy had been there hundreds of times, but the words never hung in his mind like that moment. He shook it off and walked slowly to the far right aisle and then about halfway up he came to a little chapel. It was the sacristy, where the blessed hosts were kept.

Victoria and he had lit candles and prayed there after their wedding. They had lit candles and prayed there after the baptisms of their children. McCarthy lit two little red candles and kneeled. He rested his forehead on his hands which were folded in prayer. He prayed, "God. I do not usually ask for anything, but if you could help me see the way, I would appreciate it. I feel no good to anyone. I feel like the people I serve have treated me so badly that they do not deserve my best effort. Help me." McCarthy then just went blank. He had run so far and thought so hard he could not think another thought.

He looked up finally and saw the simple gold crucifix on the beautifully crafted, but small golden altar, and it came. It was more than a thought and less than a voice. It did not feel like his thought. It did not feel like his words. It did not feel like it came from him. It felt like it came to him. It could not be his thought, because he never would have thought this could be the answer to his dilemma. The thought or answer to his prayer was so simple, but it had never crossed his mind until now. It was clear as a blue sky in July now.

The answer that came to him was this: "It will be all right."

McCarthy was no longer panting. He had lost track of how long he had been there. Two people were on pews near him, and he had not noticed them come in. He got up, a little stiff in the legs, and slowly walked out. He touched his hand to the holy water again and touched his forehead, his heart, and each of his shoulders. He looked up and his eyes were drawn again to the same pane of stained glass. "He dwelt among us."

McCarthy looked at the pane of glass and thought to himself. "The Big Guy upstairs had sent his son to live among us. He did nothing except teach us how to treat each other better, and he was hung on the cross and then he rose from the dead just to show us there was something beyond this world. He went through all that, and now I'm feeling sorry for myself because some mindless camera jockeys are talking bad about us. Get real! It will be all right! I can feel it." McCarthy left the church walking and after three steps he was running again.

McCarthy ran back toward the hotel past the one-hundred-year-old green water fountains on each corner. He stopped at the one on Fourth Street and took a drink, and it was cold and clear and tasted better than ten-year-old Bordeaux. He picked up the pace and passed the statue of the Native Americans playing lacrosse. McCarthy felt brand new. He felt light on his feet, and the stiffness in his legs was gone. Dan felt as if he could run the entire circuit again. He was renewed, and he could never explain to anyone why even though he felt he knew why.

Dan McCarthy could not wait until he could get back to work. He could not wait to hug his wife and kiss his children. He wanted to teach. He wanted his pager to go off again. He wanted to see the number 1025 again.

McCarthy did not understand how, or why, but he knew in his heart that his prayer had been answered. He could not explain it to anyone. He could not prove it to anyone. He could not even tell it to anyone, but he knew it. Dan McCarthy had rarely asked for anything before in his prayers. He thought the Big Guy upstairs was probably pretty busy, and even though he had heard GLP (God Loves Police), he still rarely asked. In his prayers he normally thanked God for his blessings in life. This time he had sincerely asked. He asked, because he was about to "tap out." He needed a backup really badly. This officer needed assistance. His prayer was answered in Saint Joseph Cathedral in La Crosse, Wisconsin. "God's Country."

Saint Joseph Cathedral
La Crosse, Wisconsin
"God's Country"

Chapter Seventeen: The Press Conference

McCarthy had managed to avoid press coverage on the shooting of Michael Mattix for the entire period he was attending the Defense and Arrest Tactics Instructor Course. He had missed the talking heads in the twenty-four-hour news game who all knew how to have avoided such obvious carnage. They speculated. They analyzed. They played the tape over and over again, ad nauseam, and it made no difference. Michael Mattix was still dead. He would never kill and rob again, but somehow, those who were not there and would never be in such a situation to face such a dangerous man knew how to handle it better.

McCarthy missed it all. Stammos and Brockman were joined by Dooley on Lake Nelson. The fishing was good, and the company was better. There was no television at the cabin. They fished from the time the loons started their sorrowful song until just before the bullheads would begin feeding along the shoreline. They would clean and cook their fish and then take turns showing off their own special recipe for walleye. They decided walleye ala Brockman was the best. They had to hand it to Brockman. He could cook walleye.

Then evenings, the boys and the wives played cribbage, dirty clubs, or the longest card game in the world called Zioncheck. It was a game handed from generation to generation in the Stammos family.

After nearly three weeks, Captain Hale contacted all four officers and said, "Chief had me call. He wants all four of you in uniform on Monday at 9:00 AM. There will be a press conference inside the council chambers at City Hall. It will be up to you whether you want to sit beside him or not, but you are welcome to."

Brockman, Stammos, McCarthy, and Dooley arrived just before 7:00 AM and beat the media onslaught. They worked out in the department weight room and then showered, shaved, and were ready for the conference.

"What are we doing?" asked Brockman. "Are we going in with him or staying out?"

"You guys stood beside me and faced down that low life piece of shit when he held a Colt 45, I don't think we should be concerned about someone pointing a few cameras at us. We did not do anything wrong. I say let's go in with the chief. Show of hands in favor," said Stammos holding up his right hand.

McCarthy put his hand up and then Dooley. As Brockman began to put his hand up hesitantly, Stammos commented, "All five fingers this time, Stanley."

Stanley laughed and put his hand up.

There was a lull and then a flurry when Chief Johnson entered the room and took the podium. Johnson was a no-nonsense chief who had worked his way up the ladder. He had done nearly every job in law enforcement there was to do, and he had excelled at all. He held a Bachelor's Degree in Criminal Justice and a Masters Degree in Public Administration.

There were a line of chairs to the right and to the left of the podium. Filing in first and sitting in the chairs to the left were Officers Brockman, Dooley, Stammos, and McCarthy. Following behind them and sitting in the line of chairs to the right of the podium was first a local celebrity Sheriff S.R. Dooley of the La Claire County Sheriff's Department. He was well known and well loved in the county. He had been born and raised in Franklin, Tennessee and came from a long line of Dooley's that were named S.R. The S.R. came from a relative who fought in the battle of Franklin in the Civil War. He stood beside his beloved General States Rights Gist, who fell in that battle, and after the war named his first son States Rights after his late great general. It became a family tradition that was passed down to the sheriff, who passed it down to his son, Dooley, who chose just to go by Dooley.

Dooley was not ashamed of his southern heritage or his unique southern name. He just felt that there was only room for one S.R. Dooley at a time in La Claire County.

The sheriff had moved to La Claire after serving in Vietnam. He came back to the states and served as a recruiter in La Claire and met his wife. They married and had a child, and she was so attached to her family that S.R. Dooley became a deputy and eventually rose up the ranks of the Sheriff's Department to become sheriff.

The sheriff had learned long ago to talk like a "Yankee," but he always reacquired his Tennessee drawl on two occasions. He talked like the boy from Franklin, Tennessee whenever he told a joke and whenever he became angry. His son, States Rights Dooley, also chose to pursue a career in law enforcement, but with the city of La Claire rather than the county.

Joining the venerable S.R. Dooley on the right of the podium was a Special Agent from the local FBI office. There was an agent from the State of Wisconsin Department of Justice, Division of Criminal Investigation and a Lieutenant from the Wisconsin State Patrol.

When the officers entered the council chambers and took the four seats to the left of the podiums, there was a buzz from the gathered mass of cameramen and reporters, followed by a flurry of flashes.

As soon as every one was seated, Chief Johnson began speaking. "Good morning, ladies and gentleman of the press. I would like to thank you for coming today. I come to you after we have completed an exhaustive investigation into the incident at the Settle Inn, which happened over three weeks ago. When I say we, I am referring to investigators from the La Claire Police Department, the La Claire County Sheriff's Department, the Wisconsin State Patrol, the Wisconsin Division of Criminal Investigation, and the Federal Bureau of Investigation. We felt more pressed by time than usual, not because there was a killer at large, because in this case the criminal was brought to justice on that day. We were pressed for time because of the inaccurate, slanderous, and irresponsible reporting done in this matter."

This brought a murmur in the crowd. Stanley Brockman sat straight up in his chair and nodded his head. Dooley, Stammos, and McCarthy sat stoic in their chairs.

The chief continued, "This irresponsible reporting started on the day of the incident. Captain Hale of our department made repeated requests to stop broadcasting live footage of this incident in progress. These requests were either ignored or disregarded, and live shots from the helicopter were utilized by the reporting news agency. The investigation revealed that the suspect watched this coverage and the feed, and this enabled him in carrying out his plan, which was to shoot and kill as many police officers as possible. This man was a killer."

"The suspect was Michael Mattix. He was a three-time loser, and he was wanted for absconding from his parole in the state of Texas. The Federal Bureau of Investigation has connected him to eighteen Farmer's Co-op robberies across the country, including one in which a branch manager in Liberty, Missouri was shot in the head and killed by the same weapon used in the La Claire robbery."

"Mr. Mattix was a desperate and dangerous man. The shooting was the result of a planned ambush of the officers. Our investigators were able to piece together the following information. Mattix robbed the Farmer's Co-op four miles from the Settle Inn. He returned to the Settle Inn but was followed by a local man, who will receive a departmental award for his bravery and cooperation. Police were notified and arrived within minutes. They were able to evacuate the area and contain the suspect before he knew of their presence. Elements of the La Claire Police and Sheriff's Department SWAT teams were on scene before Mattix was aware of the police presence. Mattix was most probably made aware of their presence by a CBN news helicopter and cameraman broadcasting a live scene shot as the situation developed. This was in turn broadcast on CBN live. Mattix watched this coverage throughout the incident."

"When our negotiators arrived and the scene was contained, they made contact with Mattix. In what appears to be a part of his plan, he threw the room phone out the window and then shortly thereafter asked for a phone to be delivered."

"Mattix then taped his Colt 45 to his hand and propped open the room door. He concealed himself under a bed after moving it into a position so that he had a clear field of fire toward the room door and also the ability to watch the live news coverage broadcast to him by CBN News."

"When the delivery team, consisting of Officer McCarthy with a ballistic shield, Officer Dooley on the MP5, Officer Stammos on MP5, Officer Brockman with a Glock 17, and Officer Carpenter, who was prepared to deliver a sturdy hard line negotiator throw phone to the suspect, which would have allowed direct line communications to the negotiators, Mattix opened fire from his place of concealment under the bed. He fired a total of nine rounds, striking the ballistic shield three times. He then, apparently, began to aim to the left and right of the shield, and those rounds struck the door frames on either side of the doorway. Officer Stammos, Brockman, Dooley, and McCarthy all returned fire simultaneously, when their lives were endangered by this withering gun fire. They all struck Mattix repeatedly. There has been much discussion about the number of times they fired. I would like to warn you that the photo I am about to show you is very graphic. There was much debate about whether or not to release this photo, but we felt it needed to be released in defense of these honorable officers." The chief then motioned toward the four seated officers. "It was strongly felt that you in the media need to see this. This is a photo of what the officers observed from the beginning of the gun fight until Officer McCarthy called 'Cease Fire,' and once again, I must warn you it is very graphic."

The screen showed the emblem of the La Claire Police Department, and with the push of a button, the photo flashed on the screen. There was a loud gasp from every non-law enforcement person in the room. The photo was the muzzle of the 45 still secured in the hand of Michael Mattix in death. The muzzle of the firearm still winking menacingly in the death grip of the killer.

"You see, ladies and gentleman, Mr. Mattix was so intent on

killing to the end, he duct taped the weapon to his hand and his arm to the bed so that, even wounded, he could still fire accurately toward any officers at the door. He never intended on talking to the negotiators. He had lured these officers into a trap. Once the officers started firing, they could not detect any change in the status because the muzzle still was directed at them, and Mattix was under the bed. This is what they saw. Four officers faced this fire and four officers fired and hit the suspect. The entire furious gun battle was over in less than ten seconds, but facing this view, it was a terrifying ten seconds for the officers in that doorway. When they approached this doorway, it was the officers' intent to deliver a phone to open up communication with Mattix."

"The photo shows that Mattix could not be seen under the bed. Ladies and gentlemen, this was what these officers saw. The threat to them they perceived was real. These officer's actions were clearly defensible and justified. I stand behind these officers and all of their actions. These officers will be decorated accordingly for their good judgment and bravery under fire. There is a fine line between having a name on an award and a name on a wall, and I am grateful to God my officers had the courage to fight back and keep their names off a wall. I'll take a few questions," said the chief.

The CBN News reporter then asked, "What about the officer that gestured toward the cameraman. Is he going to be punished for his unprofessional conduct?"

"I am glad you asked that question," said the chief while a very serious look came upon his countenance. "I considered Officer Brockman's actions very seriously. The moment he made the gesture, he had just been involved in a gun fight where he had to take a man's life. He had just realized that a cameraman in a helicopter from your network, CBN News, had just sent live shots of a tactical movement to a gunman who was lying in ambush. He had just discovered that the cameraman endangered their lives. I realize as Chief of Police that under normal circumstances, I would think it deplorable if our officers would choose to communicate in this manner, and if they did, they would most certainly face disciplinary actions. In this circumstance, I have considered that my officers' lives were endangered by your station's actions. I have considered that my captain spoke with your producer and asked you to utilize a loop or taped delay in this matter, and your producer refused. Considering the fact that my officers could have been killed and your station did nothing to help or prevent their endangerment, if not for the restraint afforded me by the calmness of this moment, I might choose to make the same gesture to you right now."

The CBN reporter then pushed the issue stating, "Don't you think that the gesture speaks to the confrontational gun slinging predisposition of those officers you have wearing those SWAT uniforms."

With that, Sheriff S.R. Dooley stepped forward and Chief Johnson yielded the podium to Sheriff Dooley, resorting to his southern drawl. "I am Sheriff S.R. Dooley of the La Claire County Sheriff's Department. Y'all want to listen to me real closely. My son was one of those brave young officers at that door. He did not fire at Mr. Mattix. He *returned* fire. Do y'all grasp that concept, or do I have to draw you a picture and give you some sort of remedial training. *Returned fire.* D'y'all understand? As a sheriff, it makes me angrier than a horned toad on a hot sidewalk the way y'all reported this here incident. As a father, it infuriates me to this moment how you endangered my son's life and his friends' lives, and that was not good 'nuff. Now y'all want to ruin his career and the careers of his friends who, in the aftermath of a gun fight, mind y'all, and I feel I have to repeat that for y'all, a gun fight! He flips a cameraman the bird."

"Chief Johnson is much more politically correct than I. He has to answer to the mayor, but I only have to answer to the people of La Claire County. In this case, I think I have one thing to say to the reporter who asked the question, the cameraman, and the producer who decided to run the footage live. Y'all put this in your pipe and smoke it!" Sheriff S.R. Dooley flipped the reporter the bird. "The rest of you, thank you for your time." Sheriff Dooley then returned to his seat.

One viewer at home, Harley David Slade, had stopped writing feverishly on a pad in front of him to watch the news coverage of the press conference with great interest. After the news conference ended, he felt truly inspired. He returned to his pad and wrote "If there is a need to take a hostage, *secure sawed-off shotgun to the hostage with duct tape!*"

Author Dan Marcou, La Crosse Police Department and
Randy Stammen, Sauk County Sheriffs Department
Oktoberfest 1979

Chapter Eighteen: Drive Through Service

Harley David Slade stepped up to the bar at the Rump and leaned forward as the bartender stepped up, as if what he was about to say was extremely sensitive and should not be divulged by the bartender even onto death, "Bud Light."

Jake was familiar with the peculiar nature of Harley David Slade and just answered, "Comin' right up, Harley."

Harley watched as his main squeeze, who he had never squeezed, Darla twirled effortlessly on the pole dressed only in a pink sequined G-string. Darla was on stage alone and had the appearance that she was the only person in the world and she was dancing for her own self gratification. She was a constant draw because Darla could be connected with every person in the room when she was on stage, or she could be aloof, distant, and unattainable like a mountain peak in Tibet. You could see her, but you could not have her. Both Darlas were sexy to the men who came to watch her dance.

Harley was mesmerized as Darla skimmed across the stage to the disco song *Midnight at the Oasis*. This was the Darla he loved. The Darla he could not have. The Darla no one could have. His head swooned as if he was placed in some mystic trance as Darla twirled down the pole upended and suspended but still incredibly erotic.

When the music stopped and Darla picked up the clothes scattered about the stage and the bills that customers had scattered in a fruitless effort to draw Darla out of the distance and bring her somewhere into the vicinity of their face, Harley cast his eyes about the room, and there he was. Harley was a man with a mission. He was a patient man who now needed help. He had tried to purchase weapons from a gun show and gun shops but could not do so because he was a felon. Records checks had prevented him from arming himself to make war on his enemy. His failures would not result in rage. He contained his rage. He controlled his rage. He cultivated his rage like his beloved marijuana plants. He could not wage war when the only weapon not recovered by the La Claire Police Departments raid was a sawed off single shot shotgun.

He saw Billy Mitchell enter the bar. When Billy saw Harley's intense gaze upon him, he nearly panicked. Billy had betrayed Harley twice. Harley scared Billy, and Billy did not know why. Harley had never been in so much as a bar fight, but something about Harley scared Billy down to his bones.

Harley took a swig out of his Bud Light and then crossed the room like a cruise missile locked on target. "Shit, here he comes. He knows," thought Billy.

"Billy, I have a business proposition," said Harley as he sat down in the seat next to Billy, without saying, "Hi, how are you, or is it all right if I join you?"

"Go ahead, shoot," countered Billy, wishing he had chosen his words more carefully.

"I need guns. I need ammo. I will pay top dollar," said Harley.

"What makes you think I can get you guns," asked Billy.

"Billy, you went to prison for burglaries. Lots of burglaries. You can get into anywhere and take anything you want. I don't see you dressing in a suit and working at a brokerage firm 9 to 5 every day. I think you still are in the business. I don't care where you get them. I need them and I will pay," said Harley as he reached inside his faded green army fatigue jacket.

Billy felt his intestines do a summersault as Slade's hand disappeared inside his jacket. He slid instinctively back in his chair but then sat forward and smiled as Slade pulled a large wad of cash into Billy's view, and cautiously only revealed it to Billy Mitchell, burglar extraordinaire.

"Can you get me guns, or do I need to find someone else?" asked Slade.

"I can get you whatever you want if the price is right," answered Billy as mesmerized with the mountain of cash as Slade was by Darla. "Just call me Billy-Mart."

"Good," answered Harley David Slade, as he jockeyed the large wad of bills back into the interior pocket of the jacket. "I want two semi-automatic handguns, one semi-automatic carbine, a 308 rifle and a scoped rifle, and one Remington model 870 shotgun," said Harley as if he was ordering a meal at a Burger King drive through. He then reached into his right coat pocket and handed an envelope to Billy Mitchell.

"Good faith," said Slade.

Billy looked into the envelope and saw a shopping list and ten $100 bills. Billy thumbed through the bills and asked, "When do you want these by?"

"A week?" asked Harley.

"Better give me two. I do not want to move too fast. There are some details I will need to work out," said Mitchell.

"Two weeks then," said Slade taking another swig out of his beer.

"What are you doing? You starting a fucking war?" asked Mitchell.

"The fucking war has already been started. I am finishing it!" said Slade with the look in his eye that was, until now, the source of Mitchell's unfounded fear of Harley David Slade. Now Mitchell was relieved. He knew the fear he had of Harley David Slade was not groundless. He was relieved now to know that he was not to be the target of Slade's rage. He did not know who and did not care who. He was happy he had worked his treachery against Slade in the dark. Mitchell lit up a cigarette and took a drink from his rum and coke and thought, "If this man knew what I did to him, I would be taking a dirt nap right now." Mitchell finished his drink and pulled out one of the $100s, just as Darla was sitting down at the table next to Billy. "Harley, Darla, drinks are on me," said Mitchell.

Slade's eyes met Darla's and then quickly darted to the floor. Darla could not help but laugh at the obvious school-boy crush Harley had on her. "Sure, Billy. I will have a Sex on the Beach."

"Bud Light," said Harley looking at his shoes with his intestines now doing somersaults.

It was thirteen days later Billy sat in a stolen Mazda RX-7 side by side with his brother Zach in a stolen Toyota.

"You have the trunk unlatched?" asked Billy.

"Check, Bro," answered Zach.

"When and where?" asked Billy.

"Ten seconds behind you and to the right," answered Zach.

"Then what?" quizzed Billy.

"I swing round and back in, trunk open. I then enter over the hood of the Mazda, being careful of glass, then I hammer," he held up the brand new craftsman hammer he had on the passenger seat next to him, "the handgun counter and grab what I can carry, dump the hammer and out I go. I dump the guns in the trunk, and when you come out with the long guns, I make sure your side is unlocked, and when you are in off we go!" said Zach gesturing with his right hand as if he was shifting an imaginary race car.

"I want to be in and out in two minutes tops," said Billy.

"What are you worried about, Bro. I got you covered," said Zach.

"Since I decided to hit this place in La Claire, I have been seeing that fucking McCarthy in my fucking dreams," fretted Billy.

"He's off tonight. I checked. I called from a pay phone and said I had some information for him, and they said he was off," assured Zach.

"What'd you do that for?" asked Billy.

"What? Are you the only one that can have bad dreams? The fucker has sent both of us up, and now we are pulling this heavy shit on his beat. I just figured I needed a good omen. He's not working tonight, and that is a good omen. Let's do it!" said Zach.

"Let's do it!" agreed Billy. He flipped up his hood on his black sweat shirt, put on his goggles, slipped in his mouth guard, and tightened his leather gloves on his hands. Then Billy slammed his car into gear and headed like a cross bow bolt shot straight at the front door of Bill's Gun Shop on Highway 41 on the edge of La Claire. He reached the double glass door and crashed through it and into the showroom of Bill's.

Like clockwork, Zach spun the Toyota around, flipped the locks on the doors and popped the trunk as he snatched the hammer off the seat of the car. Billy was out of the car and over the hood in a flash. He had large bolt cutters with him, and he dashed to the rear of the store after grabbing a shopping cart and quickly cut the cable on two gun racks. He filled the cart with 4 Colt AR-15s and two mini-14s. He smashed a case nearby with the bolt cutter and grabbed two mitts full of magazines and then went to the second rack and grabbed the Remington 870 and the Remington 308 with the scope.

He spun the cart about and raced toward the door, pausing only to toss selected ammunition on the bottom of the cart.

At the door, Billy met Zach. He was already returning from the trunk, where he had dumped as many handguns as he could carry in his arms and pockets and came back to help lift the cart over the Mazda RX-7, which was partially blocking the exit. Zach then rolled the cart at a run to the Toyota as if they were engaged in some sort of bizarre supermarket sweepstakes. Billy joined him at the trunk, and they tossed the weapons into the trunk. Billy could not maneuver the 308 rifle into the trunk. "Shit!" said Billy, and he then opened the back door of the Toyota and tossed in the rifle.

Zach pushed the cart out of the way, and his adrenaline caused it to shoot across the lot into the grass and down into the ditch between the parking lot and Highway 41. In a wink, Zach was behind the wheel and Billy was in the passenger's seat. They shot out of the lot as the timer went off on Zach's watch. "Mother fucker, we did it! Two minutes."

"You set a timer?" asked Billy.

"Yeah, man. You said two minutes," said Zach.

"What do you think this is? A dumb fucking movie? Timers make noise. We try to make as little noise as possible. That could have got our asses busted!"

"Yeah, I forgot. That's why you put the fucking door smashing silencer on the front of the fucking Mazda," said Zach. "Eat shit, Billy. You're always on my ass."

Billy thought and then laughed. "Sorry, Bro. You're right… fucking door smashing silencer. We got to get one of those things. Two minutes, Bro!" said Billy triumphantly holding up a high five.

"Two minutes, Bro!" said Zach.

Then Zach pulled into a secluded lot and pulled next to Billy's car. They transferred the weapons and left the Toyota with the keys in it. As they drove away, Billy looked at Zach and said, "In and out in two minutes. You got to love that drive through service."

Chapter Nineteen: "Phu Bai in July"

"Jesus Christ, Compton! When are you going to retire? You are setting a bad example," complained Captain Hale.

Compton looked at Hale and said, "I'm one of those old guys who went over the hill and found out that when you get over the hill, you start picking up speed." It was a question Compton got often. Rarely do cops reach retirement age and stay on. Compton not only stayed on, he stayed on nights. He stayed on the SWAT team. He stayed on being one of those people everyone counted on. Tonight, Compton was dressed in his SWAT uniform getting ready for training. He was on the computer answering e-mail and printing handouts for the SWAT training, which was scheduled to start in one hour and thirty minutes.

"Sergeant Compton," said Detective Sergeant Scott Brickson, who was the full time drug investigator.

"Yeah, Brick," said Compton not even looking up from his computer.

"I see you have a SWAT training tonight. Since every one is going to be here, how about you help us out with a warrant," asked Brickson.

"Who, what, when, where, why, and we will supply the how?" asked Compton.

"Good questions. Every one of them, good questions, but I don't know many of the answers yet. We are doing a no-knock warrant. We have a bad actor from out of town. We have information that he is staying at a local hotel. He is bringing in a quantity and will have it with him in his room. I just do not know his name, other than he goes by Dax. He is a gang banger from Chicago. He should be armed, and he is reportedly wanted for a shooting in Chicago. The bad guy may be spreading that rumor just to intimidate the local population, but we do not want to take any chances. We will get the information and do a telephonic warrant, and then we will let you know the particulars. It will definitely be a no-knock. Can you be ready to go in two hours?" asked Brickson.

"Is that in two hours ready, set, go, or two hours hurry up and wait?"

"I would like you to be ready to go anytime after two hours, but it might be a hurry up and wait," said Brickson. "Sorry, Buddy."

"That's OK. It's just nice to know whether to expect fast or slow. I'll just adjust the training. We were going to get pretty dynamic tonight. It's Maddy's first night back with the team since she returned off light duty," said Compton.

"How's she doing?" asked Brickson.

"She's indomitable, man. She's a Spartan," answered Compton.

"I'll get back with you as soon as I know something," said Brickson.

"10-4."

As the clocked ticked to 6:30 PM, the scheduled start time of SWAT training, Compton started the festivities as usual, right on time. "Well, ladies and gentleman, did you hear about guy who went to the doctor after surviving a radiation accident at the nuclear plant?"

"No," they all answered.

"The doctor says, after the patient regains consciousness, 'I have some good news and bad news… which one do you want first?'

The patient says, 'Give me the bad news first.'

'Well you have had a bad reaction to the nuclear exposure. You now have five penises,' said the doctor reading the patient's chart.

'Doctor, Doctor, what is the good news then?' asked the patient as he looked under his gown with shock and horror.

'All your pants should fit you like a glove.'"

There was a collective but uneven chorus of laughs, boos, and whistles that came from the group.

"Everybody is a critic," complained Compton. "I have some good news and bad news too. The bad news is I have to reschedule training," reported Compton.

"What's the good news?" asked Brockman.

"The good news is we are going on a call-out. We do not have the information right now, but it looks like we have to be ready to go, but we will be waiting until Brickson and Jefferson call us with the warrant. It will be a no-knock warrant at one of the hotels, but we do not know where," said Compton. "Anything you would like me to cover in the short time we have together?" asked Sergeant Dave Compton.

"Anything?" asked Dooley.

"Sure, I will cover anything within reason. I would like it to be a learning experience. We have one half hour at the most," said Compton.

"A bunch of us were talking and…"

"Go ahead," urged Compton seeing an awkwardness not usually displayed by Dooley.

"You are the only Vietnam combat veteran still on the department. Can you tell a war story with a lesson. You have never really talked about Vietnam. Can you?" asked Dooley.

"Yeah, Sergeant, how about it?" asked Carpenter.

There was a long pause. It was not that Compton did not think about it. He thought about Vietnam every day of his life. It was a part of his being. Warriors just do not babble on about war, real war, the killing kind of war. Sergeant David Compton began to speak, "I left an awful lot of brothers behind in Vietnam. It has been hard to talk about, but you guys are my brothers and sisters now." Compton leaned against the table in the front of the classroom. "A story with a lesson?" said Compton picking up his bottle of Mountain Dew. He opened it, and it made the refreshing "hishhh" sound of a newly opened bottle. He took a drink and then screwed the cap back on the bottle, set it down on the table next to him, then looked up at the team seated at tables around him in the classroom.

"Gary Carpenter, Maddy Brown, you have both learned the hard way the lesson that I would like you all to take from this story. It is a story only because I am telling you it. To me it is not a story. It is a memory." Then Compton's eyes became distant. They squinted as if he was actually straining to see the events as they were being replayed in front of him. "It was July in Phu Bai, 1969. Our troops had won every battle they had fought. We had survived the Tet Offensive and a number of mini-Tets, but it was a war that was not to be won. I did not know that then. I was a Marine and could not grasp the fact that the people back home did not appreciate what I was doing for them. Did not love me for what I was doing for them. Would spit on me when I came home for wearing my uniform with pride. I was a Marine with my war. What else could a good Marine ask for? It was July in Phu Bai. I was stationed on a hill in a fire base, and I was in a hole by the wire. I was with two buddies. One was Chet, and the other was Tex. We called him Tex because he was from Texas. Tex was a big guy. He was about six feet two and stocky… not a weight lifter stocky, but a hay-throwing farm boy kind of stocky. He always had a smile on his face. Chet was about six feet and was a quiet and serious kind of guy. Vietnam. The days were hot white, and the nights were black as a bat's closet. Sleep. I don't even remember sleeping while I was there. That night in July, I know we didn't sleep. There was a report that there had been activity. Sappers were seen the night before, probing our lines. We were watching the wire that night, three Marines in a hole, trying to hold a little piece of shit ground that I called home for one year. On that night, Chet whispers, 'I see movement.' Then Chet fired a flare off and lit the place up, and God damn, they were all over. One moment nothing, and then they were all over. We set off our Claymores. They were anti-personnel mines that were in the perfect spot to do a great deal of damage on the first wave. Chet saved our asses, boy. Then we opened up. It was so dark when the flare went out that you could only see about five feet in front of you. The only available light was muzzle flashes, and it seemed like there was another NVA soldier appearing in every flash. There was so much shooting that it was like God had set the heavens on strobe. Chet went down instantly. Tex was alive as any nineteen-year-old kid could be in the midst of all that death. He screamed and fired and fired and screamed. It wasn't a scream of fear, it was more like an eagle on the attack. He covered my back, and when the early waves came, he was evening the odds considerably with his M-16. Tex was beside me for the entire fight. Whether the fight lasted ten minutes, an hour, ten hours, I do not know. It seemed like a minute was an hour and an hour was eternity. I just kept shooting and yelling, and when I ran out of ammunition, I used Chet's. When I took his ammunition and picked up his M-16, I could see he was gone. He looked so peaceful. It looked like he just laid down and went to sleep. I could not tell where he was hit. After picking up Chet's weapon, I shot to the right, to the front, to the left, and to the rear. They were all over. It was what you would call a target-rich environment. We had been overrun. It was every Marine for himself, and Tex was beside me, behind me, and in front of me. Then, as it appeared we just might make it through the fight, he went down. He had taken a hit in the forearm, and there was arterial bleeding. I called for a medic, but all that did is bring more fire directed our way. For all I knew, we were the only two live Marines left in that little fire base. I hunkered down and put a tourniquet on Tex and gave him the morphine out of my kit, and we sat out the darkness. There were a few more moves on our position, and I just shot until there was no one else left to shoot. When it got quiet, we waited for the sun to come up to find out who had won and who had lost. It seemed like the moon was going backwards that night. When the morning came, the ground was covered with dead and wounded North Vietnamese Army Regulars. They had hit us from all sides of the fire base, and we held. From my vantage point, it seemed as if you could have walked for about one hundred feet over bodies without stepping on the ground. The bodies were strewn all over and appeared to give the ground an eerie moving effect because some were wounded and still alive."

"I checked Tex, and he was weak, semi conscious, but he was alive. I asked him 'How you doin', Tex?' And he replied, 'Million dollar wound, Compton, I'm goin' to see Texas again, thanks to you. How's Chet?' I checked Chet; there was not a mark on him. He was next to me the whole time, and it could not have been from the concussion of an explosion. He was dead, but nothing killed him. 'Chet's gone, Tex.' I said"

"Chet's death was so bizarre the Marine Corps did an autopsy on Chet. It turned out that nothing had killed him. The corps doctor came to the conclusion that he thought he would die on that hill and so he did. He just died. You guys are the first people I have ever told about this."

"You said you wanted a story that taught a lesson. I learned a critical lesson from Chet and Tex. I chose to live, or die fighting. I lived. Tex chose to live, or die fighting. When he was hit, he couldn't fight any more, but he decided to live and go home to Texas. He lived and ultimately went home to Texas. Chet was convinced that he was going to die in Phu Bai on that night in July, and he just laid down and died. He chose to lie down and die, and die he did. He just laid down and died," said Compton, looking in the distance quietly shaking his head. You could hear a pin drop in the room as everyone there hung on every word this brave warrior was saying.

Then Compton turned and looked at Gary Carpenter, seated in the front row, "Carpenter, I saw you take a shotgun slug to the chest and arm, and it didn't keep you down. You decided to get back up. You could have taken a disability, and you did not. You trained with more effort and pain than any Olympic athlete, and you are back!"

"Madison, you have rejoined us tonight for the first time since you were shot. You could have rolled over and died in that squad car. You didn't. You got up and shot that crazy bastard before he could hurt anyone else. You went through more pain than most of us will ever know, and you trained like a Spartan warrior to return to us, and now you have returned."

"McCarthy, Brockman, Stammos, Dooley, after the way you were treated by the media after the Mad Mattix shootout, you could have said 'fuck it!' You shook it off and came back. It reminded me of the way we were treated by the Vietnam protesters and the press when we came back. They spit on us and called us baby killers. I never killed a baby. Nothing we did in Vietnam justified burning the American flag or spitting on the uniform of a US Marine. You were treated the same way after that shooting."

"You have all worked hard to continue to make a difference in your city. Someone asked me tonight why I have not retired. I feel like I am on a journey in life. This part of the journey I am traveling with all of you. I have not retired yet because I am enjoying my traveling companions as much as I ever have. I'm not quite ready to take a separate path yet, but who knows what tomorrow will bring. Ever since the night in Phu Bai, I have wondered what made Tex and Chet and I put the uniform on and go off to war while some people my age stayed home to burn the flag and spit on returning soldiers. I still wonder why guys like Stammos and McCarthy and ladies like Maddy Brown and all of you strap on a gun every day, and then on your time off you come in here and strap on a gun and body armor and go through doors?"

"I have come to the conclusion it is something ingrained in us. We are honorable warriors seeking a righteous battle. When we find it, we sometimes are left standing, and sometimes we are knocked down. Warriors pick themselves up, brush themselves off, and move on to the next righteous battle."

"Chet did something I could never do. He stood guard and gave us a heads up that saved our lives, and then he chose to lie down and go quietly into that good night. Tex and I decided that we could not go quietly into the good night. We would not go quietly into that good night without a good fight. We discovered that on the other side of the righteous battle and beyond the darkness were the daylight and all the rest of the days of our lives. Chet decided to give in to the seductress, death, and Tex and I decided to fight for life. Warriors have been doing that since the days of the Roman Centurions and the days of the knights."

"I learned that night on that hill to never give up. If you give up that means you lose and they win. In our world that means you die. I learned coming home from Vietnam that when the warrior takes up his weapon to defend those who will not or cannot defend themselves that the warrior cannot expect to be loved for it. It is the way of the warrior."

"I learned that to stay safe in our world you surround yourself with good people who know and love what they are doing. I learned as a leader to help them love what they are doing. I learned that the warrior must stay strong by working to stay strong. Strength does not just happen. I learned that quitting is not an option for a warrior. Feeling sorry for yourself is not an option either, easy as it might be. I learned staying positive when you are in the shit is the best way to get out of the shit. The way to stay positive is by believing in what you are doing and know it to be important and right. After Vietnam and the Marines, I found meaning in life as a police officer. People still spit on me occasionally and try to hurt me once in a while. Most of all, I found a place where I could make a difference. I found friends and fellow warriors as brave and as honorable as the men who fought and lived and fought and died next to me on that hill in Phu Bai in July." Then… silence. It was deafening.

"I got your back."

Chapter Twenty: "Thank God, It's Da Po-leese"

Brickson walked into the classroom and was met with silence. "Who died?" he asked.

Everyone in the room thought, "Chet died," but not one said anything. There was a shuffle of movement as everyone began to emotionally travel back to La Claire, Wisconsin from the darkness, heat, and death of Phu Bai, Vietnam.

"Where are we going?" asked Compton.

"You are going to room 212 at the Motel Eight," said Brickson with an undeniable urgency.

"Now?" asked Compton.

"Now," said Brickson. "We lost him after the exchange, and he has $10,000 in buy money, and if we don't get it back it will be my... we have to get it back!" said Brickson.

"Stammos! You know the layout. We have been there a hundred times before. Make your plan," said Compton.

"Do we have keys?" asked Stammos.

"Not yet. I will hit the night manager up for a key. He might give us one, but don't count on it. I think he's hinky. I will stay with him after I ask so he doesn't call up the target. The target is Dax. That's all we know. He is armed with a semi-automatic handgun. The informant saw it. He had a female with him. Their car is back at the hotel right now. Jefferson is sitting on it. I have a no-knock warrant. The suspect is a black male in his thirties with a thin build. He is about five feet ten inches.

Stammos had stepped up to the white board in front of the room and quickly drew the layout of the Motel Eight from memory. "Right. I will take the breaching shotgun on this one in the event that we do not get the key. It will take at least two shots on these doors, so everyone plan on hearing at least two shots from the breaching rounds. No sympathetic fire, all right?"

"This is the stack!" Stammos said, writing the names in order on the white board. "I will breach, Dooley, you go in first with the MP5. McCarthy, you have hands free, and Madison, you have the Benelli shotgun. Sergeant Compton, please cover the window on the east side of the building. It is quite a drop, but it has been done before. Brockman, you join him, but you will be in the marked unit in case they go mobile. Any questions?" asked Stammos.

"McCarthy, you are driving. We are taking the van. Anyone not in the plan standby at the Safeway in the SWAT van. Call La Claire ambulance and have them standby at the Safeway. Who's got it?"

"I'll handle that and drive the truck," said Officer Jared Jackson.

"Let's go!" said Compton.

Brickson was out the door on a jog. Everyone else was right behind him.

As the SWAT van approached the hotel, Brickson came over the radio, "Can you believe it? The night manager will not give us a key. He says he needs to make some phone calls first," said Brickson.

"Ask him one more time, Brick, with a please," said Compton.

"My verbal judo did not work. He says no key," said Brickson with a laugh.

"No key it is," answered Compton. "Stammos. Lock and Load!"

"10-4," said Stammos as he racked open his model 870 shotgun, specially fitted with a ribbed extension to allow for a release of pressure when the breaching round is fired. Stammos carefully viewed the breaching round and made sure it was a breaching round, and then he cupped it in his hand and rolled it into the chamber, slamming the action home. He then took four more breaching rounds and tucked them into the magazine, making certain each one was neither a slug nor a .00 buck round. The breaching round is a frangible round that hits the locking mechanism and expends its energy immediately, blowing the mechanism into small pieces, allowing a locked door to be opened.

As the van came slowly to a stop on the north side of the hotel, out of sight of Dax's room, the entry team peeled out and stacked.

Compton keyed the mic on the radio, "SWAT is 10-23 (at the scene)."

"10-4," said the dispatcher making note of the transmission on the SWAT screen, which was one of four calls the dispatcher was working at one time. The dispatcher was juggling them like a circus act.

Stammos gave thumbs up, and as the tap returned back up the line, he breathed once in slowly and out slowly and he was moving.

"SWAT is moving," said Compton.

McCarthy had his Glock out, and the pace was a little faster than usual. It was probably because $10,000 of the Metropolitan Enforcement Group's money was at stake. Brickson had made that very clear. Forget about lives being at stake, on its face $10,000 made this call incredibly urgent.

As the entry team passed, a man in the lobby stopped dead in his tracks. He was an older gentleman whose eyes looked like two white saucers in his head with a chocolate donut hole sitting in the middle of the plate. He had not expected a SWAT team to open the door for him.

Brickson was leaning against the counter of the hotel, and the night manager appeared to be mimicking the older gentleman. Brickson had a big grin on his face. He knew he would never have to ask twice again for a key from this night manager. "212, guys. He's not expecting you, but I think he's going to leave the light on for you." No one paid much attention to what Brickson said, but they would laugh at it later.

McCarthy smelled the faint odor of cigarettes, urine, and old booze soaked into the carpets as they quietly moved up the stairs to the second floor. They avoided scraping the walls and the metal railing and were through the door immediately after it made a squeak that seemed to every team member to be loud enough so that every resident in the hotel must know a SWAT team was approaching. In truth, it blended in with the muffled hotel hallway sounds of humming lights, porn movies, and children crying.

When the team arrived at 212, it was clear what was happening inside. Dax and his girlfriend were involved in one of the fabulous five activities that drug dealers partake in. Number one was to use their drugs, number two was sell their drugs, number three was to eat, number four was sleep, and number five was to have unprotected sex with high risk partners. The female was screaming, "Yes! Yes! Yes! Oh God, Yes!" This indicated to Stammos that if he were to ask them if they knew a SWAT team was outside their door the answer would be, "No! No! No! Oh God, No!"

Stammos lined the shotgun up to the right of the door handle. "Blam, chick chick," he then quickly moved up to the interior latch, which was in place, "Blam, chick chick," and the door was open. Stammos stepped out of the way and let the entry team flow through the open door.

Everyone in unison shouted, "Police Department, Search Warrant! Get down! Get down! Get down!"

Dax was on top and his girlfriend Tiffany was on her back with both feet high in the air. In a nano-second they were both on their feet, trying to disconnect while fleeing in an awkward looking hobble, which was incredibly fast for its appearance. Their hands, for the time, did not occupy a weapon, so McCarthy went into pursuit. As the two fleeing fornicators slammed the bathroom door, McCarthy hit the door near the door knob with a flying front kick. It shattered the door and would have opened except both Dax and Tiffany hit the door with their combined weight instantly. Dooley hit the door a second time like he was a lineman with a free shot at a stumbling quarterback, and the door swung open and slammed into the wall. Dax and Tiffany toppled into the tub tearing the shower curtain down as both tried to use it to break their inevitable tumble. They both landed ignominiously on their backs jammed into the tub, with four feet in the air flailing about looking like some botched attempt at humor during an episode from Jackass.

"Police! We want to see your,..." McCarthy paused because, in the case of Tiffany and Dax, it was clear that they were absolutely not armed. "We want to see your hands."

Tiffany looked and saw two SWAT officers pointing guns at them, and she became instantly elated. "I'm not goin' ta die! I'm not goin' ta die. Thank God, it's da PO-leese. Thank da Lord, it's da PO-leese!"

McCarthy handcuffed Dax, and Officer Madison Brown was called forward to cover and handcuff Tiffany, who seemed totally accepting of the idea that she was alive and naked in front of a SWAT rather than dead and lying naked in front of one of Dax's many enemies.

After clearing the bed, Tiffany and Dax were laid on the bed. After their perceived near death experience, no Miranda Warning was going to convince either of these two suspects to remain silent.

"Man, I thought you were some brothers from Chicago who want me dead. I thought they were coming through the door shooting. I was strapped, but my piece is in my car. Thank God, you is da PO-leese."

"Thank God, you is da PO-leese," seconded Tiffany.

"I thought I was dead. I thought you were dead," Dax rolled awkwardly toward Tiffany and they kissed.

"Oh, Baby, I thought we was both dead. Oh Thank God, it's da PO-leese."

"Dax. Where's my $10,000 bucks?" asked Brickson, getting right to the point.

"It's in the bathroom. Move the ceiling tile, over the sink. The green is there, and what's left of my product is there, too. Thank God, it's da PO-lees!" Dax did not give any thought to what he was saying. He was alive and it was a beautiful world, for the moment.

"Thank God, it's da PO-lees! I love you, Babe," said Tiffany as they kissed again.

Then Dax got indignant and demanded of Stammos, "Hey man, why were you shooting at us, man? We din't do shit!"

"Just relax. No one was shooting at you. Those were special rounds that blow the locks off the doors but do not penetrate." Then Randy used his best, most empathetic voice that he could conjure up and said, "I can understand that it would sound that way, especially with half of Southside Chicago looking for you, but we were not shooting at you, Dax. Feel better?" asked Stammos.

"OK, man. It just scared the mother-fucking shit out of me! I thought my black ass was dead," whined Dax.

Then McCarthy stepped in with pen and pad, "Let's get it right the first time. What's your real name, Dax?" asked McCarthy.

"Dexter R. Redmond, and this is Tiffany A. Redmond," said Dax.

"Why you be tellin' that shit, man. Now our asses will be goin' to jail. Fuck you, mother-fuckers!" said Tiffany, her epiphany at an end.

Stammos then laughed, "Tiffany, what happened to 'Thank God it's the police?'"

"Dat was den, and dis is now! Now it's fuck da PO-leese, mother fucker!"

Dispatch then called, "255, are you 10-61 (is that person within ear shot)?"

"255, go ahead, the subject is not 10-61 (is not in the area)," McCarthy stepped outside the room into the hallway.

"255, both of those subjects are wanted out of Chicago for armed robbery and delivery of controlled substances. Dexter Redmond is also wanted for attempted murder. The warrants are confirmed," said the dispatcher.

"10-4," answered McCarthy.

Sergeant Compton heard the transmission. "Let's get these two separated and transported ASAP. Find out where Brickson wants them."

"You bet, Sarge," said McCarthy feeling the buzz every cop gets when they get a serious hit on a warrant check.

As Officer Madison Brown assisted Tiffany into some clothes and McCarthy assisted Dax into his, two criminals were meeting in a boat landing on the opposite side of La Claire. One was a burglar delivering a special order to a valued customer. The other was a drug dealer, who was on the verge of delivering death.

Chapter Twenty-one: Armed and Dangerous

When Harley David Slade pulled into the boat landing, Billy Mitchell was already waiting. He was seated on top of a picnic table with a cooler by his side. As Slade walked up to the table, Billy reached into the cooler and pulled out a cold Bud Light and handed it to Slade asking, "How is my new best friend?"

Slade took the beer and twisted off the cap and tossed it into the grass. He took a long drink and then, after belching loudly, he said, "What the fuck was that? You drive a car through the fucking front door of the place?"

"That will throw them off the trail. That is an Asian gang MO. They will never suspect me," countered Mitchell.

"Asian gangs?" pondered Harley.

"Fucking Asian gangs. The La Claire police have probably already written these guns off as being in the system in Minneapolis right now. The heat is off here," explained Billy reaching into the cooler and pulling out another Bud. "Hey, it's a nice night. Want to have a couple beers?" asked Mitchell.

"Yeah, it is," said Slade. Slade was not a very social man and had few friends. He had never had anyone in his whole life stick his neck out for him and do such a large favor. For Harley, Billy was as much of a friend as Harley had ever had.

After a long silence, Slade asked, "What is prison like?"

"Don't get me wrong. I don't ever want to go back, but it wasn't too bad. I got more in common with people in there than people out here. I don't feel like such a freak in there. None of those assholes wants to get a job and go to work every day. They all want to fuck just about everything in a skirt, but they'll make do with a thin guy with long hair if nothing else is available. They are all fucked up just like me," said Billy taking another drink.

"The chow is good. If you don't fuck with the guards, they don't fuck with you. If you keep a low profile and are not a skinny, long haired blonde guy, most everyone leaves you alone."

"I'm never going to prison. I'll die first. I'd kill first!" said Slade.

Mitchell then pulled out a pack of cigarettes. Slade had that scary look on his face. He offered Slade a cigarette.

Before he could verbalize his offer, Slade pulled out a baggie with four rolled joints. "This is my shit. This is good shit. Try one of these," offered Slade.

"Thanks, man," said Billy, putting his cigarettes back into his shirt pocket. He put the perfectly rolled joint between his lips and cupped his left hand to block the breeze, and then he lit his lighter and held it to the end of the doobie. It flamed for a second until Billy sucked in a deep breath and held it. He then breathed it out as if it was a breath of fresh Colorado Rocky Mountain air. "Man, this is some really good shit. It like feels like this shit is inhabiting my brain already. How do you do it?" asked Billy taking one more hit as Slade lit himself one.

"This isn't just weed, man," said Slade as he took a deep breath. "This is the best dope manufactured north of the Rio Grande. It's a healing plant, man."

"Healing plant?" asked Billy.

"Yeah, the government doesn't want you to know that you can heal just about anything with this shit. It would put the drug companies out of business if everyone found out how truly great this shit is. I smoke it, and I am never fucking sick, man. It makes sick people healthy and crazy people sane. The fucking government does not want us to know. It's the fucking wonder drug that would put the drug companies out of business because you can grow it anywhere. Anyone can grow it anywhere," said Slade taking a deep breath.

"Tell him about the war," said the Dark Lord.

"Yeah, I'm getting to that," responded Slade.

"Getting to what?" asked Mitchell who had lost the ability to be concerned about Slade speaking out of turn to someone that was not there after his fourth drag on his Harley David Doobie

"What do you think about the war on drugs?" asked Slade.

Mitchell laughed and took another drag from his doobie, "Right now, I feel like you and me are kick-ass winning." This, Mitchell thought, was just downright funny, and he began to laugh like he believed it was funny, which he did.

"The war on drugs was illegally declared by Richard Nixon." said Slade.

"Tricky fuckin' Dickie," said Billy laughing again at his wit. He finished taking the last drag on his doobie and it was down to a nubbin roach. "Hey, you got any more of that shit?"

Slade reached into his coat, pulled out the baggie, and carefully separated the zip lock and handed one more joint to Mitchell. Mitchell quickly lit his new joint off the embers of his first. Then he tossed the first and inhaled his second deeply.

"Nixon declared it illegally, and it is being fought illegally against citizens of the United States. I was taken prisoner in an illegal war," said Slade. "That makes me a prisoner of war — a prisoner of an illegal and immoral war. Since I am a prisoner of war, I am a combatant. Since I am a combatant in a war, I can inflict casualties. I will inflict casualties. You have performed a great service in my cause," said Slade nobly.

Mitchell took another deep drag on the second joint and then looked as seriously as he could at Slade and said, "Dude. You got to lighten up." Mitchell then laughed, but he did not know why. Mitchell thought, "I'm fucked up on the outside, but this guy is scaring the shit out of me on the inside."

"Mr. Mitchell. You have conducted a very successful mission. I thank you for your courage. I would like my guns now. I have your money in the trunk."

Mitchell got up and walked over to the trunk of Slade's car. Slade looked around and popped the trunk. He handed a bag over to Mitchell. "There is $10,000 in the bag. That should be more than enough, but you performed with great audacity and courage and deserve a medal not money. I have no medals to give so I will reward you in cash. I will take my shotgun, rifle, carbine, and two handguns as ordered, please," said Slade, now standing at attention.

"Holy shit!" said Billy "Coming right up." Billy tripped over himself heading over to his car. He took a blanket and wrapped the 308, the shotgun, and the carbine in the blanket and carried them over to Slade's trunk like they were stacked firewood. He carefully laid them in. Billy then returned to his car and took two handguns out of the trunk and placed them in an empty Styrofoam cooler. He carried the cooler to Slade's car and set them in. "Keep the cooler and blanket, man."

"Say, Harley, who is the enemy in this war on drugs that you are fighting?" asked the Billy Mitchell who was fucked up on the best weed north of the Rio Grande while the sober Billy was screaming, "Get the fuck out of here before this crazy fucker unloads." Fucked up Billy was not listening to sober Billy at all.

Then in voice that could have come from the bench in any courtroom in America, Harley David Slade proclaimed, "The first to die will be Judge Alice. She has been condemned. I will take her at her barracks. Then I will attack the courthouse and kill as many other judges and attorneys as I can. If their mindless gunmen stand in my way, I will kill them also. You are welcome to join me if you wish, soldier," said Slade as he removed the Glock 23 from the cooler and he expertly worked the action, stating, "Smooth. Nice."

"No thanks, general. Supply is my specialty. If you need anything else, I'm at your service," said Billy.

"Thanks, Soldier," said Slade placing the gun back into the cooler and the lid back on the cooler. He then slammed the trunk and saluted to Mitchell.

Mitchell was shaken. He returned the salute using the three-finger boy scout salute, which was the only salute he had ever been taught and which was all that was available to him right now since he was trying not to piss his pants and not to be killed all at the same time.

Mitchell left the other cooler on the table and hurriedly jumped into his car. He drove off looking in the rearview mirror expecting a LAS Rocket to be shot straight up his tail pipe at any moment, but he was able to get away clean. "Fuck! Now what?"

Mitchell drove to the La Claire Police Department and parked across the street. He was just about to get out and walk inside when he saw a squad car pull up. McCarthy got out of the passenger side and opened the back door. An excited black man who was handcuffed was taken out of the backseat. He was nervously talking and all Mitchell could hear was an occasional "fucker," and a "motherfucker."

Mitchell saw McCarthy calm the man down, and though Mitchell could not hear his words, he could recognize the tone. McCarthy was schmoozing him with that good guy buddy-buddy shit that landed Mitchell into prison the last time. Then Mitchell, still buzzed on the best weed north of the Rio Grande, said out loud to himself, "Fuck. If I go in there and tell them anything, I am going back to the joint. The chow ain't all that fucking good, and there are two things you can't get in there. One is Darla's poon tang, and the other is every other poon tang in the world. I'm out of here." Mitchell then signaled carefully and pulled out so correctly he could have had a "student driver" sign on top of his vehicle. He then left the La Claire Police Department far behind.

One hour later Billy knocked on Zach's door. Zach came to the door and looked both ways down the hall as he let Billy in. "How did it fuckin' go, man? Did he buy them?"

"Every one of them. Check this out. This is your cut, Bro." Billy tossed twenty $100 dollar bills on the table for Zach. He took them all off our hands for $4000. Can you believe it? $4000 for two minutes of work," said Billy proudly.

"Awesome, Dude!" yelled Zach, counting his share. "Want a beer, man?" asked Zach.

"Yeah, but you're buyin'. Let's go to the Rump. I think I want to celebrate with Darla tonight," said Billy, throwing Zach's coat across the room to his brother.

"Man, you are one lucky bastard, tappin' that ass," said Zach with envy dripping from every word.

Billy Mitchell didn't feel lucky. He had just smoked the best weed manufactured north of the Rio Grande. It did not help him at all with his sudden case of depression. Knowing that he had just cheated his brother out of his share of the take did not make him depressed. Knowing that he would make even more money on the guns he still had and that it would all be profit, screwing his brother a second time, did not make him blue. What made him intensely depressed was that he knew Harley David Slade could kill. He knew down to his soul that Harley David Slade was a dangerous man and would kill.

Tonight, Harley David Slade was not just dangerous. Thanks to Billy Mitchell, he was armed and dangerous.

Chapter Twenty-two: "He's a Hard Nut To Crack"

It had been three weeks since McCarthy and the La Claire SWAT team had arrested Dax and Tiffany. Thinking of Tiffany's shrill voice thanking God for the "*Po-leese,*" would immediately bring a smile to McCarthy's face. McCarthy had no idea that across town on that night the instruments of death had been delivered from the hands of an old adversary into the dangerous hands of a new adversary. McCarthy would meet Billy Mitchell and Harley David Slade again, but not this week.

This week, McCarthy was once again at the training facility in Angelo, Wisconsin. He was attending a one-week course to be a hostage negotiator. The trainer was a Federal Bureau of Investigation Special Agent named James Roemer. Roemer was a comical guy who could talk a pit bull down from the back end of a meat truck.

It was the philosophy of Sergeant Dave Compton's that he wanted every tactical team operator to be crosstrained as a negotiator. He would say, "If some guy shows up at a door being held by a tactical operator, I want everyone on the team to have a dialog option. I want us all to be as good at talking and listening as we are at shooting. Any time they are talking, they are not shooting."

McCarthy spent the week learning how to apply active listening skills and empathetic listening skills. He learned about establishing rapport and identifying a hook in which a negotiator can emotionally lock on to the suspect and reel him in. He learned about special concerns negotiators should have when communicating with people in crisis. McCarthy attended the school with Dooley. Dooley's wife Gloria was a negotiator, and he was happy to attend to understand what she did for the team.

On the evening of the fourth day of training, Dooley and

McCarthy went out for a pizza in La Crosse. McCarthy said, "On Third Street in La Crosse there is the neatest pizza place for adults I have ever seen, and the pizza is awesome. It's called Big Al's." When they arrived, it was early and the crowd was light.

They took a table in the front window. They ordered their pizza, and then Dooley found himself intrigued at the décor. "You ain't shittin' about it being unique. This decorating job definitely did not have a woman's touch. I've never seen that before," as he pointed to the front end of a red Cadillac sticking out the wall above the front door. "Or that," he said, directing McCarthy's attention to Orville and Wilbur Wright in the Kitty Hawk flying in formation with a World War I Sopwith Camel. Dooley just scanned around the room in awe at the decor. Lifesize three-dimensional images of the Marx brothers standing up on a balcony, the Canadian Goose dressed as Santa Clause on the wing, and the standard human-sized frog riding a bicycle, also in formation with the Wright Brothers. As the smiling waitress set the pizza down in front of the two hungry cops, she warned, "Be careful. It's just out of the oven. It's very hot."

Dooley winked at her and said, "Thanks, Sweetheart." He then gazed admiringly at her tight little nineteen-year-old backside forced in to a pair of jeans, clearly one size too small.

"Be careful, Dooley. Did Gloria give you permission to ravage that young lady with your eyes?"

"What Gloria doesn't know, Gloria doesn't need to know," said Dooley. "There is no law against looking." Then Dooley pulled a slice away from the pizza. The cheese from the piece he was about to devour held onto the pizza, in thinner and thinner strands until it reached Dooley's mouth and he took a large bite and instantly reacted. "Damn that's hot!" shouted Dooley, choosing to keep the bite in his mouth and blow out over and over in a futile attempt to cool off the piece in his mouth.

"No shit, Sherlock. What the hell were you thinking?" laughed McCarthy. "You look like you just swallowed a whole mitt full of cayenne pepper. The waitress said to be careful it's hot."

"No, she didn't," said Dooley, taking a long swig of Pepsi.

"Yes, she did," insisted McCarthy.

"No, she didn't," argued Dooley.

"You were so busy looking at that girl's ass that you did not hear her, but I'm telling you she warned us," laughed McCarthy as Dooley was bathing his tongue in the ice of his drink.

"Are you sure? I honestly didn't hear her. Maybe it was one of those acoustic anomalies or something," said Dooley.

"Acoustic anomaly my ass, it was a clear cut case of sensory overload. You could not hear anything because the ears are attached to the big head, and nothing on the big head works when all systems are a go on the little head," explained McCarthy.

"Well," reasoned Dooley, "hot ass, hot pizza, I enjoyed them both."

"Well, remember you'd get burned a lot worse if you touched the hot ass," said McCarthy. "What would Gloria do?" asked McCarthy.

"Nothing for looking, but if I ever… well, you know… like with anyone else, she would forgive me. Then she would make me a nice meal. She would tuck me in that night and then kill me in my sleep," said Dooley.

"Gloria?"

"Yeah, Gloria. She would kill me in my sleep," insisted Dooley, holding a second piece of pizza and blowing lightly on it. "How about Victoria?" asked Dooley, cautiously taking a bite of the second piece.

"I could never cheat on her. It wouldn't ever be the same. I got too good a thing going on to ever screw it up," said McCarthy taking his first bite, and after finding it manageably warm, he shoved the entire piece into his mouth. After some time, he swallowed the piece and proclaimed, "Damn, this is good pizza. I can enjoy a variety of pizzas, but I am going to stick with one woman. Like I said. I got it real good, and I would not want to screw it up because the grass ain't going to be greener on the other side."

"God, I love pizza!" said McCarthy. "I can remember one of the saddest moments in my life was when I was a kid and I had just cooked up a frozen pizza for me and my buddy. I took it out of the oven and bumped into my buddy, and the pizza flipped and hit the floor cheese-side down." McCarthy took another bite. "Five second rule doesn't apply when it lands cheese side down."

"I can see that being disappointing, but saddest?"

"Yeah. I think I got a thing for pizza because I hate in movies when they don't eat the pizza," said McCarthy folding up another piece and carefully savoring the next bite as if he would never have another.

"Like, what do you mean, don't eat the pizza. Name one," dared Dooley.

"In the first *Terminator* movie, there is a scene where Sarah Connors is this sweet young thing and she has been stood up on a date, so she tries to cheer herself up by going out and ordering a pizza. I'm thinking good choice. That'll do it. Then she gets the pizza delivered to her table, and before she can take a bite, Schwarzenegger shows up. Remember, he's the bad guy in the first one. He then shoots the place up, and she gets rescued by the guy sent from the future. He takes her out of the pizza joint after shooting up the terminator, and they run out of the place and leave the pizza behind." McCarthy then takes another bite of his pizza, and with his mouth full of pizza he says, "Man, it breaks my heart. I think often about that uneaten pizza."

"I can see that," agreed Dooley. "I hate the part in Bond movies where he is about to schtuup some sexy spy babe, and then he has to kill them before… you know," said Dooley.

"Yeah. I think they must have been getting some complaints on that because in the later Bond movies, he gets to schtuup them before he has to kill them," said McCarthy. "What the fuck is schtuup? Is that word used any more?"

"Yeah. I think it's Yiddish for poke, tap, savage, fornicate, you know. I'm kind of a refined guy. I try to vary my vocabulary," said Dooley sticking his pinky out as he ate his next bite. "Yeah, you know I never would, you know," said Dooley.

"Never would what?" asked McCarthy.

"Cheat on Gloria," said Dooley.

"Yeah. I know you wouldn't," said McCarthy.

"Yeah, Bro," said Dooley. "You know a buddy of mine once said something that explained monogamy better than I have ever heard it before."

"How's that, Dooley?" asked McCarthy.

"My buddy said that if you're married there is no reason to run around, because if you tip a woman upside down, they all look like sisters anyway," with that Dooley shoved another whole piece of pizza in his mouth, leaving the strands of cheese hanging down to his chin and well beyond.

"Dooley, you are a real refined guy all right. No wonder they call us pigs," laughed McCarthy shaking his head.

After leaving Big Al's, McCarthy and Dooley checked out Third Street and marveled at how the drunks on Third Street did the same stupid things that the drunks on River Street back home did. If La Claire and La Crosse were about fifty miles closer, they could have been the twin cities of Wisconsin. It would be Minneapolis and St. Paul on one side of the Mississippi and La Claire and La Crosse on the other side.

McCarthy and Dooley walked to Brothers' Bar, where the rest of the negotiator's class were meeting for a little farewell get together. Brothers' Bar was a well lighted, wide open, good old fashion beer from the tap, wings spicy or mild, peanut shells on the floor type of bar. The bar was highly recommended by the cops in La Crosse. It was a bar that had a good reputation as a bar they would go to on their night off. McCarthy sat down. The whole class had come to the bar, including the instructor. The whole gang pushed some tables together and sat down.

Roy Hoskins, the class clown from the Madison Police Department had not yet arrived. Stan from the Milwaukee Police Department said, "I saw Roy looking for a parking spot; he should be along in a minute. What do you think he is going to pull tonight?"

"He's been world class entertainment all week. I think every bar on this strip knows him by name. He should be charging admission," said Roemer, the instructor.

"What's he been doing," asked Dooley.

"Monday night he was giving a seminar. He had every girl in the bar gathered around him, and he was teaching them how to tie a knot with cherry stems," said Stan.

"So?" asked Dooley.

"With their tongues," said Roemer.

"Then Tuesday night at Coconut Joes up the street, he had every girl in the bar gathered around him, and he was teaching them how to make fucking swans out of napkins. He called it Oregenomi," said Stan.

"Origami," corrected Roemer.

"Origami. Whatever. Last night he had a cute little waitress at Big Al's laughing so hard she had to run into the bathroom because she thought she may have wet her pants. No shit!" said Stan.

"We were just there. What did he do," asked McCarthy.

"He took a bar towel and folded it up and told her to close her eyes and make a wish and he would make it come true. He said she should not tell anyone her wish because it might not come true. Then she says, 'OK I made my wish.' He, like, rolled the ends of the towel together and just like that it turned into a twelve-inch diamond cutter," said Stan laughing.

"Diamond cutter?" asked McCarthy.

"I'll explain it to you later," said Dooley laughing.

"So, I wonder what he's got in line for us tonight. Man, I've been just sitting and watching. Here he comes. Watch. You don't have to say a word. The show starts immediately."

Roy Hoskins was an older man. He stood about six feet one with graying hair and a slight paunch around the middle. He sat down and said "Hi, guys. Sorry I'm a little late, but I couldn't find a spot to park." He timed his entrance perfectly because the waitress had just arrived and was taking orders. Roy ordered a brandy old fashioned sweet. When the young waitress brought the drinks to the table, Roy took his drink and asked, "Honey, vat ees shour name?" As the show was obviously starting, everyone at the table got quiet and sat back to watch The Roy Hoskins Show. Roy had changed personas. He was doing a dead-on imitation of Christopher Walken as "The International" on the *Saturday Night*

Live Show. Walken would play a sleazy, old playboy, with a cheesy accent.

"Wendy," answered the cute doe-eyed blonde in the tight white sweater.

"Vendy, I vas vondering if you ever have made luff to a grandpapa?" asked Hoskins.

"Luff?" she asked.

"Oui, luff," and then he made with the kissing of an imaginary date. "Luff."

She smiled and laughed awkwardly and then answered, "Oh made love."

"Oui. That ees vat I said you luffly, beautiful, *magneeficent* creature, luff!" answered Hoskins.

"Made love with a grandfather? Why no."

"Vendy dear, vould you like to?" asked Hoskins without missing a beat.

Now the waitress was immediately blushing and grasping her tray in both hands holding it tightly to her breasts apparently as a shield. "No, I don't think I better." She was uncertain as to whether this was a joke or serious attempt at a pick up.

"Oh vell," said Hoskins sadly with a sigh, and he then began to pour his drink over his right hand.

Puzzled and shocked, the waitress asked, "Sir, what are you doing?"

In his same melancholy voice Hoskins replied, while still pouring, "Vell, Vendy, sveetheart," adding another level of camp and drama into his impression, "since you von't have me, I thought I had better get my date for tu *night* drunk."

The table first and then Wendy burst into laughter, while Hoskins merely sighed and continued to pour. When he stopped pouring, the laughter began to diminish, and then he held his hand out and everyone noticed for the first time that there were two doe eyes and a large red mouth drawn on the interior of his hand like a Senior Wentz hand puppet. Hoskins then threw his voice, and the hand puppet then belched like a Bavarian butcher and said loudly in a high pitched squeaky voice, "Oh, Señior Roy, I vant to make luff to you. Keez me good night!" The table exploded again. Wendy was laughing the loudest.

After Wendy left the table, Dooley said, "That was the funniest thing I have ever seen."

"Aw, that was nothing. I bet I can get a bigger laugh," said Hoskins.

"I'd like to see that," challenged McCarthy.

"I bet I can get everyone in this place laughing. All of them. I bet you all $5," dared Hoskins. "I lose if one person does not laugh. If that happens, I pay you all $10 and buy a round of drinks," challenged Hoskins.

"You're on!" said everyone unanimously.

"But it can't get us fired," said McCarthy.

"Or arrested!" said Stan.

"You're making it more difficult," said Hoskins, "but OK!"

When the money was in the center of the table, Hoskins then said, "I have to go to the bathroom. I'll be right back."

The group chatted like cops do about wages, shift assignments, most memorable close quarter battles, gun fights, weapons calibers, hilarious calls, as well as other various worthy war stories. After a while, they almost forgot they were waiting for Roy Hoskins' return. Then it started. It was small, at first, from the opposite side of the large round bar that filled the bar room. It started from the area of the restrooms. It was a laugh, spreading through the bar like a wave at a Packer game at Lambeau Field on a warm game in pre-season.

Dooley and McCarthy strained to see what was causing it. The bartender nearest to them suddenly started shaking his head and laughing. Then he appeared. It was Roy Hoskins. He had combed his hair, parting it down the middle and wetting it heavily with water. He had drawn a skinny little French mustache on his upper lip with what looked to be eye liner, and he was wearing an apron and had a towel folded over his arm. Then it appeared. Roy had a tail. A long tail. The tail coming from the back of his pants and was constructed out of toilet paper. Hoskins' tail was not just a dangling piece of Charmin. He went all the way. He obviously had tucked a wad of toilet paper into the back side of his pants, and it trailed from that point all the way back into the bathroom and fed under the bathroom door, where it was still connected to the roll in the stall. He had made himself up like a waiter, and he moved through the room meeting and greeting customers like a maître de. As he did this, the roll of toilet paper fed out more and more paper. The laughter spread from person to person and from table to table until every person in the bar seemed to be laughing either a "that's hilarious" laugh or a "what an idiot" laugh.

Dooley, who was laughing so hard McCarthy thought he was going to laugh up a lung, turned to comment, "God, he's killing me. He reminds me of that guy in that movie, what's his name," but Dooley just kept laughing.

"Steve Martin in *The Jerk,*" answered McCarthy.

"Yeah. That's the guy," said Dooley wiping the tears from his eyes.

When he reached his own table, his classmates were all ready to concede except the seasoned veteran Stan from Milwaukee who said, "Wait! You said everyone. That guy never laughed and you said everyone." Stan was right; there was one angry looking man, thin, but wiry, leaning against the bar wearing a "wife beaters" shirt. When he looked at Hoskins' performance, it seemed to make him seethe.

Hoskins agreed. "A hard nut to crack," said Hoskins. "Well, yes, I did say everyone, but I am not done yet," said the indomitable comedian. Hoskins then turned around and feigned shock and awe, coupled with embarrassment at the discovery of the toilet paper tail. He pulled it out of his pants and began rewinding the paper around his arm, while retracing his steps. On the return, Hoskins went back to each table saying over and over again, "Oh, I am so embarrassed. I'm sorry, I'm sorry, I'm sorry." This caused another reverse wave of laughter spreading through the bar.

As Hoskins reached the "Hard Nut To Crack," who was leaning against the bar, the man suddenly grabbed Hoskins by the arm and shouted, "Listen you fucking clown! Knock that shit off, or I'm going to kick your fucking ass. You are not funny."

Hoskins stopped in his tracks and ceased the act. His persona changed immediately, and he dropped the toilet paper to the floor and stepped into a perfect interview stance that did not appear aggressive but put cops into a position to move quickly on the defensive. Hoskins then said, "I had no wish to offend you, sir, and I have no wish to fight you either."

Wrongly sensing weakness, Hard Nut then responded, "It's not your wish that's going to fucking come true tonight. It's my wish. And it's my wish that I kick your fucking ass all the way out that fucking door, you obnoxious dickhead."

It had the appearance that in one moment the fight would be on when suddenly Hoskins' demeanor changed once again. "Wait one minute, sir. I guess we may as well fight since…"

"Peter Falk in *Columbo*," said Dooley to McCarthy.

"Peter Falk in *Columbo*," agreed McCarthy.

"… since I can't dance and it is too windy to stack BB's, we may as well fight, but first, here is a menu I would like you to look at before we proceed." Hoskins suddenly had a folded piece of paper he delivered over his arm, which still had the maître de towel on it.

Hard Nut cocked his head like a wild bull looking at himself in a full length mirror for the first time. He was drawn to the menu, by the sheer uniqueness of this experience. Hard Nut was no stranger to bar fights. He thrived on them, looked for them, invited them, and was well known for them in La Crosse. He had never received a fight menu before, for on the cover it said:

The I Have No Wish To Fight Menu

Hard Nut looked inside the menu with a serious interest and began to read.

Since it is your wish to fight and not mine, the selection is yours. Do you wish to fight a: (Check One)

South Paw

North Paw

Grand Paw

Hoskins apparently was not just a cop and impersonator, he was a rather good artist. Next to the first two selections was a drawing of himself as a boxer in the south paw stance and the standard boxing stance. In each of these he was in boxing trunks and his physique was that of a trim and muscular boxer. Next to the Grand Paw, his hands hung limply at his sides and he sported a paunch similar to his current physique.

As Hard Nut, continued to read there was a warning…

> Warning:
>
> Since I am a police officer, I must inform you that if I win I will have to arrest you for disorderly conduct and I may have to call you an ambulance.

Here was a picture of the Grand Paw Hoskins standing over a crumpled cartoon character looking like Beetle Bailey after a beating by Sergeant Snorkle with Hoskins stating, "You are an ambulance."

> If you win, I may have to call myself an ambulance and you will be arrested for a felony of battery to a police officer.

Here, Hoskins was the Beetle Bailey character lying beaten and broken on the ground, and he was saying, "I am an ambulance."

Then at the bottom of the menu were these words. Hard Nut's belligerent appearance did not change until he read this far:

> Disclaimer:
>
> This offer is void where prohibited by law!

God knows why it took so long, but as he reached these last words, Hard Nut… cracked up. He did not laugh a little, his whole body laughed, bending, twisting, shaking, and gyrating. He looked as if he had been holding laughs in for years, and finally, every laugh he had held from the time he matured to become the world class asshole he was until this moment was now being released from a Pandora's laugh box specially made to hold the laughter of macho pricks like Hard Nut. As his laugh finally receded, he reached out and shook Hoskins' hand and said, "Now that's funny. You are one funny son of a bitch. What are you drinking? I want to buy you a drink. What are you drinking?"

"A brandy old fashioned sweet, thanks. I just spilled mine. Wendy!" called Hoskins to the pretty doe-eyed waitress, "Could you take another brandy old fashion sweet over that table, this gentleman is buying me a drink." Hoskins then took the menu out of Hard Nut's hand and said, "I am glad you will not be ordering from the menu tonight. Thank you, sir, you are a gentleman."

"Yeah? Well, you are one funny son of a bitch," replied Hard Nut. "I would fight anyone who tried to say you weren't."

"Yes. I am sure that you would," said Roy shaking Hard Nut's hand one last time upon parting.

Hoskins continued on his mission to rid the establishment of excessive toilet paper.

When Hoskins returned to the table, he was met by the owner of Brothers' Bar. He was smiling ear to ear. "I saw that. I do not know if I should kick you out or hire you back for a return engagement."

"I don't generally work bars, but I do work bar mitzvahs," said Hoskins as he gathered up the hard-earned pile of five dollar bills left sitting in the center of the table.

"How in the hell did you get so crazy?" asked the bar owner.

"I'm a republican living in Madison, Wisconsin. One day the pressure got to me and I snapped," said Hoskins, not missing a beat.

Just then Wendy came to the table and set his drink down. Hoskins, who had not even sat down yet, handed her a five dollar bill and said, "That is to buy whatever he is drinking," explained Hoskins as he pointed to his former adversary. "The rest is for you for graciously putting up with my humor. Your tip." Her mouth opened wide at the pile of fives, and her big doe eyes opened.

She threw her arms around Hoskins and gave him a hug. "Oh, thank you." She showed the boss her tip and flashed a sincere million-dollar smile and left with a twirl, a bounce, and a cute little wiggle that Hoskins enjoyed all the way back to the bar.

"You gave her all that hard earned money?" asked Stan from Milwaukee.

"Yeah. Laughs are a dime a dozen; I can get those any time. Hugs like that are priceless," explained Hoskins, leaning back in his chair with a look on his face like he could die right now a happy man.

The fight menu was passed around to everyone at the table, and Hoskins explained that he had used it on the street for years. He could get no one to authorize its use. No one would tell Hoskins to stop using it either because, for whatever reason, it worked for Hoskins.

"Most of the combative dirt balls that I hand it to give up without a fight. The few that do not… well, it ties up their hands and their brain momentarily, and we move in and have them in rear compliance before they know what the fuck is happening." Hoskins took a sip out of his drink and smiled as Wendy was delivering another round to a group at the table. "Sweet. Just the way I like them." Wendy returned the smile and returned to the bar with about twenty eyes insuring her security on the return.

When the fight menu returned to Hoskins, he carefully folded and tucked it inside his pocket saying, "Like my Master Card. I never leave home without it. I pull it out more often than I pull out my weapon."

"I bet you are going to be a really effective negotiator," said McCarthy.

"I have been for twenty-three years. That's how long I have been married to my wife, and she still has sex with me. Look at this face. Do you not think that takes some negotiation?"

The group agreed.

"My wife… now that's a hard nut to crack," said Hoskins.

Chapter Twenty-three: "He's Shooting People!"

Dooley and McCarthy walked lazily back to their hotel. They were staying at a nineteenth century refurbished hotel located at Fourth and State in La Crosse. It was the Hotel Stoddard. The hotel was small by today's standards but was a huge palatial oasis of repose in its day. As soon as you entered the door, you were met by ornate oak woodwork, marble pillars, brass fittings, and a large chandelier hanging in front of a long, antique check-in desk.

President Taft, President Kennedy, and Elvis Presley had slept in the hotel. While visiting with his Wild West Show, Buffalo Bill got himself arrested there over a card dispute. The place had fallen into disrepair, but it was rescued from the wrecking ball by a developer who restored it to its former elegance. It was refitted, refurbished, and revived.

The hotel offered a very low government rate, so Dooley and McCarthy each got a room. McCarthy was on the State Street side, and Dooley was on the Fourth Street side. Both were on the second floor.

When McCarthy reached the front desk, he contacted the smiling young lady there and asked, "Can I have a wake-up call for 5:00 AM, please, for room 212?"

After pushing a few buttons, the young lady said, "You are all set. Good night," she added in a sing song tone.

As the two stepped into the old-fashioned gold-plated Otis elevator, Dooley lit into McCarthy, "5:00 AM. What the beejesus do you have going at 5:00 AM?" asked the incredulous Dooley.

"I'm running to Riverside and then along the marsh trail. Do you want to go?" asked McCarthy.

"I would tell you, 'in my dreams,' but I don't even want to be running in my dreams at 5:00 AM. Dyno, I think you need some professional help," said Dooley with deep concern in his voice.

"I've heard that before. There might be something to that." The elevator opened to the second floor and they separated. "See you in the morning," said McCarthy.

"See you in the lobby at 7:00 for the trip to Angelo. Not a minute earlier!" said Dooley emphatically.

When he reached his room, McCarthy realized that he was exhausted in spite of the six or seven Mountain Dews he had drunk throughout the evening. He had not drunk alcohol in years. He told people it was because he was on the SWAT team and subject to call out. He told people he did not like the headaches. He told himself these reasons too, but the truth was he saw up close and personal what alcohol did to individuals, families, careers, dreams, and aspirations, and he did not have any use for it. He had laughed and smiled so much tonight that his face actually hurt, and he had not had a single drink.

Now tonight, McCarthy was hotel-tired. He had been sleeping in a hotel all week and never slept well away from Victoria until about the third or fourth night, and then he would crash and sleep hard. That was what he felt like doing tonight. He brushed his teeth and then emptied about a half gallon of reconstituted Mountain Dew out of his system. He then slipped on his jogging shorts and a Packer jersey and then dialed home on the phone.

"Hi, Hon," said McCarthy. "I won't talk long. I'm going to bed. I'm really tired."

"I'm glad you called. I just wanted to say be careful," urged Victoria.

"Sure, but this is a crisis negotiator's school. It is pretty low risk up here," said McCarthy.

"Just be careful. I had a bad dream last night and a funny feeling all day. Just be careful," pleaded Victoria. "You know it's not easy being a cop's wife — especially the wife of a cop who can't wait for trouble to come to him, he's got to go looking for it all the time," said Victoria, concern dripping from her voice.

"Bad dream, huh? Do you want to talk about it?" asked Dan.

"No, just go to sleep now, Honey. I love you and be careful," said Victoria.

"I love you too. Night, Hon." McCarthy hung up.

McCarthy then turned the television on. He flipped channels until he came to the History Channel, and then he shut down the lights. He left the History Channel on. It cut down on outside noises while the narrator told bedtime stories about cowboys, soldiers, heroes, and villains and lulled McCarthy to sleep. Dan then nestled his head into the pillow and thought, "Be careful? Be careful of what? What could happen here?" In minutes McCarthy was sleeping the sleep of the dead.

McCarthy had no idea that as he was drifting off to sleep a drama was unfolding just one floor up on the third floor of the hotel.

Norberto Ruiz sat on the bed of the room. He sat quietly, breathing slowly and loudly as he methodically pushed 9 mm rounds into a magazine. He pushed until the magazine would not take another. He slammed the magazine into an Uzi and closed the action on the weapon, sliding a round into the chamber. He flipped the safety off and set it to full auto and then set it down on the bed in his hotel room.

He picked up two more magazines and, "Schnick, schnick, schnick." He filled each of them, once again, until they held no more. His player played the thumping base of *Ludicrous*. He droned on about "hos" and "drugs" and the joys of abusing them both. The pounding rap conversely spewed a venomous hatred of the "PO-leese." Ruiz was a punk. He was a gang bangin' member of the Latin Kings, one of the many gangs that had spread throughout the United States like a cancer in a terminally ill patient.

Ruiz was out of Milwaukee, and he was lying low in La Crosse because he had been skimming cash and coke from his boss, thinking, "Who counts? Who's going to miss a few thousand out of millions of dollars. Whose going to miss a few grams out of kilos upon kilos?"

Ruiz found out the hard way. Who counts? Drug bosses count.

Ruiz was given a week to make up the losses with interest, and he thought, "What the fuck am I going to do. Get a night job? Fuck this." So Norberto hit the road with his current lady, Carmen.

Today was a bad day in the life of Norberto Ruiz, and he was about to pass it on. He loaded his guns, and then he strapped on his vest. He had purchased a Kevlar vest on the street, just like he had purchased his Uzi and his Beretta on the street. He was a felon. The law said he could not have a gun. It was one more law that was not written for Norberto.

He did not obey the laws of his gang, which punished by death. Why would he obey the laws of a state where there was no death penalty? Norberto was going to commit the ultimate crime tonight. He was going out like his hero Tony Montana, yelling, "Say hello to my little friend," with a gun in each hand. He would kill anyone who wronged him. The first to die was to be Carmen.

The door knob turned and the door swung open. Carmen entered the room and set her keys down on the table and tossed her purse to a chair next to the table. The guns did not concern her. She lived in a world of guns, but when she saw the look in Norberto's eyes her blood froze. "What?"

"You fucking whore!" shouted Norberto, and he hit her hard with the Beretta, across the side of her face. Her jaw was fractured beyond repair. Her last word, not including some whimpering noises would be, "What?"

Even a condemned man is read the charges before the execution. Carmen would die wondering, "What?"

Norberto would not even take the time to tell her why she was dying so horribly. The last thing she would hear would be the man she loved saying, "You fucking whore!" He covered her face with a pillow and pressed the muzzle against the pillow. Carmen tried to speak, but no words would come. No more words would ever come for Carmen.

"Bam!" The muffled shot sent a dusty blowback into the air as the bullet passed through the pillow and into Carmen. Her fear and pain were gone. Carmen was dead for calling her sister and telling her about the quaint old hotel she was staying in with Norberto in

La Crosse. Carmen's sister would tell her boyfriend, Hector, who just happened to be Norberto's boss — the boss who wanted to kill Norberto. Carmen was dead for doing exactly what sisters do. She was dead for bragging about what a nice boyfriend she had.

Norberto threw Carmen's purse off the chair and sat down. He slid the chamber open slightly on the Beretta and let it close after seeing the chamber contained another live round. He put the gun to his head and gritted his teeth and took a deep breath. He sweated and shook and then dropped the weapon to his lap. Too bad, the world would have been a better place without Norberto. Except for Carmen, the world almost got off easy. Too bad, Norberto was a coward.

He looked at Carmen and tried to feel something for her. She had loved him. She had made him laugh. She had given up her job, her family, and her life to run away with him, and now she was dead and he felt nothing. Then he felt something that seemed to be a feeling. Well, it was almost a feeling. It was almost an emotion. It was almost human. Norberto thought, "Carmen, you fucking whore! I should have fucked you one more time. Damn!"

Norberto then tucked his spare magazines into his belt and took the Beretta in his right hand and the Uzi in his left. He stepped out into the hallway and noticed one man standing in his pajamas. The man had an ice bucket. He was trying to get his key into his door and then stopped. There is an instinct that causes the human animal, when faced with death, to fight, flee, submit, or freeze. The most difficult to understand is the freeze instinct. Scientist explain that it comes from the days when large animals would sometimes pass over immobile objects, and humans, who could not out run their predators, found freezing a viable option for survival.

In a world where the only predators that we face are other humans, this is not a viable option in most cases where survival is in question. The man with the ice bucket stood as frozen as the ice in the bucket. In those long last moments, he thought of his wife. He loved her. He thought of his children. He loved them. He thought of his God. He was about to meet him. His last word… "Why?" Like Carmen, he would never have his question answered.

Norberto aimed and shot his Beretta seven times. He hit the stationery victim seven times. The bucket hit the floor at the same time as Norberto's second victim. Norberto then sprayed the hallway with his Uzi, emptying his 30 round magazine in a frenzy. He fumbled with the magazine in his belt and reloaded the Uzi.

Two other hotel occupants heard what everyday people always hear when they hear gunshots. They each said, "Firecrackers! God damn kids and their firecrackers." A young woman stepped out into the hallway and saw Ruiz. She saw the man with his ice bucket lying dead, and she did not freeze. She fled, locking the door behind her, and Ruiz opened fire, one round crashing hard into her hip. She went down, and the rest of the rounds passed over her head. She was saved by a gunshot wound to her hip.

Her neighbor across the hall popped out and was also hit. He was hit in the abdomen and managed to crawl back into his room and lock the door.

Ruiz stood in the hallway panning back and forth, hoping for another hapless victim. The gun smoke filled the hallway of the third floor. There was so much smoke from the gunfire in such a small place that, suddenly, the smoke alarms began to sound. Norberto ran to the elevator to find more victims. He pushed the buttons, but the old elevator had new technology installed in it. It had locked down when the smoke alarms went off.

Just then, the night manager entered the hallway from the stairway. He had been summoned by the alarm. He spotted Norberto standing over the innocent man and his spilled ice bucket, and then Norberto turned slowly and brought the Uzi up. He slowly and deliberately pointed at the night maintenance man. The muzzle looked to be the size of a Howitzer. The maintenance man was a military veteran. He knew now was the time to sound retreat, when the battle was not winnable, and he fled three times as fast down the stairs as it took him to climb up. He was out the door before the next burst of gunfire rattled into the heavy wood of the old oak door.

Norberto then heard a siren, "Fucking cops!" At that moment, a young soldier on leave from the army stepped out of the room just down from the elevator. He had been sound asleep and was not quite awake. Ruiz shoved the Beretta into the soldier's face. "Back inside or you're dead!" Ruiz shoved the man into his own room and then into the bathroom. He ripped the shower curtain down and wrapped the soldier in it. The soldier was awake now. Ruiz shoved the man into the tub and yelled, "Shut the fuck up and don't move or I blow your fucking head off." The soldier laid mute in the tub.

Screeeeeee — McCarthy woke up on his feet. The fire alarm was sounding. When he realized that it was the fire alarm, he walked over to the door and felt it. It was cool to the touch. He looked out the peep hole, and the hall was empty. He was the only one that, apparently, had awakened on his floor. McCarthy threw on his jeans, his socks, a mock turtle neck, and his Milwaukee Brewers letter jacket, and out the door he went. McCarthy had remembered the fire escape route, and he took it right down to the alley. He was not surprised that he was the only one up and out. Many people ignored fire alarms in hotels. They went off so often. Unless there was a fireman at the door pounding, many people would just stay in bed.

McCarthy reached the bottom step of the fire escape and took the time to tie his shoes. He then walked around the hotel, through the parking lot, and headed toward the front lobby. Just then, an ambulance went blaring down State Street past the hotel, and it headed to Third and turned south toward Lutheran Hospital.

At that same moment, a squad car pulled into the lot of the Stoddard. The lone officer exited the squad and slung his shotgun to low ready.

"Hello," thought McCarthy. "Cops do not take shotguns into fire alarms."

McCarthy saw the officer was alone. He was hesitant to stick his nose in to another jurisdiction's business, but something drew him to the lone officer. Just then, the hotel maintenance man burst around the corner yelling, "He's shooting people! He's shooting people! You got to get in there. He's got an AK-47!"

McCarthy reached the squad, and hearing the urgency of the maintenance man's voice, he stepped forward and identified himself saying, "I am Officer Dan McCarthy of the La Claire Police Department. I can help if you need some."

"Are you armed?" asked the officer.

"No," said McCarthy.

"Here," said the officer, passing McCarthy his Glock 17. McCarthy knew the weapon well.

"Who's shooting and where is he?" asked the Officer.

In a gasping rapid monologue, the maintenance man blurted out, "He is five feet ten, stocky build, wearing a banana colored sweat suit. He is Hispanic and definitely had two firearms. There is at least one guy dead. I am sure he was dead. He's on the third floor by the elevator," said the maintenance man.

The officer then looked at McCarthy and, without hesitation, gave him his marching orders, "This is a mutual aid request. I need you to cover the lobby. We are going up to the third floor." At that time, a second squad had pulled in and a sergeant rapidly stepped out of the squad and joined the first officer. "Dispatch, I have shots fired on the third floor of the Stoddard Hotel. I have an armed off-duty La Claire officer covering the lobby in a Milwaukee Brewers jacket. We are moving to contact the suspect on the third floor. He is reportedly armed with an AK-47, and there is at least one party down. Have the next responding units cover the northeast corner of the building and the southwest corner. Call out the SWAT team." The officer expertly made this transmission on the move as he headed toward the front door and then through the lobby.

In the lobby, McCarthy saw Dooley. "He is a cop also," said McCarthy.

"Are you armed," asked the La Crosse officer.

"Yes," said Dooley.

"We have an armed man in a banana colored sweat suit shooting people. Cover the second floor." The officer then keyed the collar mic, "Dispatch I have a second off-duty officer in a Brett

Favre Packer jersey, armed, covering the second floor." With that, the officer and sergeant disappeared up the steps calmly heading toward what most people would run screaming from.

McCarthy took up a position where a large pillar gave him good cover. He checked the Glock and saw that it was loaded to capacity with seventeen in the magazine and one in the chamber. He wished he had his own weapon, but a letter for the course requested that no guns be brought to the training. He had left his weapon at home as he had been directed. He remembered what a man from Texas had said to him several years ago after McCarthy and Stammos had arrested the man for carrying a concealed weapon. The man from Texas said, "I'd rather be caught with it than caught without it." McCarthy knew, now, what the Texan was talking about. After this night, McCarthy would never have to borrow another's weapon again.

From McCarthy's position, he could cover the first floor's thoroughfares. If the gunman tried to escape from the first floor, McCarthy was in a perfect position to intercept him because he was covering the elevator, the emergency exit, and the lobby exits. Then Dan noticed the young desk clerk holding the fort. He was about to address her when a middle-aged man and his wife wandered toward him, obviously unaware of anything but the fire alarm. McCarthy showed them his badge, "Folks, there is a man shooting people in the hotel. We do not know where he is." McCarthy then ushered them into a conference room that he could watch. There was an emergency exit in the room. "Stay in here until something happens to make you feel like you have to head out that door. If that happens run out the door and do not stop."

"Yes, sir," said the woman, whose eyes made it obvious that if she had not been a few minutes earlier, she was now wide awake.

McCarthy then went to the night manager at the front desk. "Please shut down the alarm. It is drawing people out of their rooms. They are safer in their rooms, now, until we find out where this guy is. When anyone calls, please tell them to stay in their rooms and double lock the doors. Tell them the safest place to be is the bathtub."

The manager answered surprisingly calmly, "Yes, sir," and she ran to the office and returned. When she did, the ungodly screeching of the fire alarm had stopped. Then she picked up the phone, "Hello, Stoddard Hotel." The night manager listened for a minute and then the color ran from her face as if someone had just walked over her grave. She then handed the phone to McCarthy saying in a whisper, "It's for you. He wants to talk to a cop. He says… he's says he's the killer."

Benelli M1 12-Gauge Shotgun

Chapter Twenty-four: The Ice Man Cometh

McCarthy scanned the area and saw no additional officers yet, and he took the phone, "Hello. This is Officer Dan McCarthy."

"Yeah, cop. I want out or this guy here dies," said an angry voice.

"Well, it isn't all that easy. I think I can help though. My name is Dan McCarthy. You can call me Dan. What can I call you?" asked Dan in a voice as calm and as conversational as he could muster.

"My name? Fuck my name. That don't matter."

"You called me, and that means you are a reasonable man. Since you are a reasonable man, that means we can talk. Since this is a difficult situation, that means we will be talking a while, so what shall I call you?" asked McCarthy hoping that he could get a name or nickname out of the suspect. It would be a great start.

"What can you call me?" Ruiz thought of the innocent victim he had just shot and killed. He saw the image of the man standing near his door in his pajamas and falling to the floor after being shot down by Ruiz for absolutely no explainable reason. Ruiz pictured the ice bucket rolling out of the man's hands, spilling the ice onto the decorative pattern of the carpeted the floor. "Call me the Ice Man. I iced some people, man. I deliver the cold icy reality of death," said Ruiz.

McCarthy thought, "That's going to creep the hell out of me when this is all over, but not now. Not now. You have to talk to this man. Like Compton says, 'If he's talking, he's not shooting.'"

McCarthy had pulled a hotel notebook over to his spot at the lobby desk. He wrote the words "Ice Man," "hostage," and quotations around, "Call me the Ice Man," "I iced some people, man," and "I deliver the cold icy reality of death."

Then McCarthy motioned to the night manager. He ripped

out another page from the notebook and checked her name tag. It said "Hello, my name is Shelly. I'm here to serve you." He wrote on the top of the page, "Notes to Shelly," and below that he wrote, "What room?"

Shelly caught on fast. She wrote, "306."

McCarthy wrote quickly and pointed to two officers coming through the lobby door. "Tell them I have him on the phone and he is in 306."

She nodded her head and ran to the officers. McCarthy saw one headed up the stairs while the second, who was a sergeant, came over to McCarthy. McCarthy started to hand him the phone, but the sergeant motioned for McCarthy to keep talking. McCarthy realized the sergeant was right. Rapport had been established. To break off a conversation so sharply could be catastrophic.

"Ice Man, do you have someone there with you?" asked McCarthy.

"Yeah, man, and he's fucking dead if you guys come crashing through the fucking door!" yelled Ruiz.

"You sound upset. I am here to listen to you. I am here to help." McCarthy tried to say those words in a quiet and calm tone to bring the suspect down. He was agitated, extremely agitated. He had already killed, and for some reason he had stopped killing. McCarthy was in a position to exploit that pause so that more help could arrive and a response could be planned. If he was not calmed down, the man screaming these words would kill again soon.

"You fuckin' know I'm upset. I killed people, man. That's as fuckin' upset as it gets, man!" said Ruiz, who seemed to McCarthy to have come down a notch.

"You can call me Dan. You sound very upset. Are you hurt?" asked McCarthy.

"Dan, no I'm not hurt, man. Ain't nobody hurt me, man. I done hurt people. I'm the shooter, Dan. I'm the killer. I ain't hurt," said Ruiz, now speaking in a matter-of-fact tone of voice.

"Good, he's calmed down and he using my name. Good signs," thought McCarthy. McCarthy then asked, "Are you armed, Ice Man?"

"Fuckin' Chui I'm armed. I got's an Uzi and a Berette 9, and I ain't afraid to kill any motherfucker that gives me shit!" He then aimed the Beretta at the soldier lying as still as he could make himself in the tub. McCarthy wrote down "Uzi" and "Beretta" on the pad in front of him and showed the sergeant standing next to him. The sergeant passed this information on the La Crosse Police Department Emergency Response Team. They now knew that the suspect had a hostage, was in room 306, and their ballistic shields could stop what he was carrying.

The soldier looked into Ruiz's eyes and saw that he could kill. He thought, "Please Mary, Mother of God, get me home to my family safely." He had not prayed that prayer since his beloved third division had driven into Baghdad in the opening of the 2003 war.

"Say, Ice Man, you have someone with you. Is that a friend or family?"

"No, man! He's my hostage. He's dead if I do not get respect, man," said Ruiz.

"May I talk to him?" asked McCarthy, worried that he might be pushing a little too hard too fast.

"Yeah, Dan. Talk to him. You need to know I got this guy and I will kill him." Ruiz got up from the toilet and held the phone to the ear of the soldier.

"Sir, can you hear me?" asked McCarthy.

"Yes," said the soldier.

"Can he hear me?"

"No, I don't think so," said the soldier.

"I am going to ask you a series of questions and just answer them yes or no. Got it?"

"Yes."

"Does he have two guns?"

"Yes."

" Does it look like he will use them?"

"Yes!"

"Is anyone else in the room with the two of you?"

"No."

"Are you hurt?"

"No. Get me out of here. This guy is going to kill me, man!" yelled the soldier as Ruiz shoved the Beretta into his face, smashing it tightly up against the soldier's nose.

"That's enough!" yelled Ruiz, who had clearly worked himself up into a frenzy again.

"Ice Man. With a nickname like that you must be cool as ice under stress," schmoozed McCarthy.

Ruiz calmed himself again, proud of the name he picked for himself on this night. He thought it would make a catchy headline. "Yeah, I am cool under stress, man. I've been in the shit on the streets," said Ruiz, clearly calmer again.

"Where you from, man?" asked McCarthy.

"Milwaukee is mi barrio," answered Ruiz.

"Is your family there?" asked McCarthy.

"My mamacita still lives there," said Ruiz, with a heavy tone of emotion.

"When was the last time you talked to your mamacita?" asked McCarthy.

"Tonight. I called her to tell her where I was and to tell her I loved her. You know you got to say adios to your mama," said Ruiz. "I told her I love her."

McCarthy thought, "Great. He loves his mother."

"Ice Man, you must really love your mamacita if you called her tonight, which has to be the toughest night in your life," said McCarthy. "What I am hearing is that you love your mother and would like to talk with her again."

"Yeah, man. I told her to drive to La Crosse. She's on her way."

"She might be around here somewhere right now. Let's both agree not to do anything that endangers your mamacita," said McCarthy.

While McCarthy occupied the killer, the Emergency Response Team formed two shield teams with two stretchers. Shelly had been taking calls on a separate phone at the front desk. Everyone noticed how calm she stayed throughout the incident. She would later shed some light on her coolness under pressure explaining,

"My dad was a cop. Apparently, he passed down coolness under pressure."

Shelly received two frantic calls from a wounded female in 310 and a wounded male in 311. The female was in a great deal of pain, and the male said he thought he might die if he didn't get to the hospital soon.

Shelly told them both, "The police are here. They will get to you as soon as possible. Hold on. Don't give up. They are coming."

The officer in charge of the Emergency Response Team sent two teams with two stretchers simultaneously with shields, master keys, and plenty of firepower. The La Crosse County Sheriff's Department Team responded also. A mutual request call had gone out beyond Officer Dan McCarthy and his buddy Dooley. Both teams moved in stealth mode and were able to quietly make entry into both rooms. Using direct pressure and quick clots, they were able stem the flow of the bleeding, and then the shield teams provided cover while they backed down the hallway with the victims each placed on a stretcher.

McCarthy did not feel like he was negotiating. It felt less like negotiations and more like a conversation. He was having a conversation with a person like any other person he might meet on the street. The only difference was this person had just killed and was considering killing another man lying in a tub under a watchful eye. The watchful eye was the muzzle of an Uzi. McCarthy realized the most unlikely bond was developing between two unlikely people. A short-term relationship had been built between a cold-blooded killer and a cop. The killer was so cold blooded he chose the moniker "Ice Man."

Ruiz had grown to trust the man on the phone. McCarthy had come to realize that, for whatever reason, he had managed to rekindle the spark of humanity left in this man and was like a caveman with his flint, trying to blow gently on it to keep it burning. Ruiz assured McCarthy, "I won't kill this man unless you guys come crashing through my door. If that happens," Ruiz pointed the Beretta at the soldier, who cringed and closed his eyes, "Bam!" and then Ruiz pointed the gun at his own head, "Bam! Then you get nothing but a couple of dead guys." The soldier opened his eyes to discover the execution was a mock execution. He wondered what it was going to be like for him when it was real. He was certain that he would die in the bathtub. Ruiz continued, "I'm sure you don't give a shit about me, but this guy right here will be the first to get it."

"Don't talk like that. I care about you. Any man who clearly loves his mother as much as you do is all right with me," said McCarthy trying to keep the glow of humanity flickering.

"I do. My mamacita is a beautiful person, and I do love her. If I give up will you promise I can see her again," asked Ruiz, with his voice cracking with emotion.

"Yes. That is a promise I can keep." McCarthy tried to contain his excitement. The Ice Man had used the word give up without being prompted. This no longer was a conversation. This was, indeed, a negotiation. McCarthy wrote down on his pad in large letters, "He wants to give up and see his mamacita again."

The sergeant standing next to McCarthy wrote, "Our arrest teams are in place."

By this time, the rescue teams had been reformed by the Emergency Response Team Commander and were standing by on the third floor with an alternate plan for the entry into Ruiz's room or the arrest of Ruiz, which they did not think was likely considering the carnage they had already seen.

McCarthy wrote, "Transition to your negotiators?"

The sergeant shook his head in the affirmative.

"Ice Man? Can I have your real name?" said McCarthy. "Then when I meet you I can greet you like a friend."

"My name is Norberto Ruiz," said the gun man in a tone of voice indicating he was accepting his fate.

"I am going to turn you over to someone who is going to talk you out of this unpleasantness. Is that OK, with you?" asked McCarthy.

"Yeah. You promise I will be able to see my mamacita?" asked Ruiz.

"I promise on my mother," said McCarthy. "I am turning you

over to another officer from the La Crosse Police Department. He will help you get out of there tonight."

McCarthy then relinquished the phone to the negotiators who were standing by and he stepped back. He took a breath.

He then took in the scene. He realized that as he stood talking to the killer at the front desk he had wrapped himself in a cocoon of intensity in which he could only see the sergeant, Shelly, and the phone and the pad in front of him.

The lobby looked like a busy airplane terminal. He glanced about and watched the emergency medical technicians roll a stretcher by. A pretty young female was in the first one. McCarthy thought the pained expression for this young lady should be because she was experiencing labor pains for her first child. She should not have to be enduring the pain of a bullet wound at the hands of a stranger for no reason. McCarthy noticed that although she was experiencing the pain while wide awake, she was stoic. She had taken a bullet in her pelvis, and still she did not cry out.

Then a second stretcher rolled pass. Two technicians rolled the stretcher out carefully while an IV bag hung swinging from its harness. The male was also quiet. His eyes were fluttering. He was obviously hovering in that dreamlike state between consciousness and unconsciousness.

McCarthy was happy to see they were alive. McCarthy realized he had no idea if he was on the phone for ten minutes or ten hours. He was sweating like he had just competed in an iron man competition, and this was the first he had noticed it. He also realized he still had the Glock in his hand, and although it seemed that everyone knew he was a police officer, he felt a little self conscious about walking about in a Brewers jacket armed with a Glock. He slipped the Glock into his belt in the small of his back and moved the clip-on off duty badge to a spot a little more visible on his belt.

The negotiator that took over was good. McCarthy thought, "He's much better than I am. That guy should have been on the phone from the start. He's not sweating like a pig."

The negotiator was a stocky guy in his forties with salt and pepper hair. He looked like he had seen it all. McCarthy could hear that he was explaining the procedure that the SWAT officers would use to safely arrest him once he came outside of the room into the hallway. "I'm telling you this so there will be no surprises. This is all for your safety and ours," said the negotiator.

Within fifteen minutes, Ruiz was in the lobby. One of the Emergency Response Team Members was meticulously searching him while two more covered him. When the officer slid the bullet resistant vest off Ruiz, McCarthy thought, "I'm glad I did not have to face a man with an Uzi and a vest. He was more ready for this than I was tonight." Then he thought again, "Victoria tried to warn me. She said 'I had a dream.' She said, 'Be careful.' Her sixth sense is even keener than mine." He would never doubt her again.

McCarthy had said he would introduce himself to Ruiz when he came down. He felt no compunction nor need to ever talk to this man again. He watched the officers lead the handcuffed killer out of the hotel. McCarthy thought, "No death penalty in Wisconsin. That's too bad. I hope he is claustrophobic and gets a nine-by-nine cell with a six feet eight cell mate who prefers to give rather than receive and that likes it rough."

McCarthy then saw the first officer that arrived at the hotel walking down the steps, carrying a shield. He now also had a black helmet on and the black outer armor of SWAT over his uniform as he walked up to McCarthy. He set the shield down and leaned it next to the pillar that McCarthy was using for cover earlier. "My name is Dan," said McCarthy, extending hand.

"My name's Bob, Brother," said the La Crosse officer. "Thanks for the help."

"Thanks for the Glock," said McCarthy, slipping his hand into the small of his back to retrieve Bob's weapon. Then he stopped as he became a little bit concerned about being in plain clothes and pulling out a weapon in a hotel filled with cops and said, "Is it OK to do this here?"

"Don't worry. Everyone here knows that you are a cop." McCarthy then continued retrieving the weapon and handed it carefully to Bob who holstered it and snapped it down.

"I suspected you were SWAT," said McCarthy, "by the way you handled your Benelli, and then I knew you were SWAT when I watched you head into that building as calm as a clam. You made some pretty impressive decisions in a matter of seconds, and you were as good on the radio as you were with the shotgun," said McCarthy. "Nice work."

"Yeah but that's the key. I was working. Do you spend all your nights off like this?" asked Bob.

"No. Not so much," said Dan.

The two were then joined by Dooley, who walked up and extended his hand to Bob, "I'm Dooley."

"Just Dooley?" asked Bob.

"Like Cher. One name says it all," said Dooley.

"That's the truth," agreed McCarthy.

"I have to get back. It's a mess on the third floor, bodies, casings, and carnage all over. We are going to go room to room now and check to see if we have any more victims. There are two dead up there, and we evacuated two wounded. The entire third floor is a crime scene. We have to let the people know that it's OK to leave their rooms. We'll need statements from you two. Could you head two blocks north to the station and make out a statement, please?" asked Bob.

"Right away," said McCarthy.

"Say you are SWAT, too, right? Are you tactical or negotiations?" asked Bob.

"Tactical, but our commander believes in cross training us. It just so happens I was in negotiation training all this week at Western Tech. I was wondering when this thing started if it was some elaborate training scenario by the FBI instructors," said McCarthy.

"I wish. Those people upstairs are not going to stand up when someone yells End of Scenario," said Bob. "Hey, all I can say is thank your officer in charge for sending you to the training this week. It could not have been timed better," said Bob. "I've got to go now." He then disappeared into the throng that now occupied the lobby.

Then McCarthy noticed a soldier in fatigues talking to the sergeant who had stood beside McCarthy during the negotiations. The sergeant pointed at McCarthy and said something to the soldier, who nodded.

The soldier walked over to McCarthy and, with sudden and unexpected swiftness, hugged him. "Hey, man. You saved my life. I don't know what you said to him, but he was going to kill me and you talked him out of it. I'll never be able to repay you, man. You were like an answered prayer."

McCarthy awkwardly returned the hug. This, obviously, was the man in the tub. McCarthy would not be able to say afterward how long the hug lasted. It was long enough to do some thinking though. He thought of the hug Hoskins received from the waitress, and he now understood how a hug from a stranger could be "priceless."

Then he thought of Brockman and how many times he said, "Police work. TJIF, this job is fucked. What a totally fucking thankless job." McCarthy was being thanked by an American Soldier, an American Hero. He thought about how close he came to giving in to the cynicism after the gun fight with Mad Mattix. He thought about the vest, the Uzi, and the two people two floors up that were never going to be hugged again in this world. "Just returning the favor, soldier," said McCarthy.

Then he thought again, "Thankless job, my ass. TJIF, this job is fantastic. This thank you is priceless… priceless."

Chapter Twenty-five:
"Damn, 9 Iron Instead of a 9 mm"

Harley David Slade sat impatiently in his car, waiting for the condemned. He had fantasized, planned, and prepared for months for this night. Now he was ready. He sat looking at the "condemned's barracks." It was a large brick home with a pool in the backyard. It was in an up-scale neighborhood with a park across the street. He could sit unnoticed in the parking area of the park as he watched and waited. He had bought a newspaper to cover his face whenever anyone passed his parked car, but now he caught himself actually reading an article in the paper he had bought merely for a prop.

The headline of the article was, "ICE MAN KILLS TWO, WOUNDS TWO IN LA CROSSE."

As he read the article, he came across the line, "Officer Dan McCarthy of the La Claire Police Department was staying in the hotel while attending a training session in La Crosse and served a key role as the initial hostage negotiator...." Slade crumpled the newspaper and said aloud, "Fucking McCarthy!" Then Harley realized how loud he had spoken.

Slade looked frantically about and saw his outburst had gone unnoticed. He threw the crumbled paper into the backseat and picked up the sports section to use when he needed to look nonchalant. This was a great deal of work for Harley. He needed to look nonchalant. It was imperative that he look nonchalant. It was written in his plan, "Standby in your car until the arrival of the condemned and Lawyer Sloan. Then begin incursion." The plan said nonchalant. "You must be nonchalant!" ordered the Dark Lord.

"I'll smoke. OK?" Slade answered the voice.

He reached into his pocket and pulled out his baggie, zip locked to insure freshness, and removed a personally rolled marijuana cigarette. He knew that this would keep him occupied until his "targets" arrived. "I love this shit," said Slade. He placed the object of his affection between his lips then flicked his Bic and lit the doobie.

Slade took a deep drag and held it as long as he could. When he could stand to hold it no longer, he opened his eyes and exhaled, and there she was. He almost missed her. She was walking from her car, which was parked in the driveway. "The condemned has arrived," Slade said out loud.

He took another drag from the doobie, and it glowed brightly as he inhaled since now the sun was almost down. He would not need the newspaper any longer. The darkness would conceal him in the car. The darkness of the night would be his accomplice. He would wait for Lawyer Sloan. He would wait for the time to be right, and then he would strike.

It was two hours later before Sloan arrived. Slade said out loud, "There you are, Sloan, you pig. I wonder if I am the only one that knows you are sleeping with the Honorable Judge Alice at night and slipping all your cases into her court all day." Slade took another deep drag off his doobie, then let it out and said as he hacked from the smoke that he loved so much, "Slipping it to her in the day and slipping it to her at night." He then began coughing uncontrollably. The cough turned into a laugh that, if heard by anyone, would have aroused suspicion because of its maniacal nature. "I told a joke. It was a good joke. I don't usually tell jokes. I should tell more jokes. They make me laugh," said Slade to the Dark Lord.

Slade was right. This may have been the first joke he had ever told. It would be the last joke he would ever tell. Nothing Slade would do from this point forward would ever be considered funny by anyone again. Not even Slade.

Slade watched the house for hours. He watched the lights go on in one room and out in another. He watched the dim shadowy light of the television until it flickered out.

Then finally, the bedroom light went on upstairs and then out again. He waited five minutes. Ten minutes. Twenty minutes. Thirty minutes. "It's time!" said the Dark Lord.

"It's time!" answered Slade.

Slade slipped on his gloves. He checked his Beretta. He checked his knapsack: knife, duct tape, wire cutters, glass cutter, raw hamburger. Everything he had listed in his plan was there. Everything he needed to make it work was there. "Ready!" said Slade. He pulled across the street to a dark spot along the curb, where a large Hackberry tree blocked the street light and the large full moon as he made his approach.

He made his way to the black Lab named Holmes in the back and went to the cage. Judge Alice had named the dog after her favorite jurist, Oliver Wendell Holmes. Holmes had grown accustomed to Slade's visits. Slade brought him a healthy portion of raw hamburger each night that he made his reconnaissance. The Lab came to anticipate the visits. Slade could not be dangerous. He brought hamburger. No one noticed the sudden weight gain of Holmes, and no one noticed Slade.

Slade went to the phone cable, and with his wire cutters, he cut the line. He gambled that the cell phones would be out of reach in chargers. He had no choice. The hard line would be out of service. Slade then made his way to the rear patio door. He cut the screen with the wire cutters and then reached in and flipped the lock and gently opened the screen door. He then put the cutters back into his bag and immediately had his glass cutter. He put a pre-cut length of duct tape on the glass and held it while he carefully cut a circle in the glass. Slade tapped it once. Then he tapped it twice, and it came loose. He held it from falling and pulled it out with the tape. He set the glass down on the patio and reached in and turned the lock. "Chick!"

Sloan was just dozing after a passionate round of love making with Judge Alice. She was the sexiest woman he had ever been with. He felt the fact that they had decided to keep their relationship quiet might have made their relationship even more exciting, because it was almost like a forbidden secret tryst.

Sloan was spooning Judge Alice like an old married couple drifting off to sleep next to her nakedness when, "Chick!"

"What was that?" asked Alice.

"I don't know. It was definitely something," whispered Sloan, now wide awake.

"Shhhhhhhhhhnk."

"That was the patio door!" said Alice, in a frantic whisper.

She reached for the phone next to the bed and put it to her ear, trembling, while Sloan jumped out of bed and slid on his pants. "Ahhh," he exclaimed as he realized the painful truth that putting underwear on before the pants prevent some terribly painful but non life threatening injuries in men. He readjusted himself and then zipped up.

"The phone is dead!" said Judge Alice, now frozen in sheer terror.

Sloan went to the closet. He pulled a 9 iron out of his golf bag. "Damn!" He had agreed to sell his 9 mm H & K semi-automatic handgun that he had always kept next to his bed for protection when he moved in with Alice. He had bought it and trained with it because, as idealistic as he was about his job, he knew that some of the people he defended would kill without a second thought. They would kill for money, for love, for pride, for revenge, even for a pair of high top Nikes.

Sloan was not allowed to bring the gun with him when he moved in with Alice. The judge would not have a gun in her house. "Son of a bitch! I got a fucking 9 iron in my hand instead of a 9 mm. Thanks a lot, Alice!" He whispered.

"I'm sorry?" said Alice pulling the covers tightly up to her chin.

"Stay here." Sloan did not forgive her. Sloan never would forgive her. Alice was about to learn. Guns don't kill people. People kill people. Criminals kill innocent defenseless people. Alice would never forgive herself.

Sloan crept carefully across the room and opened the door. He reached out and turned the hall light on. He saw nothing. He went to the top of the stairs and yelled, "Who is down there!"

Nothing.

"I called the police! They should be here any moment."

Nothing.

"Maybe I was hearing things," he thought hopefully.

"Sloan!" came the familiar voice from behind him.

"Shit. How did he get behind me!" thought Sloan as he turned and faced a figure in a green army jacket and a mask. The man had a gun pointed and aimed precariously at the attorney. Something about the man's voice, his mannerisms, his coat, and his boots, looked familiar.

"Slade?" asked Jack Sloan.

"Slade," was all Harley David said, and then his gun barked once.

The bullet hit Sloan squarely in the chest, and he stood for a second, speechless. He looked down at his chest and put his fingers into the hole. It was such a small hole for the pain that he felt. He looked at Slade and wondered, "Why? I got you off. Why me?" He dropped the 9 iron and now realized it was not easy to breathe. He tried, but all he could hear was a gurgling, gasping sound. Sloan wondered, "Who is making that sound?" and then twelve seconds after the bullet burned its way into Jack Sloan's aorta, he fell dead to the steps. He slid, tumbled, and rolled to the bottom. His only real offense to Slade was that he was a lawyer. They all had to die eventually in Slade's war. He believed them to be, "the profiteers in the illegally declared war on drugs."

Jack Sloan was a lawyer. He was a good lawyer. Some always found it hard to believe that a good lawyer could be a good person. The adversarial system of law in this country required a vigorous defense by good lawyers on both sides. McCarthy would always recognize that the system was flawed. Sometimes the innocent went to prison, ever so rarely, but too often the guilty walk free among us. Jack Sloan was a good lawyer. Jack Sloan was a person who did not deserve this death. Jack Sloan the lawyer was an unwitting accomplice in his own death. *Jack Sloan was...*

Harley David Slade already had his gun to the face of Judge Alice when the body of Jack Sloan stopped rolling at the bottom of the stairs. Harley ripped the sheets from her grasp. He was shocked. He had not planned on this. He had never seen her long red hair falling down around her shoulders. It had always been up in court. He had never seen her eyes without those dark glasses on. The bench and the robes always hid her large natural breasts, which sagged slightly but sensually with age. She was round in all the places a woman should be round. This handsome, middle-aged woman would have aroused most men, but that was not what aroused Slade. None of these alluring characteristics in any woman, even Darla, aroused Slade.

Slade had never seen any woman cower below him in fear. He never stood so powerfully in control of a woman before in his life. This is what Slade found lit an out-of-control fire in his loins. He had to have this woman… now! "Spoils of war!" he declared. Then he took her.

After, Slade threw the judge a robe and said, "Put it on!" When she put the robe on, Harley David Slade duct taped her wrists together and covered her mouth with his hand. "Breathe!" he said. The judge breathed through her nose. When he saw she could breathe through her nose, he covered her mouth. He did not want her to die too soon. "If you resist any one of my requests, you will not be asked a second time. You will die on the spot. Understand?" growled Slade.

She shook her head, submitting totally to him now seemed the only way. She was crying quietly, trying to maintain some sort of dignity in the midst of her humiliation.

Slade slipped a pair of loafers on Judge Alice's feet. Then he slipped his hand slowly up her thigh, remembering. She closed her eyes and turned her head as his hand reached what had once belonged only to the man she loved, who lay dead at the bottom of the stairs.

Slade saw her reaction and withdrew his hand. He stood up and the pointed the weapon at her and said in a voice that was unusually calm. It was as if he was giving directions to a motorist, looking for the nearest Burger King. "Now, down the stairs, over your dead boyfriend, out the front door to the front walk, take a right at the sidewalk and get in the car under the Hackberry tree. Move now, please."

Slade took her by the arm. They reached the top of the steps, and she saw Sloan. She had loved him. She loved his confident manner. She loved his shiny suits and his fake tan, his pony tail. She saw him lying dead next to the 9 iron with a large black-looking pool of blood spreading across the polished hardwood floor at the bottom of the stairs. She thought of what he had said when he argued vainly to keep his gun for protection. "Guns don't kill people. People kill people." Now he lay there dead because she sent him into the darkness with a 9 iron.

As Slade and Judge Alice stepped over Sloan, they both stepped into the blood of Slade's victim. They slipped and nearly fell in the ever widening puddle. Judge Alice's shoe nearly fell off, but she held it on by curling her toes. She limped along as she tried to slip it back on, and then she thought, "Kick it off outside. Do not let him see you do it."

She continued to limp. The only thing holding the shoe in place was her curled up toes. As she stepped outside the house, she relaxed her foot, and the bloody shoe slipped off on the front step and lay there… unnoticed.

Slade pushed her into the front seat of the car and pushed her down in the seat. "Don't get up." He said in that still strangely calm voice.

Slade drove directly to his house. He parked in his driveway and looked up and down the street. It was very late. "No one is around. Good!" He walked around the car and opened the door. He had disabled the interior light of his car so that the darkness still served him well. He took the judge by the arm and led her up to the house. He was thrilled that his plan was working perfectly. He was so pleased with himself he did not pay attention to details. He did not notice Judge Alice was no longer limping. He did not notice the second bloody loafer was left sitting on the front step of his home.

Slade took her into a bedroom. There was nothing in the room but a chair, which was bolted to the floor. The room was painted black, and the window was boarded up. After he sat her in the chair, he took off his mask. "Slade," she thought to herself. Then she realized in horror, "Oh my God. He showed me his face. I am going to die in this chair."

"This was where my plants were. You took them away from me in your war, your illegal war on drugs. Now you are facing justice. You have been convicted in absentia. You have been captured, and now I will read the charges and soon the sentence will be carried out. The sentence is…" Slade put his head down and was silent and motionless for two minutes.

Judge Alice sat hoping, praying that he would not say what she knew he would say. The wait was unbearable. "So this is what it feels like to be a victim," she thought. "Death would be too good for this mother fucker," thought the lifelong opponent of the death penalty. "I would sentence this bastard to a long, slow…"

"Death!" said Slade. Saying the word and looking at her trembling body rekindled the fire. He looked at her nipples, hard from fear. He walked to her and slid the robe open exposing one of her breasts. "But first… spoils of war."

Chapter Twenty-six: "Fuckin' McCarthy"

As McCarthy walked into the classroom for line-up, everyone became suddenly quiet. This lasted for a moment or two, and then Stanley Brockman chimed in, "Hey, McCarthy. Did you enjoy your time off. How about for your next vacation you use my timeshare in fuckin' Darfur."

"I was thinking maybe you might like to take a cruise into the heart of the Devil's Triangle," said Carpenter.

"No peaceful disappearance for McCarthy. He likes gunfire to lull himself to sleep. I have some tickets to a kill-a-terrorist fantasy camp," said Madison Brown.

"You couldn't settle for turning this town periodically into a war zone, McCarthy, you have to take your show on the road to a peaceful little river town like La Crosse?" asked Brockman shaking his head walking over to Dan. "Fuckin' McCarthy," he said shaking Dan's hand. "Good job, Dyno. Remember now, when they give you a citation for that, what I said about those citations."

"Remind me, Stanley," said Dan.

"Stick to Charmin — the paper they use on citations is too coarse to wipe your ass with," answered Brockman. "Citations chafe."

Compton then walked into the room and set the line-up book down on the table in the front of the room. "This is kind of unique. First shift responded to another domestic at the Peterson house over on Victory Street this morning," said Compton.

"What's unique about that? The Petersons are always waging war on each other," said Brockman.

"When Tracy and Harrington got there this morning, Mrs. Peterson was beating the hell out of Mr. Peterson, and Mr. Peterson, who was sober for change and claiming innocence, reported to Harrington, 'All I did is wake up and give her a kiss and say good morning.'"

"Harrington then asked Mrs. Peterson, 'Is it true that your husband said good morning and you attacked him.'"

"'Not exactly,' explained Mrs. Peterson. 'He gave me a long, loving kiss and then said, "Good morning, Kathy," and then I attacked him, the son of bitch.'"

"'Why did you do that, ma'am?' asked Harrington."

"'Because my name is Susan!'"

"Then it says here she had to be restrained and taken to jail." said Compton. "True story."

After Compton started the shift off right… with a laugh, he hit all the bulletins, new warrants, missing persons, auto thefts, and recent burglaries. He then ended the line-up saying, "Nice job, McCarthy."

"Thanks, Sergeant," said McCarthy.

"One more thing. We are setting up another school for you in the sunny Gaza Strip. How does that sound?" asked Compton.

"No thanks, Sarge. I don't care for the Hamas cuisine," answered McCarthy, rubbing his stomach. "It gives me the Hershey squirts."

"Say, guys. It's itching tonight. You know the dirt ball barometer," Compton said, scratching a scar on his left hand that he received from a knife at a domestic many years ago. He claimed something big always happened when it itched. "If that's not enough, there is a full moon tonight."

"Did you ever notice that we are always busy when the dirt ball barometer itches?" Maddy Brown said to McCarthy.

"Oh yeah. That and full moons. I don't know if we are busy because there are forces in the universe at play that we don't understand, or if we generate more because we think things are going to happen and we are more perceptive then usual. I don't know which it is, but we are going to be busy tonight. I would bet on it."

McCarthy then thought, but kept to himself, the unwritten law of nature that cops swear by. "Look out. Shit happens in threes." McCarthy and every cop in the world knew this to be an unshakable fact. "Shit happens in threes." By McCarthy's figuring, the first of this current series was the Mad Mattix shootout. The next for him was definitely the Norberto Ruiz arrest and all of the devastation he wrought. "What next?" He did not know what, but he was certain Compton let him know when. It would happen tonight.

As McCarthy lapped River Street and Bluff Street, checking on how the bar crowd was doing, he saw a familiar face seated in a car stopped at the stop light right beside him. "I'll be damned! It's Billy Mitchell." McCarthy immediately punched Mitchell's name into the laptop in the squad.

Mitchell was oblivious, initially, of the squad, and then he felt a funny feeling on the back of his neck as if someone was watching him. He looked to his left and there he was, smiling and waving at Mitchell.

Billy panicked and gave McCarthy "the look." The look that tells a cop that something is wrong. Every seasoned veteran knows what "the look" looks like, and every court in the land should recognize it as justification for a street contact because it is as accurate as calculus in the hands of a highly trained mathematician. It is not considered grounds for stop, because people who are not mathematicians do not understand how calculus works, and people who are not cops do not understand how "the look" works.

Billy then said out loud, "Fuckin' McCarthy." He then smiled and waved back as the light changed to green, and he pulled out tying to be the perfect driver. "Holy shit, I have a gun on the seat!"

McCarthy's query came back with a ding. There was an active warrant for parole violation on Billy Mitchell. He had missed his most recent appointment for his parole agent, during which a urine test was required. Billy thought taking a urine test at this juncture to be imprudent. He skipped it.

McCarthy let Billy pull ahead, and then he maneuvered the squad behind Billy. He called in to dispatch, "255, could you verify a warrant on Billy Mitchell. The computer shows an active warrant for parole violation on him."

"10-4, 255. That warrant was just entered into the system by me an hour ago. It is confirmed, and I have a hard copy right in front of me," said the dispatcher confidently.

"10-4. I am behind him now, and he is driving southbound on River Street from Diamond. Could you send me a back-up. He usually runs and fights," said McCarthy. He held off hitting the lights. He would wait for his back-up if Billy would be patient.

Billy watched McCarthy pull in behind him. He watched in the rearview mirror while McCarthy made his transmissions. He could not wait. The gun he had on the seat was taken in the burglary at Bill's Gun Shop. He had kept it. He liked the feel of the weapon. He thought he might need it. "Fuckin' McCarthy!"

Billy grabbed the weapon and reached as far as he could and stuck the gun under the passenger seat and then straightened back up and checked the mirror again. "Fuckin' McCarthy, what are you doing?"

McCarthy saw the movement. It was obvious. The courts called it "furtive." He would now be able to search under the seat for his own protection and because he was going to make an arrest. Then he thought, "Was he reaching to hide something under the seat or reaching to get something from under the seat." It was impossible to tell.

"Dispatch, I am going to take Mitchell high risk when I stop him. There is something going on. He just reached for something or ditched something under the seat." said McCarthy.

"10-4. 257 and 259 are heading your way. They will be a couple minutes," answered the dispatcher.

"10-4," said McCarthy. "I will hold off until they get to me, and then we will set up the stop," said McCarthy.

"Fuckin' McCarthy," said Billy as he punched the accelerator to the floor. He was not going back to prison. If he could loose McCarthy and ditch the gun, he would only have a fleeing charge. If he got caught with this gun, he was going down and probably Zach with him. Billy had weighed all his options, and fleeing was his best bet at doing some short jail time rather than hard time at Waupun.

McCarthy was not shocked. He half expected it as Billy's car began pulling away, as if the squad was parked. McCarthy hit the lights and siren and breathed in through his nose and out through his mouth. "Stay calm, so they can understand you," he said to himself as he keyed the mic, "255. I have a 10-80 (high speed pursuit). We are traveling southbound on River Street at 70, now 80, now 90 miles per hour. Advise the shift commander that traffic is light and the pursuit is in reference to a felony warrant."

"10-4," said dispatch. There was a pause. "The shift commander has been advised; he will monitor the pursuit."

Billy then hit the brakes. The front end of the car was pile driven forward, and the rear end came up and began to fish tail slightly back and forth. Then he turned left, and in one block he turned left again.

Mitchell was maneuvering so fast he made both turns before McCarthy could get on the radio. "255. He is northbound on Bluff Street, now. He is traveling at 75 mph right now. Is there anyone who can get set up with the road spikes?"

"257. I will try to get into position and set up," said Maddy Brown.

Mitchell watched McCarthy and saw that he had gained on him and held tightly to him on the turn. "Fuckin' McCarthy!" he yelled out loudly in a rage.

Mitchell suddenly slammed on the brakes and turned right, sliding left and hitting the curb. A hub flew off, a tire blew, and none of this caused him to stop. He continued on his flight toward jail rather than prison. Mitchell knew the system. His parole agent would not revoke him for a pursuit. Bad guys run from cops. He would revoke him for breaking into a gun store and selling guns to a homicidal maniac who wanted to "make war" on God knows who.

Mitchell checked the rearview mirror and saw McCarthy was right on him. With a flat tire he would not out run McCarthy in this car. Mitchell slammed on the brakes, sliding his car to a stop, so the driver's door was angled away from McCarthy. Mitchell was out and running before his car even came to a complete stop.

McCarthy called out, "Seventh and Hennepin, eastbound, foot pursuit." Then McCarthy was out of the squad. McCarthy had chased Mitchell before. McCarthy's lifestyle and training schedule had been kinder to McCarthy than Mitchell's lifestyle had been.

Mitchell had started with quite a lead, and McCarthy was pulling inevitably closer to an impending collision with Billy Mitchell.

Billy Mitchell cut across a bank parking lot, which was devoid of cars because of the late hour. His lungs were burning and his legs were weighing him down. He looked around and "Fuckin' McCarthy" was gaining on him. Mitchell was running out of options. He thought as he ran, "If I would have brought the gun, I would shoot fuckin' McCarthy right now. Shit — puff puff, pant pant, puff puff, pant pant. Every time I run from McCarthy he does his judo shit, spins me down and makes me hurt — puff puff, pant pant. Fuck it! I'll fight him standing up. I think I can take this fucker standing up," thought Billy, who had one thing in common with McCarthy. He was a positive thinker.

As Billy nearly reached the far side of the parking lot he spun suddenly and got into a boxer's stance. "Come on, McCarthy. I'm sick of you fuckin' with me. Let's see what you've got!" shouted Billy.

McCarthy pulled up and transmitted into his collar mic. "I'll be involved in a 10-10 (fight) with Mitchell in the parking lot of the Governmental Employees Credit Union."

McCarthy got into a defensive stance and moved in a circle with Billy keeping his guard up. He could see that Billy was tired. Maybe back-up would get here and he would give up. McCarthy could hear the sirens, and they were about one minute or more out. A lot can happen on the street between a cop and a desperate criminal in one minute. One minute can be a lifetime some times.

Billy jabbed twice at McCarthy, and McCarthy pivoted out of the way. "Come on, Billy. Stop resisting. Get down on the ground. You are under arrest. Give it up!"

"Fuck you, McCarthy — puff puff, pant pant. I'm not going back to prison — puff puff, pant pant." Billy then picked up his right leg and thrust a pretty good looking kick in the direction of where McCarthy was, but by the time it reached where McCarthy was, he had pivoted to his left, hooked his arm to his side, and caught the leg as Billy tried to retrieve it. As Billy hopped momentarily on his left leg, he looked at McCarthy and said, "Fuckin' McCarthy!"

McCarthy hooked his second arm under the right leg of Billy and lifted up sharply, dropping Billy onto his back. McCarthy then twisted Billy's right foot, causing him to flop to his stomach and McCarthy slid smoothly into a painful leg lock. "Stop resisting Billy! You are under arrest. Give me your hands!"

The pain shot from his calf straight to his brain. He had fought McCarthy before. He had felt this pain before. He knew what to do now. There was only one thing to do. His hands shot quickly behind his back in total submission. "OK — puff puff, pant pant. Ok — puff puff, pant pant. I give — puff puff, pant pant." McCarthy slipped on the handcuffs effortlessly at this point as Maddy Brown came sliding into the lot.

Mitchell was searched and placed in Maddy's car. "Can you take him to interview room number one?" asked McCarthy.

"You bet," said Maddy.

As Maddy pulled away, Mitchell looked back at McCarthy and said, "Fuckin' McCarthy."

"Try to take on McCarthy?" asked Maddy. "How'd that work out for ya?"

"I'm like oh-for-three or — puff pant — or oh-for-four with McCarthy," said Mitchell.

Then Billy shifted gears and smiled, "I think I need to ask for a different arresting officer. How about you, Sweetheart? I'd much rather grapple with you. How about it? I'd even let you pin me," said Billy, reeking with all the charm a street urchin like him could muster.

"Be still my heart," said Maddy. "I will put you on my calendar for Friday night five to ten years from now. How's that sound?"

"It's a date. My calendar is free," smiled Billy. Then his smile waned and he added, "I hope I will be."

McCarthy entered the room about one half hour later, and Billy sat emotionless at the table. McCarthy handed him a cold Pepsi. "If I remember right, this is what you drink."

"Yeah. Thanks, McCarthy."

McCarthy then said, "I am going to read you your rights, and then I want to ask you some questions about the gun in the car. We know it came from Bill's. We checked the tapes, and I personally can say that it is you and Zach in the store. You can make us work for it or you can help yourself. It's up to you. Don't say anything yet."

McCarthy then read Billy his rights. Billy waived them and then said, "I will talk to you, but I want some assurances. I was going to come in and tell you guys anyway until you stopped me and fucked everything up. Now, I will talk. It's big. You might even prevent a murder. No murders. I am sure of it, but I need a district attorney, and I need to know I will receive some heavy consideration for my cooperation in sentencing. This is no shit, McCarthy," said Billy taking a long drink out of his Pepsi. He set it down on the table and said, "Your move, McCarthy. You like to be a fuckin' hero. Here's your chance. The shit's goin' down soon if not now. Now's your chance, McCarthy! Don't fuckin' blow it. Like they say in the movies, this is bigger than the both of us!"

Kei Satsu Jitsu

The Police Way of Combat

Chapter Twenty-seven: The Barking Dog

Holmes was lying in his pen relishing the aftertaste of raw hamburger when he heard the front door slam. His head popped up and his ears folded back. He heard a muffled cry of his beloved master and a car door slam. Holmes began to bark. Something was wrong. Something was terribly wrong. He had no clue what, but he knew something was wrong.

Holmes barked for one hour straight before a neighbor woke up and called 911.

Maddy Brown was just clearing from the station after dropping Billy Mitchell off.

"257," Maddy said.

"257, report of a barking dog at 2225 Park Drive. I will send you some additional information via computer," said dispatch. "The complainant will press charges. She wants a citation issued."

"10-4," said Maddy.

Maddy wheeled her squad toward the call, pulled up the call screen on her computer, and saw the name of the dog owner. "Judge Alice. Man, everyone else is chasing down bad guys, and I have to write a barking dog ticket to a judge. Great. This will be a wonderful career enhancer. She already hates cops in general. Now she will have a reason to hate me specifically. Shit, this is McCarthy's beat. If he wasn't tied up all the time, he would be handling his own barking dog calls. Fuckin' McCarthy."

As Maddy pulled up, she parked under a Hackberry tree to allow for a cautious approach to the house. On the night shift, certain precautions were second nature to Maddy, even on a barking dog complaint.

"Howl... howl... howl... howl," echoed through the otherwise quiet neighborhood. The dog wanted in, wanted out, wanted something.

Maddy went up to the front door, and then there it was, exactly where it shouldn't be. It was a shoe. It was a woman's flat-bottom, slip-on shoe. It was a woman's flat-bottom, slip-on dress-shoe, *covered with blood.*

"257. Send me a back-up and a sergeant 10-33 but have them come in silent. I do not know exactly what I have, but something is terribly wrong here," said Maddy, her voice on edge.

"I copied," said Compton. "I'm 10-76 (en route)."

"I'm 10-23 (arriving) right now," said Dooley, who recognized the address and was heading over. He had been there before to have Judge Alice sign search warrants.

While waiting for their arrival, Maddy Brown took her weapon out and circled the house, cautiously checking the area. She could see no movement in the house, but when she reached the patio door, she saw a round hole cut in the glass of the patio door. "I have a burglary here. Send additional units."

When Compton arrived, he positioned units covering the outside, and he took Dooley and Maddy Brown inside. "This is exigent circumstances. Stay together on the search. Watch out for suspects and also for the possibility of disturbing evidence."

The front door was unlocked. Compton entered first and was quickly followed by Maddy and Dooley. There was no doubt about what they had. Jack Sloan's lifeless body was the first thing each of them saw when they entered the house. "230. We have a 10-100 (death) definitely not natural. Call the bureau. We are still clearing the house."

McCarthy looked at Mitchell, who sat smug and determined at the table. He took the Miranda Waiver and left the suspect, locking the door behind him. He walked to the front desk, where newly promoted Sergeant Randy Stammos sat.

"230. We have a 10-100 (death) definitely not natural. Call the bureau. We are still clearing the house," said Compton on the radio.

"Where are they at?" asked McCarthy.

"They are out at a barking dog call at Judge Alice's house," said Stammos. "It sounds like the proverbial shit has just hit the fan." Stammos was on the phone, "Yeah, hello. Captain Severson. Compton is out at Judge Alice's house, and they are still clearing it, but I am pretty sure we will need detectives in here. They report they have a dead one and it is not natural." Then Stammos listened and answered, "Yes, sir, I'll give him a call right away."

"It's going to get crazy here, Dyno, what do you have on Mitchell?" asked Stammos, holding the phone, about to place another call.

"I have him on fleeing and tied in with Bill's Gun Shop, but I think he has something to do with this," said McCarthy.

"That would be highly fortuitous," said Stammos with a false haughty air. "Get what you can get, and let me know what you've got as soon as you get it." Then Stammos was back on the phone.

McCarthy listened for a bit, and when Compton radioed that they had a crime scene he called dispatch. "Yeah, this is McCarthy. Can you have Compton call me at 1119 as soon as he can. I know he's busy, but I have some information for him," asked McCarthy.

"230. When you get a chance call 255 at 1119," said dispatch.

Less than a minute passed, and the phone McCarthy was parked by rang. "McCarthy."

"Yeah. What have you got?" asked Compton.

"This is the deal. I have Billy Mitchell connected to the Bill's Gun Shop burglary. He says he wants to deal on something big that is about to go down or going down, and he will not talk until he gets a DA and certain agreements," said McCarthy. "I need to know what happened there because I've got a feeling it is related."

"Jack Sloan is dead. He was shot. It looks like Judge Alice has been abducted. She left or dropped a bloody shoe on the front door step. I have the detectives coming here. We are going to be busy. If you think you can get Mitchell to talk on your own, go ahead. It looks like the judge left here alive, and I do not know how long that will last. Take the ball and run," said Compton.

"Yes, sir," said McCarthy.

McCarthy filled Stammos in on what he had. "Make sure you have the cameras rolling," said Stammos. "Good Luck!"

McCarthy moved Billy Mitchell into interview room number two, where a camera was mounted. He started the digital recorder taping and then went over his rights again. "OK, OK, we did this. I said I would cooperate if I had a deal and some promises."

"Well, Billy, I cannot make you any promises. You told me some serious things were going to go down, and I believe you. In fact, I think they are happening as we speak. We have Jack Sloan dead, and Judge Alice has been abducted from her home. Since I believe one plus one usually equals two, I am guessing that the gun involved in the Sloan homicide is one that came out of Bill's Gun Shop. I am also guessing that when all is said and done, we will find out that you are up to your ears in this. Now, the choice is yours. Tell us what you know. This is possibly is your chance to be a hero or your chance to be an accomplice in a homicide and kidnapping." McCarthy knew he had him. Billy's eyes opened wide. Mitchell knew, but he did not know.

As soon as McCarthy finished his last sentence, Billy was giving a statement that came out so fast it sounded as if Billy's native tongue was magpie. "I didn't know. He just wanted some guns. You guys took his guns. I was afraid of the guy, so I did the job for him. I sold him some guns, and then he starts telling me about some crazy God damn war on drugs, and he was a soldier and I was a soldier and all this crazy scary bullshit. I almost came down to tell you guys, but then I thought I am truly fucked either way. Man, I didn't know he was going to kill no lawyer and kidnap a judge. Man, the guy's crazy. He's fucking nuts. He talked about war and killing a lot of people." Billy then dropped his head into his hands and began to cry.

"Who?" asked McCarthy.

"Harley David Slade," said Billy. "You busted him the night I called, when he was hanging outside my house. He was really pissed, but Jack Sloan got him in front of Judge Alice, and she let him walk," sobbed Mitchell. "McCarthy, you got to help me, man."

McCarthy left Mitchell crying into his hands and ran down the hall to Stammos. Stammos hung up the phone and then began to dial another number.

"I think the guy who did this is Harley David Slade. Mitchell says he did the gun shop for Harley. Harley told him he was going to wage a war on drugs against… whomever. Sloan was his attorney and Judge Alice was the judge he appeared in front of. Billy says he sold him guns and thinks he did this," said McCarthy.

"I am running out of people on this," said Stammos.

"How about you call out the team and get some bodies in here. I will leave Billy locked in room number two. I will swing over to Slade's house and see what I can see," said McCarthy.

"I'll call out the team on a hunch, McCarthy, but I hope you are right. This is my first night in stripes, and I don't want to loose them for at least a week or two. One night would be embarrassing," said Stammos.

McCarthy parked his squad a block down from Slade's house. As he approached on foot, he could see that every house in the neighborhood was dark. McCarthy had a great deal of difficulty staying in the shadows because the moon was high in the sky like the proverbial big pizza pie. When he got one yard over from Slade's, he could see that every light in the house was on, that is, except one room. It was unnaturally dark. McCarthy, for whatever reason, approached at a slow walk and was drawn to the dark room. He was concerned, at first, that the room's window might be open and Slade would be able to sit inside and see him approach from the darkened room. As he got closer, he could see that the room was boarded shut from the inside. "Hello," thought McCarthy.

McCarthy paused and looked the scene over. There was no movement in the lighted rooms that he could see. Slade had cheap shades pulled. McCarthy could see in through the gaps between the shade and the window frame. The curtains were not drawn.

McCarthy looked over the car parked in the driveway and Slade's van parked in the street. Then… hold… what… McCarthy saw it. It was on the front step lit up. A moonbeam shined on it like a spot light on Broadway. It was a woman's dark slip-on shoe.

McCarthy moved slowly, cautiously alongside Slade's car. He got as close to the boarded window as possible. He could hear Slade on a rant. "You have been found guilty in my court of..." and then the words were muffled. McCarthy could tell Slade was pacing as he spoke, coming closer and then moving farther away. Then there was a long silence. Suddenly Slade shouted, "Death. The sentence will be carried out at dawn! The condemned may speak now."

Then McCarthy heard it. He barely heard it. It sounded like a muffled woman's cry.

"Dawn. A little more than an hour," thought McCarthy.

McCarthy moved to the bushes and called Stammos, "Randy. I am at Slade's in the bushes to the southwest corner. He is inside and I am quite sure that Judge Alice is inside. I heard him say something about death at dawn and heard what sounded like a muffled woman's cry. I do not believe I need a warrant, but I would like some back up, a shield, and something reliable to breach this door with."

"Some of the team is already here. I called them in. Captain Jackson was unavailable, but Captain Hale is here. Just a second, here is Sergeant Compton."

"What do you have?" asked Compton.

"I have a shoe on the step outside the house. I have lights on except in the front room on the south side. That window is boarded up. I heard Slade ranting, and he said something about death at dawn, and then I heard a muffled cry. I think the judge is inside. I don't think I need a warrant to go in. We have exigency, but to be successful I feel the team should be here. Mitchell said he sold a number of guns to Slade, and there is no doubt in my mind he will use them this time," said McCarthy.

"We'll stage to the south. We'll let you know when we arrive. You know best where to be. Try not to trigger anything unless we are ready," said Compton.

"Yes, sir, Sergeant," said McCarthy.

As Compton hung up, he turned and saw Hale standing behind him.

"What's going on?" asked Hale, who had just arrived. Due to the nature of the case, he was anticipating a media blitz on the disappearance of a judge and the murder of an attorney. Since the chief, the assistant chief, and the captain of patrol were out of town at the International Association of Chiefs of Police Conference, that made him the ranking officer on the department.

"Sir, McCarthy thinks he has located the judge. He believes she is being held inside Harley David Slade's house in a boarded up room. He is at the house, and we are going to see what we can do."

"You are not going into that house and getting that woman killed with your macho SWAT team bullshit," said Hale.

"Respectfully, sir, I am officer in charge of the SWAT team, and I am responsible in SWAT call-outs to make these decisions. The chief has given me that authority. It may be advisable to hit the house when he has no idea we know she is in there with him. The opportunity might present itself, and we have to have the ability to be flexible on that issue. Sir, it needs to be the commander on the scene's call," said Compton.

"Here is the deal. You will make contact, and you will negotiate first. That's an order, Sergeant Compton! I am the chief in his absence, and that is an order!" said Hale.

"Respectfully, sir, we may do that, but we need to have flexibility here. Please do not take away my authority to make decisions on the scene. I need that flexibility," pleaded Compton.

"I am saying you may not do anything unless you first try to negotiate. Do you understand, Sergeant Compton? I'll not have another wild west shootout on my watch. Do you understand, Sergeant Compton?" said Captain Hale.

"Sir, yes, sir!" barked Compton looking straight ahead, needing to conjure up the Marine in him to restrain himself.

Compton went down to the classroom. Hale followed him and sat in the back of the room to make sure his orders were not usurped. Compton quickly drew Slade's house on the board. "We have been given a very important task. McCarthy is out at Harley David Slade's house. We suspect he is holding Judge Alice hostage.

I have sent Carpenter and Hartley ahead. They are here and here, cornering off the house. I have a marked squad already in position here in the event that he goes mobile. I will be the team leader on this particular call-out because Captain Hale has taken over as officer in charge."

Team members present looked back at Hale, who smiled and nodded his head.

"Gloria, you will establish contact as soon as we are in position and try to negotiate his surrender. We will use the Kwik Trip one block from the scene as a command post. The arrest team/entry team will stage wherever we are directed to by McCarthy at the scene. Dooley, you will be the shield man. We all know Judge Alice, and we all know Slade. Slade is known to have an AR-15 and a 308, so take the heavy shield. Stammos, I want you with the breaching shotgun. If we have to enter dynamic, we will bang (flash bang) the room on entry. I want all weapons on semi-automatic on this call. We have a hostage, and we do not want to hit the hostage. I will be armed with an M-16, and I will have it on semi-automatic. We will use McCarthy on the arrest/entry team as well. Sniper's will be posted here and here," indicating positions on both sides of the house. "Are there any questions?"

There were no questions. "Let's roll."

Captain Hale traveled with the team. He loved the sound of that, "officer in charge."

He had checked the policy, and Compton was technically right; the spirit of the policy was to have Compton calling the shots. There was a line that allowed a ranking member of the department to take over command of the team when the assigned officer in charge was absent or under extraordinary conditions. Hale felt these were those conditions. Hale had no SWAT training. He was not a trained negotiator. He had contempt for the team and thought them unnecessary. "We managed years without them."

When the team arrived at the Kwik Trip, they stacked and moved to a position in the yard next to Slade's house. The entry team met McCarthy there. They had cover of a brick retaining wall.

"How does it look?" asked Compton.

"All the lights are on in the house. Shades are pulled, but there is a gap in them on the edges, and you can see him moving around occasionally. I have heard him ranting, and the only indication I have that she is in there is when he said the death sentence would be executed at dawn I heard a muffled women's voice. The perimeter is in place, and the chase car is in place. I planned on taking him down before he got into the car if he came out before you got here. Oh, then there is the shoe out on the front step," said McCarthy.

"Hold here. I want to see that shoe." Compton climbed over the wall and moved to a position alongside Slade's car. He looked carefully over the car and then came back quickly and quietly behind the retaining wall.

"That's the same type of shoe as was left on the judge's step. It is too coincidental. I think the judge was thinking on her feet. She left us some probable cause," said Compton.

The radio then cracked in Compton's ear piece. "The suspect just pulled up the shade in the back of the house and looked out the window. He is in the kitchen at the back of the house," reported Carpenter.

Compton contacted Captain Hale. "Captain, I request permission to make entry. The suspect is in the kitchen, away from the victim."

"Negative, Sergeant Compton. We are requesting a warrant and about to establish contact. We do not know she is in there, nor where she is. Stand by," said Captain Hale.

"Be advised that there is a shoe on the front step identical to the one left on the judge's step," reported Compton.

"Standby, Sergeant!" said Hale with disgust in his voice.

Slade stepped into the kitchen to make the judge a last meal. On his reconnaissance, he had noticed she had ordered a chicken salad sandwich, and he had made some up special for this occasion. As he sliced the bread in quarters, he thought he heard something outside. He pulled the shade up and looked hard but saw nothing. He had such disdain for the police and their abilities, he could not conceive that anyone could have penetrated his perfect plan. He peered deep into the darkness and saw nothing.

He went to the refrigerator and poured an ice tea and cut a lemon and put it in the glass, just like she had ordered it. He then set the sandwich plate on a tray along with the iced tea and carried it carefully out of the kitchen through the living-room, and just before he turned into the hallway, the phone rang.

"The phone? What the…" said Slade.

Slade set the tray down and then slowly picked up the receiver. He put it to his ear. He said nothing.

"Hello. Mr. Slade," said the voice on the phone.

Slade said nothing.

"Harley David Slade, this is Officer Gloria Dooley of the La Claire Police Department. I'd like to talk to you please," said Gloria.

Slade did not panic. He had prepared for this. A man without a plan, without contingencies would have panicked. Slade had planned for this possibility.

"This is Harley David Slade, what do you want?" asked Slade.

"We would like you to come out the front door with your hands up please."

"Why? What have I done? I have been seeing my probation officer. I have done nothing wrong," said Slade.

"Harley, can I call you Harley?" asked Gloria.

"Go ahead. It's my name," said Slade.

"We would like to talk to you about an incident earlier. Could you please step outside," requested Gloria.

"No, I don't think so, and if you come in, she dies! Call me back in fifteen minutes. I have to think about this. Call me back." Slade hung up.

The police now wanted to negotiate. He would negotiate with them until he decided the negotiation would be over.

"Sergeant Compton," said Hale.

"Go ahead," said Compton.

"We have established contact with the suspect. We have confirmed that he is holding a female. We should have the warrant in hand shortly, but be advised, stand by. He wants to talk," said Hale.

"10-4," said Compton.

Compton was a good cop, but before he was a good cop, he was a good Marine. Good Marines obey orders. His instincts told him that they missed a golden opportunity to take Slade without harm to the judge, and his instincts were golden. That was all a flight that flew. He would now have to quickly grab the next opportunity. He was a Marine, and he took orders well even when the orders were from a superior who was his inferior. Compton used to tell the officers when they complained about commanders, "Hey, just relax. Your life will be much less stressful when you realize that some people have the authority to be wrong." Compton said that often. "Some people have the authority to be wrong," he thought. The thought gave him little solace tonight, even if it was a rock solid fact proven once again by Captain Hale.

Slade calmly walked to a closet at the end of the hallway and opened the door. There, neatly arranged, was his arsenal. Each weapon was cleaned, racked, stacked, loaded, and charged with each safety off.

He picked out the simplest one of all. It was one he had bought from an old derelict that frequented the Rump. It was a Savage single shot 12-gauge shotgun with a sawed off twelve-inch barrel. "Yes. This will do."

He broke the barrel open slowly and saw the magnum round of .00 buck in the chamber. ".00 buck. Nine 33-caliber pellets released with one squeeze of the trigger. That'll do the trick," he said to himself. He closed the barrel.

He tucked the phone in the side pocket of his tactical pants he bought specially for the war. He picked up the tray with one hand like a waiter and in the other he carried the shotgun along side his leg. "Now it's time for her last meal."

Slade entered the room where Judge Alice sat engulfed in her fear. He set the tray and the shotgun down.

"I made you something to eat," he said as he ripped the duct tape from her mouth.

She let out a pained cry, but he covered her bleeding mouth with his hand instantly to muffle it.

Slade picked up a quarter of the chicken salad sandwich. "Your favorite." He said as he pushed the sandwich against her mouth. "Eat!" She ate what would be her last chicken salad sandwich one bite at a time. It tasted of Miracle Whip and dread. She did not need Miracle Whip right now. She needed a miracle.

When she finished the sandwich, the phone rang.

"Hello!" said Slade.

"Yes. This is Officer Dooley. Harley, we would like you to come out. No one needs to be hurt," said Officer Dooley.

"I'm coming out. I will come out through the front door. Give me fifteen minutes. I will send her out to you. She is alive, and she will be coming out alive. I give you my word. If you come in, I will kill her," said Slade and he hung up.

Back at the Kwik Trip, Gloria had the phones wired to a speaker so that Hale could hear everything. "Yes!" he said. "He's coming out the front door and she's alive." Hale immediately keyed the radio. "Hale to Compton," said Hale.

"Go ahead," said Compton, hunkered down by the wall with his team.

"He is coming out the front door in fifteen minutes. She is alive, and he is sending her out also. The order is a red light. Stand by," transmitted Hale sounding triumphant.

"Red light? What does he mean red light?" asked McCarthy.

"He has watched too many movies," said Dooley.

Compton did not quite know what Hale meant by red light, and he was afraid to ask for clarification. He decided the ambiguity of the order served the team better than clarification. They did not need their hands tied when Slade came out the door. Compton's instincts told him Slade was not coming out the door peacefully, and his instincts were platinum.

Compton repositioned the arrest team to safely make the arrest. He put them on a line parallel to the sidewalk leading from the front door of the house. Dooley was assigned to go forward with the shield if Slade agreed to comply and go prone. McCarthy was assigned to talk to Slade and hopefully talk him into a high risk prone position. McCarthy would approach from behind the shield and handcuff. An ambulance was on standby down at the command post in the event it was needed. Traffic was closed off, and a reverse 911 line had ordered neighbors to stay off the street and stay in their basements.

The fifteen minutes came and went. Twenty minutes passed by. Finally, as the sun started coming up, McCarthy turned to Compton and said, "Dawn."

SWAT
Blue Knights in Black Armor

Chapter Twenty-eight: Dawn

There was a noise at the front door of Slade's house.

Compton shook his head with concern on his face. "Dawn. Shit. Dawn!"

"Be ready. Here he comes," whispered Compton.

The front door opened. "We're coming out!" shouted Slade.

The door opened, and Slade pushed the judge out of the door. "What the…?" said Dooley.

The judge was dressed in her bathrobe and barefoot. She was heavily duct taped about her mouth and neck, and the tape connected her to the muzzle of a single barrel sawed off shotgun. Slade had duct taped his hand to the grip of the shotgun. He boldly walked out of the house and then tripped and nearly fell over the shoe left by Judge Alice.

He looked at the judge and cursed, "Damn you!"

Slade stopped. His eyes fluttered as he tried to regain his composure. He did not want it to end yet. He took a deep drag off the marijuana cigarette he held lit in his left hand.

"If any one shoots, she dies," yelled Slade.

McCarthy stood behind Dooley and the shield. He didn't quite know how to start. He could not say drop the gun. "Harley. It's Dan McCarthy of the La Claire Police Department. I can see that you are upset. What has got you so upset?"

"What's got me upset, you ask? You, McCarthy! Cops! Judges! Lawyers! You come into my home and shut down my business. You take my money, my plants, my whole reason for being, and then this bitch arrogantly sits on a bench looking down at me holding my fate in her hands. The worm has turned, now, hasn't it, your honor," Slade said pushing her to her knees with the shotgun.

The sniper had a clear shot, but he did not quite know how to process the combination of the uniqueness of the situation coupled with the order "red light." He did nothing but look through his scope and hope. He had been trained that there was no such thing as a "red light." There was no such thing as a "green light." He had been trained that he was to make his own decisions. He was trained that taking a life was his decision based on each situation, but the sniper heard the words from a captain, "red light."

"Shit!" was all he could say.

"This is your war on drugs. You declared war on me, so I declared war right back. Waging an illegal war in America against the citizens of this country is treason. Treason in time of war is punishable by death. When the sun comes up, she will die," rambled on Slade.

The judge looked around hoping... praying... and then when nothing happened, she gave in to despair.

McCarthy aimed, but the shot was too long for a handgun. If he was off by an inch, he would not totally and instantaneously incapacitate, and Harley would kill the judge in his last desperate act. Something had to be done. Slade was going to kill this woman.

"Slade, drop the weapon. Do it now. Let the judge go!" shouted McCarthy.

"Sniper to Captain Hale. You said 'red light.' I would like to take a shot. Request permission to shoot," said the sniper, not believing his words as they came out of his mouth.

The radio was silent. Hale was silent.

"Well, your honor. We did not get a call from the governor. I guess your sentence will be carried out," said Slade, smiling.

"Crack!"

The round went into the left ear of Harley David Slade, expanded instantly and considerably, and continued through his brain stem. It stopped just short of Slade's right temple.

Slade crumpled limply to the ground like a house of cards. He was dead instantly, before the bullet even reached its final resting point inside his demonic skull.

"Suspect is down and 10-100," said Sergeant Compton calmly over the radio. "All units stand by and hold your positions. I need an ambulance right now in front of the residence."

Compton then stacked the team behind Dooley's shield, and they made their approach cautiously and quickly. When the team reached her, Judge Alice lay quivering on the sidewalk next to Slade. She was still attached to the shotgun and convinced that it still might go off at any second. She was right. If she had moved at all to pull away she would have died.

Compton let his M-16 hang from its bungee sling and put it on safe. He took his search and rescue knife out of its sheath and said soothingly, "Please, your honor, stay as still as you can. Do not pull in any direction." Compton then carefully cut the duct tape away from the muzzle of the shotgun. "Can you walk?" he asked.

She shook her head tentatively.

"Dooley. McCarthy. Take the team and clear the house. Watch out for accomplices, booby traps, trip wires, etc." Dooley had been holding a position between the judge and the house and they moved instantly.

"Are you OK to walk, your honor?" asked the Compton.

She shook her head yes.

"Compton to command post, have that ambulance park one block south of the scene. We still have not cleared the house."

Compton put his arm around the judge. He cut the tape freeing her hands and she instantly threw her arms around him and began to cry. She held him tightly around his vest. She stumbled when she got to her feet, so Compton picked her up and carried her to the ambulance. He laid her gently onto the stretcher.

As he started to leave, she took him by the hand and held it. She looked at the soft warm blue eyes under the hard, cold black helmet and she sheepishly said, "God bless you. Thank you so much."

"You're welcome, ma'am," said Compton. "You'll be all right now. It's over."

As Compton turned and paused, she watched him. She watched all of them. She looked at them through different eyes. She had never been a victim before this day. She had never looked into the eyes of a killer before this day. She would never again look at many things the same way she had just twenty-four hours before.

She looked at Compton framed by the door of the ambulance. There was a time she thought SWAT officers were mindless jack booted macho thugs. She felt her main purpose as a judge was to protect the public from their heavy-handed over-zealous tactics. On this day, she was thrust into the real world by Harley David Slade. Now, all she could see was she had been a damsel in distress and she had been rescued by knights in black armor.

Colt M-16 in the hands
of a modern knight in black armor

Chapter Twenty-nine: Marine

It was over twenty-four hours before most of the officers involved in the kidnapping of Judge Alice, investigation, and rescue would lie their heads down on a pillow. The only one that slept well when they did was Sergeant David Compton. Slade was an easier kill then any of the North Vietnamese soldiers he had killed in Vietnam. Compton had great respect for the enemy he fought in Vietnam. Soldiers who answered their country's call many times learn to give respect to a noble, hard fighting enemy.

Compton had given little thought to the shooting of Harley David Slade, other than whether he had proper sight alignment, breath control, and a good smooth trigger squeeze. It was one of the easiest kills he had ever made with an M-16. He was twenty-five feet away, and Slade was turned sideways and stationery. No Vietnamese adversary had ever been so obliging to Compton. Harley needed killing, and Compton was glad to oblige him right back. As far as Compton was concerned, Slade had been a righteous kill done by an honorable warrior.

Hale slept well also. Hale continued to keep his incompetence a secret. It was a secret to absolutely no one but himself. The cat would soon be let out of the bag.

One who had difficulty sleeping that night was the sniper, who had been given a "red light," when he knew there was, "*No such God damned thing in real SWAT!*" he told his wife, when he came home. "*There is no red light in SWAT!*"

McCarthy had trouble sleeping. He didn't quite know why. He told Victoria, "I know I did not have a shot yet. I am concerned, though, because of the Mattix shooting that I might be gun shy."

Victoria said soothingly, "Dan. Don't you belong to a team? Didn't you call them because you knew on this one you needed the team's help? Weren't you assigned to talk and then cuff? I am sorry,

Honey, but living with you has apparently given me more insight on SWAT than you because even I know 'long guns for long shots' is how that one was supposed to be handled." She finished with confidence in her answer.

"How did you get so smart?" asked McCarthy.

"I have always been the smart one in this marriage. You have just lived with me long enough to get smart enough to realize it," answered McCarthy's most ready and available back-up.

"Wow. I married a sexy blonde with brains," whispered McCarthy kissing her soft red lips. The two slipped under the sheets, still kissing.

Judge Alice was hospitalized and was heavily sedated. Her life had been changed forever in less than eight hours. She did not know if she could be a judge again. She did not know if she could practice law again. Before the sedatives allowed her to sleep and dream her horrible dreams, she did not know if she would even be able to get out of the bed she was in and ever face the world again.

Judge Alice had been victimized in every way a woman could be and still live. The problem with being victimized so horribly and still retaining life is the victim has to learn how to live again. This type of victimization is as damaging as a stroke. The victim has to relearn how to do everything that was so automatic before. They have to gain the strength to get out of bed, they have to learn how to dress themselves, how to put one foot in front of the other and walk through a day. They have to learn how to communicate with people they know and especially those they do not know. It would not be easy, but she was a strong woman. She would have help.

A debrief was scheduled the day after the killing of Jack Sloan and the abduction and rescue of Judge Alice. Chief Ray Johnson flew back immediately from the chief's conference in New Orleans to attend the debrief. The entire SWAT team, detectives, and the night shift were present, as was Captain Hale.

After the synopsis of the night's events was read by Sergeant Compton, he asked if anyone thought improvements could be made or special recognition should be given to actions taken.

Detective Sergeant Joe Darnell raised his hand and said, "You know, when I arrived at the scene, patrol had been all through the house. Valuable evidence is lost forever when patrol officers tromp through a crime scene. They do it all the time and they never learn."

Compton knew what he was going to do. He had listened to pompous asses too long to listen to them anymore. "Sergeant Darnell. Thank you for your input, but the initial responding officer was Officer Maddy Brown. She was not responding to a homicide. She was responding to a barking dog. It was because of her keen observation and follow-up of those observations that led to the discovery of the body of Jack Sloan. At that time, they had to do a protective sweep of the scene to determine if there were anymore victims or a possible suspect still at the scene. To do that, the scene had to be entered. I respectfully disagree with your application of your perennial complaint about every crime scene you have ever come to. When you arrived at the scene, the scene was secured, and you were debriefed on the location of evidence observed, what areas were ventured into during the sweep, and who entered those areas. That is the best we can ever do during a crime scene in progress. Anything else, Detective?" asked Compton.

Carpenter raised his hand.

"Yes, Gary," said Compton.

"Why did we not make entry when I saw Slade in the kitchen making a sandwich, if we knew the judge was in the front bedroom? The door was busted from our last entry. We could have been on him like stink on shit before he got back to the judge," asked Gary.

"Captain Hale," said Compton.

"That was your call to make Sergeant Compton," said Hale.

"I respectfully disagree, Captain. You specifically ordered me not to make entry because you wanted to try negotiations first and you wanted to obtain a warrant first," said Compton. "You were the officer in charge in this action, and you made the decision to not go at that time," said Compton.

"Well, I uh... decided that there might not be enough information to substantiate that the judge was in the house, and I did not want to jeopardize a future p-p-p-prosecution," stammered Hale.

"If I might ask one question," said Chief Ray Johnson, "why were you in charge of a SWAT action, Captain Hale? You are the Director of Community Services."

"Well, policy dictates that a ranking officer can take over command of the SWAT team during certain emergencies. I felt that this was the type of situation that called for rank and experience, not just experience," said Hale sticking out his chest. "I felt it was too big for a sergeant."

"Since I signed the policy and helped write that policy with Sergeant Compton, I can tell you that you have misread and misinterpreted that point of the policy. The intent was that a person of rank may take over command of the team in absence of the officer in charge or the officer in charge's designee. I do not care how big an emergency a situation is, I want that man handling it!" said the chief emphatically gesturing toward Compton. "There is not a better man in an emergency on this department than him."

There was a buzz in the crowd and arms uncrossed and re-crossed and heads were shaking in agreement.

"In your honest assessment, Sergeant Compton, do you think this might have ended differently if you would have entered when Slade was in the kitchen?" asked Chief Johnson.

"Frankly, sir, it may have and it may have not. We did enter that house once before, and Slade managed to make it down that hallway before we got to him. It may have ended with a shooting in the kitchen. We may have been able to go hands on with him in the kitchen because we did not know and still do not know whether or not he had access to guns at that point. He did have access to knives. It is a long answer, but the short answer is it may have ended the same, better, or worse. We cannot know now. I can say when any option is taken off the table in a team action, it may result in a missed opportunity. This was a missed opportunity," said Compton.

"By the way, Sergeant Stammos, good call on calling in the team," said Chief Johnson to Stammos.

"Thanks, Chief," said Stammos.

"Anything else we need to discuss, for better or worse," asked Compton.

"Yes sir," said Officer Chuck Hansen, one of the team snipers. "Why was a red light given? I felt I had a shot and my hands were tied."

"Who gave a red light on this one?" asked Chief Johnson looking at Hale.

There was silence.

Stammos answered, "That is no secret. I heard it from the station. Captain Hale said, 'Red light. Stand by.'"

"I said red light because we were trying to establish communications with Slade. I did not say red light when he came outside with the judge. I certainly would have given a green light then if I was there and saw Slade come out with a sawed off shotgun taped to her neck," explained Hale.

"Sergeant Compton, could you give us a short session on why there is no such thing as red light or green light in SWAT," said Chief Johnson.

"Respectfully, sir, I would like to ask Officer Hansen, our sniper, to explain that with your permission and his OK," said Compton.

"Go ahead, Officer Hansen, if you would like," said Chief Johnson.

Hansen stood up quickly. "You see, sir, red light and green light are Hollywood terms. It is not used by trained tactical personnel. Scenes are too dynamic and communication is sometimes broken and slow. Every man and woman is bound by the same deadly force criteria, even SWAT team members. To shoot someone, I have to perceive at the moment I squeeze the trigger that the person I am going to permanently stop with my match grain 308 round is presenting imminent danger of death or great bodily harm to someone else, myself, or the community at large. The suspect has to have a weapon or be a weapon capable of delivering these things, shown or communicated the intent, and is activating or about to activate the delivery system of the weapon."

Hansen took a breath and realized he was not nervous. He was speaking in front of his chief and half the department, and he was not nervous.

"You see, if someone at a Kwik Trip gave me a green light at a scene one block away and I saw that the person put his weapon down and his hands up and I shot him because I was following an order, I would go to prison. By the same token, when someone gives a red light at a Kwik Trip one block from a scene and then someone shows up with a gun to a victim's head, I now am stuck with a quandary. I now have to ask myself, should I shoot and disobey an order, or should I not shoot and let the victim die. The decision to use deadly force is a personal decision and has to be in almost all cases, with very few exceptions. When someone uses the term red light and green light, it tells everyone that they have watched some SWAT movies but have never taken a SWAT course." Hansen sat down. He took a deep breath. He still did not feel great, but he felt much better.

"Hell. If my saying red light did all that, then why did Compton shoot? That must mean he disobeyed a direct order from his superior," said Hale clutching at this one last straw.

"Sergeant Compton?" asked Chief Johnson.

"Sir, I knew this team has never operated under a system which its members needed to specify a red light and green light. To this team, therefore, such an order in the case of a deadly force decision had no meaning. It could not be an order. I knew Captain Hale had never been at any of our trainings nor had he been to any other SWAT training, so his order meant something to him but was confusing to me. Therefore, since there was no explanation, I had to interpret what his order 'red light' meant. I decided it meant do not make an entry. There would be no possible way that I could interpret that it meant do not shoot Slade. Let him shoot the judge. I know Captain Hale would never give such an order," Compton said. "I took the shot because I had a weapon that I have handled and fired more times than I could ever count. The Marines prepared me well to use it, and my department prepared me well to continue to use it. I had justification and knew if I didn't take a shot an innocent person was going to die at the hands of a killer who had just finished killing another innocent person. It was an easy shot for me. I am not going to criticize Captain Hale for anything he did. If he would not have stepped in as officer in charge, I would not have been in a position to take the shot and make the shot. I have learned to not argue too much with success as long as it has been honorably achieved. I will say that if Captain Hale promises not to take over my beloved SWAT team again, I will not bring my SWAT team over to his next bike rodeo and order the children down on the ground." Compton paused and smiled.

"Deal," said Hale.

"We have an awful lot of people on overtime here. Does anyone else have anything to say?" said Johnson.

No one said a thing because the chief was about to let everyone go home after one hour, while they were receiving a minimum of three hours time on the big clock.

"I have this to say," said Johnson, "we have to have these debriefs to polish the diamond so to speak. I will tell you all this, though, I am proud of you every day, but the way you handled this one just about brings a tear to my eye. You're excused." Everyone applauded and the chief interrupted, "I said, 'just about,' now God damn it, don't be going out and telling everyone that the chief cried in front of the SWAT team."

As everyone began filing out the door, Chief Johnson called, "Captain Hale. I'd like to see you in my office."

"Yes, sir, Chief Johnson," said Hale.

McCarthy said to Carpenter, upon hearing the exchange, "Couldn't happen to a nicer guy."

Carpenter added, "His fat ass can afford to have a bite or two taken out of it."

"Or three or four," said Maddy Brown.

"Maddy, what are you looking at Captain Hale's ass for? I thought you were kind of stuck on me?" asked Brockman.

"Stuck with you, Brockman. I'm not stuck on you, Stanley, I'm stuck with you," said Maddy giving him a playful slug on the arm.

After the debriefing, Compton left since he was on administrative leave pending the result of the post-shooting investigations. He did not worry about such things. Long ago, he had decided that worrying was a wasted emotion. He had prepared for the shooting and its aftermath long ago. He knew he was right in his actions, and in Compton's world, that was all that mattered.

He sensed though that someone needed help, and he could be the one to give it. He sat quietly next to her bed. He looked at her. He wanted to help her, but there was something more. He had not felt this for two years. Not since…

She opened her eyes. She should have been startled to see him, but she wasn't. "My knight in shining armor," she said with a smile.

"Hello, your honor," said Compton.

"No. You can never call me that again outside of the courtroom. I want you to call me Alice," said Judge Alice.

"You can call me Dave," said Compton.

"It was nice of you to come," said Alice.

"I wanted to make sure you were OK," said Compton.

"Do you do that with all the damsels in distress you rescue?" asked Alice.

"No, I don't… I just…" Compton had no more words.

"I don't want to get too personal, but aren't you old enough to get off the SWAT team or off nights?" asked Alice.

"I'm old enough to retire if I wanted to. I do it because I still have something to offer. The kids on nights are like my kids. I'm their law enforcement father, and I just can't run off and leave them. I like being their dad. The members of the SWAT team are like my brothers and sisters, and you just don't run off and leave your family. They are really the only family I have," said Compton. "I'm not ready for soap operas and game shows."

"I didn't come here to talk about me though. I wanted to ask you how are you doing?" asked Compton tilting his head and leaning forward to look deep and see what her eyes were saying. "God, she has beautiful eyes. A man could nourish himself forever looking into those eyes," he thought.

She smiled and looked away, and then her lip started quivering and she began crying. It was what she did most all of her waking hours. She had managed to hold it together when visitors came in, but she felt she no longer needed to. She felt she could cry in front of this man. She could never have cried in front of Sloan.

Compton put his hand on top of her hand and gently patted it. She took his hand and held it.

"How do people go on after something like this?" asked Alice.

"They just go on," said Compton.

"That's easy to say, but I don't think I can," sobbed the judge.

"That's OK. Cry. That is an important part of the going on," said Compton.

"How do you know? How could you know?" sobbed Alice holding Compton's hand so tightly that it hurt.

"I know. I've had to go on," said Compton.

"When?" said Alice, who even now was more interested in someone else's pain than her own.

"In Vietnam, I lost some of the best friends a guy could ever have. They had their whole lives ahead of them, and now they are just a memory and a name on a wall. I moved on. Twenty years ago, my wife and I lost the only child we were ever going to have together. It nearly killed us both. We finally decided we had to move on. We moved on together. Then two years ago I lost my wife… my best friend," the emotions caught the marine off guard like a well-planned flank attack. It welled up from inside like a volcano erupting. The Marine held them in. He dropped his head and covered his eyes and collected himself. After all, he was a Marine. He was SWAT. He could not let a judge see him cry.

Alice said, "I am so sorry." She sat up in bed for the first time since she had arrived in the hospital.

When Compton was able to recover and speak again, he said, "Thank you. I had to move on again alone. You chose life, Alice. Now you have to move on and live it," said Compton.

"I didn't choose life. I was helpless. If it wasn't for you I'd be…" She could not say the word. It was not that she feared death. She felt that she lived and Jack Sloan did not. She felt she had been responsible for all of it. She felt that she had been Harley David Slade's accomplice in the death, the rape, the terror — all of it! She had released him from jail. She had suppressed the gun he had been arrested with as if it never had existed. She had suppressed the truth as if the truth had not existed. She knew in her heart of hearts that it was a close call, her call. She knew she could have ruled the stop legal, and Harley David Slade would be in prison. Jack Sloan would still be alive. She would not be lying in this bed feeling guilty, so very guilty. She had disarmed Jack Sloan with her arrogant platitudes and made him face Harley David Slade with a golf club. She wished it was her dead on the floor at the bottom of the stairs, not Jack.

Compton interrupted her rapid downhill slide toward psychological self flagellation. "You did choose life. If it wasn't for you, we would not have found you. That shoe did not accidentally land on your front step. Its pair did not accidentally land on Slade's front step. That was a courageous act that was deliberately done. It brought me to you," said Compton.

"But Jack's dead and it should be me. I'm the one that let that crazy man out. Me!" and she covered her face with her hands and began to sob.

"Listen. Surviving when someone you love doesn't is unbearable. You ask yourself over and over, 'Why them? Why not me, Lord?' There is no answer to that question. You can ask it every day for the rest of your life and there is no answer to that why. You just have to move on. As far as you being responsible for this, let's get something straight: Harley David Slade was a killer his whole life looking for a victim. He was a dangerous man. He did this. I didn't do it. You didn't do it. Jack Sloan didn't do this. We were all doing our jobs the best we saw fit to do at the time. Harley David Slade is responsible for this tragedy. It won't be easy, but now you have to move on. We all have to move on," said Compton.

The judge uncovered her face and looked slowly up at Compton. He had saved her once, and now he had come to this room to save her again. She looked at him for a long time. He had dark but graying neatly groomed hair. His face was handsome and as chiseled as his muscular body. "God, he looks like someone," she thought. "Of course. He looks like Superman, without a cape."

She held out her hand on the bed. "David. I usually don't have trouble sleeping, but I have been so frightened of the dark since… it happened. Can you stay with me until I fall asleep? You make me feel safe."

"I would be honored to, Alice," said Compton, who had to once again suppress the welling up of emotion inside, surging, pushing, and fighting to get out as he struggled to keep it in. His wife, his best friend, was the only one who called him David.

Then as Alice felt sleep was about to become a gentle friend once again, she looked one more time at her guardian angel, who had rescued her from a horrible death, and she saw it in the reflection of the so very dim light of that hospital room. She saw what few people see. It was there glistening like a diamond in church. It was one small tear on the cheek of a Marine. Not just any Marine. From this moment and for the rest of her life, he would be… her Marine.

Epilogue: Blue Knight in Black Armor

Over a year had passed since the glare of the national media spotlight had flickered out in La Claire. The citizens of La Claire could even be heard to occasionally say, "Nothing ever happens here in little old La Claire," without triggering an argument.

La Claire's population would be down one for three to five years. Billy Mitchell had taken a plea bargain on the burglary to Bill's Gun Shop. The career criminal had been given consideration for his timely cooperation with McCarthy, which ultimately led to the successful rescue of Judge Alice.

The award ceremony at the annual Police Memorial Day Service had to be held at a ballroom at the La Claire Civic Center due to the number of people attending and the number of award recipients. Two Unit Citations were given out to the La Claire SWAT team. One was given for the Mad Mattix incident and another for the rescue of Judge Alice. McCarthy received a citation for his actions in La Crosse at the Stoddard Hotel.

When Stanley Brockman received a citation for his actions in the Mad Mattix shootout, the proud look on his face made it clear that the citation would not be causing Stanley any chafing. After the ceremony, Stanley even did an interview for the press, during which he ended by waving all five fingers at the cameraman while he smiled.

The last award of the night was witnessed by a retired Los Angeles Police Officer, whose daughter Maddy was his proudest accomplishment in life. She received a purple heart for her wounds and a Medal of Valor for the action taken under the worst conditions. Diane Lambheart did not cover the event on "Prime Time Special." The next story on police heroism that Diane Lambheart would do would be her first story on police heroism. Maddy didn't care. Her father was there.

Young Officer William "Shep" Shepherd watched from the audience picturing the day he would be walking across the stage after performing some magnificent act of bravery. He was satisfied now, though, with the fact that he had just been released from his probationary status and he was now officially a police officer in good standing with the La Claire Police Department. He knew that there may be other police departments as good as his, but none better.

As the days passed, Alice and David Compton took time to get to know each other to find out if the intense love kindled in that quiet hospital room after that terrible night would survive the passage of time. They discovered that not only did the love survive, but it also grew.

Now a cluster of police, family, and friends gathered about the gazebo in Gibbon Park, where Judge Alice and Dave Compton stood gazing into each other's eyes reciting their vows together for all to hear. No one on the La Claire Police Department had ever seen David Compton nervous before, and no one had ever seen Judge Alice demure before. Compton nervously recited along with Alice the following words while gazing into each other's eyes:

As we stand here today, before family and friends,
We proclaim that we have found a love without end.
Now we'll travel from here toward life's great unknown
Knowing we'll never again travel life's path alone.

We know whatever life offers we can weather
As long as our hearts are bound forever together.
Through sadness and joy the worst and the best,
Our love will withstand all and pass every test.

So I vow to give you my heart, my soul, and my hand.
Nothing can put asunder a love God must have planned.

After the brief ceremony, McCarthy stood with his wife Victoria on the carpet of green next to the gazebo at Gibbon Park.

It had been a civil ceremony in front of a judge.

Victoria asked Dan, "Those vows, where did they get those vows?"

"I'm pretty sure they wrote them," said McCarthy.

"They were beautiful. They made me cry," said Victoria dabbing a lace handkerchief to her eyes.

"I'm sorry, Hon," said McCarthy.

"No. That's a good thing. The words were so meaningful. So beautiful," gushed Victoria as she dabbed at the corner of her eye with the handkerchief.

"Yeah. I suppose," shrugged Dan, scooping a ladle of punch from the bowl and pouring it into a crystal cup.

"Why are they having the ceremony now and the reception in two months?" asked Victoria.

"The judge could not clear her calendar until then, and they wanted the reception to coincide with their honeymoon," said McCarthy as he handed her the crystal cup filled with punch.

"Why didn't they just have the ceremony at the same time as the reception?" asked Victoria.

"They couldn't wait. They didn't want to wait. They were saving themselves until marriage. There's a bun in the oven. I don't know. Why? They just wanted to get married," said McCarthy.

"A bun's in the oven?" asked Victoria.

"No. There's no bun in the oven. I just don't know why. They just did it this way," answered McCarthy.

"Don't you men ever talk about these things?" asked Victoria.

"No. I don't think so. What things?" asked McCarthy.

"Never mind," said Victoria, frustrated by the manness of men. "Who is that man talking to the groom? He's the distinguished looking guy with gray hair. He looks familiar."

"He should be. That's the Secretary of Defense Charles Walker, former Senator from the State of Texas," answered McCarthy. "Compton's known him a long time. He calls him Tex."

"Where did Dave Compton have an opportunity to get so close to the secretary of defense?" asked Victoria.

"Phu Bai," answered McCarthy, taking a drink from his punch

while Victoria wiped the stain it left off Dan's mustache.

"What's a Phu Bai?" asked Victoria.

"It's a long story. Do you want me to tell you now?"

"No, not right now, is that Sandy with Stanley Brockman?" asked Victoria.

"Yeah. They've been dating for about three months now," said McCarthy.

"How did that happen? Stanley Brockman, of all people, with Sandy. Talk about your odd couple. Stanley looks different. Why does he look so different," asked Victoria.

"Everyone says that. You have just never seen him when he was smiling. Stanley has made a real turn around lately. Compton says the old Stanley is back. The one he knew before he turned into a ROD," said McCarthy.

"What's a rod? Never mind, explain that to me later when you explain about the shoe fly and knowing the senator. How in God's name did Stanley Brockman hook up with Sandy?" asked Victoria incredulously.

"Sandy has been single for as long as she has worked at the police department. Guys have been hitting on her, and when that didn't work, women started hitting on her, and she just turned them all down without any explanation," said Dan.

"Just so you know, this is the kind of long story I like. Continue," said Victoria anxiously awaiting more.

"Really? OK. I guess," said McCarthy.

"Continue. Come on, come on," said Victoria impatiently.

"OK. Well, Stanley has been bringing her coffee, newspapers, picking up lunch for her, and basically hovering about her like a lovesick puppy for years. She never even noticed him. He was the only single guy that didn't hit on her on the whole department."

"Yeah, baby. A story from Dan McCarthy where no one gets shot or arrested. I'm loving it. Keep going, babe!" said Victoria, her eyes lighting up.

"Would you like me to continue?" asked Dan.

"Yes," shot back Victoria.

"Do you need me to continue?" asked Dan.

"Yes," answered Victoria.

"Well then, how about I fulfill your needs now and you fulfill my needs later," asked McCarthy.

"Listen, Mister, you get fulfilled plenty. It's my turn now so tell me how it happened right now or there will be no fulfilling for a very long time," said Victoria.

"OK, OK," said McCarthy as he continued. "Well, apparently, Sandy had been involved in a long-term relationship with an international buyer for Pier One Imports," said Dan.

"Pier One Imports? An international buyer for Pier One Imports? I love that store," said Mrs. McCarthy breathlessly.

"Do you want me to get his number? I can ask Sandy because he is available now, I believe, for short term meaningless relationships. I think it says so right on his business card," said McCarthy acting as if he was about to walk over to Sandy and ask.

"I love the store, not the man. Shut up and keep talking," said Victoria.

"Shut up and keep talking? That's going to be difficult," teased McCarthy.

"Daniel McCarthy! Remember what I said? Very long time. No fulfilling?"

"All right. All right! Sandy gets tired of the routine of him being gone a month and in town for five days and no commitment. She finally gives him an ultimatum, 'Hey Mr. Fancy Schmancy Pier One Import International Buyer, it's either my way or the high way.' She says, 'Right now, we pick the date that is going to be our wedding anniversary or there's no mystery you're history.' She used those words exactly," said McCarthy emphatically on the last point.

"Yeah, right. OK, keep going."

"Well, he ums and ahs and then explains that he is married," said Dan.

"Really! Oh my God, that poor thing. I feel so bad for her," said Victoria in a whine like she was talking about a kitten with a broken leg.

"Yeah. Well, she takes a couple of sick days to stay at home and cry. Then she comes back to work, and when she sits down at her desk there is a little plant and a card saying, 'I missed you. I hope you are feeling better. Love,' and its signed 'Stanley.'"

"Did he know what had just happened to her?" asked Victoria.

"No. No one knew. She kept her private life private. Well, she opens the card, looks at it, and then there is Stanley Brockman standing there with a cup of chicken soup instead of coffee. She looks up at him and says, 'Thank you, Stanley. You are always so nice and thoughtful. Did anyone ever tell you that you have a very nice smile.' That's all it took. Stanley has been smiling ever since," said McCarthy.

"There! There! That's the kind of story I want to hear. Your cop stories are OK, but can you scrounge up a story like that every once in a while, dear," said Victoria, kissing him on the cheek. "We better mingle and congratulate the bride and groom."

The romance between Judge Alice and Sergeant David Compton rocked the criminal justice world. It began immediately after the Slade incident. There was no attempt to hide the fact that they were a couple and in it for the long haul.

As Dan and Victoria approached the throng around the bride and groom, they joined the line behind Randy and Jody Stammos. "What do you think about all of this?" asked Jody.

"I would have never pictured it a couple of years ago," said Dan.

"No way," said Randy. "She's even changed in court. I actually look forward to going to her court. She smiles, greets you by name, and treats you like you're not a lowlife scum bag for arresting lowlife scum bags," said Stammos. "Remember when we used to call her court Wonderland? She was Alice in Wonderland," commented Randy.

"What do they call it now," asked Victoria.

Stanley Brockman turned, "Thunder Land. I thought of it myself," he said proudly as Sandy smiled and squeezed his arm.

"Why Thunder Land?" asked Jody Stammos.

Stanley then explained, "I was in her court for a sentencing. This guy we arrested for armed burglary had transferred into her court deliberately because of her reputation for being a criminal's dream judge. Let's face it. She was a soft touch for the criminals and a hard ass for us. Well, this guy walks up saying all the right things. He found Jesus, he was sorry, he was seeking treatment so that he could become a valuable member of society, blah blah fucking-blah, wah wah fucking-wah," said Stanley.

"Stanley. Your language." cautioned Sandy.

"Sorry, Honey," said Stanley. "I'm trying to improve my vocabulary," said Stanley winking at McCarthy.

"Anyway, the judge listened, and then she lowered the boom. She hit him with the maximum penalty. She went higher than the recommendation of the District Attorney and suggested that charges be pursued in the future on criminals like this man, who use a weapon in a crime, in federal court where there would be no possibility of parole. I wanted to jump up in the air and say to the judge, 'Wham bam! Thank you, ma'am,' but I'm pretty sure she would have taken it wrong," said Stanley.

"I concur, Stanley," said Stammos. "Good call."

"Anyway that's when it came to me. She struck like Thor's hammer. This isn't Wonderland any more. It's Thunder Land, and I like it!" said Stanley popping a whole cracker in his mouth that contained an unidentified paste on top of it.

"It's not like she's a push over," said McCarthy. "She's just been fair. She sentences like every judge can. She always says, 'My first concern is the safety of the public.' Wow! What a novel concept. I love it," said McCarthy.

"It's too bad she had to suffer so much to arrive at the philosophy," said Jodi.

"If it doesn't kill you, it makes you stronger, Compton always says." said Stammos.

As the line moved up to Mr. David Compton and Mrs. Alice Compton, Dan McCarthy shook Compton's hand and said, "Hey, Sarge, I am so happy for you."

"Thanks, Dan," said Dave Compton, pulling him in by the hand and giving him a fatherly hug. "Come here, kid. You're not getting away that easily. Thanks for being here."

"Thanks for inviting us," said McCarthy, patting the groom on the back. Compton then moved to Victoria and hugged her like she was his own daughter-in-law.

McCarthy then approached Judge Alice and said, "Your honor, I'd like to say something I would never say in your courtroom because you would scream, 'You're Out of Order.' You look lovely today."

"I would never think a compliment like that was out of order, but I would like to say something I could never say in court. Thank you, Dyno." They hugged, and she held him for a long time and said quietly, "Thanks for everything." When Alice released Dan, she had to wipe a tear from her eye.

McCarthy was deeply moved and thought, "Thankless job my ass."

"Beep. Beep. Beep. Beep," sent McCarthy, Brockman, Stammos Carpenter, Hartley, Dooley, Gloria, and Maddy Brown scrambling for their pagers.

McCarthy pulled it out and looked at the pager.

"What does it say?" asked Compton.

"1025," said McCarthy.

"What does that mean?" asked Alice.

"I'm sorry, but it means that we have to head to the station immediately. It is a general call-out for all available SWAT team personnel," answered Dan.

"Stammos!" said Compton. "You fill in for me as officer in charge. They'll understand why I can't be there," said Compton.

"Now wait just one minute, David," said Alice. "We planned on getting married today. Mission accomplished! What would have happened the night I needed you if you would have had something more important to do. I have you for the rest of our lives. Someone else needs you right now. They are calling for the best, and that's you, so you go with the rest. We'll manage without you until you get back," said Alice.

Compton was shocked. He stood for a moment dumbfounded, and then he said the first thing that he was inspired to say, "I love you." He kissed Alice tenderly and then turned abruptly and took off at a run, stride for stride with McCarthy.

"You can hop in with me," said McCarthy. "Victoria and I took two cars just in case."

Victoria and Alice watched their men sprinting across the park in their tuxedos after six other men in formal wear. Gloria Dooley and Maddy Brown had kicked off their heels, and both had their long dresses pulled up to her knees, managing to keep pace with their teammates. Then Victoria and Alice shouted simultaneously, "Be careful!"

Compton looked at McCarthy and McCarthy at the man who had been teaching him how to be a cop nearly his whole life, and they said to each other simultaneously, "Bad guys better be careful!"

"Are you ready to be the wife of a cop? More accurately, are you ready to be the wife a SWAT cop?" asked Victoria.

Alice watched as the team ran toward the unknown as they always did, together. She pictured David Compton on the night she fell in love with him forever. That night, he came to her in the hospital and held her hand and spoke softly to her, rescuing her a second time. He had rescued her body and then he rescued her heart.

She would always be able to picture him sitting on the bed in her hospital room, relieving her suffering and enduring his own. He sat so stoically on the edge of that hospital bed, and his secret suffering was betrayed by one glistening tear on his cheek.

Then Alice said, "Ours was like a fairy tale romance. I was a damsel in distress, and he was my knight in shining armor. I fell in love with that SWAT cop. It's who he is, and I will always love him for it. I saw firsthand what they are capable of and how important what they do is. They are literally the difference between life and death."

Alice watched as McCarthy and her David drove quickly out of the parking lot and onto Highway 41. She turned to Victoria and said, "The fact that they are willing to put their lives on hold at the sound of a pager and rush toward what everyone rushes away from is one of the things I think that attracts us to them. If it wasn't, we would ask them to quit. I couldn't ask him to quit."

"I wouldn't ask him to quit," agreed Victoria.

Alice then sighed and watched McCarthy's car disappear over a rise in the highway and said, "David has said, 'Being SWAT is like being a Marine. Once you're a Marine, you're always a Marine. Once you're SWAT, you're always SWAT. That is the way it is for me.' They saved my life. I thank God every day they came into my life when they did. I owe every day for the rest of my life to them. To most people, they are just SWAT. To me, they will always be my *Blue Knights in Black Armor.*"